THE GUMIHO KING'S BRIDE

BEX GIL

SERPENTS & DOVES PUBLISHING

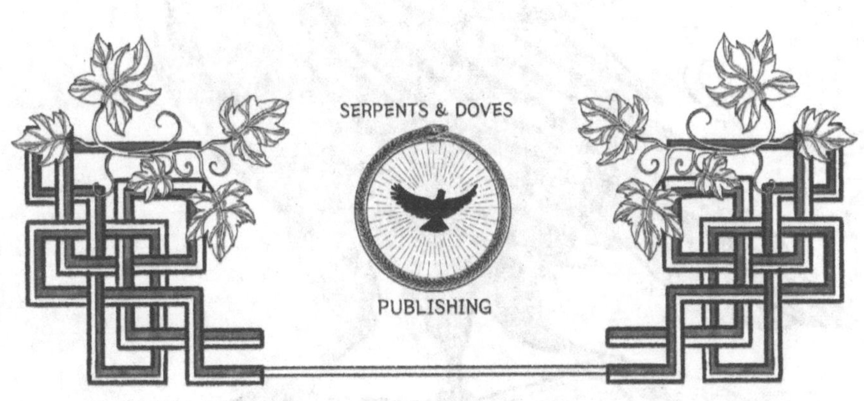

The Gumiho King's Bride

Bex Gil

A Note From the Author

Thank you for picking up *The Gumiho King's Bride*. This book is intended to be an ode to my husband and I—a South Korean native and American respectively. I grew up with fairytales, and Disney's *Beauty and the Beast* was my favorite princess movie. As an adult, I grew to love Korean culture and history, so much so that I majored in International Studies (which meant years of Korean language, history, and culture classes) and lived in South Korea for a few years as both a student and English teacher. Of course, I also love kdramas, but there just aren't enough fantasy ones! So I took all those pent up passions and wrote this book. I spent a long time researching the different mythological creatures—many of which we don't know much about as they were lost to time and different ideologies. This is not meant to be a text book, but I do hope it will introduce you to Korean myths and spark a personal interest that will spur you on to research the rich culture and history. The National Folk Museum of Korea is the one of the best online resources available in English where you can learn about everything from the history of hanbok to no longer celebrated holidays.

The female main character in this book has cerebral palsy—inspired by a relative. I asked said relative questions about their experience because although I have my own disability, I know our experiences will not be the exact same. I do think all of us struggle with feeling valued in a world that ties our worth to our productivity, and of course, being in pain is hard to endure. I hope that no matter one's body/health, that you would all feel loved, seen, valued, and worthy of being the object of epic fantasies and swoony romances.

Content Warnings

This book includes mentions of child abuse and on page attempted SA.

To my husband,
two cultures coming together,
a tale of true love

Phoenix Realm
MYTHICAL LANDS
Kaesong
MORTAL LANDS
Gumiho Realm
Haetae Realm
GORYEO
Dragon Realm

This is the legend of the Gumiho King.

A night of bloody revenge, returned on his head in the end. Negligence, the seed of greed, of humility he was in need.

A centuries spanning curse, for a woman he does search. Hearts to consume, without one, he is doomed. From those whom he hates, one will rescue from his fate.

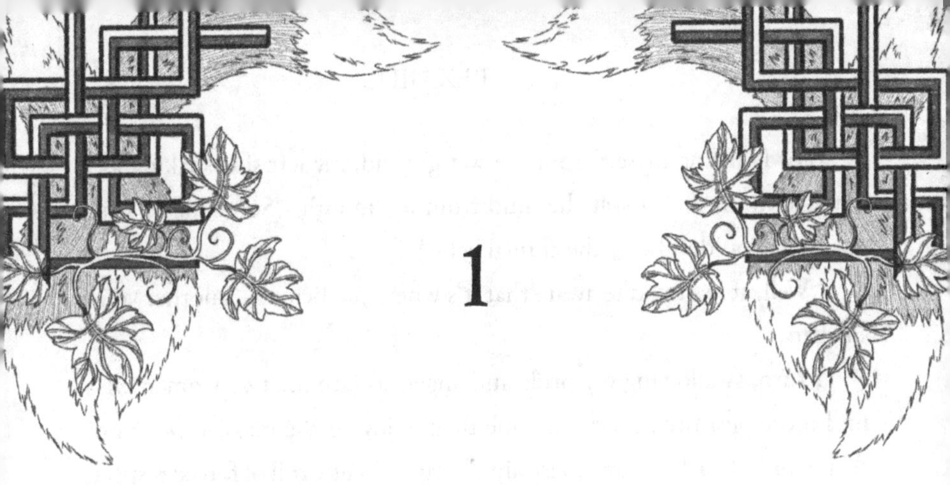

1

MY LIFE WAS RUINED from the moment it began. A broke girl with a broken body and a broken family. The only difference between me and the pig I am feeding is that someone cares whether it lives or dies. It's going to be someone's food at least.

The mud sucks at my shoes, the snorts of the hog stuffing himself full of the scraps rumbling in my ears like grunts of thunder. Despite the musty smell of the muck, my mouth begins to salivate as I stare down at the remaining food in my wooden bucket. On top is a rib, chunks of beef still remaining on the bone. How could they have thrown it away when there was still so much meat left? I glance around, checking if any other workers are around, but aside from myself and the animals tucked in the far corner of the estate, there is not another living being in sight. No one would notice if I took it. I trust the pigs to keep my secret. Reaching into the bucket, I grab the rib and bring it to my mouth.

Once I get past the slightly sour taste coating it, the beef flavor comes through, and I have to stop myself from moaning. It's been months since I've eaten beef. Before anyone happens upon me, I reach down again, taking a handful of rice that had long gone dry and tuck it into my pocket. When I reach to grab another handful, a hard pair of hands shoves my back, and I careen into the muck, moist soil and dung smashing into my pants and shirt.

"If you're going to eat like a pig you should live like one too," a familiar voice sneers behind me, eliciting a grimace of my grime covered face.

Slowly lifting myself from the wet ground, my left side shaking as I struggle to my feet, I spit the mud from my mouth. "Someone of your position shouldn't be by the animal pens."

"Well, at least you're aware that it's where *you* belong," another voice snickers.

I turn, swallowing my pride and anger, to face the two women who find more pleasure in harassing me than enjoying the massive wealth of their family. "Taehee-nim, Taeri-nim," I say, my voice full of forced respect, my strong hand clenched into a fist by side. "Is there something I can help you with?"

Behind them stands a short man, from the Yoon family if I recall correctly. I've seen him following them around on many occasions, but just like those times, he remains quiet, eyes averted from me. Whether he pities or loathes the sight of me, I am not sure. Either way, his only goal is to avoid displeasing the Song sisters, perhaps hoping for an advantageous marriage for his smaller noble clan.

Taehee, the elder sister, steps forward, careful to hold the hem of her skirts clear of the sludge. I am sure she can afford to dirty her shoes and buy a new pair everyday. "Those scraps are meant for the animals, not you." She pauses, peering at the pigs snorting behind me before drawing her gaze back to me. "Although the resemblance is striking."

I shove the desire to grab her by the hair and thrust her face into the mire deep down, knowing it would only offer a temporary satisfaction and reap more serious punishment upon myself. Another idea sparks to life. The corner of my lip twitches, and I lurch towards her. As I fall forward, I force a faux exclamation from my lips. "Oh no!"

On my way down, I make sure that my muck covered hands meet the fabric of her skirts, marking it with chestnut streaks. I don't intend for more to splash on her, but when my body collides with the mud, more splatters, brown spots dotting her pale face. Perhaps the heavens are on my side for once.

Taehee screams, and her hands fling into the air, her skirts dirtying even further when they meet the ground. The pigs snort, seeming to laugh at her. Red blooms across her face like a rash while Taeri and her male companion gape at the sight of Taehee covered in mud.

Scrambling back to my feet, I bow several times, gushing apologies, "I am so sorry, Taehee-nim. Please forgive me. It was an accident." Which isn't a complete lie. I never intended to get mud on her face, only her dress.

She cannot decide between anger and embarrassment, but once more, the heavens help me. A caw sounds above, and a white substance splatters on the top of Taehee's head. Taeri and the young man both gasp again, and Taehee reaches a trembling hand to the top of her hair. When she brings it back down, a scream of disgust rips from her lips. Bird feces cover her fingertips. A laugh threatens to escape me, but I fold my lips together to contain it.

Casting one more glare my way, Taehee storms off, her younger sister and male companion following after, heads tucked into their shoulders. They may hold more power, yet they are fragile, defeated by a bit of wet dirt and a bird. I glance up to thank the crow, but it is gone. The sun hangs low, dusk draping across the sky in hues of blue and pink; it is time for me to go home. I check to make sure the rice scraps are still in my pouch and then limp out of the estate and off towards the sector of the city where my father and I reside, happy despite the soil caking my clothes and skin.

The Song estate is in the nobles district of the city, my house on the opposite side. However, it is not the first time I am traipsing through the streets covered in mud, but knowing that the eldest daughter of the Song clan had to return to her silk draped rooms and trunks full of jewels with bird poop on her head makes me feel like I am the victor today. Is this how soldiers feel when they return victorious from a battle, covered in filth but adorned in a crown of triumph? I ignore the looming threat of retaliation from the Song sisters, instead basking in today's win.

The buildings I pass are all tapered and tiled roofs, the tallest building being the magistrate's office that stands three tiers high. Apparently, the capital has a pagoda as tall as a mountain. Or at least that's what the other commoners say, not that any of us will likely have enough coin in our measly mortal lifetimes to visit Kaesong and confirm it.

Red ribbons wrap pillars, and crimson lanterns hang above my head, the decorations marking the Year of the Maiden. It's the first time I'm experiencing the event that only happens once every seventy years. Not that it will affect me one way or another, as I am not of the nobles who are required to send a woman to the Gumiho King, nor am I able to afford any of the treats that are sold during the festivities. At least the decorations are pretty to look at.

Walking past the tea shops emitting warm floral aromas, food vendors steaming with boiling chicken and dumplings, and clothing stores bustling with noble daughters, I stop by a stream that cuts through the city to clean the grime coating my face. The few trees dotting the bank whisper with a gentle autumn breeze, and the creek giggles in greeting. My clothes will have to wait until I reach my house, but the cool water refreshes me while it washes away the dried mud from my skin.

Across the stream sits a familiar face, cheeks plump as a peach and pink garments embroidered in yellow lotuses. "I take it Song Taehee was in quite the mood today?" Yuna asks, her long hair half up in a braid, the rest flowing as freely as the water in front of us.

"Isn't she always?" I grumble, scrubbing at the stubborn mud under my nails.

Yuna picks up a nearby stick and pokes the water. "Did you at least give her a little of what she gave?"

"Of course. My pride may one day be the end of me though," I reply with a chuckle, washing the dirt from my neck.

"Good. I am glad she didn't get away with her antics," Yuna's voice drops, a wistfulness to her words. "I wish I was as brave as you. Maybe then when she came into father's shop, I could have stood up to her. Then maybe father wouldn't have had to replace all those shattered ceramics."

"As a merchant, your family needs to appease the nobles more than I. It's probably for the best that you remained silent amidst the Song storm." But deep down, I wish Yuna would have stood up to them. It is because everyone cowers to the Song clan that the sisters wreck havoc freely in the city. The king may be far away but a tyrant reigns here all the same.

Yuna tosses her stick into the water, watching it float away. "I suppose you're right. Still, I would have liked to see whatever you did today."

I grab the end of my mud-crusted black braid and dip it into the water. "I won't lie. The satisfaction was immense." The rest of my hair will have to wait, and I curl it like a snake on the top of my head.

Yuna giggles. "I must be going now. See you around," she says, waving before she wanders off down the street back towards her father's shop.

We are of different classes, yet Yuna often comes to this section of the stream. I speculate she is just lonely and likes talking, and we can bond over our mutual dislike of the Song family.

I splash water once more over my face for good measure. As I spit the muddy water from my mouth, I feel the burning stares of the patrons of nearby shops. Two women, bejeweled hair pins shining in the remaining light, scoff at me, their lips curled up at my soiled pants, wrapped top, and plain hair piled atop my head in a bun. *If only the prettiness of their clothes could seep into their hearts.* But the thoughts of the Song sisters and the uppity wealthy merchant women flutter away when a caw echoes above my head.

Gaze tilted to the tree branches, I smile. "I see you've been waiting for me."

The crow cocks its head and shifts on the bough, black feathers shimmering blue in the rays of the setting sun.

"Yes, do not fret. I saved you some morsels." I bring out the rice I'd scavenged and toss some of it onto the ground. The bird flies down, pecking at the granules. A few shrikes and magpies come to join, and I adjust myself onto my knees, wincing when my left leg protests. Hand held out with the remainder of the rice cupped in my palm, I lure the crow towards me. He is different from the rest, an intelligence glittering in his golden eyes, a color that I have never seen before in a bird. Maybe he is different, just like me. He hops forward hesitantly.

We've been at this for months now, and each day he gets closer and closer to eating directly from my hand. "Don't be scared," I whisper.

As if he can understand my words, it does the trick, and the crow hops all the way to my hand, its pecking tickling my skin.

"Were you the one to come to my aid today?" I ponder, tilting my head as a soft smile tugs at the corners of my lips.

Of course, the bird does not reply, too busy gorging itself on the rice. When it finishes, it peers its gilded eye up at me.

"I'm sorry. I don't have any more, and I must go now. See you tomorrow."

The crow caws farewell as it launches into flight and disappears into the coming night. Slowly, I get to my feet, the wetness of the mud causing the brace on my leg to chafe. With each step, I wince. I'm glad I didn't take the long way home just to avoid the stares. The nicer merchant district gives way to patchwork homes, the first row leaning against the existing wall of an old drinking house, the other huts and shanties leaning against those in a way that if one plucked out a shack, the rest would collapse to the ground, and on and on it goes for several more rows. I weave down the slim alleyways, lines of water mixed with things I never like to imagine trickling down the slight slope.

"Songhee, is that you?" a shaky voice calls out from one of the humble homes.

Letting out a sigh, I smile and turn to the hut to my right. A rectangular gap between slanted walls serves as the door, and an old woman hunches in the entryway.

"No, it's Jiwon, Halmeoni," I reply, softening my voice.

"Oh, do you know when Songhee is coming back?" she inquires, hobbling forward with one hand braced on the wall.

I step forward, helping her sit on a wood crate that resides next to her doorway. "I'll ask around," I say.

It's a lie.

Everyday she asks, and everyday the answer is the same. If one answers honestly, that her daughter is dead, then she cries, mourning Songhee all over again. I'm not fond of lying, but in this case I think it's the best thing to do. If a lie will save her from drowning daily in a new wave of grief, I will spill such falsities gladly.

"Thank you, Jiwon-ah," Halmeoni Hyesun says and pats my hand with wrinkled fingers.

"I'll check on you tomorrow," I promise, telling myself to see if I can scrape any meat together.

There is a butcher who sells some of his leftovers—all the bits the wealthy don't want—at a cheap price. The problem is making it to his shop before it closes, and with my bad leg and work at the Song's, it can be hard to get there before the other common folk. But Halmeoni looks skinnier by the week. I bite back the curses forming in my mind. After feeding many of the children in this poor part of the city, only a few ever take the time to come check on her and repay her kindness.

I'll need to ask Seojun and Bora if they've seen Minah, I mumble in my mind. Ever since that ungrateful girl became the concubine to a son of the Baron in our town, she's turned her nose up at all those who are reminders of where she came from. I saw her last week with a luxurious garment and jewels in her hair. Just one of them could buy a pig and feed Halmeoni Hyesun for a month. If it wouldn't end in me getting flogged, I'd march up to her myself and spit on her nice dress. But alas, then I'd be unable to work and unable to obtain food for Halmeoni Hyesun. One cannot sustain themselves on pride alone.

Bowing as I leave, I start planning on what to do for dinner. When I left this morning, all we had was a few scoops of barley and one nearly rotten fish from when my father actually decided to try to help feed us a few days ago. I'd been portioning out what he'd caught, but if I wait any longer, the fish will become inedible.

Our home is a shack, like all the rest, although we used to have a little house on a little piece of land in a little village outside the city. I remember it from when I was a child, although the memories are a bit fuzzy after fifteen years. After my mother passed, my father gradually became fonder of drinking and eventually picked up gambling. One night led into every night, and by the time I was eight, we had to sell the house and land to pay his debts.

Still, that time was precious because one of the village women helped me. I was born prematurely, and my body was not normal. She helped me train and stretch my muscles, and her husband even carved me braces, replacing them when I outgrew them. Now I work, not only to keep a roof over our heads, but also to pay someone to make my braces. The training of my leg and arm only did so much, and I'll never be able to fully use them. Even now, my left hand is curled in a loose fist—its natural state. Pain, of course, is always present, sometimes dull and sometimes severe, my muscles cramping like a hand stuck into freezing water.

The fraying woven door signals I'm home. A sigh leaves my lips. I'll have to ask my father to fix it. The air is stale and still sour from when he urinated the other night in his intoxicated slumber. My nose scrunched and my lip curled at the stench, I walk past our little cupboard and fire pit that sits inside next to the entryway and head to where my father normally is at this time of day.

"Appa, I'm home," I say, pushing aside the tattered curtain that serves as our shared bedroom.

But he is not here, and there is only ever one type of establishment he goes to when he leaves the house in the evening. My pulse quickens like a deer who just noticed a tiger, breaking out into a panicked sprint. I rush to my well worn blanket, fingers finding the hole where I hide my wages. My father has found every other place I've hidden my money—a box under a pot, an upside down cup in the corner, even a hole in our dirt floor—so I shouldn't be surprised that he has now found this one. Still, my heart drops to my stomach at the absence of my coins.

Rushing to change out of my muddy garments into my only other clean set of clothes and brace, I can only hope he hasn't spent it all already. I hurry as fast as my leg allows out the door and head back into the streets.

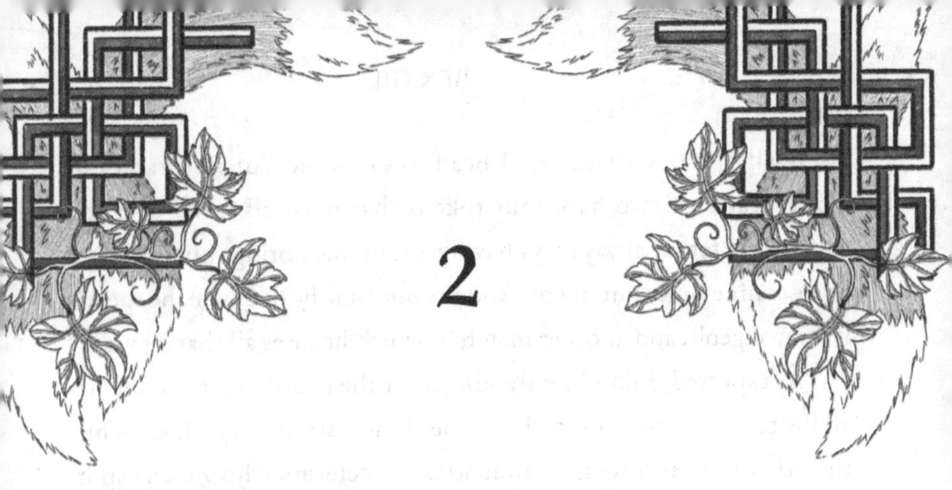

2

T HE GAMBLING DEN IS a quaint structure, at least the one the lower class uses. Perhaps the nobles patronize one dripping in silks, pretty men and women serving meat on gilded dishes. This one is nothing like that, the acrid smell of vomit and urine and cheap alcohol leaking from the very walls of the place. Although the customers of the upper gambling establishments would have wealthy family members to bail them out of their debts, my father only has me, and I have only the money I earned from taking care of the Song clan's animals. Which is to say, not much at all.

Angry wives drag their husbands away, their scoldings disappearing down the street. As I enter, a drunk man bumps into me, and I lose my balance, my leg barking in pain. Luckily, I only slam into a wall and not the ground. The belligerent man doesn't apologize, doesn't even bother to look back, just continues stumbling down the steps and mumbling under his makgeolli-ridden breath.

And this is why I'll never touch a drop of that cursed rice-wine, I grumble to myself.

Rubbing my shoulder, I enter the bustling building and weave through the bodies. Men are shouting their bets around dice tables, and a fight breaks out in the far corner before two burly men known as the Collectors escort the offenders out without a hint of gentleness. I ignore the lewd comments made by passing men and search for the face of my father. I suppose after a couple of bowls of makgeolli, even someone such as myself appears attractive. I head towards the Yut-nori tables in which teams of two have four tokens that must all travel over the course. My father always says having a teammate brings him luck, yet he loses nine times out of ten. And the one time he does win, he spends it on makgeolli and another match in which he loses all that he won.

As expected, I find him standing over the board of circles. He has all his tokens traveling together—the riskiest strategy possible. While the other team throws their four sticks to determine how many spots their tokens can move, I position myself next to my father. It will do no good to tell him to leave. He never leaves in the middle of a game. The last time I tried, he threw me to the ground and continued to play while I held my injured arm and tried not to cry in the crowded building.

My breath stills in my chest, and I pray that the opposing team rolls poorly. Eyes fixated on the sticks as they fall onto the table with a loud clacking, I dig my nails into my palms. Four sticks facing down. *Mo.* My heart plummets along with my hopes that I would get to leave this place with at least some of my money. My father's arms began to shake while his partner's shoulders droop down. The opposing team advances one of their tokens five spaces forward—right to where my father has all his. Now that they've landed on the same circle, my father and his partner have as good as lost. Their tokens are removed from the board; meanwhile, the opposing team smiles triumphantly, their remaining three pieces not far behind. They'll finish the course with all four before even one of my father's tokens can.

My father's partner says nothing and just downs the rest of his makgeolli. My father curses, slamming his fist against the table, the tokens and sticks jumping.

Placing my hand on his arm, I say softly, "Let's go." My money is gone by now. No use getting angry about it.

I support my father with my good side, the scent of rice-wine wafting off him. We turn to leave, but one of the men from the opposing team rushes around the table to block our path.

He is a tree trunk of a man, his face dark with little lines running along his skin like bark. "Not so fast," he growls. He sticks his thick, calloused finger in my father's face. "You still owe me."

My eyes dart between them. "Did you keep going after using all my money?" I sound like a parent scolding their child for eating too many sweets—not that I've ever had the experience of having enough sweets to over eat–and in this case, the consequences are much more serious than an upset stomach.

My father says nothing, gaze refusing to meet mine. He's only done this once before, and after I kicked him out of our house, he promised not to do it again. I shouldn't have accepted him back, seeing as he still takes my wages from time to time, but he is all I have in this world. The only thing worse than being poor is being alone.

Saving my scolding for later, I face the man in front of us. "I don't have any money on me right now, but I can bring you what he owes you tomorrow." I get paid tomorrow, but that means we won't have much money to get us through to the next pay day. Looks like there will be no chicken for Halmeoni Hyesun. But perhaps we could spare her some barley...

The man leers forward, reaching up a hand to brush my arm as he inhales. "You smell terrible, but you're not so terrible to look at." Two of his teeth are missing, and several others are the dark color of decay. Truly a rotten man.

My stomach roils, and my shoulders stiffen. "I said, I'll bring you the money tomorrow."

He steps forward, and I look to my father to defend me. But he does nothing, even taking a step away, although that could be from the alcohol. My good hand curls into a tight fist.

The man continues, his eyes dropping to my legs and back up to my face. "I'd hate to get the Collectors involved in this."

Chills creep along my spine like a winter frost. I glance to where the two burly men who just threw out the brawlers stand by the entrance. I've seen how they deal with those who refuse—or who are unable—to pay their debts. Peering back at the man in front of me, I weigh my options. My chances of escaping by running are nil, and this man has made it clear he will not accept delayed payment, and the Collectors have no qualms harming women. Just last week when I came to get my father, I saw them break a woman's hand for trying to swipe some coin from one of the tables.

I have to go with the option that allows me to still work tomorrow. Just when I open my mouth to answer, I feel a hand on my arm. Hope blooms inside me, and I turn my face. But it is not my father who comes to my aid. Instead, a stranger stands next to me. The new man's clothes are far too fine for such a place as this, his voice and hands too soft to be amongst such hardened people. Then I notice a black clad guard with a mask and sword standing next to him, and now I understand why he is not nervous, although why he is here remains a mystery.

"I will pay the debt," the new man states calmly and reaches into his voluptuous sleeve to pull out a pouch of silver stones.

My jaw nearly drops at the sight of so much silver, but I manage to keep it shut and keep some dignity. The man from the opposing team doesn't waste another look at me, his eyes lighting up at the currency of the rich. The noble looking man plucks a silver stone from his pouch and places it into the palm of the other man, who scurries off with his small fortune. Although I wonder what it would be like to hold a piece of silver instead of the common coins I'm paid in, I quickly reach for my father and tug him back towards me.

Doing my best to bear my father's drunken weight, I dip my head. "Thank you," I say sincerely, albeit a bit rushed, before I start dragging my father out.

Nothing in life is free. Someone always pays the price, and I don't want to know the price of this strange noble's help.

Despite my bad leg and belligerent father, I manage to lose the noble man amidst the crowd of gamblers, drunks, and threatening men demanding their payments. We break out into the street, and I take the chance to look over my shoulder. The man is straining his neck like a crane, searching for me. I smile and turn back around, limping forward while my father slurs something unintelligible. When we turn the corner, a body blocks our path.

The guard who was accompanying the noble man stands in front of us, arms crossed and sword tucked under his armpit. Is the displeasure portrayed by his furrowing brows his normal expression or his annoyance at our poor attempt at evading him and his master? I glance at the sword, hoping it's the former.

The noble man catches up and says, "I do not wish to harm you. I simply have a proposition."

Very few people help others without expecting something in return, and the wealthier they are, the more they demand. My eyes scan our surroundings, looking for something—or someone—to aid us. But who would help a lame and a drunk, especially at the cost of angering a noble?

No one.

A rich man on the other hand...

"You're giving away silver stones?" I shout as loud as I can, the heads of those nearby whipping towards us.

Just as one can count on greed, one can count on desperation. The guard behind us curses as people begin to approach, dirt covered nails reaching towards the man in fine clothes. The noble says nothing when people press upon him, his eyes only widening for a fraction of a second before a smirk tugs at his lips. His guard quickly loses interest in my father and I, switching to protecting his liege from the crowd that continues to grow by the second.

"Please, sir, I need medicine for my mother," one young child says, fingers tugging the noble man's sleeve.

An old man holds out his wrinkled hand. "I have not eaten in two days."

There is no lack of sad stories in this section of the city.

I take the opportunity to push through the sea of people, holding tightly to my father lest he get lost. Glancing once more over my shoulder, I see the strange man dip his head, as if acknowledging I've won our even stranger game. I turn my face away, hoping there will not be another match. Unlike my father, I do not test Luck, for I know she does not often choose me.

Stumbling through the alleyways, we make our way to our shack of a home.

"You look like your mother," my father slurs, the statement accusatory.

"I know," I grunt, trying to ignore the pain—my body protesting his heavy weight.

"You took her from me," he adds harshly despite the way the alcohol gives him a lisp.

"I know."

How could I forget, when every time he drinks, he reminds me? For twenty three years I've heard those words, and even after all that time, it stings. One may become accustomed to pain, but it never stops hurting. Instead of focusing on my aching heart, I fixate on the throbbing of my leg, my unwanted phantom companion that makes its home on my entire left side. Today the right side hurts as well, strained by having to make up for the other half of my body.

The woven door to home appears before us at last, and I let out a breath. My leg didn't have much strength left. I release him and allow him to stumble his way to his own worn blanket and straw mat. Hopefully he will not vomit like last time. The stench haunted our shanty for a whole week, even worse than the urine.

My cup overflows, but the drink is bitter.

Once I hear the deep, drunken snores of my father, I allow myself to cry.

❀ ❀ ❀ ❀ ❀ ❀ ❀ ❀ ❀

A few days later, I head out early, stopping by Halmeoni Hyesun's house to drop off a small cup of barley porridge made from a few chicken scraps I found discarded behind an entertainment house.

"Halmeoni?" I call out.

Shuffling sounds inside, the dawn light unable to illuminate deep inside the shack. A wrinkled face pops from the shadows.

"Jiwon-ah!" she exclaims, reaching to drag me inside. Her memory always starts off well enough, but by the evening, she always calls out for Songhee.

I enter and hand her the porridge, her face brightening more than the sunbeams cascading above the city wall. She sets it down on the leaning table by the section that serves as her kitchen—not that she has much food to use in it.

She hobbles to a worn woven mat and gestures to it. "Sit, sit. Let me do your hair before you go to work."

I wave my hands in front of me, shaking my head. "No, please eat first. It tastes best warm, and I have time to wait."

She acquiesces and picks up the quaint dish, sitting on the mat where I join her. Knowing that she will have eaten today will make it easier to work. A glob of porridge sits on her chin, and I lean forward to wipe it, putting it back in the bowl. I do it twice more, and when I see that the bowl is completely clean, I turn around and finally allow her to braid my hair as she does most every morning.

A low hum emits from her lips as she twists locks of hair together. Songhee used to sing all the time, humming as she walked. Her music put a smile on everyone's faces, including hers. No one would have guessed that she was so sad on the inside...

But everyone has their limits, gets tired. I can't say I haven't had such thoughts, but there is something stubborn about me, a spite at the thought of letting life get the best of me. It's what has helped me endure. That and the kindness of people like Halmeoni Hyesun. There are people in life who stoke your fire, keep the embers burning, even as others try to smother the sparks.

After she finishes tying off the ends, Halmeoni Hyesun leans forward, pressing a kiss against the back of my head. I turn around and grab her hand, the backside full of ravines and her palm as rough as coarse sand.

"Thank you, Halmeoni. I'll come by this evening after I finish my work." I know she won't remember by then, but at least in this moment, she will know she is cared for.

"Alright. Be safe. Don't let those Song girls bully you," she says, sending me off with one more smile.

Using the wall to help me to my feet, I give her a grin back. "You know I never do." And with that, I head off, hoping that my father will not find my new hiding place for my money. I've longed since learned to split up my stashes, so although he spent all that was in the blanket, he did not find the one I had tucked into a hole in our ceiling. Now there is some hidden in a crevice between our wall and the next door neighbor's wall. My hand just barely fit when I shoved it there this morning while my father was still sleeping off his intoxication.

When I stop by the stream to wash my face, four women are drawing water from the creek. They're talking about the Year of the Maiden.

"This is the one time I'm grateful to be poor," the oldest one says with a light laugh.

"Oh, I don't know. I've heard the Gumiho King is stunningly handsome. Sounds like whoever is chosen is one lucky woman," a wisp of a woman says wistfully.

"Are you mad? Gumihos are beautiful, but they're deadly," the chubby one scoffs.

The old one adds, "I heard they eat human hearts."

"I heard they dig up graves to consume livers," the chubby woman says.

The wispy woman frowns. "But I thought if they bite a human, that person becomes a gumiho too."

The petite one giggles. "How romantic, getting to spend centuries together with a handsome nine tailed fox."

"I wish I could volunteer to go," the wispy one says with a sigh.

Bursting into laughter, the chubby one says, "Maybe I should try. Can't be worse than being with my husband."

The old one shakes her head at the comment while the petite one giggles and the wispy woman looks shocked that such a comment was even made.

Suddenly, the petite one changes the direction of the conversation. "Isn't it the Song clan's turn to offer a daughter?"

My eyes widen. Each noble clan is responsible for providing the sacrificial woman each century, but I didn't realize the Song clan were the unfortunate ones for this year. Unlike some of those women, I have no fantasies about the Gumiho King. Anyone who forces someone to marry them is a beast without a heart. Maybe that's why he has to consume them, to make up for his lack of one. Or livers. Either way, what he eats has nothing to do with me, but it is the first time that I pity Taehee and Taeri. All the other women in the Song clan are either already wed or too young to. But their reprehensible personalities cut my pity short.

I look up to see the sun has made its way well above the city wall. Time to head to the Song family estate. Leaving the women to continue their speculation of the Gumiho King and his future victim, I walk through the bustling city streets, fellow members of the working class scurrying to and fro before those of the noble and wealthier merchant class awaken.

In order to avoid the crowds, I turn down a less busy street. Two men appear in front of me. Normally, I'd ignore them, but their eyes fixate on me as they stalk forward. I quickly turn around and head down a side road. Danger dances along my skin, leaving goosebumps in its wake. Two more men appear, and panic churns my insides. What do they want with me? Certainly they're not intending to sell me to some brothel. No one wants a broken plaything. Is it the man from the gambling den? But he got his silver, so there is no need to come after me. No matter who it is, it does not take a scholar to deduce their devious intent. I take the only road available, hoping it won't lead to a dead end.

I glance over my shoulder to see if they're following.

Nothing.

I let out a breath. I've lost them.

Smiling, I turn forward. Cold grips me, the smile falling from my face.

A man towers in front of me, and behind him with a maniacal grin to match a dokkaebi, stands Taehee. The men who were following me appear now, grabbing both my arms. It appears that the eldest Song sister is here for revenge. I do not scream, for no one would come to my aid. I do not beg, for I am no coward. I do not cry, for I will not give her the satisfaction.

I simply grit my teeth as a smirk slithers along her lips, and she orders, "Let's go."

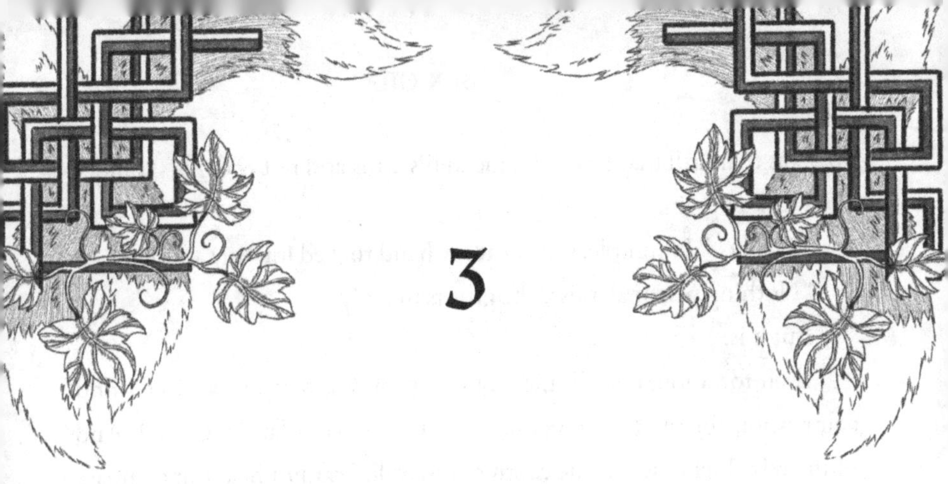

3

N O ONE TELLS ME anything as we walk, not that I ask many questions for fear that I reveal how nervous I am, but I recognize the direction we are going: the Song estate. We pass by a plethora of people, but aside from a few puzzled looks, none interfere. A daughter of the Song clan versus the daughter of a gambling addict. Not a difficult choice to make.

"Can't you move any faster?" Taehee snaps.

"You know I have a bad leg," I reply dryly, not bothering to use honorifics.

She glances over her shoulder, assessing me as if I was a bolt of silk or a bag of rice and not a person. "Carry or drag her, I don't care, but I want to get back before the sun is too high. I forgot my parasol."

I wonder why she came at all, but the only answer that comes to mind is that she relishes in seeing people squirm under the power of her family name. Other people's humiliation tastes better to her than the sweetest pastry. Any pity I had earlier for her and her sister as the potential sacrifices for the Year of the Maiden are whisked away, and now I pray that she is the one to go to the mythical monster. She'd make a good gumiho and they a fine pair.

The burlier of the two men who've been walking on each side of me stops suddenly. For a moment, I want to protest in order to save myself some dignity, but I know I will never be able to keep up with their pace. My pride tastes bitter when I swallow it. Not resisting when the man picks me up, I am thankful that he carries me in his arms and not over his shoulder like a sack of grain.

"Thanks," I mumble, staring at my hand tucked into my abdomen.

"Nothing personal, miss," he grunts in reply.

But it is.

Even for a job, one should not compromise their morals, yet I find compassion for the man because I am sure he has a family to feed. And ultimately, Taehee is the one causing this. Still, I cannot help but compare him and Yuna. It is because people are always cowering to the noble clans that such injustice persists. A little voice whispers in the back of my mind, pointing out my own act of cowardice by allowing my father to continue to live with me while he drains my wages.

I squash the small voice. We are not the same.

At last we arrive at the Song estate, a walled mansion with animal pens, gardens, and ponds, and even a small stable with horses and carriages. It is almost a city within the city. As expected of the Marquis.

We enter through the gaping gate, servants coming and going about their duties, a single guard stationed on one side of the entrance. None of them look our way, and I know it's because they're used to not asking questions of their masters. None of them have spoken on my behalf before, so it is futile to expect it now. Maids rush out of Taehee's way, heads bowed. The way she walks with the entitled expectation that all should move out of her path, like a rock breaking the flow of a river, makes me want to slap her. One young girl is unable to move fast enough under the burden of her basket of laundry, and Taehee bumps into her. The girl and her clothes fall to the ground.

Taehee looms over the trembling thing. "Can't you see where you're going? Your salary will be deducted this month."

"Mistress, please forgive me," the maid begs, crawling and clutching the hem of Taehee's voluptuous skirt. "My mother requires expensive medicine, and I cannot afford to have my wages deducted."

Glaring as if the maid was no better than the pile of dirty clothes, Taehee chides, "Then learn your lesson and don't make such mistakes in the future. And if you question me again, you shall find yourself the subject of a much harsher lesson."

No one comes to plead on the maid's behalf. Since Taehee is already mad at me, and whatever she is going to do to me can't get any worse than what she has done in the past, I call out, "I thought the Songs were a noble household, full of mercy and grace even to those beneath them. I wonder what the city-folk will say knowing the eldest daughter of the Song family refused to grant grace to a poor maid's ailing mother?"

I swear the guard holding me starts to smile, but before it can fully form, Taehee glarcs daggers our way. My bravery withers beneath her wrathful eyes, and worry wrestles inside me, tensing my shoulders as Taehee breaks out into a smirk again. Maybe she does have something uniquely terrible planned for me.

"Very well." She points to another maid passing by. "You, make sure to spread the word that I spared this servant's mother despite her grave mistake." The woman nods and hurries off, while the maid bows at Taehee's feet.

"Thank you, Mistress!" she exclaims, pressing her forehead to the ground.

Taehee's lip curls at the sight, but she says nothing else, striding towards one of the buildings nearby. I've never been inside any of the residential areas of their estate, so I am utterly lost and unsure where we are going. We stop in front of a room facing a courtyard, full of well trimmed bushes and pruned trees, the leaves gold at the behest of autumn. The burly man sets me down gently while another opens the sliding door.

"Wait here," Taehee hisses, spinning on her heel and striding off around the corner.

Not wanting to be forced inside, I amicably enter, the door hissing closed behind me. I take in the room. On one side is a bed of thick blankets—ones without any holes. Shutters cover every window, and tables and cabinets fill up the other wall opposite of the bed. This is far too nice for a prison. Did she bring me here to be some concubine? I immediately dismiss the idea. Only the most beautiful of commoners would be chosen for such a position, and I am certainly not that, at least not with my rags for clothes and thin frame from lack of food. Maybe to some my face is pretty to look at, but still, nothing good enough to catch a noble man's eye. There was that one man at the gambling house... I also dismiss that thought. One more sinister takes its place, and I look once more around the room.

Is Taehee bringing me here to set me up? Accuse me of stealing her jewels? I could have my hands cut off for that.

An ahjumma enters, her hair in a bun behind her head, pulling on her skin so that there are almost no wrinkles on her middle aged face. With her are two other maids and two men carrying a wooden tub. More enter behind them carrying buckets of water.

"What is the meaning of this?" I ask, wrapping my arms around myself. Did she order them to drown me? Even Taehee can't have reached the point of murdering people. At least not with her own hands in her own home. Setting me up is more the Song style.

"Our orders are to get you ready," the ahjumma replies in a monotone voice.

Ready for what? But I know there is no use in asking the question, the ahjumma's stony face telling that she will provide no further answers. She glances at me with eyes full of disgust before tearing her gaze away. She must be rather indignant to be here serving some girl from the streets. The men leave after placing the tub and filling it with water, but the ahjumma and two maids remain.

"I can bathe myself," I mumble.

An annoyed expression forms on the ahjumma's face. "We have been entrusted to make sure you're prepared to a certain standard."

She waves the maids towards me, and without waiting for my consent, they start stripping me. They are not gentle when they shove me into the cold water—courtesy of Taehee, I'm sure—and scrub my skin until it feels sunburnt. Silence suffocates the air in the room, nothing but the sounds of small splashes of water and the occasional instruction from the ahjumma.

Once they're satisfied that I'm as clean as one can get in a single bath, they pull me from the tub and bring out a pair of fine clothes—a persimmon-colored top that a noble woman would wear with a matching soft sunset-yellow skirt. Gold lines the hem of them both with a matching gold waist sash binding it all together. Before they dress me, I point to where my brace was strewn onto the floor. "I can't walk well without it, and if you don't plan on killing me, I expect I'll be needing it at some point."

The two maids look at the ahjumma for permission, and after a few seconds, she nods her head. One of the girls fetches it for me, and I mutter a thanks. After so many years, I've gotten accustomed to putting it on myself. As soon as I am done, the two maids resume their dressing. While they wrap me in fine fabrics, the top going down to my thighs and tied off with a billowing ribbon, another person enters. Two persons actually.

Taehee crosses her arms and snickers, "A pig in nice garments is still a pig."

"Shouldn't we be nicer to her? She is going to marry the...creature, instead of us," Taeri mumbles, eyes darting between me and her older sister.

"She's going to die, even less reason to waste favor on her," Taehee states as if I'm not even in the room.

Footsteps echo, and the Song patriarch—Song Talhae—enters the room. "Girls, please leave."

Taehee steps forward, grabbing her father's sleeve while her bottom lip protrudes in a pout. "Abeonim, I—"

His voice is low, his eyes narrowing. "I said go. *Now.*"

With a humph and one final glare thrown my way, Taehee stomps out. Taeri at least offers a feeble smile before exiting after her sister. In my looming death, she seems to find some sympathy for me. I do not want it, although I suppose it makes her slightly better of a person than her sister. Their father grunts, gesturing for the ahjumma and maids to go as well.

As soon as they leave, Song Talhae lifts his head high, eyes sweeping from my head to toe and back up. "The servants did a good job dressing you up. No one will know you were a girl plucked from the streets. Remember, you are the daughter of a deceased cousin of mine. Song Jinah, daughter of Song Jaeyoung. If anyone asks, the Song clan has fulfilled their obligations."

"What are you talking about?" Why would I need to lie that I am from the Song clan? His words add on to the confusion of the situation, and I am still unsure as to my purpose of being here.

His brow rises. "Your father didn't tell you?"

My heart drops to my stomach, knowing that whatever is said next won't be good, but no matter how harsh the truth is, I will not shun it. Even if it comes as a blade, I will embrace it. Though it slay me, I will not shield my eyes from it, for I am no coward.

The confusion must be clear on my face since he continues before I can answer. "Your father gave you to us in exchange for a pouch of coins."

And slay me it does.

My knees buckle, and I collapse to the ground with a loud thump. I'm brimming with questions and tears, but neither come out. Why does my own father despise me so? Meanwhile the Song family is willing to do anything to protect their daughters from being sacrificed. My chest constricts, and it hurts to breathe. I feel like a sputtering candle in need of air.

"Remember the story I gave you, and for the sake of your father's life, you should keep the details of our transaction to yourself. And of course, it goes without saying, if that is not enough incentive for you, then remember that your life will be forfeit upon your unwelcome return." He waits for a response, but all I can manage is a subtle nod. "Good. There is someone else who wants to see you, and then my servants will send you off," he states, seemingly unconcerned at my pain both internal and external.

He must be quite satisfied, having successfully saved his daughters. The current Song patriarch is not actually the eldest, and rumor has it his political scheming gained him connections that allowed him to argue that he'd be best as leader of the clan. Seeing the shrewd man now, I think those rumors are true. People are pawns, and power is protection. He has no qualms using others for the benefit of his clan. Such a corrupt man has no business being a Marquis. I am only glad that he does not seem to know of my connection with Halmeoni Hyesun, for my father is a poor threat against me, my life only slightly better.

"Wait," I call out, and he pauses in the doorway. "How much did you give my father for me?" My voice comes out so feeble. I hate it. I wish I didn't care. I wish I could sever any remaining love for my father, yet a fierce reluctance refuses to cut that final thread.

His face softens, pity forming in his eyes for the briefest moment when he answers, "Fifty coins."

The thread snaps.

He leaves me with the crushing weight that I was only worth fifty coins to my father. I make ten in a month working for the Song family. Five months of my hard labor is the cost of my life. I do not have the strength to get up, not with the burden of truth bearing down upon me. Perhaps I was a fool for asking. I could have at least imagined that he gained a house, land, and years worth of money for me, or that they threatened his life. Two shoes come into view, cutting off all the things I wish were real and all the things I wish were not.

"Hello, again. You cost me a pretty pouch of silver, what with paying off the debt and all those poor people," a voice belonging to the pair of feet says with more amusement than anger.

Looking up, I am filled with no emotion. Not fear. Not surprise. Not happiness. I am empty. Nothing matters. *I* do not matter.

The same man from the gambling den is here, his masked guard with him, too. Why he feels his guard's presence is necessary in the middle of the Song estate, I cannot guess. Perhaps he is not a noble but a prince in need of constant guarding, and if Fortune was ever on my side, he would be here to rescue me like the romantic tales. Tragedy seems fated to be my ending, though.

"Who do I have the pleasure of addressing?" I ask, the only words that come to mind at this moment.

"You can just call me Woosung," he says, giving a soft smile.

There is kindness in his gaze. Is he truly here to come to my rescue again? No, not likely. I narrow my eyes, realizing he has not provided his last name, but I suppose I don't need to know it. All the nobles are the same anyways.

After a few moments of silence, he assumes correctly that I have nothing to say. "And you are Song Jinah."

"That is not my name," I growl.

He cocks a well groomed brow. "Oh? I thought it was the Song clan's turn to offer a bride."

"A bride?" That is an interesting term to apply to the women sacrificed to the Gumiho King.

"Did they not tell you what your purpose is?" He seems to enjoy that he possesses information that I do not.

At last, I get to my feet, smoothing out the luxurious skirt. "They did not. Nor did they pay me, so I will not lie on their behalf." Song Talhae can kill my father for all I care, for my father has sent me to my death.

His smile widens. "What is your name, then?" he inquires.

I do not appreciate the way he wields my ignorance like a weapon over me. "What do you mean 'bride?'" I cross my arms.

"Answer me first." His smile grates my patience. There is something subtly arrogant about it.

I have no energy to play his games. "Baek. Baek Jiwon."

"Not of noble birth, then." A statement. Not a question.

"I think you could've surmised that when we met at the gambling house."

He shrugs. "I thought you were simply a fallen Song relative, seeing as Song Talhae has been mentioning you being the sacrifice for the past month or so. Certainly would not be the first of noble birth to gamble their fortune away."

"For the past *month*?" I gape.

I had always wondered why the Song family had hired a girl such as me who works slower than others, and it seems that now I have the answer. Song Talhae knew his clan's turn had come to produce a sacrifice, and he had schemed for a decade on how to ensure his blood would not be sent. That explains how this man found me, and why he was interested in me in the first place. Why the Song patriarch chose me is not difficult to deduce. He chose me because no one would miss me, no one would recognize me. Halmeoni Hyesun would have already forgotten about me, and my father obviously didn't want me.

Something is more pressing to consider. "So what did you mean when you said I was going to be a bride?" I demand in a tone unbefitting my inferior station. But what more can happen to me that hasn't already?

At one time, the nobles possessed the knowledge of the Year of the Maiden's origin, but such information was lost long ago. Now, we can only speculate. One of the more outlandish theories is that he needs a mortal woman to mate with in order to create the nine-tailed shifting foxes. But I've always thought it was mere myth. Perhaps it is not.

"What do you know of the Gumiho King?" Woosung asks, fingers tapping on his bicep.

"That he demands a woman every seventy years, and the women are never seen again. No one from my station is ever chosen, so I'm not particularly familiar." I don't even know the names of all the women who've been sacrificed, not sure if anyone remembers aside from some royal scholar. The Year of Maiden feels like it's always been and always will be, much like the seasons of the earth.

"Do you know what he does with his brides?"

"Didn't I just say I didn't know much?" I retort, my voice revealing my lack of patience. I'm about to be sent to my potential death, as unlike the wispy woman from the stream, I have no romantic ideals about the Gumiho King.

He cocks a brow at my bluntness but continues, "The Gumiho king is powerful, the keeper of the forests. One day, centuries ago, a beautiful mortal woman captured his heart, and so he stole her away to his den deep in the woods. When the woman's husband came to take her back, he killed both of them and ate their hearts. Ever since then, every seventy years he takes another woman, addicted to the beauty of mortal women, their hearts particularly delectable. Who knows what horrors occur in his obsession?"

"If it is beauty he seeks, he'll surely be disappointed when I show up," I scoff, rolling my eyes.

"At least you have an accurate appraisal of yourself," he mumbles. Speaking more clearly, he adds, "But after a few weeks of good food, a few baths, and a new set of clothes, you can become a fair beauty."

Anger pinches my face, and I raise a pointed finger, ready to unleash a barrage of insults that I'd been stockpiling over the years. They were intended for Taehee, but this will have to do.

He shoves my hand down as if I were nothing more than a contemptuous child and states, "Some say he feeds off their blood, using their lives to feed his power."

"My blood won't be of much interest to him, seeing as the body that houses it is so feeble," I say with a laugh.

He frowns. "This is serious, Jiwon."

"You're not the one being sacrificed," I grunt, leaning against the wall to take off the pressure on my left leg.

He has a lot of patience for a noble man, and he continues his speech, "One thing for certain is, his brides are never seen again. I am of the personal belief that he likes to eat their hearts to maintain his own beauty in his human form."

"Wonderful." Acting so nonchalant is the only thing keeping me together in this moment. I have thought about killing myself before, but now that I am faced with death, I find myself eager to live. Perhaps it is because if I die, I want it to be my choice and not one that is made for me, especially by the Song family.

As if he can see past my apathetic facade, he says in a serious deep tone, "I have a way for you to live."

I eye him with an obvious suspicion. "Why should I trust you?"

He steps forward, leaning towards me and whispering, "I am not actually a noble."

My eyes widen. "B-but you're so wealthy."

"Simply a savvy merchant." He leans back, crossing his hands behind his back and smiling. "I do not promise you wealth nor love, but purpose. If you kill the Gumiho King, you will be known as the savior of the kingdom instead of the broke girl with a broken body, good for nothing more than mucking pig pens."

Indignation overwhelms me, goading me into speaking a sharp retort, but whether it is at the use of the word "broken" or the fact that I desire to be valued, I am not sure and decide to entertain the idea. "I am no warrior. How could I possibly kill someone so powerful?"

"With this," he says, eyes glittering when I don't immediately refuse him, and pulls out a sharp pin that resembles what the wealthy women put in their hair. "It is made of red pine. Stab him in the heart, and he will die like a common fox." He gestures with his chin, eyes urging me to take it.

The wood feels mundane, not magical. How could something so simple kill a gumiho?

"Those more familiar with the more mystical parts of our world refer to it as one of the three godwoods. Gingko, zelkova, and red pine all hold certain properties that seem to have an effect on creatures such as dragons, gumihos, and dokkaebi."

"How do you know so much if you're not a noble?" It's strange to have so much knowledge. Is it all fabrication? Money is a key to knowledge though, and with his overbrimming riches, he can certainly pay to obtain much information, even that which was thought lost.

He shrugs. "It is a personal interest of study."

Ultimately, how he knows any of this makes no difference to me. He's been more generous with both his money and information than anyone else.

The door slides open and in steps the ahjumma from before, her unpleasant expression seemingly a permanent position of her face.

"Looks like my time is up. Good luck," Woosung says as he heads out of the room. "We will see each other soon."

"What do you mean? How? When is 'soon?'" I rush to ask, my hand raising to reach out to him despite him already being halfway out the door.

He continues walking, shouting over his shoulder, "You will know when you see me next."

What kind of asinine answer is that? He disappears around the corner, and I am left alone with my questions.

The ahjumma beckons me forward. "Follow me. I will take you to the carriage." She does not wait for a reply and heads back outside.

I scramble to follow, passing by a sneering Taehee and somewhat sympathetic looking Taeri. Or maybe the sun is just in her eyes.

My father must have been ignorant of the Song clan's intention, not that he would have cared even if he'd known. Whether I became a concubine or was killed, did he even spare a thought? I shouldn't be surprised, but I am hurt. I thought that he loved me in his own broken, bitter way, yet apparently, fifty coins was all it took to throw me away. I bet he didn't even bother asking for more.

The silks that kiss my skin are soft and smooth, a stark contrast to the coarse fabric I have been allotted the past decade. I don't even remember the last time I wore a skirt.

Staring straight ahead, I whisper, "This is not the end."

Life is a series of problems for me to solve, and this shall be no different. I have survived through so much, and my story will not come to a close from some sadistic fox.

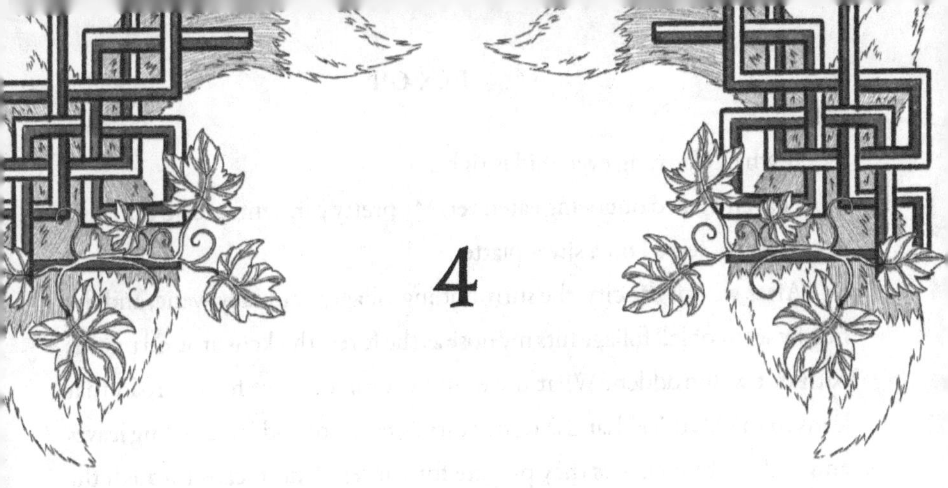

4

UNLIKE THE NORMAL GRAND sendoff that the noble ladies who are sacrificed receive, I am silently sent off through the back door in a nondescript carriage and no attendants aside from the driver. I wonder what excuse they will give the people for the lack of the traditional parade. Normally, blood orange chrysanthemums are tossed as the carriage drives through the city, the woman's family following the procession. Many even keep the thrown flowers for good fortune or protection, for the flowers used on the Year of the Maiden are said to keep away the malevolent mythicals that breach the borders and wander into the human lands.

Perhaps the Songs will send an empty adorned carriage through the streets for pretenses. Smart of them if they truly do so. It is a safer plan than allowing me to be in the procession where I could peek my head out and show the false sacrifice they're making. The Song patriarch didn't get his position from being careless.

When we come to the city gate, large arches carved out of the stone wall with watchtowers situated on top, a few people shout excitedly as we pass. Others hush them, pointing out that this carriage is far too mundane to carry the Maiden. If they knew I was one of them, some poor woman plucked from the streets, would they be so excited? Maybe they would. Maybe they'd like the idea of one of their own being chosen for what is reserved for nobles. Everyone loves a story of one rising above their station. But I do not go to marry a human royal who fell in love with me at first sight; I go to marry a monster.

If what Woosung even said is right.

I haven't ruled out being eaten yet. My pretty garments are no different than poultry served on a silver platter.

After we exit the city, the surrounding villages gradually wane, and the musky scent of fall foliage hits my nose as the forest thickens around us, this path not well trodden. What use do most humans have for the road that leads to the Mythical Lands? Red squirrels hurry to and fro, rustling leaves and shaking branches as they prepare for winter. A deer leaps through the brush, startled by our jostling carriage and snorting horse. I wonder what creatures exist in the Mythical Lands? Soon I will find out.

When we reach the edge between the Mortal Lands and those of the Mythicals, the carriage jerks to a halt. I push back the curtain and peer out the window. The trees are surprisingly normal, as are the plants, rocks, and small river serving as the border. The two sides match seamlessly except for one thing; the creatures standing on the other side are those of legends.

Two girin, cobalt scales shimmering in the midday light, stand in front of a wood carriage trimmed with gold and tassels. The paintings I had seen in various drinking and gambling houses that I'd pulled my father from did them no justice. Their horns and beards are like those of the sea dragons, their long tails like those of an ox, and their horse-like legs ending in deer hooves. One of them shakes their head impatiently, gold mane fluttering.

The driver's voice breaks my trance. "Miss, it is time to go."

Miss? Does he know who I am and just pretending? Or did the Song's tell him I am one of them?

Swallowing, I let the curtain fall back down in a whisper and crawl to the exit. The driver holds out his hand to help me down—a last kindness before I am sacrificed. I give a small smile in return, grateful for the assistance as my bad leg buckles when I hit the ground. The driver steadies me, dipping his head before quickly hopping back onto the carriage and flicking the reins. The horse rushes into action, apparently as equally eager as its driver to put distance between itself and the mythicals across the river.

I don't watch long, wanting to get the next part over with. Attempting to escape does not even cross my mind. A breeze whispers through the trees, telling them where I head, and in response yellow leaves fall like gold tears, branches waving in farewell as I approach the bridge. When I reach the crest, I am able to better see the woman standing by the two large girin. She is beautiful like the moon—pale with sparkling stars in her eyes. Her features are sharp, but what grabs my attention the most is her red hair. Her tresses fall like flames—or a river of blood. My stomach twists, and I gulp. I think I prefer the former comparison.

After I cross the wooden bridge, the width large enough for two carriages to cross at the same time, I come to a stop before the woman. Her nostrils flare, and she tilts her head. When she opens her mouth to speak, two sharp canines protrude from the rest of what look like human teeth. I do my best not to stare as I listen.

"Please, have a seat. It is about an hour ride to the palace." She dips her head and gestures to the carriage.

So we speak the same language, albeit her accent is different. "Thank you," I reply.

When she turns to move out of the way, a long, luscious white tail tipped in scarlet greets me. I cannot help that my eyes widen at the shocking sight, but I do not allow myself to gawk, instead smiling and climbing onto the carriage. Taehee had said I was going to my death, but this fox-lady has been nothing but kind. There is no reason to treat one about to be killed so well. And then there is this opulent carriage.

Gold leaves crust the outside corners, and red silks drape from the windows. Crimson cushions cover the floor, and I situate myself comfortably atop them. Why send such a beautiful mode of transportation for the one you intend to harm? Maybe I am being too optimistic. Humans can pet a cow one day and eat it the next. My previous poultry comparison comes back to mind.

The carriage jolts forward, my heart lurching along with it. On the ride here, numbness stole every emotion from me, but now in the silence of a carriage being driven by a half-fox-half-human and two girin, every feeling creeps in at once. I want to cry, to scream, to break something. My skin heats up and my heartbeat grows wild. I need a distraction. I will not shatter, will not show weakness in front of this potential predator.

"What's your name?" I call out to where the fox-lady sits on the lip of the carriage, body swaying with the movements of the girin. Despite my nerves, my voice sounds normal after years of training myself not to reveal my fear in front of monsters. Before now, they just happened to come in the shape of two girls.

"Shinhye," she replies, softly shouting to be heard above the noise.

"Thank you for coming to get me. My name is Jiwon. Baek Jiwon." I wonder if she will be shocked that I am not a Song. But do they have different naming customs amongst gumihos? Will she even notice?

"Why are you thanking me?" she inquires.

She mentions nothing of my family name. Won't the Gumiho King feel cheated? "Because you could have killed me right away or made me wander until I died in the forest. You could have even made me walk the whole way, following behind you on the carriage."

"You are a cynical one," she comments, neither a critique nor compliment.

"Kindness is rare, and favors are expensive," I mutter back.

Some strange yipping sound comes from Shinhye. I think she is laughing. "You are a wise one, then, too."

I've only just met this fox-woman, and yet the compliment feels genuine and fills me with warmth on such a difficult day. Maybe the Mythical Lands will be better than my own. I squash the thought because I have yet to meet the Gumiho King, and he may quickly change my perception of this place. My thoughts today are as fickle as my father, changing from hope to despair and apathy to fear with each rotation of the carriage wheel.

Suddenly, the air becomes stuffy inside the carriage, the walls closing in on me like a shrinking cage. I crawl forward, sliding the curtain to the side. The crisp autumn air washes over me. Shinhye looks at me from the corner of her gold eyes but doesn't question me.

"Can you tell me about your king?" I ask, situating myself into a more comfortable position.

Shinhye shifts, perhaps unsure with what information to divulge.

I offer lightheartedly, "I promise not to run off no matter what you tell me."

Her posture relaxes. "My Master is..." she pauses, mulling over her words. "Cold but kind. He tends to keep others at a distance, but it is because he is afraid of being hurt."

I nearly laugh, folding my lips to keep the sound from coming out. That is nothing like I've heard, neither from tall tales nor what Woosung relayed to me. No human alive has met him that I am aware of, but Shinhye is his servant and could be biased. I tuck her words in the back of my mind with a safe layer of suspicion.

"Does he eat people's hearts?" I ask, letting my curiosities run free.

Now it is her turn to laugh, that same yipping sound as before. "Not human ones, no," she says in the same way a parent might talk to their child who is afraid of a monster hiding in the dark.

Although it may be silly, her response comforts me. One less thing to be anxious about. I pull at the layers of fabric, my skin flush. I crawl forward, sitting just behind Shinhye.

"And what is your name?" I ask the girin.

Shinhye covers her mouth, but I can hear her smiling as she says, "They cannot talk."

A frown tugs my lips and brows down. "Oh."

Heat spreads across my face and down my neck, one that even the autumn air cannot cool. How am I supposed to know what creatures here can and can't talk? Something catches my attention, and I careen my head to get a better look. A creature dangles from a tree branch from a snake-like bottom half while its cat-like head watches us go by.

Without looking away, I ask, "Shinhye! What is that thing?"

She doesn't even need to turn to know what I am speaking of. "A myodusa. Half-cat and half-snake. But do not fret, they are one of the nice animals here."

I glance at Shinhye. "So that means there are not nice ones, too."

I rush to peer once more at the myodusa, but we are too far away now for me to see it.

"Yes. So it is best not to go out at night, and even during the day, you should always have someone accompany you. Humans make easy prey here in the Mythical Lands," she explains far too casually, chills creeping along my skin as I imagine terrible beasts tearing me apart. She continues talking, seemingly oblivious to my nerves. "But if you ever come across a myodusa again and you happen to have food, you should give it some. If you feed it, it will do you a favor."

"I can't say I am not the same. Feed me and I will be a grateful girl," I joke. It earns a yipping laugh from the half-fox.

We spend the rest of the ride discussing the difference in animals that inhabit the two lands. Daltokki—rabbits pale as the moon with glowing star-like eyes, bulgae—dogs with fiery fur, and gyeryong—chickens with the bottom of a dragon, all roam the lands. And those are only the non-human-like ones. Dokkaebi wander without a kingdom to call their own. They're the most human appearing ones, and they are also the most conniving.

"They are able to cast short but immersive illusions," she warns. "You cannot trust what you see or even hear around them. They can even trick your sense of smell and taste, but it can only last ten or so minutes at a time—at least in my experience."

"In your experience?" I press, curious about her run in with the mischievous creatures.

"I met one once, and it got me to bite my own tail by making me think it was a juicy deer leg," she says with a slight hiss to her words.

To save her further reminiscing on her embarrassment, I ask, "So are there mundane animals here too? The ones found in the human lands?"

She nods. "Of course. Animals do not stick to borders like humans do. Mythicals of any kind are allowed to travel freely within our region of the peninsula. Only the main courts where the rulers reside tend to be homogeneous, but in the Mythical Lands, you will find villages of haetae, gumiho, and dokkaebi all living together. The dragons are far too fond of their water to live inland unless there is a large lake."

"So can girin shift?" I question, glancing at the great beasts pulling us and imagining how huge they'd be as humans.

"No. Only mythical breeds with pearls can. Simply put, you may categorize all mythicals into a pearl-less and pearl containing kind."

My head hurts from the flood of new information.

Our conversation ends when the palace comes into view, the walls similar to ours, except gray and moss covered, as if it has existed since the land was formed, growing up from the soil like a tree. Pillars supporting tiled and tapered roofs line the top. A sharp gate yawns before us, two lanterns hanging like fangs from the arch of the entrance. The carriage passes through, but no bustling royal grounds greet us. It is eerily quiet. I glance at Shinhye. Are gumiho customs different from those of humans? But who takes care of it all? Peering around, it doesn't appear they do much tending. A variety of foliage and flora consumes the courtyard, ancient trees crowned in flaming orange and glimmering gold line the path the front entrance, and brown buildings peak between the trunks.

Shinhye stops the carriage at the front entrance of the palace, reddish-brown pillars guarding the entrance while cyan rafters support dark gray tiles tinted with blue. I didn't know what I was expecting. A cave perhaps. However, this is quite similar to human architecture. Two gumiho statues stand as sentries at the top of the stairs, their eyes  almost sentient. I shiver. Although the building is similar to a human-made structure, the atmosphere of this place is certainly *other*.

When I get off the carriage, Shinhye stares, perplexed with her head tilted and eyes searching, a question clearly on her mind. Her white brow curves like a feather on her forehead.

"Is there something you want to ask?"

"You didn't scream or balk." At first I don't know what she is referring to, but then her fox-tail curls around her leg, coming into view.

Lifting my skirt, I reply, shrugging, "I know what it's like to be pitied for it, feared for it, and even loathed for it."

This time, it is her sharp eyes that widen as she gets a good look at the wood brace that goes from just below the back of my knee down to my ankle where it disappears into my shoe. I can see that she is trying to think of what to say, and there is a strange satisfaction in knowing that I have made a mythical speechless.

She clears her throat and finally speaks, "I see. You are not like the others."

Ah. I had forgotten that I am not the first mortal woman sent here. "And what were the others like?" I wonder if she will even answer.

"Some cried, some screamed, some fought, and some died." She lists it off so casually, as if their lives—whether or not they met their deaths prematurely—were nothing of import.

A new cynicism drapes over all the information she divulged on the trip here. These gumihos may intend to kill me, and they might not even believe they're doing something wrong. For her master to kill mortals and for her to still consider him kind...

A sudden dread grips me like fierce animal claws.

"Shinhye, I see you've brought the mortal," someone says from the top of the steps.

I turn slowly, gulping, my heart beating as rapidly as a rabbit. It has been a long time since I've felt like cowering. Even in front of the Song sisters, I never let myself run. But now, seeing him, I desperately wish for a pair of healthy legs that could take me far away from here.

The Gumiho King of the forest has come to claim his woman.

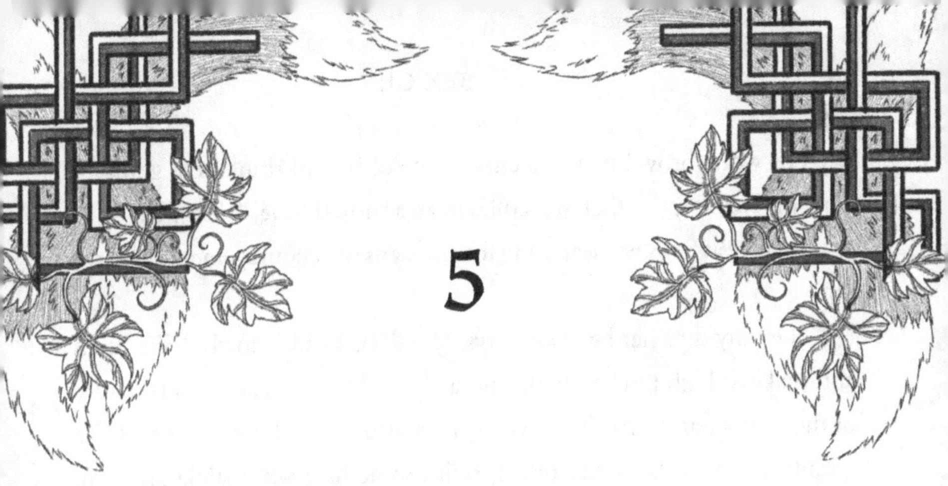

5

Even in his human form, his features remain sharp, his glowing golden eyes pointed at the ends, his jaw sharp like a fox's snout, and his ears are... Absent? No human ears rest on each side of his head, and instead, two pointed white furry fox ones jut from the top of his head. His flowing garments with voluptuous sleeves are like that of human nobles, black fabric trimmed in red with a matching long scarlet vest. He belongs in a painting, not reality. That otherworldly beauty is what makes him the most frightening. The Song sisters are beautiful on the outside but vile on the inside, and with the coldness I see in his gaze, I know he will be the same.

I recall what Woosung said about the Gumiho King consuming mortal hearts to maintain his beauty, and it suddenly seems like the most accurate theory. Courage flees from me for one the few instances that I can remember. The pin he gave me burns against my chest where I tucked it in my underlayers.

The Gumiho King doesn't even bother to look at me when he says, "Shinhye will give you a tour of the palace." His gaze rests on the palace wall, seeming to be as uninterested in me as a noble passing a beggar in the streets. Does he find me so repulsive?

My courage flickers back to life, anger silencing any suggestions wisdom might make to speak with more respect. "Don't you think it would be more appropriate for the master of this place to guide me?"

His white brow lifts like a curved line of frost. I think he is going to deny my request, but then he replies in an annoyed tone, "Very well."

I glance at Shinhye, searching for any signs of encouragement or warning.

She only dips her head and says, "I will be inside shortly." She turns and makes a high pitched bark, and a cloaked being appears to take care of the carriage and girin. The two begin chatting, but due to the hood, the gumiho remains obscured from my sight. Something white sticks out from the cloak, but I cannot make it out clearly from this angle.

"Well, are you coming or not?" Inha's sharp question yanks my attention back to him.

I take a deep breath and slowly ascend the stairs.

The Gumiho King looks down on me as I struggle with each step, and he crosses his arms. Is he irritated that I am taking too long? The immature side of me wins, and I purposely slow my pace, adding in a few grunts for good measure. His fingers begin tapping on his biceps, and it makes me smile. When I reach the tenth and final step, he does not offer his arm nor any other pleasantries, and he simply spins on his heel and enters the building. I rush to catch up, regretting my earlier stunt. Petty revenge tastes sweet at first, but it is most often followed by a bitter aftertaste.

Seemingly eager to conclude his coerced guiding of the palace, the Gumiho King does not wait for me. His pace is far too quick for my shorter appendages, my left leg struggling to stay just behind him. The lower limb burns, begging for me to slow down, but I will not ask this gumiho for any such favors, will not admit weakness in front of this predator. His steps are as silent as snowfall, while my shoes slap against the smooth dark green jade floor. I wonder how they got so much jade to create it? He says nothing as we pass by pillars, images of running gumihos and hopping rabbits carved into them. One pair even has a few myodusa on them.

"Won't the jade be cold in the winter?" I ask, my curiosity greater than my fear of the lithe gumiho next to me.

His ears flick, his tail, a twin to Shinhye's, swaying with his steps. "We have warm water running beneath the floor in the winter. Despite our fur, foxes like being warm, too."

Another commonality with humans. My gaze lifts upwards to where brown-red rafters cut like claws through the darker wood ceiling. While watching, I trip over my own feet and careen towards the jade floor I was just appreciating. A hand grabs the back of my collar, halting my fall. An unflattering choking noise comes from my throat, and he yanks me back.

I cough, glaring at the gumiho as he releases his grip on my garment. "Thanks," I grumble, rubbing my neck where the cloth cut into it.

He shakes his hand as if he were casting away dirt before he drops it back to his side. "It is best to watch where you are going."

"How should I call you?" I ask, ignoring his jab.

"Inha."

"Jiwon."

"I didn't ask."

"I know."

He grunts softly, but I am not sure if it is in humor or annoyance. The hall gives way to a large room with more branching corridors—left, right and center. He pauses and points. "Straight ahead is my throne room, right is the West Wing, where you are allowed to walk freely, and the left is the East Wing. You are never to go there. Anywhere outside the palace but within the walls is also fine."

"What? A whole half of the palace is restricted?" I sputter. For some reason, that seems even more outrageous than not being allowed outside the greater walls. I'm still not certain what my purpose being here is.

His lip curls, a single fang flashing a warning. "I could always confine you to your rooms."

"I'd rather you kill me." I cross my arms, titling my head to meet his gaze.

In an apathetic voice, he says, "That is still under consideration."

I lift my chin up at a proud angle. "You cannot. Shinhye has become attached to me already."

He cocks a brow, his voice a soft, unbelieving grumble. "Is that so?"

"Feel free to confirm it with her." I shrug.

His narrowed eyes bore into mine. "What if you're lying?"

I do not retreat from his stare. "I don't like to lie."

"All humans lie." His tone is cold, sucking the warmth from the room—not that there was much to begin with.

"Some more than others," I admit. "And it would be dishonest to say that I never have and never will. I'm not perfect, after all, but I try my best not to."

He turns his face away from me and mumbles quietly, but not so quiet that I cannot hear him, "They sent a strange one this time."

Did he see my leg brace when I showed Shinhye? Or is he referring to my personality? Either way, I don't particularly care about what he thinks of me. "Shall we continue the tour?" I ask, wishing to move on.

He takes a step towards the right, but I put up an arm to block him. Despite knowing that I would have been caned for such an action to a noble back home, and that I just might be inviting him to use those sharp claws on his fingers against me, I do not lower my arm and immediately apologize. All of my forbearance was left in the Mortal Lands; it's not like adhering to social etiquette spared me any trouble. I endured so much from the Songs, and I still ended up here. There is a strange liberation that comes with teetering upon the precipice of death. If he is determined to eat my heart, then my lack of decorum will not affect the matter. I've spent my whole life biting back sharp retorts, and now that the doors have opened, I do not desire to shut them.

But how much can I push this gumiho before he shows me what those sharp claws and canines of his can do? I feel like one of those children who uses flower petals to decide what to do, except for me, each pluck of a petal switches between wanting to live and wanting to give in to the dark fate awaiting me. To slay or to be slain. It feels like it's the only choice I have in this situation.

A low growl emits from his throat, his eyes narrowing.

"I'd like to start with the throne room," I say, feigning ignorance of his irritation.

"Very well," he replies with a slight hiss, his clawed fingers twitching at his side.

He leads me straight down the corridor towards the arching entrance in the shape of a gumiho, tails splayed around it with a pointed snout resting at the top, wooden eyes peering down at me. We pass under it, a chill crawling down my spine as if the carved wood came to life and the gumiho blew air down onto us. A square room, decor matching the halls we just wound through, waits on the other side.

A seat of gnarled wood serves as his throne, roots digging into the mound of moss covered ground that juts from an area of the floor devoid of jade. It's a little piece of the earth in the middle of a manufactured room. The back of the tree-like throne reaches towards the ceiling, branches covered in flaming fall foliage. It calls to me, beckoning me to touch it. I walk forward, arm slowly lifting. Before I can take more than a few steps, a clawed hand clamps down on my forearm, waking me from my trance.

"What do you think you're doing?" he snarls, yanking me back to face him.

I shake my head, casting off the last of the strange feeling. "I–I'm not sure. I thought it was calling to me."

Inha's eyes widen, and he releases me. "Calling to you?" he rasps, disbelief clearly written across his face. He peers at the throne with what I can only describe as a sort of longing, although I do not understand why.

I press my palm to my forehead. "I think I'm just tired. Perhaps we should head to my rooms."

We make our exit, but I take one last look at the enchanting throne before we turn around the corner. The desire to touch it is already gone, and I wonder if I imagined it. Maybe I really do need to sleep. As I follow Inha, I observe his white hair, a spill of moonbeams down his back. His ears draw my attention next, two snowy mountains capped in crimson.

Once more, my curiosity bursts. "You look human except for the ears and tail," I comment. There is also the fact that claws exist where fingernails should, and his canines are as sharp as any predator.

Reaching up to touch one of his ears, he says, "Mortals are such lowly things, and my ears and tail are a reminder that I'm not of them."

I roll my eyes. "Why not stay in your fox-form, then?"

Said ears flatten, and his tail twitches erratically. "Don't forget that you are not to come into the East Wing of the palace." If he had any fur on the rest of his body, I am sure it would be bristling.

Silence blankets us the rest of the tour as he explains that the kitchens are down one hall, and the servants' quarters are located behind that, and down another hall are some guest rooms that are never used. I wonder what is in the East Wing, but I know now is not a good time to ask. Perhaps later Shinhye will be able to answer my questions.

My leg brace is beginning to chafe. *How much further to my rooms?* I whine to myself, not quite that brave to complain like a child to the Gumiho King.

Soft footsteps sound behind me, and I turn, smiling at the arrival of the fox-woman from before.

Inha clasps his clawed hands together. "Ah, Shinhye, it is about time. You can take it from here. You will be attending to the mortal woman from now on."

"It's Jiwon," I remind him.

Inha eyes me but does not correct himself. He snorts a burst of air from his nostrils. "Like I said, if you need anything, ask Shinhye." Then he stalks off.

I don't bother watching him leave.

Shinhye gives a sympathetic smile. "Please, do not take it personally."

"I learned long ago that one's rudeness to me has less to do with me and more to do with them," I say, shrugging.

She claps her hands together, noticeably devoid of the long claws that are on Inha's, and says cheerfully, "Well, why don't we get you settled in your new room." She slides open the door in front of me.

Apparently, where we had stopped was my room. Was Inha really that eager to get rid of me that he couldn't even open the door in front of us and finish the tour?

But when I see my new living quarters, my mouth drops open, my eyes nearly popping out of my head. I step over the threshold, letting out an awe-filled gasp. It is even more luxurious than the room I was dressed in at the Song estate. Two windows are cut in each of the two outer facing walls, the other two walls covered in tapestries and paintings of landscapes. A canopy of scarlet cascades from the ceiling to the floor, surrounding a thick pile of white blankets on the ground, a silk pillow embroidered with pink peonies situated at the top. The Gumiho King must really love red.

"I take it everything is to your liking, then?" Shinhye asks, leaning forward to study my expression.

I nod, unable to speak. It's all so...*human*. "Do all gumihos live in structures like those of humans?"

"It depends entirely upon the individual gumiho. Some prefer to stay in their fox forms, and thus tend to enjoy caves or dens, while those who spend more time in their human forms follow the fashion of mortals."

Raising my arm, I pinch the fabric of the canopy, running my fingers down it. "I see. And what do they do for work?"

"Some, like myself, serve the master here, while others live a simple life, hunting and foraging for their sustenance, and the ones that I mentioned—the ones who are inclined to mortal forms—will learn crafts in order to trade with other mythicals and the bolder ones venturing to do business in the Mortal Lands."

My mouth drops open again. "You mean there are mythicals living in the Mortal Lands?"

Her tail swishes. "Perhaps a rare few reside there, but most of the time, they live here and just conduct their commerce with brief visits. Although there is no official law prohibiting it, it is generally looked down upon for mythicals to move to the Mortal Lands."

I rub my left arm. "Interesting. I wonder how many mythicals I've met unknowingly."

Not seeming to hear my comment, she continues explaining and points to the right where a screen acts as a wall to another room. "You can bathe in there. The water comes from a hot spring, so it is always there, always warm."

I close my eyes, imagining dipping my aching body into a warm pool of water. "That sounds amazing," I say, nearly moaning.

"Would you like help undressing?" she asks, already moving towards me with her hands raised and ready to peel off my garments.

Waving my hands in front of me, I decline, "No, thank you. I didn't mean right this moment. For now, I think I would like to eat and sleep."

"Ah," she says, lowering her hands, "I see. I will tell the others to begin preparing dinner then."

Before she goes, there is something I want to know. "Shinhye, when I asked the king about why he doesn't stay in his fox form, he seemed upset."

Her body stiffens, a faint grimace gracing her fine face. "Oh. Yes. It is best not to bring that up."

"Why?"

Chewing on her lip, she hesitates but at last answers, "He is cursed."

"Cursed?"

"Yes. The curse took from him his tails, along with most of his powers—including the ability to shift. However, when our King was cursed, we were too. Whatever form we were in is the one we have stayed in. My mate is still in his fox form—far more fortunate than I, stuck appearing as a mortal for decades." She glances at me before adding, "No offense, of course." She continues, looking over her shoulder lovingly at her white tail tipped in red, "I am just glad I had one of my tails on before I got stuck in this state."

What a harsh curse. I wonder what they all did to deserve it. "What is your husband's name?"

"*Mate,*" she corrects. "His name is Taejoon."

"How many gumiho are there?" My finger traces the curtains encompassing the bed of blankets. Did they make it this way in order to create the feeling of a fox den?

"A little over four thousand. Since the curse, there have been no newborns. It is difficult to reproduce because our pearls—"

Her words are cut off when Inha enters the room. What is he doing here? He was so eager to rid himself of me just moments ago. His tail twitches behind him, and he opens his mouth to speak but closes it as if to gather his thoughts. "I... I wanted to invite you to dine together," he stammers harshly at last.

He should have taken longer to choose his words, and more importantly, practiced on how to say them. I frown. "I would like to eat dinner in my room." He treats me as if I was a burden, even though he is the one who wanted a human here, and then he orders me like a prisoner, unable to freely wander the palace. Now he wants to *invite* me to dinner? *I thought foxes were supposed to be clever.*

His tail stops moving, and I swear his golden eyes grow dark. "Of course." Ears flattened back, he hisses, "It must be too difficult to dine with a beast." Before I can correct him, he storms off, leaving Shinhye and me alone.

"I'm just tired," I explain, letting out a sigh and rubbing my forehead.

Shinhye grimaces. "Don't take it—"

"Personally," I finish for her. "I know."

After giving me a long, assessing look, she says, "Maybe you're the one."

"The one?"

She gestures to my bed. "I shall explain later. I will bring you your dinner shortly."

I nod, too tired to argue.

Later, alone in my new room, I sit by the window and stare out into the eve, wondering if Halmeoni Hyesun has eaten today, if my father has already spent all the money he received by selling me, and if the Song sisters have found a new victim. Two good things about being here are that they can no longer harass me and I am well fed. I think back to the dinner Shinhye brought me—rice porridge with huge chunks of chicken and fresh vegetables, pickled cabbage with spices the way humans like, and buns full of sweet beans.

It seems after centuries of mortal brides—if that is in fact what we are sent here for—they've gotten quite good at cooking our food. What did they serve the first one? Raw meat? What do gumihos even eat? I cannot avoid dinner with Inha forever. Maybe tomorrow I will find out. I gulp. Hopefully not human hearts. Despite Shinhye stating the contrary, I still doubt if it is the truth. Maybe I should keep the pin Woosung gave me in my hair at all times.

The crescent moon climbs slowly, hanging just enough above the palace walls for me to catch a glimpse, and I lean my head against the side of the window. My life is a multitude of glimpses, wholeness just always out of grasp. Throughout the day, I tried to ignore my emotions, to stay calm, but they're a shadow that clings to me. In the solitude of my room, I fear that I cannot avoid them any longer.

A caw echoes outside, followed by the whispers of flapping wings. Scrambling backwards, a shout of surprise bursts from me, the crow landing on the wooden sill with a soft click of its talons. The scent of freedom wafts from his feathers.

Gaining my composure, I crawl forward, slowly lifting a finger towards the creature. "Hello there."

The bird turns its head, providing a good view of its eyes.

I gasp. "It's you!"

Golden eyes twinkle, a sprinkle of sun in the night, but something is new. As he adjusts himself on the window, a third leg comes into view, and I suck in a breath. Was the third leg always there? How could I have missed it?

"How are you?" it asks.

I jerk backwards, mouth dropping open and my hands slapping against the floor. "Y-you can talk?"

"Of course. All samjok-o can speak," it replies nonchalantly, clacking its beak.

The betrayal of my father and the strange turn my life has taken gnaws on my patience. "You say it as if it's common knowledge," I snap and reach for the nearest object. My hand finds a ceramic vase housing a single orchid, and I chuck it at the crow and shout, "You deceived me this whole time."

The samjok-o screeches, hopping out of the trajectory of the incoming vase. My throw was weak and my aim poor, and the vase smashes into the base of the wall. The pieces clatter like chimes, the water snaking out towards me. The only innocent one in all of this is the orchid, laying in the broken remains of its once home.

The water reaches me, the end of my skirt absorbing the liquid and turning the fabric a dark yellow. Even when I went to the crows covered in mud, I never lifted my voice at them. I wince and mumble, "I'm sorry. I'm just a little tired."

A soft coo. "Understandable. I did not intend to deceive you, but I was not permitted to speak then."

I stretch my hands towards him, and he allows me to stroke his smooth feathers with my finger, accepting my apology and perhaps a subtle way of his own. He is a bit of familiarity in this strange place, a small comfort on the worst day of my life.

"Have you met the Gumiho King yet?" he asks.

Inha's image in my head—beautiful face, cold eyes, and sneering lips—is hard to forget. I glower. "Yes. He was beautiful but not particularly warm."

"Ah, yes. He has never been my favorite of the rulers."

"Rulers?" I pause my petting, perplexed.

His talons click against the wood as he adjusts his perch. "Do you know anything about the mythicals?"

My tone is sharp. "I'm illiterate and poor, spending most of my time working. I didn't really have the opportunity to learn besides hearing street stories or witnessing the occasional painting."

He snaps his beak—not enough to hurt—at my finger. I wince but accept his scolding, and he continues explaining, "Well, in brief summary, there are four rulers in the Mythical Lands. The Gumiho King is of the forests, the Phoenix Queen of the skies, the Dragon King of the seas, and the Haetae Queen of the mountains."

"What about the other creatures I've heard about? Like dokkaebi, bulgae, and daltokki? I even saw a myodusa on the way here."

"They all exist, but none of them are rulers. Much like the girin, they are spread over all the land. Although there is a small group of dokkaebi that ventured into Mortal Lands a few decades ago. But that is something I need to worry about, not you."

"And what exactly is it that you samjok-o do?" I inquire, suddenly curious as to why the crow has watched me since I was in the Mortal Lands.

"We are messengers between the earth and the Celestial Realm."

"Then is there truly a Celestial Realm?" I scoot forward, leaning closer to the window sill. If I had not been sent on behalf of the Song sisters, I wonder if he would have ever been allowed to speak to me. I suppose I was never important enough to receive a message from the Heavens.

"Why of course. There are always things occurring in the Heavens that those here are ignorant to. Alas, I must go. I've got one more visit to make before I return to the Celestial Realm."

Without the chance for me to protest, the samjok-o flies off into the night, his black feathers melding with the darkness and taking away the little bit of familiarity he brought with him.

Now that he is gone, and without Inha's irritatingly aloof and gorgeous face to fuel my ire, or the Song sisters' torment to ignite indignation, the strength seeps from my soul. The heavy weight of life slams into me, my breathing labored by the crushing feeling of my chest. A flood of grief and sorrow fights against a fire of resentment and rage. The tears come soft at first but quickly shift into sobs. Bunching the blanket up into a thick chunk, I shove my face into it and scream. It is muffled in the room yet loud in my head, a screeching sound that scrapes against my skull.

I am alone. So alone.

I hate my father.

It's the first time I even allow myself to say it in my mind. Deep down, that feeling has festered, but I always tried to ignore it, always tried to please him, to take care of him. It was all for nothing. *I* am nothing to him.

Throwing the blanket aside, I walk over to the screen that separates my quarters from the bathing room. My fist punches through it. *I hate him.* Again. *I hate the Song clan.* Again. *I hate these mythicals and this life that constantly pours misfortune upon me.* Again. The screen is full of holes, and splinters dig into my skin, causing more tears to form. The only comfort in this pain is that it is a pain I chose to inflict upon myself.

A knock sounds from the door, but I don't want any visitors. I don't want to hear Shinhye tell me not to take anything personally, for I've heard it far too many times today, and I do not wish to be ordered around by that infuriating fox who couldn't care less about me. In the darkness, my hand gropes in the dark, searching without prejudice for something to throw. I stumble into a desk, my fingers curling around a ceramic. With all the strength I can muster, I chuck it at the door, shouting, "Leave me alone." I do not see it, but I hear the ceramic shatter and fall to the floor.

Whoever knocked does not do so again.

Collapsing on the floor, my whole body shakes as I weep. My clenched fists tuck into my chest, my knees following suit. No one in this palace will care about my tears, nor will anyone outside of it. Halmeoni Hyesun would if she could remember me. Who will take care of her? I can only hope the other children she fed alongside me will return her kindness and care for her in my absence.

Tomorrow, I will determine my next steps, but tonight, I grieve. Mourning for Halmeoni Hyesun and myself. I pray she will be alright, and despite his betrayal, I pray that my father will be, too.

I go to where I hid the godwood pin in the pillow while Shinhye was fetching me dinner. I do not want my end to be at the hands of that rich, beautiful monster. But could I kill him like Woosung asked? Moreover, *should* I? He has yet to harm me. So far, his only crime is being cold to me. I slip the pin back into the pillow and lay my head upon it. Sleep embraces me quickly, and my dreams are filled with forests, foxtails, and fangs.

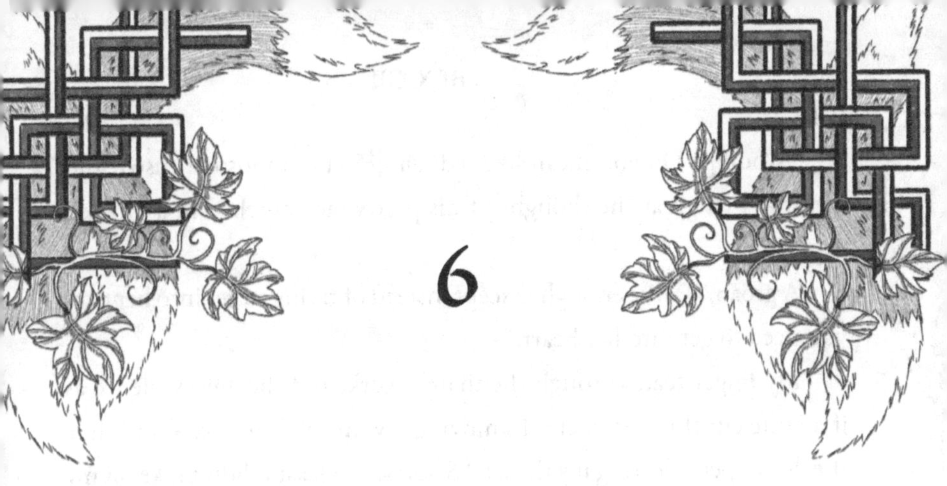

6

T HE NEXT MORNING, I hear voices outside my room when I wake. Walking past the poor screen that I punched into an oblivion, I softly shuffle towards the door, careful to avoid stepping on the broken ceramic, and put my ear against the thatched part. The words are muffled but identifiable.

Shinhye mutters, careful to keep her voice low yet not low enough. "You should be nice to her. We *need* her."

With footsteps quieter than their voices, they probably shouldn't be talking about me right outside my door, no matter how softly they try to talk.

"Do you really trust a mortal to help us?" a male asks incredulously. Although our interactions have been brief, it can only be the Gumiho King.

"She is different," Shinhye insists.

"In the past, only one has even tried. *One.* And she gave up after the third trial," Inha shoots back, but more than anger, I hear hurt and disappointment in his voice.

Shinhye lowers her tone even further, so I have to lean harder against the door, my palm pressing against the thin fabric. A splinter from last night digs deeper, but I muffle a hiss and ignore the pain.

"I think she can make it until the end," she insists.

"Mortals and mythicals are not exactly friends, let alone—"

With an exasperated sigh, Shinhye interrupts, "Try wooing her."

"Wooing? Do you mean like seducing?" He sounds confused, and I muffle a laugh at the thought of his pretty face pinched in a puzzled expression.

A groan. "Close enough. Except instead of trying to get into her bed, you need to get into her heart."

My finger tears through the thatch work, and the voices silence as if a knife cut through them. Removing my finger, I step back and slide the door open, clearing my throat. "S-sorry." At least I didn't take off my outer garments from the previous day. I don't need more embarrassment heaped upon this moment.

Inha stiffens, a frown forming on his face. Shinhye smiles, giving him a soft shove with her shoulder, foxtail twitching behind her.

"How was your first sleep here?" he asks awkwardly at last.

My fingers bunch the fabric of my skirt. "Fine. Thank you." I don't know what else to say. I was expecting to be dead by now in all honesty, but instead the fearsome Gumiho King is inquiring about my sleep. I'd believe he was genuinely concerned if he'd actually look at me instead of staring off into a distant place where he is probably dreaming I am not present. Still, it's better than being shredded by his claws.

"Good. Then you can join me for dinner tonight," he says, a harsh bite to his words that lets me know he is not asking this time.

Although I slept well, my patience still runs low, and the wounds of my father's betrayal are still fresh. "Is it not enough for me to be a prisoner here? Must you also demand that we play pretend with pleasantries?"

His upper lip curls, revealing both of his pointed canines. "You will—"

Shinhye interrupts his snarl, elbowing his side and conveying some message through her eyes. Inha growls before releasing a long gust of air and relaxing his shoulders.

He clears his throat. "Would you please grant me the honor of joining me for dinner tonight?"

I glance at Shinhye, meeting her gaze. Eagerness blazes in her eyes, and she nods her head in encouragement.

Although I have only known her for a day, I am fond of her. I have no desire to disappoint her. I look back at Inha. Some immature part of me wouldn't mind disappointing him though.

"I'd rather eat in my room." And then I slam the door shut, not wishing to see a crestfallen Shinhye or raging Inha. Disappointment cannot compare to dignity, and I will not grovel at the Gumiho King's feet. He is equally to blame for my presence here as the Song family and my father. None of them deserve my time.

"Fine! Then you can starve for all I care," Inha shouts through the shut door. "I told you it was pointless, Shinhye."

Shinhye speaks softly through the door, "Please, do not take it personally."

"I don't. But I also won't accept his anger either," I reply dryly.

Quiet.

Just when I think she, too, has gone, she says, "I hope you will give him a chance."

I know this time, the silence means she is gone.

A chance? A chance for what? To eat my heart? To turn me into some kind of pleasure prisoner? My body shudders at the very thought. My heart will never belong to the Gumiho King, literally or metaphorically. Perhaps there is a third option, one that doesn't include me nor Inha dying.

Escape.

If I can get Shinhye to show me around the palace grounds, I can make a mental map. Later, I can scout out the surrounding area. Once I reach the Mortal Lands, I could get Halmeoni Hyesun and take her to a new city, one where I won't be recognized and incur the wrath of the Song clan. Because ultimately, there is nothing keeping me here. I am not of the nobles, required to sacrifice myself. I am certain the Gumiho King will not be pleased, but that is for the Song clan to deal with.

I dress myself in a lilac skirt and cream top, using my teeth to aid my good hand in tying off the long straps. I can knot things fine enough, although the tie is nothing beautiful to look at, but it will keep my clothes on me. I leave my hair unbound and open the door to find a tray of food waiting for me. My stomach growls. Mapping out the palace can wait until after I eat.

After scarfing down the rice porridge and eggs and tucking a few chunks of food into my pocket in case I meet any creatures who'll let me go for the price of a snack, I head back out into the hall, searching for anyone who could show me around. I should have asked where Shinhye's room is. By the time I reach the main hall that leads to the throne room and East Wing, I still have not seen another being.

Turning towards the entrance, I decide that I might have better luck by just wandering the grounds alone, and that way no one will distract me with idle chatter or question my desire to explore the area. I chew on my finger, trying to suck and pluck the splinters out while I walk. With a grunt of triumph, I manage to remove two of them. Too preoccupied with the final one, I nearly run into Shinhye when I turn around the corner.

"Oh," we exclaim in tandem.

My mind rushes to find a good reason for my random wandering. Guilt pricks me as if I am a child caught disobeying their parents. "Umm... I was looking for Inha." That was a terrible excuse, but it's too late to change the words.

She smiles, looking rather pleased that I want to see him. "He received a message from the Phoenix Queen and went to her court."

"What about the curse? I thought he couldn't leave his lands?"

"The curse demands no such thing. His...reclusive tendencies are of his own volition."

Whatever royal responsibilities demand the Gumiho King's attention is no concern of mine, and it provides the perfect opportunity to explore for a future escape. His annoying and arrogant eyes will not be prying for at least the rest of the day.

Shuffling in the direction I want to go, I mumble, "Well, if you don't mind, I just want to go for a stroll around the palace."

"Would you like me to accompany—"

"No," I rush out before realizing how suspicious my rejection is, but I am now committed to surveying the grounds by myself. A shadow darkens her gold eyes, her lips pursing. Quickly, I add, "No, thank you. I would prefer some alone time. But maybe tomorrow you can show me around the palace grounds?"

Her expression brightens up again. "Very well. I will make sure to let the Master know you wish to see him upon his return."

"Thank you," I say, swiftly striding away before she can say anything else.

I walk outside, staring at the stairs I ascended only a day ago. Is there something wrong with me that I find this whole place normal? If it weren't for the fear that Inha is going to eat my heart, I think I would quickly become accustomed to this place. A home. Not that I'd ever expect to find love here amongst the gumihos. But I think Shinhye is genuinely kind, and given time, we could become friends. It certainly has more potential than that shack with a drunken and deadbeat father.

However, a pig living in luxury is still destined to be slaughtered. My end will not be at the hands of the Gumiho King. I carefully climb down the stairs, the fresh scent of soil hitting my nose. There is a beauty to this place, the way it cohabitates with nature instead of fighting it. In all the paintings of the royal palace, everything is perfectly placed, not a wild flower or stray tree to be found. As I gaze at the walled land, I see coves of trees and patches of fall flowers that made their home of their own accord. Vines crawl up buildings and barriers, a sea of leaves covering the ground.

Now is not the time for sightseeing. I shake my head and regain my focus. I look left and then right. Where to start? Should I just leave straight away? I look down at my skirt, knowing the brace covered leg that hides beneath the fabric. I can't outrun a human, let alone a gumiho. Maybe if I can ride a girin...

To the stables then.

Yesterday I saw that other fox-man hybrid come from the left side of the main palace, so I head the direction he had appeared. I pass by the windows of the East Wing, all of them shuttered. I fetter my curiosity though, since I don't need to know the entire palace layout, only the path to escape. It doesn't take too long for me to find the stables with a pasture full of several girin, ranging from the cobalt pair I saw the other day to a teal that matches the palace rafters to a grass colored hue. All of them share gold manes though, and I wonder how such majestic creatures could become domesticated. I suppose humans did the same to horses, and perhaps girin are just as mundane to other mythicals.

I walk towards the towering fence, the height matching the size of the girin who stand higher than that of a horse. How can I possibly get atop one of them? The fence in front of me could be used as a makeshift ladder. For now, I simply need to see if the girin will allow me to approach them. If they scare, or worse, are aggressive, I need to find a new method of transportation.

Ducking under one of the lower rungs, I enter the pasture. There is something familiar about the scent of the soil and the animals, and it takes me back to the days of laboring at the Song's estate.

A simpler time. One before betrayal.

I shove away the thoughts of the past, as they do me no good in the present and weigh down my future. Slowly, I approach the grazing girin, careful to keep within their eyesight lest I inadvertently sneak up on them and receive a kick from their powerful appearing hind legs. As I draw near, a few of them padder away. Only two remain. I pick the jade colored one because he is the closest and I'm going to have to do a lot of walking today.

The girin looks up, golden eyes glittering in the morning sunlight, pieces of grass protruding from his soft looking lips, a stark contrast to the scales that cover the rest of its body. Maintaining calm and steady steps, I get within arms reach of the creature. It does not draw closer but neither does it back away. Stretching my hand towards it, I pray it does not secretly have sharp fangs and a pension for meat, hoping that the grass it chews means its teeth will also resemble the cows and horses back home.

It suddenly snorts, startling me. I bite my lip, swallowing the shout that nearly bursts from me. I flinch but manage to keep my movements contained. Inhaling, I creep closer. My fingers meet the cool and smooth surface of the creature's neck. It steps closer, pressing against my palm. I stroke its face, and the girin nibbles at my clothes.

"That's not food," I scold it, laughter bubbling to replace the nerves from a few moments ago, relieved that it seems more interested in my clothes than my flesh.

I glance around, checking for any foxes, humans, or hybrids in-between. With none to be seen, I reach down and tug up bunches of grass. I slowly walk backwards towards the fence, luring the green girin with my bounty. Every few steps, I allow it to eat some, until finally, my back bumps into the wooden fence. I give the remaining handful to the creature and turn to the fence. With my good hand clutching the wood above—ready to take the majority of the weight off my bad leg—I put my stronger leg up on the lower rung and launch myself upward. I repeat the action until I am high enough to mount the girin who continues to graze right next to me. At least something in my life is working out in my favor.

I hook my arm around one rung, reaching out with my stronger side towards the creature. My fingers tangle in its coarse, gold mane. *One.* I bend my knee. *Two.* I take a deep breath. *Three—*

"What are you doing?" a voice shouts and breaks my concentration.

I lose my grip and begin to crash towards the earth. Hopefully, the girin won't get startled and stomp on my head. Before my body hits the ground, a pair of milky-white furry arms catches me. The owner of the arms grunts with the brunt of my weight barreling into him, but neither of us falls.

"Thank—" My gratitude wilts, my eyes widening at the sight of a snout. I did not see it so clearly yesterday due to his cloak.

The fox-man sets me down, and I am able to see his entire body now. The upper half is completely that of a fox—save for some strange human like furry fingers—while the bottom half is that of a human. Shame quickly wells inside of me for staring for so long. I hope he will not take offense at my shock.

I bow. "Forgive me. I did not intend to be rude."

His ears lower in what I assume is shame. "Nothing to apologize for. Normally, I try to stay out of sight of the master's women."

I straighten back up, the corner of my lips curling down. "That sounds unfair to you."

He shrugs.

"What is your name?"

"Ah, yes. I forgot that I know your name but you do not know mine," he says, chuckling. "You can call me Gunoo."

"And how do you know my name, Gunoo?" I ask, perplexed. I only just arrived yesterday evening.

"Shinhye informed us all last night. She speaks rather highly of you."

"Oh," I exclaim, a smile spreading across my face.

But then he adds, "She says that about most of the human women who come though. Shinhye is rather optimistic."

"Oh," I say again, frowning now.

Gunoo, ignorant of my displeasure, continues babbling, "You see, each time one of you comes, Shinhye is the one to greet you—she is the nicest and one of the more human looking of us. Well, of course, I am always willing but if I was the first one you see, you would probably run away screaming." Again he breaks out into a boisterous bout of laughter, a foxlike hand resting against his belly.

As his chuckling begins to fade, I interject before he can start another long monologue, "If you will excuse me, I have something to attend to."

He takes a step forward. "If you would like, I can accompany you."

Waving my hands in front of me, I blurt, "No, thank you though."

Not wishing to provide a chance for him to further insist, I scurry off, guilt prickling me for rejecting him. He seems nice, but unfortunately, I can only plan my escape if I am alone and undistracted.

While I walk down the main path to the palace gate, I wonder what other variations of gumihos live here. Are they too embarrassed to show themselves? Are they nocturnal like their common fox cousins? No matter the reason for their reclusion, I am grateful for it right now because it makes slipping out unnoticed quite easy. Every once in a while, I glance over my shoulder to make sure no one is following me. Even if they are, it is not a crime to go for a simple stroll.

The lanterns hang unlit, the arch of the gate less ominous in the morning light, or perhaps it is because I am thinking of escape that they lack their carnivorous intimidation. I pause outside the exit. Curving to the left is a well worn road, wheel divots digging into the dirt, the forest forced to creep along the edge of the path after years of being beaten back. To the right the forest is thin, but no trail is visible to my eye. I think the girin—unencumbered by the carriage—will be able to traverse the lesser traveled path, but it would also run faster on the unobstructed road. Which will be better for a hasty escape? I head to the right side, leaves and twigs crunching underfoot, releasing the musky scent of autumn into the air.

If I find this trail too hard to traverse, then I can simply follow the road. Inha is not exactly the most welcoming of creatures, and I doubt there will be many paths to his palace. I was too dazed on my journey here to recall everything perfectly, but I don't remember any forking trails.

Something crackles in the bushes, and I freeze. It won't be a bulgae, will it? From the brush, a familiar creature emerges. The myodusa has golden eyes like everything else here, black dots mark its tan fur, and bark brown scales wrap around its serpentine bottom half. It meows, giving me a glimpse of its forked black tongue.

I crouch down, and the myodusa slithers closer, its front paws working in tandem with its lower snake half. Slowly so as not to startle it, I reach out a hand, palm up, revealing a piece of meat from the porridge this morning. Do myodusa even eat meat? I should have asked Shinhye.

It pauses, nostrils flaring. Then it darts forward lightning fast, a flash of brown and beige.

"Oh!" I exclaim, bemused as it gulps down the meat. It's a fast little thing.

Having finished its snack, I smile, and the creature rubs its head against my hand. I scratch between its ears, a purr vibrating into my fingers. 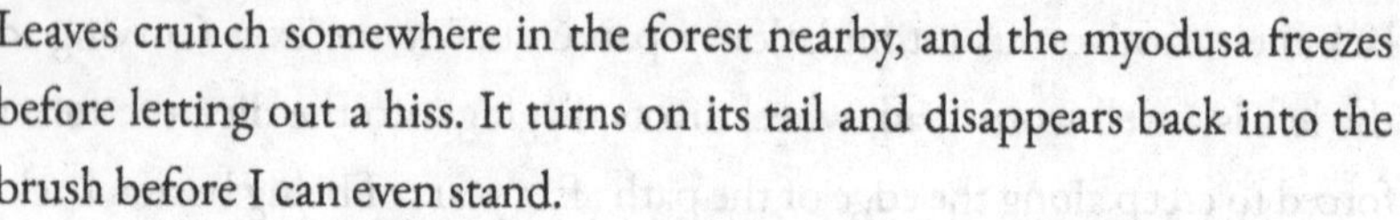 Leaves crunch somewhere in the forest nearby, and the myodusa freezes before letting out a hiss. It turns on its tail and disappears back into the brush before I can even stand.

Whatever scared it off can't be friendly.

Worried about what frightened the myodusa, I get up and start heading back towards the palace entrance as fast as I can. A twig snaps. A tree branch swishes. Something big is coming. My heartbeat increases as does my pace. Regret gloats over me; I should have begged Shinhye to take me outside the walls instead of sneaking out.

"Jiwon!" a man quietly shouts.

A human.

Or a monster who speaks like one.

How would it know my name? I whip around, raising my fists in front of myself in a feeble attempt to ward the potential assailant. A familiar face appears out of the foliage, masked guard in tow.

I let out a breath, the tension in my back dissolving, but then my apprehension is replaced with confusion. "Woosung, how did you get here? What are you doing here?"

He motions for his guard to keep a few steps back, the masked warrior's eyes darting around like an anxious deer.

"How are things going? Are you alright? Did he hurt you?" Woosung rambles off his questions.

My heart back to its normal pace, I shake my head. "No. I am fine. But you didn't answer my question." A peeving habit of his. "Why are you here?"

"I am relieved to hear it. But you must not forget what he is. I could not be honest with you last time, since there could have been ears listening. I know the true reason he wants mortal women."

Seems a strange reason not to tell me before. What could he know that the nobles don't—or can't—know.

"He is cursed, you see, and he will ask you to help break that curse. Agree to it, and you will gain his trust. Once you have his trust, you can use that pin I gave you." Woosung's eyes bore into me, searching for signs of hesitancy.

I cross my arms. "Why should I when I can just escape? Why should I put my life at risk?"

Taking a step closer, he asks, "What about the woman who will replace you? No noble is of the stock to be able to kill a gumiho, let alone the king of them all. Only someone who has grown up fighting, who knows what it takes to survive in a harsh world, can do this."

He has a point. If I run away or even if I submit to fate and die at his hands, there will only be another woman sent here in my stead several decades later. But *killing*...

"Can't you do it?" I ask, still uncomfortable with the thought of taking a life other than that of animals for food.

Shaking his head, he replies in a serious tone, "I cannot get close enough. Only you can. And if you succeed, I promise to rescue you and give you enough money to start a new life with your father."

My back stiffens at the mention of the man who sold me like some piece of livestock. "I have no desire to share money with him, let alone my life."

Woosung waves his hand in the air. "Very well. My point is, if you do this, you will not only be a hero, but you will also be rich."

I never thought myself a greedy person, and due to my father's gambling addiction, I never dared to imagine what I could do with my life given a small sum of money saved up. Now, a hefty amount of wealth dangles before me, and for the first time, I have the ability to dream. Even without the promise of money, Woosung makes a good point. Imagining either of the Song sisters trying to butcher a chicken, let alone kill a gumiho, is laughable. Maybe it was some sort of divine orchestration that brought me here. I am the perfect person to risk their life to kill the Gumiho King. Someone with nothing to lose and everything to gain. Someone who has known hardship and has had to skin and prepare their own meat. Someone whose hands are calloused but heart is not. My heart begins to beat faster.

I swallow.

He sees my thinking and must interpret it as hesitation, anticipating a rejection. "I did not take you for a coward, Jiwon."

It's the final shove. A fire flares to life inside of me.

"Alright," I declare. "I'll do it."

I head back to the palace, all thoughts of escape having melted away. It is only midday; my absence was relatively brief. Hopefully, no one will have noticed that I was gone and they'll just think I refused to leave my room, or in the worst case scenario, that I took a short stroll. Since Gunoo saw me, the latter seems like a good story.

My hopes are dashed when I see Inha brooding by the gate, his piercing eyes pointed at me.

He doesn't walk towards me, just stares as I approach him with a cold face and even colder eyes. I am glad he cannot read minds, cannot possibly sense my rebellious intent. Or can he? He is the *king* of all gumihos after all. I shudder. Certainly no creature possesses such abilities.

When I reach him, he growls, "Escaping already?"

"I wasn't running away. I was just going for a walk. Or am I not allowed to roam outside the palace walls?" I ask, indignance—or guilt—writhing inside me.

"I do believe I said as such the first day you arrived." Annoyance radiates off him like heat off the rocks in summer.

"Oh," I mumble, red warming my cheeks. "I must have forgotten." It's not a lie. I don't remember that rule. What is the difference between walks inside versus outside the palace?

A muscle bunches in his cheek, and his ears flatten backwards. "Make sure you do not forget again." He spins on his heel and storms off towards the entrance of the palace, white hair waving in the breeze like snow in the fall.

I follow after him, replaying Woosung's words in my head. The next time I leave these walls, it will be my last. Inha will not be so forgiving a second time, and after what I plan to do, I'll be lucky to leave alive. But if I succeed, I will be the savior of the Mortal Lands and have enough money for Halmeoni Hyesun and I to begin a comfortable life in a new city far away where the Songs cannot touch us. The thought hardens my resolve.

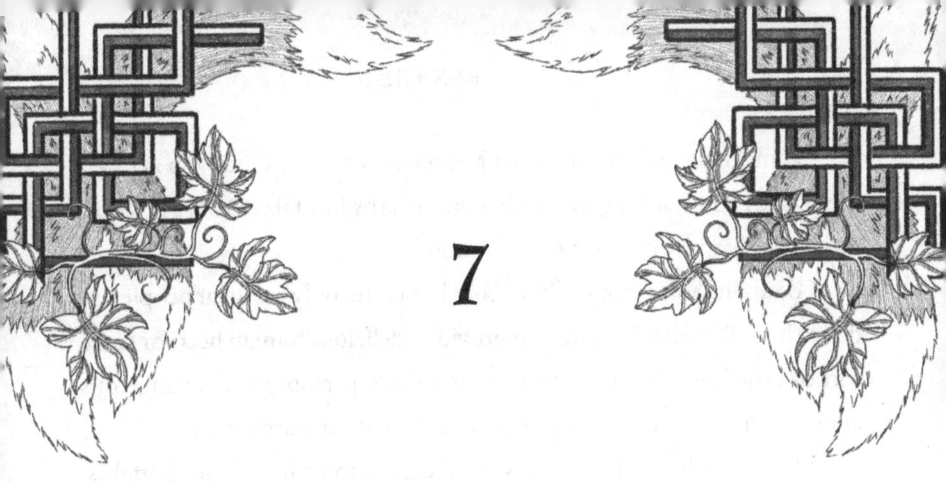

7

THIS TIME I DO not refuse Inha's offer to eat together. Dinner with a gumiho—the king of all gumihos to be exact–not even the greatest storyteller could have contrived something so fantastical. But more than a romantic dream, this is a nightmare. All the women who have come here and died, whether naturally or early as Shinhye implied, consume my thoughts.

All the insults about mortals, the cold glares and barking orders that Inha has given me help solidify my choice. I may not have been able to take my revenge on the Songs or my father, but I can take it against him. *He deserves this.* Had he been even the least bit kind, perhaps he could have saved himself from this fate. If he is bad enough to bring a curse upon himself, then death does not feel inappropriate either.

Maybe I was born for this purpose, to slay the Gumiho King and be a hero for the women of the Mortal Lands. If all goes well, Woosung will be there when I escape, waiting with a large sum of money and my future.

Shinhye enters, softly sliding the door open. In her arms she carries a full and fluffy scarlet skirt with more layers than an onion and a long, black top embroidered with scarlet spider lilies, as if someone splattered it in blood. Do mythicals also bleed red? What will it be like to feel someone's blood on my hands? I've bandaged minor scrapes and cuts, even helped skin a rabbit with Songhee before. I force such thoughts from my mind. They'll do me no good.

"I am so pleased you accepted Master's invitation. Once you get past the..." she pauses, setting the clothes on a nearby low table. "Cold exterior, he is actually quite pleasant to be around."

I doubt it. Something tells me that Inha cares only for what people can do for him. Whether I am here to provide a delicious human heart or some sort of other pleasure, he cares not for me as a person. He is a dangerous animal, one that needs to be put down before it can harm others.

My stomach suddenly turns nauseous. I don't like these thoughts. They feel slimy, like I am back in the pig pen at the Song estate and covered in grime, but if I don't think like this, I won't be able to carry out Woosung's instructions. But isn't this what the Song sisters did to me? Convince themselves I deserved their harassment, that I was lesser than them?

No. This is different. I am different. I am doing this for the greater good.

No matter what I tell myself, I still feel dirty.

Shinhye doesn't help, her hands deft as she helps me change. Tossing the worn garment over the new screen—the old one having been replaced while I was out on my walk—the she-fox doesn't ask about the damaged furniture. She has been nothing but kind to me, and I am going to hurt her by hurting her master. I wouldn't have to if he hadn't preyed upon human women for centuries. *This is justice.* The words ring hollow in my head. Why am I having such a hard time believing that?

That small voice hisses in my mind, *Coward.*

I do my best to ignore it.

Shinhye finishes off tying my top in a neat knot.

"Umm... could you braid my hair too, please?" I ask, trying not to let my nerves show.

Halmeoni Hyesun used to do it for me, and on the days she couldn't, I would simply tie the ends together. Anything more complicated was too difficult for my hands. I hope she is eating well, that someone else from our section of shacks is caring for her.

Shinhye nods, using her fingers to brush through and separate my hair into pieces. "I only know how to do a simple one."

I wonder if she learned from doing her own hair or from all the women who came before me. Seeing as her hair is worn loose, it seems to be the latter. Did she befriend them all like she is doing with me?

"All done," she says, letting the braid flop against my back.

"Thank you." I cannot get myself to look her in the eyes, and I only hope that my voice sounds normal.

When she is not looking, I slip the wooden pin into my braid. It sticks parallel to my head so that the wood is completely hidden, only the decorated end protruding just in case they recognize the material as that of a godwood tree. If she asks about the strange placement, I can just say that it is a new trend in the human lands. A sour tang coats my tongue. I hate lying. If I think about the women before me and those who will come after, it's a little easier to bear. Enduring a little bitterness now is worth the sweet future. I let out a breath. Each time I attempt to convince myself that what I am doing is different from the Song sisters and that I am doing the right thing, I know deep down it is not.

The little voice wins.

Quickly, before Shinhye looks back, I remove the pin and shove it under the nearby blankets, hoping no one will find it until I can properly dispose of it. Already I feel lighter, the tension in my shoulders and stomach releasing. The fact of the matter is, I know neither Woosung nor Inha well, nor do I know well what became of all my predecessors. Too angry at the Songs, at my father, and at life, I was willing to trust Woosung despite not knowing him well, ready to pour out all my rage and frustration onto Inha. I was a fool for trusting Woosung and no better than my father, willing to sacrifice morality for some money. Not that Inha is completely undeserving of some sort of ire, seeing as he demands mortal women, but the real reason I am here is the selfishness of fellow mortals.

Mortals? I can't believe I used that word.

Shinhye turns around, pulling out a small pouch from her waistband. She offers it to me, my eyes tracing the carefully embroidered orange camellias that contrast the teal silk they're stitched onto. A floral scent drifts from it.

"Master is fond of the smell of flowers," Shinhye explains, smiling.

I am not entirely sure why that matters—no amount of an aroma Inha likes will change how he feels about me—but it is no burden to wear it, and the smell is pleasant. She ties it on the knot of my top, the sachet and strip of fabric draping together.

She leaves my worn clothes in a pile on the floor. Now that I think about it, the other day my bed was made and the dishes from my meal cleared away by the time I returned to my rooms. Does Shinhye do it all? Are there others here that are hiding from me like Gunoo was? I should have thought of a better hiding place for the pin. Swallowing, I hope Shinhye and any other potential servants will be too busy with dinner to make my bed.

Her voice shatters my tirade of worries. "Are you ready? Master is waiting."

"Yes," I say, clearing my throat and casting away thoughts of the pin. My stomach has settled significantly since I discarded it.

She slides open the door, revealing Inha. I didn't realize she meant he was waiting outside my room. Inha's nostrils flare, and his gaze darts to Shinhye. His eyes narrow, but Shinhye gives an innocent smile and shrugs. He returns his attention to me.

I gulp, glancing down at my traitorous hands. They're shaking. I shove them into the voluminous fabric of my skirt. There is no way he knows what I was planning to do. No crime was committed, only considered.

"Doesn't she look beautiful, Master?" Shinhye asks.

His face yields no emotion. "She looks" —his eyes rove from head to toe before I can finish a breath— "fine for a mortal."

My nose scrunches. "Thanks. I think." My hands cease shaking.

Inha pivots, gesturing down the hall. "Shall we?"

I dip my head and we walk step in step, Shinhye trailing behind us. We walk in near silence, only Shinhye forcing us to converse through her probing questions.

"Does not Master's hair glimmer like moonlight, Jiwon?"

"I suppose," I reply, sparing only a quick look.

"Jiwon smells nice, yes?" she prods Inha.

His tone is apathetic. "Yes, but you knew that already."

It does not slow Shinhye down. "You two look lovely next to each other."

Neither Inha nor I reply, but our glances meet for a brief moment before running away and returning to the hallway. Inha guides me down a new corridor, and we enter a large room with space for at least a hundred people. Pillars break up the vastness of the area, and large rafters support the teal ceiling. It looks almost exactly like the throne room, except instead of a giant throne, two lonely low tables sit in the middle of the room. The air is cold and stale as if the room has not been used in a long time.

Shinhye scurries in front of us, shoving the two tables closer. "That's better," she mutters. Clapping her hands together, she says in an enthusiastic voice, "Now, hurry and be seated, and I will get the others to bring in the dishes."

Inha lets out a long breath and strides towards his table, lounging behind it with his elbow laying across his propped up knee. I follow after, sitting on the cushion behind the other table.

At last I see some of the other servants, each of them different in appearance. One that is similar to Gunoo—a human pair of legs and head broken up by a fox torso—carries in a big bowl of soup, steam curling from the top as she places it in front of me. She only wears a pair of pants, the top half of her body furry, and I wonder how hard it is to carry things with her fox fingers. Her pink hair is braided behind her, her face as pale as Shinhye's and Inha's. Next, a deep scarlet haired human looking one enters holding a platter with an uncooked chunk of meat. The metallic scent creeps into my nostrils. One more enters, pale pink hair in a bun on his head and a tail like Shinhye's jutting behind him, except that there are three of them. He sets a plate of meat on my table. I glance down at my own dish, thankful that they've cooked it for me—albeit it is rather charred. Better burnt than bleeding.

Shinhye enters, bringing a small plate of pale kimchi and a petite bowl of purple rice. She sets them both down on my table and orders the other servants out. "Thank you, you may head back to the kitchen."

The three gumihos bow and leave without a word. Even their footsteps don't make a sound. Since foxes are quiet creatures, it only makes sense that their mythical relatives would be the same.

"Please enjoy your meal. I will be here if you need anything," Shinhye declares, slowly backing away and positioning herself by the entrance.

Is that her way of giving us privacy? I am not sure if I want her to leave or not. My eyes fixate on Inha's clawed hands and fangs that are currently tearing into the meat. If Shinhye goes, he may kill me and eat my heart–or liver. Whatever gumihos eat when there isn't a human watching. Maybe I should have brought the pin with me just in case he is as cruel as some say. I may have decided not to kill him, but I do not know if he shares the same sentiment towards me. I no longer trust Woosung, but that doesn't mean I trust Inha either.

I startle at the sound of Inha's voice.

"Is the food not to your liking?" he questions, a faint growl to his words. "Or is it the company you find repulsive?" This time, his voice is softer, almost...sad.

I shake my head and pick up my spoon, lifting the seaweed soup to my lips. "Do not put words in my mouth," I chide before sipping the broth. It is surprisingly delicious. Our city is too far from the sea for commoners to have access to seaweed, but Inha's land is a bit closer, and I am sure he can afford to have it brought inland. "Both are fine," I say quickly, shoving another spoonful into my mouth.

Glancing up, I catch sight of a slight smile tugging the corner of his lips. He reaches towards me, and my breath catches in my chest. Is he going to slice my neck with those sharp claws? Was he lying when he said he doesn't eat human hearts? Contrary to my fears, he does not harm me, his touch gentle as a claw whispers against the skin right next to my mouth. When he sits back down—a rice grain on his claw—I let out all the air I was holding.

Inha wipes the rice onto the edge of his plate and tears a chunk of meat off and chews it thoughtfully, red juice dribbling down his jaw.

I blink, still processing what just happened. What is he pondering in that pretty head of his? He didn't kill me this time, but that doesn't mean he isn't planning to later. I scratch the back of my neck. How can I escape? For the first time, I doubt if I should.

The meat now swallowed, he speaks again, and I freeze. "Jiwon, I have something I want to tell you."

Bringing my hand back down, I eye him, slowly nodding for him to continue.

With a cloth, he wipes the blood from his chin and sets it back down on the table. I am staring at the red stains on the fabric when he says, "You may leave if you so wish."

"Master—" Shinhye interjects, but Inha raises a hand, cutting her off.

He is looking at me now. "I can tell that you do not like me nor that you are particularly pleased to be here. And I am no longer one to hold hostages."

No longer.

Which means he did at one point.

But what is his purpose in letting me go? Am I that undesirable? Not beautiful enough like the other noble women before me? Or does he think he is being kind? Without the money that Woosung promised, I am not sure how I can start a new life in a new city. If I return home, the Song family will certainly have me killed to hide their deception. Even a Marquis cannot meddle with the Year of the Maiden.

"I'd like to stay," I say, panic rising at the thought of being without a home in the looming winter. Leaving this place sounded like my only option, but now that he is letting me go free, I am more confident that he must not intend to harm me. Maybe in the spring I can leave with what little valuables I can scrounge up here over the next few months and take Halmeoni Hyesun somewhere. Even if we wander a while, sleeping outside in the summer is preferable to winter. I hope he will let me stay until then, and I am also glad I decided against killing him. How close things were to ending in disaster due to my foolishness.

Inha's and Shinhye's eyes both widen, both gaping at me.

"What?" he rasps, disbelief clearly displayed on his face.

Meanwhile, Shinhye's expression is one of hope, although I don't understand why she is so jubilant at the thought of me remaining here.

"I said, I want to stay," I repeat, eyes darting between both of them.

He tilts towards me, like a moth drawn to the light of a lantern. "You—You're serious?"

There are so many things I do not know, like why they need mortal women. If it is not to eat my heart, or liver, or any other body part, then what desperation drives him to demand a woman every seventy years?

Hands firmly planted on the table, I say, "I am being sincere. But I am curious about—"

Our conversation is interrupted when a servant I haven't seen before scurries in, bending down to whisper hurriedly in her master's ear. She looks human, her hair the darkest out of all the ones I have seen here. A red that is nearly brown. As she speaks, she casts a glance my way and slips a hand into her sleeve. My eyes widen, my breath stalls in my chest, and a feeling of doom, heavy and cold, grips my stomach. The object she withdraws is the godwood pin.

There is no hope in Inha's eyes now. Only hatred.

"Take her to the dungeon," he snarls, his claws scraping against the wood of the table with an earsplitting screech.

Scrambling to my feet and shaking my head, I urge, "Please, I can explain."

"If you feel the need to offer an explanation, then you know what this thing is," he growls, snapping the pin in half and tossing it on the floor.

What can I possibly say? That I was planning to kill him but had a change of heart? Despite it being the truth, it is hard to believe. "I-I—"

He raises his hand in the air, silencing me. "I don't want to hear it. Take her away. *Now.*"

Shinhye is gentle with me as her hands grip my arms and pull me back. I look at her face. Not angry. Just...disappointed? I cannot blame them, seeing as I betrayed them by bringing such an object here. Still, I did not know them, did not know that they intended me no harm.

"I am sorry," I say, voice strained and eyes begging for understanding.

She doesn't reply, avoiding my gaze while leading me out of the dining room. I twist my neck, catching one more look at Inha. His shoulders hunch, his hands hide in his lap, and his face fixates on the broken godwood pin on the floor. He looks as though I really stabbed him. Then he disappears from sight as we walk around the corner. Shinhye brings me down another hall branching from the one we came. I've seen very little of this vast palace with its maze of corridors. It doesn't matter anyways. I am not leaving this place. My mind races, wondering if I should remain silent, try to defend myself, or beg for mercy.

We reach a dark brown wooden door, and Shinhye twists the lock mechanism open, metal whining as it opens. Dusts coats every surface, and the must of rooms not often used permeates the air. Guilt swells inside me, churning waves making me nauseous. The despondent image of Inha haunts me.

Shinhye opens the creaky cell door.

For the first time, I resist, turning to face her. "Shinhye, please let me explain. I wasn't going to hurt him. I mean I was at first, but—"

In my panicked attempt to explain, I've said the wrong thing.

A shadow slithers across her face, her gaze and voice hardening. "There are few things I cannot forgive, and harming my Master is one of them."

"You don't understand what this is like for me!" I shout, anger bubbling and blood beginning to boil. "I never wanted to come here. I was sold by my own father, my life traded, deemed less valuable than the noble woman who was supposed to be sent."

Confusion flickers in her eyes, her cold expression thawing.

I continue, my lip quivering from frustration and my hands buried in my skirt, "Humans know little to nothing about mythicals. Most of what I heard was tales of the Gumiho King consuming human organs or kidnapping beautiful women to use as his playthings. Someone gave that pin to me so I could defend myself."

Her eyes darken again. "So you judged us without ever meeting us."

I open my mouth to retort, but I hesitate. She is right, but it's also not fair. I've taken too much time to respond though, and Shinhye gently shoves me back, closing the cell.

As she leaves me in the dank dungeon, she mutters, "I thought you were different."

For some reason, it feels like someone stabs me in the heart. I spin around and sit on a damp pile of straw in the corner. It was foolish of me to act on so little information. Neither Woosung nor Inha have done anything to make me trust them. Fueled by fears founded in mere rumors, I'd intended to kill Inha, genuinely considered it. I judged him, just like so many have done to me. Despite my self loathing and the guilt gnawing my very bones, I am not ready to die. I want to make up for my mistake. I want to live, want to restore the brightness to Shinhye's eyes. Despite what it appears to them as, the truth is, I decided against harming him. Death is too harsh a punishment for ignorance. Then again, what would mythicals know of the hardships of humans?

The dungeon door we entered through whines shut, swallowing any remnants of light. There are no windows here, and darkness devours me. Yet even now, with the heavens hidden from my view, I close my eyes and create my own night sky, painting tiny stars.

"This is not the end," I remind myself.

Somehow, I will survive this.

Cawing wakes me the next morning. I slowly sit up, stretching my stiff and aching limbs. The cold of the cell crept deep into my bones during the night. It feels like waking up back in my drab and dank home back in the Mortal Lands. How I rose and fell so quickly from luxury's grasp.

"Couldn't you have let me sleep any more?" I groan.

"Well if someone had not attempted to assassinate the Gumiho King, they would be in a nice warm bed of blankets instead of a dungeon," the samjok-o chides.

Blinking the sleep away, the three-legged-crow comes into view, golden eye peering at me between the bars. "I didn't try to kill him. I would have thought that a messenger of the Celestial Realm would have more accurate information."

"You thought about killing him, though. You certainly killed his trust—and his hope."

"Did you have to say it like that?" I grumble. What hope is that anyways? I saw it present in both Inha's and Shinhye's faces, but I still don't understand why. "Did they send you here to torture me?" I snap, casting a glare at the samjok-o that somehow flew down here. Is there a window in one of the other cells? Impossible. It was as dark as ink when Shinhye left me.

"I believe what you mean to say is thank you," he squawks.

"For?" I lean against the cold wall of the cell.

"For negotiating your release."

Nothing comes free in life. My eyes narrow. "What do I have to do for you?"

He clicks his beak. "Not for me. For the Gumiho King."

My spine stiffens. "What does he want?" My heart? My liver? Although I find it unfair, I understand why he'd want me dead. By all appearances, it looked like I was here to assassinate him. I just hope he uses his claws to cut my throat so I don't feel the pain for long.

Muffled, low voices echo in the stone corridor.

"He will tell you himself," the bird states.

Inha comes into view donned in black and gold robes, Shinhye following behind him in a forest green pair of garments with a pattern of white leaves. He gives me a cold, appraising look and says, "You tried to kill me last night."

Brows pinching and bottom lip pouting, I reply, "I did not."

A growl emits from his throat, and he pulls something out of his voluminous sleeve. The bifurcated pin clatters on the floor.

My shoulders rise to hide me like a turtle. "I am sorry about that. But I didn't do it. I stopped myself."

He crosses his arms, a look of clear disbelief painted on his face. "Ah, yes. Shinhye told me of your excuse."

I come back out of my shoulder shell. "It wasn't an excuse. It was the truth."

A strange noise comes out of the samjok-o. Is he laughing?

The cell unlocks with a high-pitched whine. "Follow me," Inha grumbles.

Shinhye crouches down, stretching out her forearm towards the crow.

"Thank you," he coos and hops up onto her arm.

No one helps me up. Shinhye refuses to look at me, and mistrust fills Inha's eyes. The blame lies as a blade in my chest, twisting into my heart. I should have never accepted that pin in the first place. Beguiled into thinking I would be some sort of savior, I only ended up making a hypocrite of myself. How am I any better than my father when I was willing to sacrifice someone else for my own gain?

We walk through the halls and rooms I've been before, and eventually we come to the main entrance. Instead of stopping we continue on. He is taking me into the Eastern Wing, and my stomach starts somersaulting. What lies in the forbidden section of the palace? We pass by a few doors until we reach a red one, as if it was painted in blood. Is it some sort of torture room? But it makes no sense to be here. It's more practical to keep it next to the dungeon. I cast away the silly thought, swallowing my paranoia.

My muscles tense as Inha casts open the door and strides inside. I follow after, entering an ornate room. To the left lies a bed of blankets much like the ones that were in mine, and to the right, cabinets full of papers and scrolls cram the wall, a low sitting desk sitting in front of them. Inha stalks straight forward towards a small table with a white cushion lounging upon its top. Shinhye, the samjok-o flying off her arm and landing on the window sill closest to the cushion, walks behind me.

A dull bead, a dark and dirty red, lays nestled in a small cushion.

Raising a brow, I ask, "Is this some lackluster jewel?"

The samjok-o makes that same, almost laughing noise, while Shinhye glowers.

If Inha was in his fox form, I am sure his fur would be bristling. "It is a fox pearl."

Pearl? "I thought only dragons had those." At least that's what the tales tell. Shinhye's words from the carriage ride reenter my mind; she mentioned something about the pearl have and have-nots.

"We shifting mythicals all have them. They're the source of our power," Inha explains like an annoyed older sibling. Not that I'd know from experience. Just observation.

"No need for that tone. It's normal for humans not to be well versed in the lore of the mythicals," I retort, not bothering to hide my irritation.

His voice drops an octave. "I don't think someone who attempted to murder me should be commenting on my tone."

"I told you, I wasn't—" His cold glare freezes my words. There is a strange mixture of shame and indignation roiling inside, and I do not know if I should continue to argue or appease him. I glance at Shinhye, recalling her hurt expression the other night, remembering the defeated image of Inha hunched into himself with the broken pin on the floor in front of him. "Sorry," I mumble at last, shifting my feet.

A burst of air shoots out of his nostrils, and Inha explains, "Mine came out when I was cursed, along with the loss of my tails—and most of my powers."

"What does this have to do with me?" The crow had mentioned Inha was cursed, as did Shinhye, but neither have explained why or how.

With a look that reveals how much he loathes his situation, he tells me, "I need your help to get them back."

"Me?" I ask, flabbergasted. How could I possibly help? My eyes drop to my left arm and leg.

Inha gestures to the crow. "He can explain." The samjok-o opens his beak to speak, but before the first word comes out, Inha snaps, "Later."

The bird clamps his beak shut, shuffling closer to Shinhye who reaches over to scratch his head in comfort.

My patience has run out, annoyance melting away the last of my guilt. Crossing my arms, I demand, "Someone needs to explain why I am here. Why do you want me?" If he finds me so grating, why doesn't he expel me?

"I do not *want* you," he growls. "I *need* you." The words are almost romantic, but his tone is anything but.

Shinhye quickly adds, "Mortal women are sent here in order to break the curse."

I'd never heard such a tale before, although the more idyllic rumors said the Gumiho King required a bride. Does that mean he needs a human woman to marry him to break the curse and all the ones before me refused? With his personality, I can't blame them.

The words don't come easily. "So do we have to be...joined together?" I lock my pinky fingers together.

He casts a look of disgust at me, lip curling to show off his sharp fangs. "We are not mates."

My face scrunches. "Do you mean married?"

"Close enough." He shrugs, the disdainful expression still on his face.

That's a relief. The very thought of being bound to this gumiho sends shivers down my limbs. "So why do you demand a human woman every century or so?"

"I demand no such thing. It is simply a part of my curse."

The crow interjects, "It was the will of the Celestials for the Gumiho to require the assistance of mortals."

"Did I not tell you to explain the details later?" Inha barks, his wrath palpable in the air around us. His glare is sharp enough to draw blood, and wisdom beckons us to silence. Even the samjok-o says nothing.

8

WHEN I WAKE UP the next morning, I am grateful to be back in a bed of warm blankets rather than that dank dungeon. Shinhye comes to fetch me, helping me to change into a new set of clothes. Back home, I only had two pairs of pants, two shirts, two braces, and one outer patchwork coat for winter. While one was washed and drying, I'd wear the other. Now in the cabinet of my room, there are several sets of clothing in a rainbow of color including two cloaks, one of them being fur-lined. So much wealth. Whether this is a dream or a nightmare remains to be seen.

"Thank you," I say to Shinhye as she ties off the knot of my top.

She is silent, only dipping her head in acknowledgement. Betrayal stands as a barrier between us, which I hope to tear down soon. She guides me back out of the palace where we wait in front for I don't know what, but I am not left long wondering, the samjok-o soaring overhead before swooping down to land on the head of the gumiho statue by the steps.

"Has 'later' finally arrived?" I inquire, crossing my arms. "If I am needed to help break some curse, I should know what the method of breaking is."

"You must undergo the Maeum Trials—tests of the heart and tasks to reveal your virtues, or lack thereof," the crow explains.

"I know I am not perfect, but any vice I may have developed is from my unfair lot in life. Isn't it too much to ask of me to be patient while in pain? Or to help others when I don't have enough for myself? If the Heavens wanted me to be generous, then they should have made me wealthy," I grumble. If he wanted someone perfect, he should have had a princess be sent as the sacrifice, someone with enough money to erase all worries and a family that cared about her. It's much easier to cultivate virtue when the soil is moist and well tended versus ground that is dry and rocky. Then again, the Song sisters have a father who cares and enough riches to buy whatever their heart desires and they're still feckless creatures.

If I had the wealth of the Song clan or the Gumiho King, I would wield it much better than they, I say silently to myself, hoping the messenger of the Celestial Realm cannot hear my thoughts.

Perhaps he can, for his next words feel like an admonishment. "Vice and virtue are but a choice, a difference of being led or leading. No matter one's circumstances, the choice remains the same. Mortals and mythicals alike are tempted towards vice."

Some more than others, I say in my head, glancing at Shinhye and comparing her and her annoyingly aloof and arrogant master. "So what do these *Maeum Trials* entail?"

"You shall see soon enough. Today you will undergo the first trial," the samjok-o states.

Will I have to slay some sort of vicious beast in a show of bravery? Or beat a street scammer at his own game to prove my intelligence? I am rather ordinary in intelligence and below average in physical aptitude. Noble women would have at least received some sort of education, and other poor folk would know how to use a hatchet and knives for daily tasks. For me, even cutting an onion or carrying the bucket of scraps for the animals required a significant amount of effort. Defeat begins its mocking chant.

No. I will not fail. I will win my freedom along with the gumihos. Even if I have no affection for Inha, Gunoo and Shinhye are too kind for such a curse. I glance down at my right hand, the lightweight wood of the pin still tickling my palm. I need to atone for my own sin as well. For even if it had only been for a day, I'd been willing to murder someone, and that terrifies me.

"Your Master is late," the bird remarks, staring at Shinhye.

"He will arrive shortly," she replies curtly.

The three-legged-crow clicks his beak but says nothing further and neither does Shinhye. What is taking Inha so long?

Restless and wishing to bridge the gap between us, I ask Shinhye, "You mentioned you had a husb—mate." I'm glad I corrected myself because her expression softens a bit. "Do you have any children as well?" I am not sure what they call their offspring.

"We have a pup—a daughter," Shinhye murmurs softly, sorrowful longing dusting her face as her eyes gaze beyond the palace walls. "She was born right before the curse. She doesn't even remember what my fox form looks like. I fear when the curse is broken, she will not recognize me."

My brows pinch together in a puzzled expression. "Can you not visit her?"

"Our master forbade those who are fully foxes from coming here. They remind him too much of his pain, of all that he has lost." Her gaze tears away, as if imagining the outside, her mate, and pup are too painful to bear.

Scowling, I say, "That doesn't seem fair. He is inflicting more suffering on you for selfish reasons." My eyes are drawn to her foxtail, the only sign of her being a gumiho apart from her golden eyes and flaming hair.

Her voice weighs heavy with sadness, a shadow sliding across her face. "His mother and father were good gumihos and good rulers. When they passed on the throne to their son, they retired to the forests. Some poachers got them. Feeling that his own negligence brought his parents' early deaths, he retreated further into himself and into his castle, and the land suffered all the more for it."

The crow interjects, "Sometimes we self-fulfill our own greatest fears."

Shinhye's glare silences him for the time being, and she reiterates, "He blames himself, and that was when the shame distorted his carelessness into coldness."

"You are being too lenient," the crow caws. "Rather than face his fault, he let guilt chain him, leaving others to the same fate as his parents."

"Sometimes you are too harsh," Shinhye retorts.

The samjok-o ignores her, continuing, "The Gumiho King was to guard the forest and its inhabitants, but his long life allowed for greed to grow. The fact of the matter is, his poor protection played a part in their premature demise. If he had spent less time gallivanting around as a fox and more time tending to the border and organizing his subjects, those poachers would not have dared to enter. He heaped more guilt upon his head by hiding and refusing to embrace the responsibility of a ruler."

Shinhye bristles at the criticism of her master, her fingers twitching in tandem with her tail.

Peering at the crow, I muse, "Then are hunters at fault? Is it some sort of crime according to the Celestial Realm to kill a creature for food?"

The bird clicks his talons against the stone of the statue. "Of course not. Just as a bear must eat a fish and an owl a mouse, so must man eat. But poachers...they will kill without gratitude for the life that was sacrificed. They kill a fox for just his tail or a deer only for his antlers, leaving the rest to rot. Sometimes they even take a part without killing, abandoning the creature to die in great anguish. That is an abomination to the heavens."

Shinhye mutters quietly, "It was Master's guilt that drove him to withdraw deep into himself and his palace. That much I can concede."

For once, I pity the Gumiho King. He sounds more broken and negligent than malicious and cruel. But my sympathy only stretches so far, for he is still guilty of cowardice. He should have faced his mistakes and changed his ways. "So why take his tails and pearl?"

"The tails are his pride and the pearl the source of his power, but power without virtue is dangerous," the crow croons.

The bird makes a good point. One's suffering is not an excuse to pass pain onto others, and ruling comes with greater responsibility. "Well, why doesn't he have to prove his worth? Why can't he be the one to atone?"

"Because then it is not grace, and he could claim that he deserved all that he has. But if another does it on his behalf, it is not by his honor that it is won," he replies.

I counter, glancing at Shinhye, "If it was his wrongdoings that earned him the curse, why were his fellow gumiho affected?"

Shinhye shifts next to me, and I wonder if, despite her previous words, she does hold some resentment towards her master.

The crow replies, "Because the actions of a leader create consequences that trickle down to his people—or mythicals in this case."

Does he ever *not* have an answer for something? Are the other samjok-o like him? Gunoo appears out of nowhere, startling me from my thoughts. I didn't hear him approach, a trait that all the gumihos—no matter their form—seem to share.

Gunoo smiles, revealing sharp and slightly yellow fangs and bright eyes. "Came to wish the mistress well."

My nose scrunches. "Mistress?"

He peers at me with such innocent eyes. "How else should I address the Master's woman?"

My lip curls. "I am not *his* woman."

"I am sorry. Did I offend you?" His words come out as a whimper, almost as if I had kicked him.

I sigh. "Just call me Jiwon."

He perks up. "May fortune favor you, Mistress." If he had a tail, it would be wagging.

I chew on my cheek, and the crow guffaws, amused by my annoyance. Shinhye gives a sympathetic expression, Gunoo the only one ignorant to my irritation. Still, I'm touched that they came to encourage me.

It shouldn't bother me that Inha isn't here, yet it does, his absence pricking me like a splinter. I lean towards Shinhye, lowering my voice so that the crow can't hear. "Is he not coming?"

Her eyes soften, and she reaches out to pat my shoulder. I know the words she will say before she even speaks them. "Do not take it personally."

"Right," I reply, giving a determined nod. But despite my consideration to kill him, shouldn't he be invested in my success? He has everything to gain while I have little to lose.

"Well, we cannot wait any longer. The insipid little fox should have informed me if he did not intend to come. Wasting all this time while I have so much to do." The crow launches off the statue and hovers overhead. "Are you ready to begin, Mistress?"

I shoot a glare his way, but my scowl only seems to please him as he coos, "If you cannot take a little teasing, you will surely fail the task ahead."

"I've endured far more than you can imagine, you underdeveloped raven," I retort.

His feathers ruffle, blooming satisfaction within me. "How dare you compare me to those common birds!" His screech pierces my ears painfully.

I gesture ahead. "Care to begin? Or are you going to keep squawking all day?"

He dives faster than I can react, pecking my head. "Ow!"

Shinhye gasps, rushing towards me and parting my hair to check for any injury. It stings, but I do not feel the wetness of blood.

"You are too harsh," she scolds the samjok-o.

"Humility is often developed through pain," he sings back. I never thought a bird could fly with haughtiness, but somehow he manages.

She glares at him, but says nothing, checking one last time that I am not hurt. My heart warms. Despite my betrayal, she still cares, and my resolve to break the curse hardens. Shinhye deserves to see her family.

I look into her golden eyes. "Thank you for your concern, Shinhye. I'm fine."

She pats my hair into place. "May fortune favor you, Jiwon."

Fortune has never favored me. We are not friends. Yet I have survived without her, and I will succeed without her.

"I don't forfeit easily," I say with a smile.

Light sparkles in her eyes as she steps away, and I follow the crow down the path a few steps. *Breathe in. Breathe out.* I lull the storming waves of my stomach into a calm. No matter the trial, I will overcome it.

"Try not to faint," the crow caws condescendingly.

I open my mouth to spit a snarky reply, but before the first sharp word leaves my mouth, the retort withers. Perhaps he was not patronizing, because a strange arch of a substance like water forms out of nothing. The sunlight catches it, reflecting a rainbow of colors.

"What is that?" I gasp in awe.

"A portal," he answers matter of factly. "I shall go first."

Then, with a single flap of his ebony wings, he is gone, swallowed by the portal. I can make out the palace walls through the mostly translucent door, yet he has completely disappeared. What strange things exist in this world, magic that I was ignorant of, that is mere myth in the Mortal Lands.

Glancing back one more time, Gunoo and Shinhye watch me with hope filled expressions, but Inha is still absent. A puff of air bursts from my mouth, and all my previous pity for him melts away. *So much for being eager to break the curse. Can't even be bothered to show up on the day of the first trial...* I bottle the indignance and use it as fuel, turning forward and stepping through the portal.

I emerge at the foot of a large mountain, forest surrounding us and sprawling up the massive mound of earth. When I turn around, the portal is gone. There is no going back, not until I fail or succeed, but much like fortune, failure is my adversary. I do not need the former, and I shall beat the latter.

Scanning my surroundings, all I can see are trees with yellow leaves interspersed with evergreens. Rocks and no buildings, birds and no people. What trial requires me to be in the middle of nowhere? Do I really have to slay some sort of beast?

The samjok-o answers for me. "The task is simple. Climb the mountain."

I scoff, thinking it a joke until the noise dies on my lips when I see that the crow is serious. "But—" I protest, pulling up my skirt to show the wood brace underneath.

"You can give up, go home and never do another trial," the crow goads.

Maybe the beast slaying option is better.

I don't even know what Inha will do to me if I fail since I forgot to ask when we made our bargain. But what I want more than to not fail is freedom, for Shinhye to be free to see her daughter and mate, freedom for all the gumihos to be able to shift again, not stuck in forms they hate, and freedom for myself to go where I wish and to be with whom I wish. With a humph, I roll up my sleeves and rotate my neck and shoulders, reaching down to tie my skirt into temporary pants. They could have at least granted me the opportunity to change.

"I'll climb this stupid mountain, and then I'll cook you into some crow soup," I mutter under my breath.

Unfortunately, the samjok-o has excellent hearing. "I would like to see you try," he screeches, feathers ruffling.

Whether he is referring to the mountain climbing or the soup making, I don't know, but if there is one positive attribute I possess, it's my stubbornness. The same determination that helped me endure the Song sisters and not give up despite my limited limbs is the same fire that will fuel me in this trial. I take a deep breath and begin my trek up the steep incline. At the end of summer, the cicadas ceased their humming, and only the song of birds keeps me company while I trudge through the trees.

Not long passes before my chest and my muscles are burning. I'd been working for the Song clan—taking care of their animals—for years, but I always avoided hills, let alone mountains. Even my brace can only do so much. By the time I reach a quarter of the way, tears of frustration build in my eyes. My body hurts so badly, and my left side is shaking. I look up at the long looming path. Isn't this too much? Couldn't the trial be changed to accommodate my condition? Collapsing on the nearest boulder, I allow myself to rest.

"You can always quit," the samjok-o says in a sweet sing-song voice.

The sweat wiped from my brow and my teeth gritted, I hiss, "Never."

Pushing off the rock, I begin my hike once more. My gaze fixates on my feet. *One step at a time.* If I look ahead at all the toiling that remains, I will not make it, and if I look behind and see unsatisfactory progress, I will not make it. I need only to focus on the next few breaths and the next few strides, and before I know it, I'll reach the summit. Although I take breaks when I need them, I never tarry too long lest I lose my will. Motivation runs through fingers like water, but instead of focusing on the leaking, it's best to refill it. I visualize Shinhye and Halmeoni Hyesun, for love is one of life's best fuels, but when that is not enough, spite will do, and I imagine the Song sisters' jeers, my father's unremorseful face after stealing my money and gambling it away, and keep going.

Every joint and muscle blazes, limbs trembling under the strain. My chest burns, each inhale hurting, but I force myself to breathe. *In. Out. Left*

foot. Right foot. Do not look up. Do not look back. Do not think. Just move.
I push against the tree trunks to propel me forward, grabbing at rocks to
haul myself up. Thankfully, the years of hard labor have made my palms
calloused, so they do not cut easily against the rough terrain. Woosung
was right, although not about everything. How could a noble woman ever
complete such a task as this? They have palanquins, carriages, and horses;
I'm sure they've never had to make a trek like this.

A wet drop plops against my face. Then another. And another. It is
raining. Did that inane crow cause this storm? Is he purposely trying to
make things harder? As the soil and water mixes, the mud sucks at my
shoes, the very earth turning into my adversary. I want to shout, but I can
barely breathe as it is. Failure sings to me, whispering so sweetly to just give
up.

"If you quit, I can portal you back to your rooms at that fox's palace,"
the samjok-o caws through the pelting rain.

Isn't it unfair of him to interfere?

Breathe. Just breathe. My wet brace is chafing my skin. *One more step.*
Everything aches. *This is just a temporary torment,* I remind myself.

In response to my attempts at optimism, nature decides to deliver
a dose of humility, and a stray branch thwacks me in the face, my skin
stinging. Cursing, I shove it out of the way, lamenting my lot in life.

Gritting my teeth, I continue trudging. Time stretches on, and still I
do not stop. The summit is certainly nearer than it was several steps ago.
Halmeoni Hyesun's humming fills my head, and I hold on to the warm
hope the old woman brings me. I stumble over a rock, yelping in pain as
my wrist lands the wrong way. I will not give up, not like my father did on
me and on life. Pushing myself upright, my legs lurch forward, every limb
scrambling in a desperation to keep me moving forward. This is the biggest
mountain on earth. The rain erodes my patience, and if that crow talks one
more time, I'll—

"Look up, Jiwon," the crow says overhead.

I shake my head slightly, the movement fettered by fatigue. "No," I manage to grunt. The terrain is nearly flat now, but I am afraid that it is a false summit. My hope is already cracked, and if it is met with disappointment, it will shatter completely like the vase I threw at the samjok-o. If I see how much remains, I will not be able to finish this test. Whatever it is in fact testing.

"Jiwon," he says again, "*Look up.*"

And I do.

When my gaze meets the open sky, I fall to my knees, my whole body shaking. I am at the summit, the land sprawling before me like subjects beneath a king's dais. Tears flow freely, mixing with the rain-drops so that I cannot distinguish between the two.

"I did it," I rasp, unable to shout, every bit of energy sapped from my body. My chest heaves, sucking in precious air, a metallic tang on my tongue.

The rain suddenly stops, and the sun peeks through the volup-tuous gray clouds. Rays of gilded light like fingers reach towards me, a gentle warm thawing my soaked and cold skin.

The crow lands on a rock next to me. "Congratulations on com-pleting your first trial."

The first.

There are eight more.

But that is a worry for later.

For now, I bask in victory, imagining the expression of joy on Shin-hye's face when I return, along with a significant amount of satisfaction at showing the Gumiho King my capability.

The samjok-o flaps his wings, and the portal appears, extra bright from the sunlight. Somehow I find the strength to stand and stumble into it. As soon as we pass through, a familiar set of faces meet us; Shinhye and Inha are waiting inside my room. My legs cannot hold me any longer, and I collapse into the wall, grateful the crow made the portal exit next to it. Perhaps he is considerate of me after all.

Shinhye gasps and rushes to my side, "Jiwon! Are you alright?"

I nod, relieved to be resting and hoping I'll never climb another mountain again. If only I had been born in a flatter place full of grass plains and not the mountainous terrain of the Goryeo peninsula.

"I take it she passed?" Inha asks the samjok-o, once more not even bothering to acknowledge my presence.

"Indeed. To both of our surprise, she succeeded," the crow replies, chortling.

Is he really going to ignore me?

Anger wins over exhaustion, and I exclaim, "How could you say that while I am right here?"

His golden beady eye turned to me, the bird asks calmly, as if inquiring about my eating preferences, "Would you prefer us to speak about our lack of confidence in you when you are not here?"

"I'd prefer you not to say such things at all," I snap. If I had the strength for it, I'd throw another vase at him. It is only now that I notice that my room has been completely cleared of any objects that one might throw, and I suddenly feel guilty for destroying that which is not mine. Then again, a few vases is a small price for my life and my help in breaking the curse.

The crow replies apathetically, "That is not an option."

Shinhye says softly yet sternly, much as I suspect a mother would, "You need to warm up and rest."

Despite my abundant amount of anger, my legs are not so sturdy, so I acquiesce with a nod and a soft grunt, Shinhye helping me hobble towards the bathing room before I collapse. "Can I put in a request to the Celestial Realm for a different samjok-o?" I ask over my shoulder.

Inha and the crow answer together.

"If I could, I would have exchanged him for another messenger long ago." "No, once one is assigned, one must complete the mission."

The samjok-o turns his attention to Inha, the two glaring at each other. I thought messengers for the Celestial Realm would have to be gentler in their manner of speech. Then again, a week ago, I didn't even know they were real, simply mythical tales told around teahouses and tiny shacks.

"Let us get you into a warm bath and then to bed. I will have someone bring you some food," Shinhye says, supporting my weight and nearly dragging me behind the screen. She twists to look over her shoulder and barks in a voice I imagine her using with her daughter, "And you two need to take your bickering outside and let Jiwon rest."

Surprisingly, the two leave without any protest, their arguments saved for each other. Their voices fade as they walk out and down the hall, and I whisper my thanks and limp the final few steps to the stony bath, steaming tendrils curling from the natural hot spring. Moss clings to some of the rock, appearing more like a giant hand scooped it from out in nature and plopped it into the palace. After stripping, Shinhye helps me into the water, warmth soaking deep into my bones and chasing away the last chills from the storm.

While Shinhye untangles my rain soaked hair, she asks, "How was it?"

"One of the most physically daunting things I have ever done in my life," I groan.

"What did you have to do?"

I tilt my head back to look at her. "Climb a mountain. A very large one. So I take it you don't know what happens in the trials?"

She shakes her head, fingers brushing through my tresses. "No. All I know is that they are tailored to the one who undergoes them."

"So all the other women had to do different ones?"

"Not all. Just one."

The conversation I overheard between Shinhye and Inha comes back to me. Didn't Inha say only one woman had ever attempted them? I wonder why the others refused. Shinhye had also mentioned something about some of them dying, implying that they did not die naturally. Did

Inha kill them before or after they refused? I tilt my head forward. I do not think she will be willing to answer my questions so soon, even though I succeeded in one of the trials. Trust, once broken, is not so easily regained. It will take time, but there are many mysteries surrounding the Gumiho King. By the time I complete the trials, I hope to have uncovered many of them, but I wonder if I will regret not listening to Woosung.

As she continues to do my hair, a question crosses my mind that I forgot to ask when I first arrived. Why is she the one helping me dress and bathe and fetching my meals? Aside from that one catastrophe of a dinner with Inha, I haven't seen the other gumihos again. It's so silent for such a big palace.

"Are you in charge of all things concerning me? Including cleaning and cooking for me?" My hand swishes in the hot spring, creating little ripples.

Watching in the reflection of the water, I see Shinhye shake her head. "We used to have an array of servants to attend to the mortals sent, but we found out quickly that they were quite uncomfortable with...more of the fox looking servants. And even for those who are stuck in their complete human forms, it can often be overwhelming with a new place and new people, so I became the one to interact while the others worked unseen."

"Could you please tell them that they don't have to hide anymore?"

She smiles and nods, voice light and warm. "I shall be sure to pass on your words."

9

TRIAL TWO

I SPEND THE NEXT day sleeping, only getting up to eat, bathe and relieve myself. Every part of me protests when I try to move, and I wonder what the point of the trial was other than to torment me. It is wise of the samjok-o to stay away. Even if I cannot throw rocks or vases at him as I wish to right now, I can hurl a volley of vicious verbal insults when I want. Shinhye checks on me often, bringing me meals and offering company. I accept only the former, my head throbbing too much for conversation. Curse this broken body of mine.

Later when I am lamenting alone in my bed of blankets, I hear a soft knocking.

"Enter," I call out, grimacing when I shift onto my right elbow.

My brows shoot up as a new gumiho enters. Shinhye must have relayed my words to the other servants. She looks entirely human, not a foxtail or ear to be seen, her hair a red so dark it looks brown in the shadows. It is only her golden eyes that give her away as a mythical. Recognition hits me; she is the one who came carrying the pin during that dinner. She must be the one in charge of tidying my room.

When she opens her mouth to speak, her teeth are that of a human, not a sharp fang to be seen. "Mistress, I am Minji. I am in charge of maintaining your quarters." She bows low.

"I am no one's mistress. Please just call me Jiwon." Being the one served and not doing the serving still feels strange to me. I wonder what Taehee would say if she could see me now. Would she regret having me take her place? Yet for the sake of all the servants here, I am happy they will avoid her ill temper.

"As you wish," Minji acquiesces, dipping her head.

She does not offer conversation while she dusts and gathers garments to be laundered, and I make no attempts at idle chatting. I only speak when she picks up my discarded, mud covered brace. She pinches it at the top corner, holding it far away.

With protesting muscles, I sit up slowly. "Oh. It's for my leg. Is it possible for you to wash and dry it?"

"Of course," she replies and carries the mud crusted brace out with the other laundry.

I close my eyes, hoping sleep will offer a haven from my sore and aching body, serene dreams without gumihos and curses.

The next day, I wake to find two braces resting on the nearby table. I limp over and inspect the new one. The wood is of finer quality than the one I brought with me, dark and smooth. A smile spreads across my face.

The door to my room slides open, and Shinhye enters. In her hands she carries a tray holding a steaming bowl of stew. I devour it in mere minutes, Shinhye's lips curling into a smile as she watches me consume the meal. I finish and thank her.

Now that the aching in my body has dulled, boredom takes over. Although I no longer plan to escape, it would be nice to become more familiar with what will be home for next few months or however long these trials take, and movement will help work out some of the stiffness in my limbs.

"Could you help me get dressed?" I ask.

"Of course," she replies with a pleasant tone.

Shinhye dresses me with deft hands since she has, after all, had centuries of experience helping women like me. Finishing braiding my hair, she ties it off with a red ribbon that matches the black and red skirt and top from the day of the disastrous dinner. It is freshly cleaned, not a smear or bad scent left from the night in the dungeon; it even smells like jasmine.

"I'd like to take a walk around the grounds," I say, not sure how the rules have changed since my sort of assassination attempt on Inha. Am I still allowed to walk around the palace on my own? Is Shinhye or Minji supposed to watch me every waking moment? Even if it's the latter, at least they make good company.

"Very well, so long as we do not leave the walls," she replies, standing and fluffing her own skirt, fox tail peeping through a hole in the back.

I hardly even notice it now, the appendage just like another normal limb. She hands me a cloak before we leave the room. She doesn't wear one though, and I ask, "Won't you be cold?"

Pulling on the end of her sleeve, she spares a quick look at the remaining cloak in my cabinet. "I do not get quite as cold as mortals—or the more humanistic gumihos."

My nose scrunches. "What does that mean?"

"I suppose you have seen much more strange things already, including Gunoo," she starts with some hesitation.

A laugh bubbles up, and I hope she will not be offended. "A walking and talking man with a fox head is certainly strange, and I am not sure that there is much left to surprise me after these past few days."

Turning to face me, Shinhye reaches towards her shirt and slides the wrapped top off her shoulder. Her smooth pale skin gradually blends into the snow colored coarse hair. So that's why she doesn't need a cloak. "Most of my body is covered in fur," she explains.

"I'm jealous," I say lightheartedly. "Such a thing would have served me well during the winters back in the Mortal Lands."

Shoulder covered with her shirt once more, she says in a voice that sounds like she is pitying me, "You must have lived a hard life."

Emotion clogs my throat. I do not want to talk about it right now, and I especially do not wish to cry in front of her. "Let's go," I say a little too harshly.

We walk silently through the halls, awkwardness clinging to us. The autumn air fights against the barging winter, the sky a bright blue while the air nips at my nose playfully. I pull the fur-lined cloak tighter around me.

"Would you like to return inside?" Shinhye asks, tone full of worry.

She's perceptive. Must be the fox in her.

I shake my head. "I've spent many cold seasons in much thinner garments, patchwork jackets and pants from scraps I scrounged." The words come out without much thought. So much for not talking about my life.

She nods, not offering any protest. We continue our walk, stepping on leaves underfoot. Only a few manage to cling to the newly barren trees, nearly all the foliage falling overnight.

To my surprise, we happen upon Inha out by the girin pasture, a bow in his hand and aimed at a stack of straw with a black feather protruding from the top. He nocks an arrow, raises his weapon, and pulls back the string. I don't realize that I am holding my breath until he releases the arrow. The projectile whooshes through the air faster than a diving crane and makes contact with the feather. I don't see where they go as they disappear behind the pile of straw.

I let my chest collapse, air rushing from my mouth. "That was amazing," I whisper.

"He cannot fight as well in his current form, so he has taken to the weapons of mortals," Shinhye explains.

Inha sets another arrow against his bowstring, turns and raises it. It's aimed right at my chest. My eyes narrow, a scowl forming as irritation replaces awe. I know he will not kill me, not while he needs me, and if by chance he is overcome by the desire to end my life, I am certain he'd use his claws and not a tool of man. Shinhye mumbles under her breath. I think she is complaining about her master's hospitality or something of that nature, but I do not catch it all as I stride towards him. Wisdom whispers to be more cautious, but I am so tired of enduring torment and teasing. Wisdom drowns beneath the rough and roiling waves of Indignation. Even though I decided against killing him and chose to help him break this curse, I do not like him. Our eyes clash, each step fueled by fire.

If there is ever a trial about keeping my temper in check, I am doomed.

Once the arrow tip is pressed against my chest, I halt. "I think you should practice more. Bows are effective at long range."

His eyes flash with flames, but his voice is eerily calm. "That is what these are for."

And before I can even register what is happening, his bow is down and his claws are splayed in front of my face. I force my body to still, not allowing him the pleasure of seeing me flinch.

Shinhye shouts, "Master! What are you doing? Put your hand down!"

I slowly raise my own, wrapping my fingers around his wrist and rotating it gently. He does not resist as I place his open palm to my throat. "For a fox, you are a bad hunter. The neck is for the kill."

At last his eyes widen, and he yanks his hand away as if my skin singed him. Satisfaction sparks within me. I surprised him—a pleasure I don't think I will ever tire from.

His eyes burn into me, searching into the depths of my soul. "I do wonder, little mortal, if you hold the key to free me from my chains, or if behind that meek facade, you bring more bindings."

My stare meets his in defiance. "Unleash me from my chains, and I will break yours." I don't even know what I meant, but it sounded good.

"A mortal cannot be trusted. Self serving creatures you are." His judgement stings more than I should allow it to.

"Not all of us."

"But enough are. You were not the one intended, yet here you are. Such a deceptive trick you all played on me this time." He leans back, seemingly satisfied at his analysis of me.

How did he find out? That samjok-o probably told him. Or perhaps Shinhye, since I now remember mentioning it to her the day we met. It doesn't matter. "And yet you are the reason I am here. The one who demands mortal women, is it not you?"

"As you are well aware of by now, it is the Celestial Realm who dictates the terms of the curse and how it is broken. I am certain you will lose heart, just like all the rest."

"I don't like losing. Even during the times I wished to stop living, I would not, for that would be to lose." Why did I mention that? I bite my tongue to keep from spilling any more information about myself.

The flames in his eyes sputter like a breeze calming a candle. "That's a sad way to live."

I have no need of his sympathy. Lifting my chin, I harden my tone and ask, "And how have you been living the past centuries?"

His only reply is a grunt, a puff of air shooting from his nose as his lips protrude in a pout. "Humans are strange," he grumbles, stalking off to where Gunoo waits with a quiver of arrows, eyes big as the sun. He looks between me and his master before bursting into laughter. Inha is none too pleased and takes a swipe at his head. Gunoo ducks, but his laughter continues.

If Inha wants to be more intimidating, he should take lessons from the Song sisters. But there was something I wanted to ask of him, and now is as good a time as any since I do not foresee our relationship improving with time.

Swallowing my pride, I race after him, grabbing his sleeve. "Wait."

He pauses, head turning to stare at my hand gripping the fabric of his garments.

I quickly let go. "I was wondering if I could have some clothes and money—"

"Of course," Inha scoffs, "the mortal shows her greed at last."

Anger begins to boil inside me, but I do my best to stay calm. "I was going to say it is for an old woman back home. She is poor, and her health is ailing," I explain through gritted teeth.

"Oh." The cocky expression melts. "Well, I suppose that could be arranged."

"Thank you." I bow. But when I turn and begin walking away, I mumble. "It's not like mythicals aren't capable of the same greed."

"I heard that," Inha snaps.

Curse those ears of his. "Good," I holler back. "You'll find the same vices are shared with humans and mythicals alike. You're the perfect example."

His face reddens and he points a clawed finger at me, sputtering, "You— You—"

"Remember you said you would send those supplies. I hope you will not prove yourself a liar!" I hurry off before he can find the words for a retort, scolding myself for unleashing my temper. I hope he will still send the supplies to Halmeoni Hyesun despite my insult.

My worries are eased when Shinhye inquires about the address of the old woman later that day.

The crow only gives me a few days of rest to recover from the mountain trek, but it feels inadequate. My body is still sore when he appears again to begin the next one. He rests on the sill, cool late autumn air creeping inside the open window.

"What does goodness mean to you?" the samjok-o inquires.

My brows pucker, and my lips pinch together into a thin line. What a random question. "I don't know. I haven't really thought of it before."

He ruffles his feathers. "Think now, then."

I scowl at him, before forcing my face to relax as I ponder his question. "I suppose..." I begin slowly, "That it means being kind and courageous."

"Courageous? Why would goodness include that?" He seems rather taken aback by my answer.

"Because it takes courage to stand up for what is right, for what is good. Sometimes it is easier to be bad or to look the other way when others are. No coward can ever be completely good." Like the Yoon boy and Yuna. Like my father. Like Inha.

He clicks his beak together. I still haven't figured out if that means he is annoyed, amused, or approving. This time at least, it appears to be the last one.

"I like that. Remember that as you enter your next trial."

That sounds ominous.

This time, we do not go outside. A portal appears in the middle of my room, and he flies through the translucent, waterlike door. I follow after, still not used to the nearly instantaneous transportation.

The crow flies off immediately, leaving me alone in the middle of a city, although not the one I used to call home. It's far larger, bustling with wagons and workers. Noble women stroll with their entourages while guards patrol the streets. One seller calls out to those passing by, another shoves his accessories into the face of some rich looking woman. A flag bearing the royal emblem waves atop a nearby guard tower. Perhaps it is the capital, Kaesong? But which city I'm in is irrelevant because to the right of me is a horrific sight, one that makes my blood boil.

A man leers over a woman, her face bruised. No one pays heed to her trembling nor the man's domineering posture and sneer. At best, a few cast glances and whispers before moving along with their business.

What excuses do they give themselves? That they're too busy to bother with a domestic dispute? That it's none of their business? That if the woman wants help she should go to the local judiciary? That it certainly won't escalate past a few coarse words?

Cowards, all of them.

I move forward without thinking, rage replacing any other thought of caution. I've seen this same scenario in the noble district and shack sector alike.

People are the same in every place.

The man reaches for the woman's hair and drags her into an alleyway, disappearing from my view. I increase my pace, ignoring my protesting leg. I turn the corner, and the man has one hand around the woman's throat and the other hiking up her skirts. My eyes quickly dart around, searching for anything to use as a weapon. I'm brave, not stupid. I have no chance of beating the man with one good hand. All I find is a rock. I pick it up, take a few more steps forward, and chuck it at the man, hitting him square in the back. He grunts in pain, releasing the woman and whipping around.

Alright, maybe I'm a little stupid.

There is a line between bravery and brashness, and I tend to flirt with the latter. The man looks more angry than injured, and now I have no rock.

My body stiffens, bracing for his wrath. His ever reddening face pinches in anger as he steps forward, but all of a sudden, he stops, a strange grunting-gurgle emitting from his mouth. His eyes rolling to the back of his head, his body topples into the dirt, revealing the woman I just helped holding the rock I'd just thrown. Her chest is heaving up and down, and her arms are shaking.

I lurch towards her, taking the rock from her hand as she stares, eyes wide with shock, at the unconscious man. Tossing the stone to the ground, I grab her hand and urge, "Let's go before he wakes up."

"Did I kill him?" she whispers, unmoving.

I look back down. There is a little blood matting his hair, but his back rises and falls. "No. He will live, but hopefully he will think twice before doing something so terrible again." Unfortunately, the more probable outcome is that he will wake with more anger than humility.

If I was queen, I'd command that anytime a man abused his innate physical advantages over a woman, he would be castrated. I've seen farmers and nobles put down livestock and pets alike that hurt a human, and it's only right that a person who commits harm against another is held to a higher accountability than a mere animal.

Grabbing the woman's wrist, I tug her. "We should go before he wakes up."

Her eyes are still wide, her hands still trembling, but with another tug she at last moves. We rush out of the alleyway and into the streets. I drag her along, bumping into bodies as we weave through the bustling streets. I miss the quiet and peace of Inha's palace, already accustomed to the serenity. My own city was puny in comparison. I've never seen so many people in my life, never had to fight for a path to walk. When the crowd wanes and we've put a comforting distance between ourselves and the unconscious assailant, I slow down and spare a look over my shoulder. No one pays us attention. We are but two women amongst a sea of people in a vast city.

I turn to the woman. Her face is pallid, but at least she's stopped shaking. "Are you hurt?" My eyes scan her body for visible injuries, but the only blood on her is the man's. There are bruises blooming on her arm and neck, but I worry more about the ones on the inside.

Her lips quiver, the words hard to hear above the city noise. "I-I think I'm f-fine."

"Would you like me to walk you home?"

She shakes her head. "No." At least her voice is firmer this time. "Thank you for helping me."

"It was the right thing to do," I mumble, shrugging. But I also know that many people are unwilling to do the right thing when it may cost them, when it may end up with themselves getting hurt.

"I'll keep in mind that trick with the rock," she says, a slight lilt to her voice.

"Make sure to knock him out with the first hit, unlike my poor attempt," I reply with a feeble laugh. In a more serious tone, I add, "Don't forget to bite. They often try to cover your mouth, so use your teeth."

Understanding flashes in her eyes. "Did the person who saved you give that advice?"

"No one saved me." My voice is hard, but better to crush my emotions before they can crush me.

"Oh," she murmurs softly. "I am sorry."

"Not your fault. Just make sure to intervene for others as I have done for you today." I hope she will not ask me any more questions, for I have no desire to linger on that nightmare of a memory.

She gives a solemn nod. "I promise."

Wings flap over our heads, and I look up, catching the familiar gold eyes of the samjok-o. Tilting my gaze back down, I dip my body into a shallow bow. "I must go." As I rise, arms wrap around me, and my body freezes from her unexpected embrace.

"Thank you. I will never forget your courage," she whispers, sniffling.

I awkwardly pat her back. She pulls away and bows, and then we go our separate ways, the samjok-o following in the sky. We leave the walls of the city, incoming merchants entering under the watchful gazes of the guards. They pay no mind to me though. When we reach an area void of people, I stop walking.

Glaring at the crow, I ask with a sharp tone, "Why would you let that happen?" I am not sure if I am asking for the girl's sake or my own.

"There are times for divine intervention, but the harsh truth of the matter is, humans are given free will. That agency includes the ability to harm others, and it is the choice of others to ignore or intervene on behalf of their fellow men. Or gumiho."

"A little on the nose, no?"

Again, that strange almost laughter.

"You are far too pleased with yourself," I chide with a roll of my eyes.

"I am adequately pleased with myself."

I bend down and pick up a small rock. "Careful. I am quite accurate with my aim."

A portal appears suddenly, and I fall into it with a shout. When I burst through the other side, I whip around to unleash all my irritation, but the crow is gone. I toss the rock to the ground and stride up the palace steps.

Mean old bird. He didn't even transport me to my room.

Inha waits outside my door, arms crossed and long claws tapping against his bicep. Upon seeing me, he pushes off the wall. "I take it you were successful?"

I lift my chin. "Of course I was."

"Good. Come with me."

A long breath escapes my chest. "Where are we going? I'm exhausted."

In a flash of white hair, my feet are off the ground, my body is pressed into his, and his arms hold me tight. He is surprisingly warm.

"What are you doing?" I hiss.

"You said you were tired," he replies nonchalantly. In the epic romantic tales, this would be a sweet scene, but he holds me as romantically as a pile of laundry, his face passive instead of passionate.

The feeling is mutual, and I squirm in his grip. "I can still walk."

"This will be quicker."

I do not see the portal for some reason—maybe because it is too dark inside—but we exit into a forest clearing, a waterfall humming about fifty strides away. The water slithers through the earth, disappearing into the dark forest, moonlight reflecting off the river and making it appear full of stars. Although most of the broad trees are barren, a few cling to their yellow leaves, and firs remain covered in their cloaks of green. Despite fall nearing its end, flowers bloom. Shrubs dotted in shades of red and tufts of brush blush pink cover most of the earth around us. Amaranthus peaks through, which are the only ones I can identify because they are edible. They stay alive until the first frost.

Inha sets me down, the pink grass brushing against my hands and tickling my skin. "I never knew there could be so much color left this late in the year," I comment, rubbing my fingers against the brush.

Why is he doing this? He's shown no interest in me during these two trials, so what is his aim? I already agreed to try to break his curse, and just the other day, he pointed an arrow at my chest. This must be the effect of Shinhye's scolding. A scowl forms on my face, and Inha takes notice.

"Are flowers not something you humans like?" he asks, ears twitching and white brows bunching. A piece of grass is stuck in his tail. I don't remove it for him.

"Not me. They wilt too fast, trample too easily." I look up at the forest surrounding the meadow. "Trees are sturdy. They weather storms and provide shade, fruit, and materials for people. Flowers are only pretty." I would be able to appreciate his attempt at kindness if it came from an altruistic heart, but I know he doesn't care for me. I am a means to an end.

Our bargain comes with a mutually beneficial result, along with a way for me to make it up to him and Shinhye for my betrayal.

He bends down towards a shrub, tracing a petal with unexpected gentleness, careful not to cut the fragile flower with his claw. "One might think that after nearly a thousand years of life, such things would be mundane to me, as unremarkable as a blade of grass." He plucks a reddish-pink one, a yellow drop of sun nestled in its center. "These are called camellias. Different kinds bloom at different times, some even into winter. You think they are fragile, yet they survive late into the year when other plants retreat from the cold."

"I don't think a flower can compare to a tree," I mutter under my breath.

His ears turn back towards me, followed by his face. "Maybe many of the flowers you have seen are the ones people care for, but there are wildflowers, too. They are able to thrive in harsh conditions, and even if the sun scorches them or the winter freezes them, they always return. Is it not more impressive for something deemed weak to survive rather than that which is strong? There is an extra layer of beauty in the act of defiance that these flowers perform, refusing to give up their claim in the world."

Something forms in my throat, my chest tightening. I cannot help but squirm under his piercing gaze. I think I preferred him pointing an arrow at me over whatever this is.

"If you want to reward me for my success in the trials, I'd recommend actually asking what I like instead of choosing something you like," I suggest, allowing my tone to match the autumn chill.

His hand curls, crushing the flower in his fist. "Very well," he growls. "Then I shall not bore you anymore with such uninteresting things."

Without another word, he shoves me, and I careen backwards. The world around me changes in a single heartbeat, and I end up falling onto my backside on the floor of my room. I hadn't even seen a portal.

I am left alone, guilt gnawing my conscience.

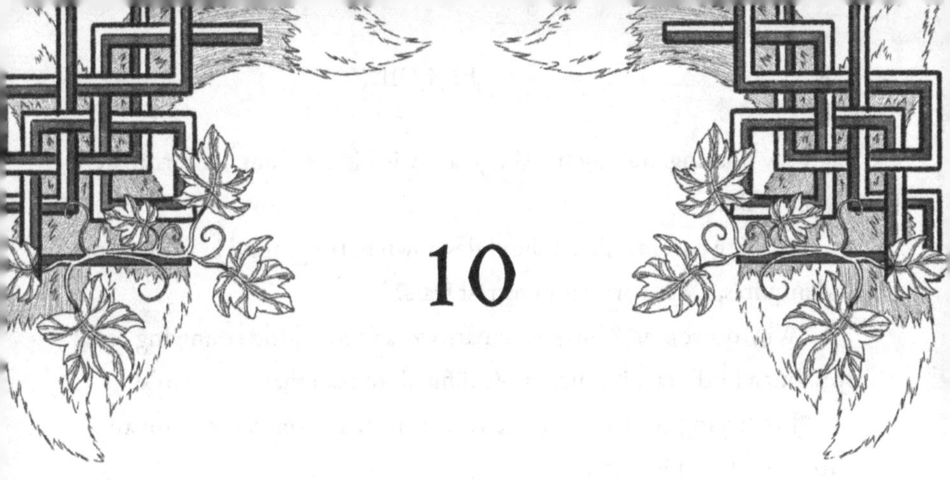

10

TRIAL THREE

U NLIKE THE FIRST TRIAL, the second leaves me emotionally exhausted. Phantom hands haunt me in my sleep, my screams scraping against my skull. I wake in the middle of the night, sweat drenching me despite the coolness of my room. Rather than calling for Shinhye, I find the fur-lined cloak in my cabinet of clothes and wrap it around my shoulders.

I need to get out of this room. I need air.

Forgoing putting on my brace, I stumble through the dark halls. The weather has turned colder, so all the shutters are closed and only the tiniest specks of moonlight creep through the cracks. Breaking out into the night, I rush down the stairs, nearly falling. I suck in cold air, my heart slowing with each deep gulp. I lean against the closest tree and slide down it into a crouch. A clicking sounds above me, the shadowy figure of a bird barely visible amongst the branches.

"Do you never sleep?" I groan.

The crow replies in a matter of fact tone, "I do, just less than you mortals."

"Is it time for another trial already?" It's the middle of the night; surely he does not intend to put me through another one right now.

"No. Just here to talk."

I say nothing, hoping he will go away if I ignore him. Unfortunately my plan fails.

Brushing past my silence, he glides down to the ground in front of me and inquires, "What are your greatest fears?"

"Why do you ask?" My gaze narrows at those little conniving crow eyes, but a bird's face is much more difficult to read than a human's.

"Just trying to help distract you from whatever caused you to be outside in the middle of the night."

I am not sure how asking me about my fears is a distraction, but right now talking about anything else besides my nightmare is appealing. "Taehee locked me in a rice chest for two days."

"How did your father find you?" the crow asks softly, dare I say, sounding sympathetic.

My voice cracks a little. "He didn't. Halmeoni Hyesun did. That was before she started losing her memory." My body shivers of its own accord, and I look up to the sky to remind myself that even in the night stars still shine. "Dark and cramped spaces are tortuous. One or the other, I can endure for a time, but the combination..." My words fade along with feelings I force from my mind. It is a common enough fear, I suppose, but I don't tell him about my other fear. That one is better left unsaid, locked deep inside where I hope to forget it.

The samjok-o rustles his feathers, his beak clicking. "I must go."

My mouth drops open. "What do you mean? We are in the middle of—"

But he doesn't let me finish and flies off into the darkness cloaked sky.

A leaf crunches behind me, and I turn, shocked to see Inha. That insufferable bird. A necklace hangs from the Gumiho King's neck, a red orb—the glow so soft I think I imagine it—fixed at the end. Since when did he start wearing his fox pearl?

"How much did you hear?" I ask, standing to my feet to save myself some dignity. I don't need him towering over me along with his pity.

"The worst parts, I presume," he mutters and takes a step forward, tail drooping low to the ground.

I cross my arms. "Not the worst."

"What could be worse than that?" He tilts his head, frowning.

"My father sold me. Sent me to what most presume would be my death. He's probably gambled away all the money by now." My voice manages to stay steady, but my heart aches. I look away, afraid of what I will see in his eyes. If I see sympathy, my emotions will come spilling out, and I will not allow that, especially in front of the Gumiho King.

"I knew you were not a noble, but this..."

A sniffle draws my attention back to him. My eyes widen and my lips part in a circle of surprise at the sight before me.

"I am a gumiho," he rasps, voice rough as he lifts a clawed finger to his face. "We do not shed tears so easily as you mortals."

But when his finger meets the wetness under his eye, the truth confronts him, one neither of us can hide from. He is crying. He is crying for a human. He is crying for me. For some reason, this moment feels monumental, and a few tears become a river directing the trajectory of my life.

My hand moves before I realize it, my finger tracing the wet shimmering line running down his pale skin dusted in moonlight. He does not shy from my touch but neither does he lean into it, frozen in his sorrowful state. There is pain in his eyes, and I see my reflection in his glistening golden irises. Is that a tear slipping down my own face or simply the water of his own eyes?

With my palm cupping his cheek, I run my thumb under his eye. "You may not have your pearl, but you have your heart." I'm not sure why I say it, but it feels right. This is not love nor even affection, but a reflection of humanity, an acknowledgment of hurt and hardship, much in the way one can sympathize with another's sorrow even without having experienced it themselves.

"It has not been used in so long, that I forgot it existed," he mutters almost mournfully.

There is so much I do not know about this gumiho, and suddenly so much I wish to. "I never did properly apologize to you for sort of trying to kill you. Or for my rudeness last night."

The corner of his lip curls upward, his ears facing forward. So the gumiho can also smile—another attribute learned.

I continue, "I am sorry for judging you. I'd heard that you had no heart—only ate human ones. I thought that you were cruel, holding human women captive for some malicious means. I acted not only out of ignorance, but out of fear. It is one of the greatest shames of my life." The one thing I never wanted was to become like my father—selfish and afraid.

It seems like there are some things that he is afraid of becoming too, or at least, things he wishes he wasn't.

The wetness of the tears on his skin appear like a shining gem under the moonlight. Even when he cries, he looks magnificent.

"I..." He pauses and reaches up to cover my hand with his. "I forgive you, Jiwon. And I hope you will forgive me for being so indifferent—aggressive—towards you."

"Master, is everything—"

We break apart, revealing Shinhye halted at the bottom of the stairs. Eyes wide, she gapes at us. She covers her mouth and exclaims, "Oh! My apologies. I thought something was wrong, Master. I didn't realize—" She spins on her heel, tail whipping behind her like a flag in the wind. "I will leave you two alone," she shouts as she disappears back inside.

Heat burns my cheeks despite the chill night air, but I cannot grasp why. I clear my throat and say, "It's cold. I'm going inside." I walk briskly, embarrassment locking my neck so I don't look back. I hurry to my rooms, casting my cloak off and curling up under the blankets.

It feels like there has been a shift in our relationship, one in which we can move past annoyance and into an amicable acquaintanceship. Friendship remains far off, but I do not expect any more arrows pointed at my chest.

When sleep returns, I dream of a white fox dancing in the forest, but when his glowing gold eyes meet mine, I am not the least bit intimidated. He radiates warmth, lulling me deeper into a sanctuary of slumber.

The sadistic samjok-o only grants me one day of rest before the next trial. He visits me right after eating a breakfast of beef and radish soup. Much better than the last beef I had. At the sight of the samjok-o, it turns sour in my stomach, and he immediately starts spouting some sort of Celestial Realm wisdom. It is much too early in the morning for such nonsense.

His voice drips in a scholarly dullness. "Peace is not the absence of troubles, but overcoming them. It is a battle of the mind, not external circumstances. Anxiety is the anticipation of bad while peace is the anticipation of good."

I press the palm of my hand into my forehead. The only thing that sounds good right now is crawling back under the blankets and ignoring the looming trial. The thought of having to slay some beast is more appealing than whatever this deranged bird has planned. If he takes me to another mountain, I'll earn a worse curse than Inha's with what I'd do to him.

Without ceremony, he portals us into the wilderness. This time, just like the last, he says nothing, flying off and leaving me alone with the sounds of the birds and a few squirrels scrounging more supplies for winter. It's a serene scene of seasons merging before the true cold comes.

Then all sounds cease, that which was tranquil turning terrifying.

A large black serpent slithers out from the shadowed forest, red eyes sparkling like gems. An imugi. I have heard two different stories, one that tells of imugi being dragons who have yet to fully form, in which they are benevolent. But by the sinister sheen to its eyes, I feel inclined to believe the second: that imugi are cursed dragons, full of malice and spite.

Like a line of ink, it spills across the earth. I expect its voice to be harsh and biting, but instead it is smooth and sultry, fit for a lullaby despite the maliciousness of its words. "I am your fears made flesh."

My eyes search around for a way out or something to defend myself with, but it is no longer a forest but a rocky cliff that surrounds me on three sides, the only path of escape blocked by the imugi. My pulse picks up, and panic seizes my body.

"You're afraid," it taunts. "That which awaits is dark and dreary, not lasting long, you'll quickly grow weary."

If only Inha were here. I may not be fond of him, but his claws would be of great comfort in this moment. I walk backwards until my shoulders hit against rock, creating as much distance as possible between me and the creature. This is all that samjok-o's doing. I am going to kill that insipid bird. The imugi towers above, leaning its scaly head towards me and devouring the little space I had made. My limbs stiffen as its breath washes over me in a wave of the odor of decay—of death.

"Your fear brings me great pleasure, a euphoria without measure," it says, nearly moaning.

I do my best to infuse calm confidence into my words. "I am not afraid." Whether it is true or not, I cling to the hope that I cannot be killed in these trials. Certainly the Celestial Realm would not require such a thing.

It smiles, revealing two rows of sharp fangs. "But you will be, yes, you shall soon see."

Then the rock bracing my back disappears, and I stumble backwards and land hard on my backside with a thud, my bones rattling. The last thing I see is the serpent's sinister smirk before the darkness swallows me. My heart begins to beat faster, pounding so hard I can hear it like a drum set against my ears. My breathing is rapid and shallow, and my chest begins to burn. I can't get enough air. My skull is throbbing.

Not. Enough. Air.

Panic consumes me, a vicious hound that refuses to release its hold. A black abyss surrounds me, not a single line of light permeating the cave. A monsoon of anxieties pelt me, drowning me in a flood. Thoughts flash through my mind, but I am unable to hold onto any single one of them. *My breathing is too fast. I am going to run out of air. I am going to die. I need to get out.*

I need out *now*.

Crawling on my hands and knees, I follow the cold stone ground until my fingertips bump into a wall where I search for any loose rock that might be movable and lead to a tunnel out. After what feels like hours of futile searching, I forfeit and shift into a sitting position, leaning against the rock wall. In this cave of darkness so tangible, with bitterness coating my tongue and despair singing in my ears, all the thoughts I've tried to ignore creep out from the shadows.

Taehee's voice manifests in my mind. *"Something as ugly as you is too painful to look at. Locking you up will be a favor to everyone."*

The acrid smell of the urine that soaked my pants for those two days fills my nostrils. My throat dries, recalling the painful scratching sensation after hours of screaming for help. Two days of terrifying solitude.

Halmeoni Hyesun cannot save me this time.

Will Inha come to rescue me? Not likely. He obviously is only tolerating me for what I can do for him. The other night, we may have seen a reflection of each other's pain, maybe even come to some sort of empathetic understanding, but there is no affection between us. Even if I fail—even if I die—he will just have to wait a few decades for another woman. And what is a few decades to a mythical who has been alive for centuries? My own father didn't want me, so why should Inha?

I am alone in this place, in this world. If I were to perish, not a single person would mourn.

And even if I succeed, what is left for me? Inha will have gotten what he desired and discard me, and I have no home to return to. Woosung will not help me, seeing as I refused to do what he asked. With each labored breath, hope withers, and with each heartbeat, another cruel thought claims me.

Life has been unkind, but perhaps death will treat me better…

The darkness is not eternal, Halmeoni Hyesun's voice whispers in my head like a weak lantern daring to fight against the heavy night.

A memory tickles my mind.

When we first moved into the city, back when Songhee was alive, they both took great interest in the girl with the wood on her leg and the father who never seemed to be around.

Tears mixed with the dirt dusting my face, and my stomach grumbled. My father was not there to hear either. A hunched figure shuffled in, blocking the little light that peaked through our doorless entryway. Her voice was soft like a hug on such a sad and lonely eve.

"Oh dear, that tummy of yours rumbles louder than thunder." Her eyes scanned the small shack, and upon realizing that I was alone, she shook her head and tsked. She held out her rough and wrinkled hands, sunspots dotting her skin. "Songhee made some rice and radish soup. I think there is even some rabbit in there."

Licking my lips, I grabbed her hand and walked with her down the alley to her home. It was the same as ours, except hers was not empty. Her daughter, Songhee, set down a pot of steaming soup, followed by five bowls of rice mixed with some beans and barley. Besides myself, there were three other children present whom I'd never seen before.

She pointed to the bigger girl. "This is Bora." Her finger switched to the boy. "This is Seojun." And lastly to the smallest of them all, a girl younger than even myself. "And Minah."

Dipping my head in greeting, I mumbled, "Hello."

They did the same in return.

Songhee smiled at me before announcing, "Let's eat."

Halmeoni Hyesun groaned, her knees cracking in protest as she sat, and I sat next to her, watching the others. Seojun didn't wait to be told again, grabbing his bowl of grains and shoveling them in his mouth while Bora, more slowly, followed suit, Minah taking her portion after the older girl. Halmeoni Hyesun noticed my hesitation and grabbed the bowl of rice and plopped it into my right hand. Saliva formed in my mouth, my stomach barking—demanding I eat. Lifting the bowl to my lips, I savored each sip.

After a few mouthfuls, Songhee asked, "How long has it been since you last ate?"

I sank into my shoulders, mumbling, "I haven't seen my father since yesterday evening."

Songhee's lips curled. The words she used next were foreign to me, but I knew nonetheless that they were sharp condemnations of my father.

Halmeoni Hyesun hushed her daughter and peered down at me with affection filled eyes, rubbing my head. "If you are ever alone, hungry, or scared, you come here, alright?"

My eyes watered, and I sniffled. "I don't like being alone in the dark."

"The dark is not eternal, my dear. No matter how long it feels, even if the stars and moon are hidden, the morning will come. Fears have a way of feeling like forever, but it is not the end. Only in hindsight do we realize how brief they are, only big in the moment."

I clutch those words, holding the memory in my heart as if protecting a feeble candle against the fierce wind.

Cold seeps into me, and I focus on it. It means I am alive. The same stubborn fire that helped me endure the pain of my body, the bullying of the Song sisters, and neglect of my father sparks again.

This will pass. This is not the end, I tell myself.

I repeat those two sentences over and over until my heart begins to calm and the roaring dies down in my ears. Taking a deep breath, I beat back my anxious thoughts. That slimy serpent shall not get the better of me. I will not give him the satisfaction, just as I never gave Taehee and Taeri the gratification of seeing me grovel.

The darkness and solitude twist time into a meaningless entity, eternity eclipsing the present. I do not know how many minutes or hours I have been here, but eventually after I calm my racing thoughts and heart, sleep comes to grant me a reprieve.

A cracking like a great splitting of rock wakes me. I slowly blink, sunlight biting my eyes. A familiar caw. The samjok-o. Using the cave wall to brace myself, I stand. The forest waits outside the cavern, and I squint until my eyes can adjust to the brightness. When my vision adjusts, I spot the crow sitting on a low hanging branch closest to the entrance.

"You know," I pause, making sure he can see the irritation flaming in my eyes, "when you asked me what I was afraid of, I didn't expect that you'd use it against me."

There are other fears I possess, like water since I cannot swim. But being in the dark is a torture, painful memories emerging to haunt me, and a heavy feeling of isolation that can reach deep into my chest and crush all hope. This time I managed to fight back and cling to some semblance of peace. It doesn't mean that I enjoyed it nor that it was easy, and I certainly have no desire to experience something like that again—twice in my life is more than enough. However, there is satisfaction in surviving, a victory that goes beyond the trials.

His tiny three legs shuffle further up the branch. "You can always give up," he reminds me with a little too much smugness.

"I'm craving poultry tonight," I growl.

He ruffles his feathers and shrieks, a smile spreading on my face. Serves him right. He portals me back to the palace, not bothering to stick around. Looks like he is learning, too.

After completing the third trial, I spend the rest of the day with Shin-hye, talking about her family and eating dried persimmons, and when it is time to sleep, for the first time in a long while, my slumber is serene. No nightmares and no waking in the middle of the night.

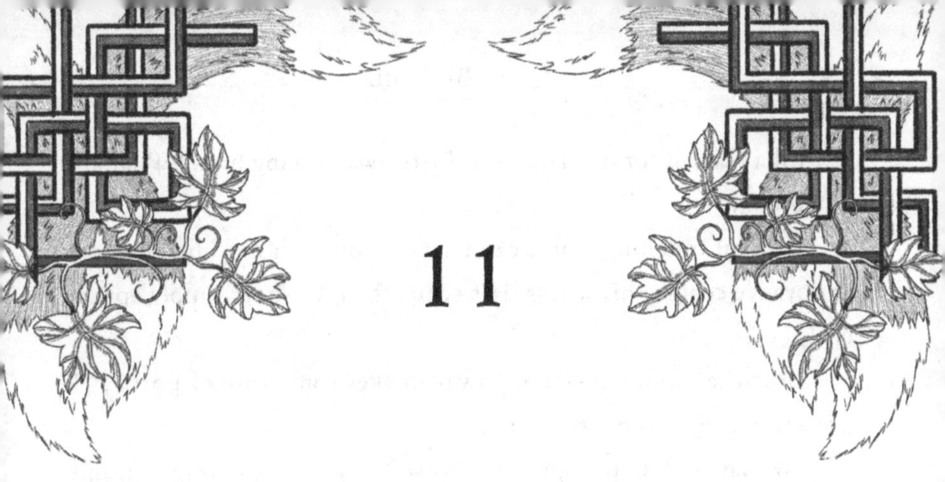

11

A SOFT KNOCK RAPS against the door. I stand and slide it open, surprised to see Inha waiting on the other side. His pearl is brighter than the first time I saw it, or maybe I didn't see it properly the previous time, or perhaps the lighting is different.

He scratches his head, his words coming out with some hesitancy. "I have some news for you."

News? What could it possibly be? I have no family as far as I'm concerned, and it is not like there is anyone left in the Mortal Lands to remember me.

When he speaks, it all rushes out quickly as if spitting out a too hot sip of tea. "Your father is dead."

I take a step back, my legs nearly buckling before I catch myself on the wall. "What?" My voice sounds like someone else's, like I am listening from above.

"Seonghwa told me."

"Who?"

"The samjok-o."

I didn't realize I never knew his name, but that is unimportant right now. "Take me to see him, please." My voice is monotone, my face dry. Shouldn't I be sobbing? Am I a terrible daughter for not immediately wailing? I suppose if my father had wanted my tears, he shouldn't have sold me, shouldn't have spent my lifetime betraying me in a thousand little ways.

Inha reaches for my hand, but I jerk away, eyeing him. "What are you doing?"

"If I am touching you, I can teleport you with me," he explains, annoyance coating his words. His sympathy is of short supply apparently.

"But the samjok-o—Seonghwa—makes some sort of portal," I protest, taking another step back.

"We have different magic." He doesn't wait for me to respond, and ignoring my protests, grabs my hand.

When he took me to the flowers, I thought I had just missed the portal somehow, but apparently, it never existed in the first place. The magical methods of mythicals are far too complex to solve right now.

The world around us blurs, my head becoming dizzy, but it is over in a heartbeat. Instead of my room, we stand in the trees just outside the city I used to call home. Night drapes over the world, silence blanketing us. I twist around, checking our surroundings; we are completely alone. A fresh mound of dirt catches my attention. My chest tightens, my stomach churning. I lurch a few steps forward, collapsing beside it and curling my fingers into the moist soil.

"Do you know what happened?" I ask, my voice still that stony cold apathy.

Inha's tone is unexpectedly gentle now, like a light touch brushing against my skin. "I do not think you will want to hear the details."

He is trying to shield me, but my father never did. There is no point in turning my face from reality when I've met with it my whole life. "Tell me," I demand, my voice breaking at last.

"Very well," he replies softly. "Seonghwa said that some debt collectors came, and when your sire—father—could not pay and the collectors had discovered that you had also "died" and would be unable to cover what he owed, they decided it was best to make sure he could not cause any more losses for their business. Whether they meant to fatally injure him or not,

I am not sure. One of your neighbors took pity on him enough to bury him."

Pity was probably not the purpose of the burial. Dead bodies become dangerous once they decay, spreading disease—one thing that noble and commoner alike fear. Whether it was truly some collectors or if the Songs decided to eliminate the only other person aware of their scheme, it no longer matters—the gambling debts or the Songs. Neither are my concern.

Anger and grief wrestle inside me. I yearned for his love, begged for his attention, and yet all he did was gamble away my hard earned money. I can't help but wonder if I was born normal, would my father have loved me?

Why? Why did you loathe me? Why was I never enough? I scream inside.

The pressure inside my chest increases, crushing my heart and threatening to break my bones into pieces. So many drunken nights of gambling with my hard earned wages, so many meals foraged and cooked by me, yet never once did he utter a kind word my way. He abandoned me long before he sold me to the Songs. The inside screams burst out, a gurgling and grunting ugly sound. With my good hand, I pound my fist into the dirt, my resentment unleashing itself upon the earth.

When I have no hatred remaining, I sit back on my knees, sliding to one side to take pressure off my bad leg.

Actually, I am glad that he is at rest. He was a broken and bitter man, and there is no point allowing his burdens to become mine. I have enough of those in my life. Having already stolen so much from me, I will not allow him to continue so in death. He made his choices, and it cost him everything. He may have been a terrible father to me, but at least he taught me important lessons. I will not become like him.

I have been mourning him all my life, and I want to bury my grievances with him.

The dead have no business haunting the living.

Water is beginning to form in my eyes, sorrow finally taking root. Slowly, I uncurl my fingers, dirt flecks falling to the ground as I stand. My hands brush against each other, casting away the remaining soil.

"I do not know what humans say during such occasions," Inha murmurs, tail curled around his legs as he stands beside me.

"Sometimes silent company is the only comfort one can accept." For what words are there that wash away grief? All sound and no substance, platitudes dull no pain. They will not bring my father back, not that I'd want him back. The father I loved never existed in the first place.

He takes a step forward, our shoulders brushing. He says nothing, not even as quiet tears leak from my eyes. I never let people see me cry, but he is not people. He is a gumiho. So maybe this once, it is alright.

We do not bring up that night again. Some wounds will only be healed when we reach the Celestial Realm, but I did my best to bury them in the ground next to my father. Whether or not they will resurface in the future, I cannot be certain. But perhaps if they do, he will stand silently by my side while I cry. Aside from his arrogance, the Gumiho King is quite good at being quiet.

❈ ❈ ❈ ❈ ❈ ❈ ❈ ❈

When the crow comes the next day, it is not for a trial. He seems to know what has taken place and allows me more time before the next task. He lands on the fence I lean against while the girin in the pasture prance around, scales shimmering in the sunbeams. The sun is weak against winter's tight cold grip on the land, and I am thankful to have such a luxurious cloak to keep me warm.

"How are you doing?" Seonghwa inquires.

I pull the cloak tighter around myself. "Aren't you omniscient?"

"That is a big word for someone who came from poverty."

Tilting my head to see him from where I sit on the bottom rung of the fence, I glare and growl, "I'm illiterate, not stupid."

He clicks his beak. "You are short-tempered is what you are."

I throw a small pebble at him, careful not to hit him.

Seonghwa shrieks and flaps his wings, shooting off the fence and hovering above my head. "You have proven my point," he squawks.

"I never said you were wrong," I reply, a smug smile curling my mouth.

"I usually am right, although I am not all knowing. I am merely a meek messenger of the Celestial Realm."

"Meek is not a word I would use to describe you," I mutter, eyes rolling.

He dives down and pecks my head. I fling up my arms to protect myself, but he is too fast.

"Ow!" The spot he hit stings like someone flicking my skin. I rub the spot, casting a glare at him.

"Pain is often the catalyst to humility," he coos, mischief flaring in his golden eye.

"If you're so perfect, why don't you complete the trials?"

"That is not how things work. The curse and the cure are clearly stated. A woman of mortals—the kind that the Gumiho King so loathes—must be the one to save him. I can appreciate the irony." He chortles at the last sentence.

"I don't appreciate you," I retort, shooting a burst of air through my nose.

"After all I have done to help you?"

"You used my fears against me."

"That was *one* time."

"My greatest trial is talking to you," I grumble.

"You are by far my most irritating mission yet," he fires back.

"So you don't only interfere in my life?"

If a crow could look offended, it would look like Seonghwa does now: feathers ruffled and beak dangling open. "Interfere? I would not use that word. But ignoring your poor phrasing, no. I have one other mission running concurrently with yours. Once I even had three missions occurring simultaneously. That was the worst year of my life."

I cock a brow. "And how long has your life been?"

He squints. "I hope you are not dreaming of it ending."

"Never." The mischievous smile on my face contradicts my words.

He eyes me suspiciously but answers nonetheless, "Two-thousand, three-hundred, and seventy-four years."

Sounds too long. Life is hard, and that near immortality is more curse than gift. "I wonder why humans live such fewer years," I muse.

"What you all lack in time you make up for in proliferation. Mythicals cannot breed like you mortals, not even like other mundane animals. They are but few in number, each only producing one or two offspring in their lives, three being the most I have heard of."

The fact is comforting. If the mythicals banded together, they'd still pose a large threat to the Mortal Lands, but at least there are millions of mortals. We'd stand a chance even against the larger and more powerful creatures. Not that I can ever picture Gunoo or Shinhye harming a human, nor Inha, now that I have gotten to know him a little.

"And what of your other missions?" I ask next. This is a rare opportunity in which the samjok-o is divulging information.

"Ah. That is none of your concern. Just a girl and a dragon."

So much for divulging information. But I am not one to back down easily. "A girl? As in a mortal?" I press.

He shifts on the fence. "I am not allowed to speak of my other missions. Especially to mortals."

The last part is quite unnecessary, but I ignore the jab. "Well, then you shouldn't have mentioned them. You've piqued my curiosity."

"Then you shall be left unsatisfied. Ignorance to all the ways of the Celestial Realm is part of life. You should make peace with ignorance." And with that, Seonghwa flies away, dissolving into the horizon.

If only I had full use of both my arms, then I could shoot the bird with a bow.

"Do you not also loathe it when he does that?" a voice asks from behind, startling me.

When I twist around to face Inha, I hate the way my heart leaps when my gaze lands on his snow white hair and honey filled eyes. But the heart is a fickle creature, and it is only reacting to the sight of a handsome gumiho. I am not so foolish as to confuse it as anything else. "Does what?"

He lowers his gaze from the sky, settling it on my own. "When he speaks cryptically or divulges only partial information. He has always gotten on my nerves."

I lounge against the fence post. "How long have you known him?"

"Before the curse, I only saw him a handful of times, but after—with each woman that came—he appeared in order to oversee the trials. Except only one ever partook in them, so even then it was not a lot. Yet concerning him, even that amount is too much."

"About the other women..."

Inha freezes, his limbs locking while a coldness creeps into his eyes. "I do not wish to discuss them with you."

I don't feel like prying. I wouldn't want him to ask about my past either. Some things are better left buried, and only someone I trust will ever be allowed to see the graves.

But he adds something I could have never expected. "If you complete six trials, then I will answer any question you ask me."

"Why not make that promise for nine?" It makes no sense to offer me some sort of reward for not even breaking the curse.

"Because by that point, I think you will need to know. If we do not trust each other by then, then you will likely not be able to complete all nine anyways."

I don't understand his reasoning. Since I have already completed three, I can ask soon enough, so I shrug and say, "Alright."

The coldness melts, and his posture relaxes. Holding out his hand, he walks towards me. I take it, and he gently pulls me up. In such a short amount of time—and despite my almost assassination attempt—our relationship has morphed into something I might call friendship. No more glares or arrows pointed at me. We have a strange companionship, one based on an agreement but slowly developing into a mutual understanding. We both have our scars, and we both can admire the strength it took to survive. He may have been born into the royalty of his kind, but suffering comes for mortals and mythicals alike, death demanding of both noble and commoner.

12

W ITH EACH TRIAL, I gain more trust from the gumihos, and thus more freedom around the palace. These days I can walk around without an escort, so long as I stay within the palace walls. It is on such a stroll in a small grove of trees, mostly just a patch of evergreens, within the grounds that I happen upon the last person I'd expect.

"Woosung! What are you doing here?" I had nearly forgotten about him since there has been so much demanding my attention. The pin he gave is long broken and disposed of, his request forfeited and the trust it destroyed slowly rebuilt.

His eyes dart around us. The masked guard stands a few steps away with his sheathed sword in his hand, but unlike the previous times, his other hand grips the hilt, ready to unsheathe it at any moment, as if an enemy could leap from the small section of trees at any moment. Is something wrong? Is he worried about one of the gumihos?

"Jiwon," he says in a strained voice. His gaze roves over my body as if checking for injuries. "Are you alright? I am so relieved to see you alive."

"Of course I am fine," I reply, crossing my arms. I had also forgotten his personal opinion of Inha, how he fears him, and I wonder why.

His expression shifts ever so slightly, his face now scrunched in a scowl instead of concern. "Why have you not done what I asked? Do you still have the pin?"

My brows furrow. "I..." How should I explain what has happened?

He steps forward a little too eagerly. "Then has he refused to meet you?"

"No, it's not that. I—"

"I do not have much time, the illusion will not last long." Once more, he scans the shadows for some secret threat.

"Illusion? What do you mean? Did you sneak in here?" I need to tell him that I want no part in his scheming. Wherever and however he gained his information is irrelevant, for he is wrong about Inha—not that I like him, but I do not hate him let alone fear him. I will not repeat the same mistake twice.

"There is no time. I have to go. Just remember what we talked to you about. You will be the hero of all the Mortal Lands, and no more women will have to be sacrificed to that monster." He moves back towards where the wall lies.

"I won't do it," I rush out before he can disappear.

He freezes. "What?" His voice is as cold as winter.

Crossing my arms, I reiterate, "I will not harm Inha. I am not sure why you believe he is evil, but he isn't." Because he took me to see those flowers—however poor an attempt it was to make me happy—and he took me to my father's grave, something he didn't need to do.

Woosung rushes towards me, hands grabbing my arms before I can step out of his reach. "Has he beguiled you? I told you he is dangerous. He has no love for humans. He *will* cause your death."

I shake my head. "If you only met him, you'd know that's not true." His grip tightens, and I wince and squirm in his grasp. "Let go. You're hurting me."

He leans his face forward, and for a moment, vague marks form on his skin. But in a blink, they're gone.

"Ask him about what happened to the other women. Ask him if he has ever *killed* one of them," he urges.

Those strange marks may be a figment of my imagination, but the cold darkness pooling in his eyes is real. What does he know about Inha that I do not? He knows more than he is letting on; he has been deceiving me from the day we met. However, the truth can sometimes come from a liar, and Woosung has successfully planted doubt. I need to ask about the other women before it can sprout into something more serious. When I asked before, I was content to leave Inha's past to himself, but curiosity haunts my mind. I've earned back some trust from Shinhye and Inha, but I am not sure it stretches that far. Can I afford to wait three more trials for the answers Inha has promised me?

When I open my mouth to ask more about what he knows, his nostrils flare, fear flashes in his irises, and then he and his guard are gone, swallowed by shadows. I turn around, looking for what it was that scared him off. It is a few moments before Shinhye rounds the corner. These gumihos are always too quiet; I never hear them approaching. But how did Woosung know? She hadn't even come into view when he got startled off. Perhaps he has an incredible sense of smell?

Shinhye waves me over, and I begin limping back towards the main palace. Although I thought I could handle not knowing, Woosung's words linger. Like an itch one tries not to scratch, I cannot ignore it. I glance back over my shoulder to the small grove of trees.

When I reach Shinhye, I blurt out my burning question, "Can you tell me more about the women before me?"

Her body stiffens before she visibly forces her shoulders to relax and creates an awkward smile. "I think that is something you should ask the Master about."

"I asked once, and he refused to answer," I mumble.

Pursing her lips, her face contorts in contemplation before answering, "Give him a little more time. Once he feels more comfortable around you—trusts that you will not run away—I am sure he will answer your questions."

Run away? That is not exactly increasing my confidence about the situation. What doesn't he want me to know? Suspicion, once sprouted, is not easily weeded out.

Shinhye breaks my bundle of worries, explaining the reason for her seeking me out, "Master would like to see you."

"Oh? What for?"

She smiles, replying, "It is a surprise." Gesturing back towards the palace, she says, "Please follow me."

My head throbs, and nerves knot my insides. I need to rest. I need time to figure out why Woosung is so set against Inha, what happened to the other women, and consider if I made a mistake in trusting the Gumiho King. If he is some woman killing monster, I don't want to help break his curse—not sure why the heavens would provide a way to break it at all. My opinion of Inha is as fluid as a river, turning every time it hits a rocky bank of new information, but I am doing the best I can considering the circumstances. Just because I wish to be loved and to be safe, to have friends, does not make this place and these mythicals so. If only there was a way to prove that they care, that they're not vicious and vile, but for some reason, only I am the one undergoing trials of virtue. It's unfair.

Those concerns aside, my body aches, begging for a long, long sleep. The skin of my leg is red and angry under my brace. I've been so consumed with the trials and life in the Mythical Lands that I haven't been taking care of myself. I used to pick heartleaf and use it to help my skin when it got irritated by my brace. Since arriving here, I have not been able to forage it, but maybe Inha will let me go outside the palace walls to scrounge some other herbs that have yet to die from the frost.

Shinhye brings me back to the dining room, and the last and only memory I have here slams into me. However, this time there is something new. Besides the tables, Inha, and a couple of servants, a small tree in a ceramic pot sits next to the Gumiho King.

Why is that here? My thoughts flit away when Inha stands, expression bright as the lanterns in the room. I think he has been staring at me ever since I entered, or at the very least, he stares now with an uncomfortable intensity whose source I cannot guess.

He inquires kindly, his lips curled up at the corners, "Are you hungry?" A growling from my stomach answers on my behalf. He smiles and gestures for me to sit. "Bring the stew and the bean paste buns," he says to the waiting servants who bow and rush off to follow his order.

After I take my seat across from him, I say, "Inha, I have a favor to ask you." Although I wish to inquire about the other human women sent here, I do not think the timing is right, but certainly he won't refuse my request for rest. I just need a few days to gather some herbs, which might take some time this into winter since all the heartleaf will have already died at the beginning of fall.

His body tenses, but he nods for me to continue, eyes glancing at the potted tree before returning to me.

Letting out a breath, I say, "These trials are taxing, both emotionally and physically. I need a little break, and I was wondering if we could ask Seonghwa for a brief reprieve."

His hands curl into a pair of fists. "You want to give up." The words come out as an accusation as sharp as a blade.

Why does he think that? Shaking my head, I insist, "That's not—"

He cuts me off, a fiery fury blazing in his golden eyes, one that I cannot understand. "You mortals are always so pathetic. Lying and breaking promises are what you are all best at."

My vision turns red, blood burning my ears. "How dare you? After all I have done for you. Are three trials not enough to show my commitment?" I ask, seething. In a vulnerable moment in which I admit my weakness, he throws it back at my face like the Song sisters threw mud when we were younger.

"You are lying." He slashes at the branches of the potted tree, tiny twigs flying through the air.

Shinhye shuffles forward, voice soft but pleading as she urges, "Please do not take it personally, Jiwon. He just has had a bad experience—"

"Quiet, Shinhye," Inha snaps, and the she-fox sinks into herself, sealing her lips.

"If this is how you are to someone who is trying to help, then you deserve your curse." I stand up and storm towards the door.

"Jiwon, please, do not go," Shinhye nearly shouts as she scrambles towards me and grabs my cloak, her eyes begging me to understand, to stay.

"Let her go," Inha orders, his eyes cold and his tone even more so.

I glare at him before shifting my attention to Shinhye, my voice softening. "I'm sorry, but I cannot stay here." Returning my blazing gaze back to Inha, I hiss, hoping my words wound him like knives, "Not *for* him. Not *with* him."

Inha has mentioned before that gumihos do not feel emotions like mortals do, but I am confident now that he just thinks so as a way to create a difference between us. He wants as much distance between himself and that which he loathes. His anger can certainly match my own.

I remove myself from her grasp and stride out the door, a thin thread tugging me and tying me to this place. I cut it as I exit the dining hall, passing puzzled servants carrying food who cast confused glances at each other. In my anger, I don't even bother going to my room to collect any belongings that I've obtained since coming here. I want nothing that was given by *him*. After everything I have endured for him, after all those moments we shared, I thought we were becoming friends at the very least. But I was wrong. He cares for no one but himself, and that night by the graveside was all an act. He could have been mocking me in my moment of mourning for all I know.

With only the fur cloak on my back, I stride down the path and out the gate, heading down the road that leads to the Mortal Lands. *That insipid, selfish, ungrateful fox! If three trials isn't enough for him, then nine certainly won't be.* A multitude of furious thoughts run through my mind until eventually numbness takes over. Although that could be from the cold.

Now that my emotions have ebbed, the pain sets in. My skin barks at me with each limp forward. Should I push through, rest, or turn back? With my well of rage empty, rest wins. I lurch towards the forest lining the edge of the road. Then my stomach growls. I should have eaten first, then asked for my favor. But how was I supposed to know he would get so upset? The grumbling sounds again, and I sigh. With only proper use of one hand, setting up traps to hunt would be useless, and it would likely take less time to walk back to the Mortal Lands than it would foraging for the few plants that are edible and still alive. Herbs make poor meals.

Darkness paints the sky above, only the barest rays of the setting sun singing farewell on the western horizon before the night fully takes over. Suddenly, I feel foolish. I shouldn't have let my temper and pride get the best of me, should have tried explaining myself further. I've always prized dignity, even at the risk of discomfort. Now, I am hungry, hurting, and alone. Pride does not keep one full.

Come on, Jiwon. Why do you have to be like this? I press the heel of my palm against my forehead as I continue scolding myself. My hands rub against my face as if they could scrub away my ire and idiocy. When Inha offered to let me leave before, I had a list of reasons as to why the timing was bad—an unfavorable season being chief among them—and those reasons remain just as true now. I am such a fool. Needing a fresh victim, my frustration turns to the world. *If my mother hadn't died, if I had a different father, if I wasn't born with this stupid body, then I wouldn't be in this position. I never would have been sold off as a sacrifice. It's not fair!* I pull at my hair as if I could tear away the injustice of life.

All of a sudden, rustling comes from deeper within the woods, my body tensing. I hope it is nothing dangerous, but as a precaution, I pick up a large nearby rock, praying it is not a wild boar, tiger, or some type of mythical beast more vicious than the other two. The creature causing the sound emerges, and I let out a breath of relief.

The myodusa I fed a few weeks ago appears now; at least I think it is the same one. I can't say I've met enough of them to know how their looks differentiate. It slithers forward and coils around the hem of my skirt. I crouch down to pet it, a purr emitting from its cat's upper body. The pleasant sound cuts off, and the myodusa's ears flatten as it hisses at something I cannot see before unraveling itself around me and quickly slithering off into the brush. What scared it off? Whatever it is, it cannot be good. Standing, I scan my surroundings, but I cannot make out anything in the twilight. Another reason I shouldn't have left. Indignance won't keep me warm on a winter night.

A crackling like snapping flames sounds from behind, and I turn, surprised to see a glow through the twilight darkened forest. Who would create a fire in the middle of the forest? All mythicals, much like most animals, should have good eyesight even in the dark, and why would a non-human need the warmth of a fire?

But then the glow moves.

And then another.

Two walking fires creep closer, and my skin prickles with danger. I slowly walk back the way I'd come, my eyes trained on the approaching light.

A snarl.

Without warning, two beasts leap from the shadows, black fur tipped in orange flames. They must be bulgae, the dogs who chase the sun and moon, although at the moment they are more keen on chasing me. Why can't there be more cute and kind mythicals? Why do they all have vicious fangs and dangerous claws? I curse again at Fortune's lack of favor for me; a twisted sense of humor she must have.

A dark figure looms behind the pair of fiery hounds, but I have no time to confirm if it is simply the shadows cast by the flaming beasts or some other creature. The dogs snarl and stalk forward, and panic grips my insides, my heart beating erratically while my brain rushes to decide what to do. I have no hope of outrunning them, even if I had two normal legs. I'm not certain I could haul myself up a tree, and I also don't know if the fire on their fur would catch on the crispy and dry autumn foliage that still coats the ground, now brown and drained of all color.

Water!

The river is not far off. I turn around, breaking out into my best version of a sprint. The bulgae are ignited by my running, crashing through the forest behind me. I don't dare look back, the heat of their coats singing my skin through my clothes. Something wet hits the back of my neck, and I imagine that their snapping jaws are close. The only reason I am not already dead is because their big bodies will be finding it difficult to traverse the thick forest.

Relief floods me as the sound of the river reaches my ears. Soon it comes into view.

"Almost there," I pant, urging my legs to keep going. The skin beneath my brace screams, but I ignore it, knowing the pain of the brace is nothing compared to the beasts behind me. *This is not the end. It can't be. You can do this, Jiwon.* I can't swim, but there must be a boulder or branch I can cling to. Drowning seems better than being torn to pieces.

A clawed paw catches my heel, and I tumble to the forest floor. Luckily, it was my leg with the brace, and the wood caught the brunt of the blow. I twist onto my back, my heart beating as rapidly as the river. The bulgae snarls and snaps its jaws at me, slobber sprinkling my face. Lurching back just in time, I scramble away, but it is not enough. I am going to die alone in the middle of the forest, and the gumihos will think that I truly abandoned them. Which, to be fair, I almost did.

The great flaming beasts crouch on their haunches, preparing to pounce upon me and finish me off. I swallow, my legs trembling, too weak to move.

Death has decided to claim me today.

A screeching hiss sounds as the myodusa returns, flinging its body at the fire hound's head. It distracts it for a moment, and I scramble to my feet, limping backwards towards the river, clutching desperately at this final chance to live. But Death, ever infatuated with me, does not give up. The other bulgae charges at me, and I prepare for pain, my limbs locking together.

White flashes in front of me, followed by a red blur. Inha swipes at the face of one of the bulgae while Shinhye attacks the other.

They came. They really came for me.

Growls grapple with each other, claws clashing with claws, except Shinhye does not have any, only her fangs and a foxtail and fierce desire to protect. The myodusa comes to her aid, its little lithe form slithering up the back of the bulgae, cat claws and tiny maw of sharp teeth digging into its flaming pelt. I am not sure how the cat-snake creature does not burn, if mythicals are immune to the fire of the bulgae. Inha grabs one of the fire hound's paws and sinks his long canines into its leg while one hand holds its throat, keeping back the barrage of beastly fangs aiming for his head.

The fight feels like it stretches on forever and simultaneously like only a few breaths have passed, but it ends when a low, long whistle echoes from somewhere in the forest. The two bulgae give one last snarl before limping away, blood nearly black dripping onto the soil. One of them has an eye swollen shut, viscous liquid oozing from it, and maybe it's just my imagination, but their fiery fur appears duller.

A smile spreads across my face, my shoulders relaxing as my gaze sweeps across the alive Inha, Shinhye, and myodusa. All of them pant, but aside from a few shallow scratches, they appear fine. And me. I didn't die alone in anguish in the middle of a forest in the Mythical Lands.

The Gumiho King sways on his feet.

Thump.

Inha's body is crumpled on the ground, blood seeping through his clothes.

I rush over to him, calling out to Shinhye, "He's hurt!"

She whips around, eyes wide, and sprints over to where I cradle his head. There are three gashes across his chest and punctures in his left sleeve. Shinhye wastes no time, yanking him up and supporting his weight, ignoring the red that pours from a cut on her head.

"Shinhye, you're bleeding," I say, concern cracking my voice.

"I am fine. It is just a scratch," she grunts as she begins dragging him back to the palace.

I wish there was something I could do to help, but all I can manage is taking care of myself. Except I cannot even do that. If they hadn't arrived when they had...

Shivers run down my spine.

The walk back to the palace is the longest walk of my life, guilt weighing down each trudging step.

Shinhye carries Inha all the way to his room, my pitiful self trailing after. Another male servant with fox ears is in the middle of organizing Inha's desk when we burst in, and he scrambles to his feet, eyes wide with worry.

"Changbin, fetch medicine and bandages," Shinhye commands and lays Inha onto his bed.

The servant—Changbin—rushes out without formality. While we wait, I search for a cloth, finding the discarded one the servant was using to wipe Inha's desk. I grab it and fold the dirty side in on itself and shuffle over to Shinhye who is crouched beside her Master.

I kneel next to her and tap her shoulder. "You're bleeding."

"I am fine," she snaps in a tone I've never once heard her use, eyes fixated on Inha's unconscious form.

Ignoring her words, I lean around to peer at the wound on her forehead and press the cloth to the gash. "Thank you," I murmur.

"After I explained to him that you were not going to abandon us—at least before he lost his temper—and that he should have heard you out, he felt bad and decided to go after you. Even in his half human form, he is not as weak as a normal mortal, does not know how taxing this all must be for you. He tracked your scent. He did not even hesitate to protect you." Her voice is so low, breaking at the end.

I can see in the way she stares at Inha and the tenseness in her shoulders that she fears for his life, but even in her worry, she stays focused, always the loyal servant. She rushes to check his arm, but the skin is not punctured, only the fabric of his sleeve torn. Meanwhile the blood seeping through the garments on his chest is indicative of a dangerous injury. Shinhye presses her hands to the wounds as we wait for Changbin in a severe silence. My mouth is dry and my throat itchy, but I do not reach for water. I have collected more regrets in the Mythical Lands than I ever have in the Mortal Lands. I don't know what to say, so I stick to a guilty quiet and continue to press the cloth to Shinhye's wound.

When Changbin returns, Shinhye hurries to take the supplies and help Inha, but I stop her.

"You should take care of your..." I pause, pointing to the laceration on her forehead. "Scratch." The blood has clotted, only a small line trickling down her temple, but there could be more injuries under her slashed clothes.

She hesitates, gaze darting between me and her master. "Do you know how to dress wounds?"

I nod. "Of course. I have had a lot of practice."

Surprise flashes in her eyes, and she looks like she wants to inquire more about my experience. But fatigue settles in, and she relents. "Very well. Changbin will be outside the door, so call him if you need anything."

"I will," I say, grabbing the tray of medicine and bandages from her hands, propping up the bottom with my stronger arm. She turns to leave, but before she exits, I say once more, "Thank you. For saving me. For trusting that I wasn't going to run away." I shift on my feet, the ceramics clacking together. "Well, that wasn't my original intent anyways. It's hard not to take what he does personally."

She pauses in the doorway, dipping her head in acknowledgement. That is her only reply, and she disappears, sliding the door close behind her.

Turning back to Inha, I let out a long breath. It's true that I've helped patch up my father on many occasions—usually after debt collectors paid us a visit, but I've never had to treat another man. My cheeks flush as I untie Inha's top. Perhaps if the circumstances were different, I could appreciate his lean and lithe form, but the three crimson cuts across his chest cause a pang of pain in my heart. His current condition is my fault. If only I had been more patient, tried talking until we came to an understanding...

My chest tightens, the hand of guilt squeezing my insides with a vicious grip.

I remove the lids from all the ointments and tinctures, sniffing their contents. I start by washing the wound with warm water, gently dabbing the open areas. An old scar, mostly white but dusted with pink along the edges, sits just under his left collarbone. What caused it? My hand freezes when Inha groans. His eyes remain closed, and my hand resumes applying the medicine.

Several minutes later, he finally comes to, his eyelids slowly fluttering open. At first his expression is contorted in confusion, eyes glazed and head rolling side to side, but when his gaze lands on me, his features relax in what looks like relief.

"You are still here," he rasps, wincing with each word.

"Did you think I was wanting to run away when I asked for a break?" Reaching for a cup of water, I bring it to his lips. He tilts his head up and takes a few sips.

He swallows. "Yes."

"I promised you that I would get you your tails back. I haven't fulfilled my vow," I mutter, looking away from him.

Hisses escape his gritted teeth as I press into the open wounds in order to remove some dirt.

"Sorry. Bear with it a little while longer," I say, lips protruded and brows pinched in focus.

"This would not have happened if you had not run away," he grumbles, pain prying complaints from his lips.

Through narrowed eyes, I reply dryly, "I only ran away because you were so frustrating and ungrateful."

"I thought you were trying to back out of our bargain."

"I said I wasn't. You should have listened!" I throw the wet cloth to the ground where it lands with a slap.

"You should have controlled your temper," he chides. But the effort causes him more pain, and his tone mellows when he mumbles, "Quite a lot of rage for such a small body."

Ironic, considering his own. Even if mine is more vicious than his, a small fire is still a fire, all flames able to injure the same. I cast a cold glare at him. "I've been through a lot."

He pushes through the pain and says, "Have not all of us? I do not understand your temper, having all these outbursts. But I suppose that is just how many mortals are." He prattles on, unable to see his own hypocrisy, "Such sensitive beings, swinging from sobs to singing to serious bouts of fury. You will find gumihos much more monotonous. We experience emotions, of course, but nothing like the range you mortals do. Although I think you were personally created with an extra amount of anger."

Again he paints mortals as beneath mythicals, but he is the one who is cursed, whose own anger or greed caused his tails to be taken.

My ire boils over. "Because I'm in pain!" The words explode from me, and now that I've started, I cannot stop the flow of feelings flooding out. "My whole life, my father loathed my existence. I didn't ask to be born" —I hike up my skirt and gesture to my leg and then my left arm— "didn't ask for all of this. It isn't fair! Other people get normal bodies with normal families and normal lives. I am at the mercy of some mythical who thinks I am lesser than, who doesn't care how badly my leg or my heart hurts." Traitorous tears trickle down my face.

His face softens, sympathy painted in his golden eyes, and his hand crawls closer, his fingertip resting against my knee. "Anger feeds agony, a pain that spills over into others around you. Take it from someone who raged for a few centuries, it cures nothing. Bitterness saps the joy from life, a curse of isolation and self pity and shame. My chains existed before the curse came upon me."

He speaks of his anger as if it is a thing of the past. "You don't come across as particularly joyful," I grumble, sniffling and hurrying to wipe the evidence of my emotions away.

I regret my words right away when his expression changes. Seeing his somber soaked features and eyes shadowed with sorrow, I realize that I may be broken on the outside, but others are broken on the inside. He assumed many things, but I have not put in the effort to understand him either. We've both done inconsiderate things to each other, but nothing that cannot be forgiven. Despite the distance he is constantly trying to put between us, he came to find me, risked his life for me.

And just like that, a little flower blooms in my heart, pink petals unfurling, a drop of emotion in its center—the color of golden eyes.

"I'm sorry," I say and set the medicine back in the box. Grabbing the roll of cloth, I hold it in the air for him to see. "I need you to sit up if you can."

He nods and slowly rises, groaning and grimacing with every minute movement. I use my good arm to help pull him into a sitting position, his skin warm to the touch. "This is going to hurt at first," I warn and wrap the bandage around his torso, using my weak hand to press the cloth in place. "It might be a little loose since I can't tie it as tight as someone with two good hands." I bite my lip when I see a section of bandage drape. "Maybe Shinhye should do this part," I murmur and begin to lean back.

A hand wraps around my wrist, grabbing my focus. My gaze goes from the pale-clawed hand gripping my arm to the pallid face of the Gumiho King. The sudden contact makes my heart flutter like a startled bird.

"If it is alright with you, I would like you to do it," he says softly, eyes asking and not ordering.

Swallowing, I nod and continue wrapping the bandages around him, now keenly aware of his breath, of every brush of my fingers against his skin. For some reason I cannot comprehend, I purposely make a mistake, restarting a stretch of cloth. As I lean in again to reach around his back, his nose whispers against the top of my ear, sending chills down my spine and tingling down my limbs. Heat blossoms through my cheeks. Maybe I'm more a coward than I'd like to admit, because I rush the last bit, tying a poor excuse for a knot and tucking it under another section of fabric.

I scramble backwards and to my feet before I make a bigger fool of myself. Only a couple hours ago, I was running away from this place—from him. I used to dream about leaving, now I dread the thought of it. I bid the

Gumiho King goodnight, rushing past his puzzled servant on the way back to my room.

13

S EONGHWA MUST PITY ME since he visits right after I wake to let me know I have a week before the next trial. The visit is brief and that is the second sign of the samjok-o's sympathy. I hope he will grant me the same period of reprieve between all the remaining tests. I tell myself it is because I need to rest and not because of a slowly blooming affection between myself and a gumiho. I have been a fool in so many ways, and I will not allow some imagined notion of romance to ruin me for a second time.

Soon after Shinhye comes to my room, a bandage wrapped around her head. Minji arrives only to grab some garments to be laundered and disappears back out the door.

Once Shinhye and I are alone, I point to her forehead. "How's your wound?"

She shakes her head. "Nothing to worry yourself with."

But I do worry because her posture is stiff, her jaw clenched, and her tail is dropping so low that the tip touches the floor. "Is something wrong?"

She shuffles, slowly approaching. "I just wanted to come to help you pack your things."

My brows furrow. "My things?"

"The Master said you may keep all the clothing and accessories in this room, and a carriage and a few years worth of silver will be sent as well."

She opens the cabinet and begins pulling out garments and piling them on the table.

My eyes widen. "Are you kicking me out?"

Her expression changes from concern to confusion, her hands pausing their packing. "What? Of course not. The Master was under the impression that you still want to leave."

"I did, but not now. I want to stay," I say quickly. Reasons I give in my head include poor timing and the wish to repay Inha and Shinhye for saving me from the bulgae, refusing any other proposed notion such as romance.

Her face lights up. "Really?" She rushes forward and takes my hands in hers, her fox tail swishing excitedly. "So you are staying?" Shinhye asks, eyes twinkling with hope and happiness.

I nod. "I shouldn't have left like that in the first place. Even if Inha is a bit...irrational sometimes." Because he is also kind, more than I initially wished to give him credit for.

Ignoring the insult of her master, she throws her arms around me.

My eyes widen at the unexpected gesture, but I reach up and pat her back. "Is everything alright?"

She rubs her cheek against my shoulder. "Thank you," she whispers the two words once, but the gratitude is expressed for a multitude of things. When she pulls away, she suggests, "Maybe you would like to deliver the news, along with some medicine, to the Master?"

"Oh. Alright." I smooth my hair down. Is it knotted in the back?

Springing into action, Shinhye jumps to her feet, instructing as she hurries out, "Wait outside the Master's rooms, and I will have the medicine brought to you."

I reach out towards her, the words dying on my lips as she disappears. Letting out a long breath, I make my way to Inha's quarters where I find a tray of medicine and bandages waiting on the floor in front of the door.

Shinhye, you clever she-fox. Smiling and shaking my head, I pick it up and brace it against my hip, rapping on the door.

"Inha, it's—"

"Enter."

The door slides open with a whisper, and I step inside. Inha lounges on his bed of blankets, propping himself by his palms. He only wears a white pair of pants and shirt—undergarments usually covered in robes. A blush brushes my cheeks and neck. I swallow and shuffle forward.

Desperate for a distraction, words begin spilling out. "I should check your wounds. The bandages should be changed once a day as well as ointment applied. Drinking tea can help with recovery as well." My eyes fixate on my feet, then the blankets, then the wall right behind Inha. "How are you feeling? Are you hot? Do you have chills? I suppose there is always a chance for infection." At last I spare a quick glance at Inha, jutting my chin at his torso. "Please remove your top."

"Is that not something you are supposed to do?" he inquires, voice husky.

Eyes widening, I gasp, "E-excuse me?"

A wry smile slinks across his face. "It hurts to move too much still. My skin feels tight and itchy."

Clearing my throat, I give a curt nod. "Ah. Yes. Of course." Scolding myself for interpreting his words in such a sensual way, I kneel beside him, setting down the tray of medicine and begin untying his top with fumbling fingers. To distract myself from his nearness, I say, "Such sensations are normal. It means your skin is healing quite nicely." I brush his clothing off his shoulders, careful to avoid touching him.

The skin around his wounds is puckered and pink, brown scabbing forming gradually over the clotted gashes. Turning towards the tray, my hand hovers above the creams and serums, searching for the right one. I pluck a tincture with an oil to help with the irritation and encourage the body's rejuvenation—at least I think that's what it's for. Many of the medicines are of higher quality than the ones I made or bought with my meager wages, the ingredients only those the wealthy can afford.

When I twist back towards Inha, I continue avoiding his gaze. I am not sure why, but I am having a harder time focusing on his treatment, his taut torso demanding admiration. I fear what lure his face would bring.

Get a hold of yourself, Jiwon. He is simply a patient.

Yet each time my fingers brush his skin, fire sparks, and I fight the urge to jerk my hand away.

Once I finish and start putting the tinctures away, he once more grabs my wrist and twists. His fingers gently tug my hand towards him, the heel of my palm scraped with red lines. "You are injured."

"It is nothing compared to yours," I mumble and try to tug myself free. He does not let go at first, a scolding in his eyes even though he doesn't say the words aloud. He shouldn't be worried about such a small patch of scratches; I have been through worse, his own wounds far more severe.

My protests ignored, he grabs the ointment I was just using and starts to apply it to my scraped skin. It stings like a thousand needles. As soon as he is done, I whisk my hand away and tuck it to my chest.

"Are you scared of me?" he asks abruptly, his voice barely above a whisper as if he is afraid of my answer.

"No," I say, shaking my head. "I have seen men act more like wild animals for nothing other than their personal pleasure." For levity's sake, I add, "You're not scary. Maybe intimidating. Definitely annoying." What I don't say is that he is attractive, growing more so by the day.

A chuckle begins but quickly fizzles out into a grimace. "Are you trying to injure me further?"

All mirth melts away, shame creeping in to take its place. *That's right. He is in pain because of me, because I am so useless. I am not worth someone risking their life.*

His hand gently touches mine, and this time I don't pull away, although I cannot get myself to meet his gaze. Honesty springs forth unbidden, as if his hand unlocked a chest I wanted to remain closed. "I feel guilty. You got hurt while protecting me, and I wasn't able to help." Water begins to form in my eyes. Infuriating tears. They do not listen to my wishes, forming despite my protest. The next words I say come out so soft, so broken. "Maybe my father was right to throw me away." I thought I had put away grief, yet that wretched creature comes for me again, clawing at my heart. I hate my father, but right now I hate myself even more. My very existence is a burden.

"Look at me, Jiwon-ah." The way he says my name tugs my face back to him. His expression is soft, golden irises glowing like a welcoming ember. Inha whispers, "I would always choose you." His hand finds mine, his fingers wrapping around my own. "At first I worried whether you would stay, now I worry about whether you will leave. I would fight those bulgae all over again if I had to."

What guilt does he carry for him to say such words? It is hard to believe that he means them about me. Are we both trying to prove our worth, our right to life and love?

Water wells in my eyes, spilling over and down my cheeks while my lip quivers. "I-I—"

There are no words for how I feel. Aside from Halmeoni Hyesun, I have never had someone say that, had someone *mean* it. And isn't that what love is? A dedication, whether romantic or platonic, in which another's well being is put above your own? One could argue that Shinhye and Inha and even that little myodusa saved me because they needed me for their own benefit, but what good would it have done if they had died protecting me? They'd gain nothing, and even if they'd been confident in their abilities to fend off the bulgae, Inha is worried about me being frightened of him. What captor worries about what their prisoner thinks of them?

I have found more love in the Mythical Lands than I ever did in the Mortal Lands. Although they made it clear I am free to leave, it is too late. Instead of my body, Inha has captured my heart. I've never been in love—well, one that wasn't a lie—but I wonder if this is what it feels like. My gaze retreats again, lest he read the emotions written in my eyes.

Once more, he calls my name, and he says it with such warmth that I want to melt. "Jiwon, would you let me kiss you?"

Swallowing, I slowly form my answer. "I don't think you're in the proper condition to..." My voice trails off, my protest dissolving. Because I don't want to deny him. I want him, want to kiss him.

"Is that a no?" he asks.

"No!" I rush out, twisting and accidentally laying my hand on his abdomen. But then embarrassment overtakes me, and I quickly remove it, heat crawling along my face and down my neck. Composing myself, I add, "If you want to, I wouldn't be against it."

With a muffled groan he adjusts his position, wincing as he leans towards me. I should tell him to lay back down, but right now I want to be selfish. Our faces creep closer, the heat moving into my core. I can see the honey flecks in his eyes, each notch in his lips. My heart thumps erratically in a wild dance to drums.

The door slides open, and we scramble apart.

"I just wanted to check on how the Master is doing," Shinhye says as she enters, oblivious to what was about to happen.

Inha's voice comes out hoarse, and I wonder if it's from the pain of his healing wounds or from the moment that we shared. Why did I say he could kiss me? Is it guilt? Perhaps I feel bad for him, like he is some wounded pheasant. That's not right. No one kisses a bird. A handsome gumiho on the other hand...

I shake my head, banishing the strange thoughts. Sympathy lowered my guard, his pitiful state luring me. It certainly had nothing to do with his sharp gold eyes full of sunlight, or his snow white tresses inviting one to play in, or the hard angles of his face that my fingers wish to trace. Clearing my throat and my mind, I head back to my rooms. By the time I reach them, I still have not fully convinced myself that compassion nor gratitude was the source of my desire.

The next trial offers some distraction from my fickle thoughts. Even if I have to spend the whole day climbing another mountain, it will offer a respite from the war taking place in my mind. I still am not certain if I love Inha, and I am even less certain how he feels for me. I do not know that'd I'd recognize love in the first place. Halmeoni Hyesun loves me like a mother, and Shinhye loves me like a friend. But what is this that is blooming between Inha and I? A dream or a danger, it seems like something one can only decide in hindsight.

"Are you ready?" Seonghwa asks, wings whooshing by my head, breaking me out of my cave of contemplation.

Inhaling in a deep breath, I release it and nod. "Yes."

He caws, and the familiar arching portal coalesces in front of us. The sheen shimmers in the sunlight, and this time I do not wait for Seonghwa and step through it. When I exit through the other side, a quaint village greets me, the silhouette of a larger city a few miles off, nestled in a nearby mountain range.

Seonghwa flaps his wings furiously, hovering in front of me. "I am supposed to go first," he squawks, sparing no indignance at my perceived audacity.

I shrug. "Fly faster next time."

Using his wings to thrust a gust of air into my face, he says, "I am going to enjoy today's trial."

Which means I am going to hate it.

"Gentleness is a virtue," he coos.

Today is definitely going to be the worst one.

Perhaps I think too highly of myself, but I have always been kind. Patience and gentleness on the other hand...

Well, life beat most of the gentleness out of me, and patience has eluded me since birth. If I am interpreting Seonghwa's mocking comment correctly, today will require both, but also knowing Seonghwa and this asinine curse, the trial will only count for one of those ever elusive virtues.

I follow Seonghwa as he guides me towards one of the houses. I am not sure if this is a real place or simply an illusion, but if it's a facade, it is a very accurate and well constructed one. Blurred memories of the village I was born in form in my mind. For a moment, I think I can picture my mother, but then the fuzzy figure dissolves completely. She died in childbirth, so any image I have of her is a wistful imagination. A sudden pain pinches my chest, doing nothing to help my poor mood.

We come to stop in front of a small house, the roof covered in straw and a porch in need of new wood. A middle aged woman exits, hair braided behind her head and a scowl painted on her face. She glares at Seonghwa. "Crow's a bad omen. But I was told your help would be free, so I guess I shouldn't pay no mind."

I glance towards Seonghwa, his gold eyes and third leg clearly visible to me. Perhaps he is using an illusion to appear ordinary to the woman. "You're right," I say. "Crows are a nuisance." I swat at Seonghwa, and he screeches, flying higher and out of reach. If I have to deal with this cantankerous woman, it would be best if he wasn't here to jeer. Turning my attention back to the woman who watches me with hands on her hips, I smile. "How can I help you, Ahjumma?"

She looks me up and down, squinting at my fine clothes, and barks a question, "Can you climb?"

"Not particularly well." I lift my skirt to show my brace.

Rolling her eyes, she scoffs, "Some help he promised."

I step forward. "Excuse me, but who is 'he?'"

"Some man came by the other day—a good looking young man—and said he had a friend who was trying to pay some sort of penance or some nonsense. Thought it was a scam, but here you are."

I have never seen Seonghwa's human form, and I am still not entirely sure he has one, but it only makes sense that he is the culprit of my free labor.

"Follow me," the ahjumma orders, already striding around the side of her house. She leads me to a giant pile of fresh straw, points and explains, "Need to switch out the roof before the first snow." She gestures to a ladder leaning against the wall. "Since you can't climb, you'll hand me the straw."

Shimmying up the ladder with more speed than I expected for her age, she pauses at the top and twists to look down at me. "Hurry up now."

"Oh. Sorry," I mutter and scramble to grab a bundle of straw, the pieces prodding my skin. I step on the first rung to reach her, and then she takes the straw from my out-stretched hands and tosses it on the roof. We repeat the process until all of the bundles once on the ground are situated on the roof. She makes quick work of spreading them out before  swiftly descending down to the ground while I scratch my itching skin. A piece of straw even poked my eye. Still, this is by far the easiest trial yet.

Straightening my clothes, I say, "Well, I am glad I could be of service and—"

She cuts me off. "Next is the inside," she grunts, already heading around the corner and into the house.

A sigh. It was foolish of me to assume the test would be so easy. Seonghwa did mention patience, and as I follow the middle aged woman, I know I am going to need a lot of it. Sunlight pours in through a hole cut into the wall, dust dancing in the rays. The floor is completely covered in wood, a luxury compared to the dirt floor I spent most of my life sleeping on.

"Grab that pile of blankets. We'll take them to the stream to wash them." The ahjumma grabs an armful and walks swiftly back outside.

I struggle to carry the remaining load, my breathing labored as I try to keep pace with her. Luckily, the stream is only a couple minutes away, and we find a large rocky area to place the laundry on.

She pulls out a sack and asks, "Would you prefer to scrub or to wring?"

Both of those sound hard, but one is easier to do single handed. "Scrub," I reply, trying not to let my frustration show in my tone nor my face.

She tosses me the pouch. I release a breath, relieved that I didn't drop it and successfully avoided being scolded. Sharing the same tub, I sprinkle in some of the soap powder. I submerge the first cloth in the soapy water before kneading it on a large rock next to me. Then I rinse it in the stream. We wash the blankets for two hours, the skin of my hands wrinkling—matching the ahjumma's face. I can't even feel my fingers, the cold water chilling my very bones. In an effort to work warmth into them, I shake my hands in front of me.

Surely this concludes the trial? Or do I have to sacrifice my limbs to the cold water?

"We'll leave them here to dry on the rocks, and while we wait, we can do some more chores inside." The woman is already walking off back to the house before the final word leaves her mouth.

In such a short amount of time, I've grown accustomed to not having to do such chores. If only Minji and Shinhye were here to help, then again, I suppose that wouldn't serve as a true trial for me.

I don't know if Seonghwa is watching, but I wish I could see him. I'd love to throw a rock at him. Groaning, I get to my feet and limp towards the house, and as soon as I cross the threshold, the ahjumma is already ordering me around.

Shoving a broom into my hands, she tells me in a gruff tone, "I'm sure even you can do this."

My mouth gapes, eyes wide. She does not seem to care about my weaknesses, and it is unfair of her to demand of me the amount of labor one with four functioning limbs would do. I think of Halmeoni Hyesun and the chores I would occasionally help her with. Maybe something is wrong with this woman too. Some diseases are of the heart, eating away at the kindness and consideration of others. Or maybe she is having a bad day like I am, in which case, getting upset won't change anything besides making us both more miserable.

Alas, I am mortal, so when I turn my back to her, I make faces and mouth all the snarky words I wish to say. It helps relieve some of my frustration, and I wrangle my anger and try to encourage myself. *It's just one day of hard work, Jiwon. Nothing you can't handle.*

Besides, this woman is still better than working for the Song sisters. At least she hasn't locked me in a chest.

She barks at me to hurry up.

Hasn't locked me in a chest *yet*.

The bristles of the broom hiss against the wood. In order to distract from the complaints about how slow and useless I am and the sharp stares of the ahjumma, I begin imagining the broom as a giant paint brush. Streaks of white form before peaking with two red tipped triangles, and two gold dots nestle underneath the snowy tresses, and a nose crests from a pale face. Flirtatious fangs peak from behind a pair of plum lips. Quickly, I brush the broom over the imaginary image, the colors clumping into one giant pile of dust and leaf bits, and remove the remnants of my painting out the door.

Scanning the house for any more debris, I nod my head in satisfaction at the dirt free floor. Certainly this must be—

"Help me organize the kitchen," the woman barks.

My shoulders slump as I shuffle to where the ahjumma stands by a table covered in dishes and cooking utensils.

"Put that jar on the table." She juts her finger to a small ceramic on the ground, brown crusting around the lid in what I can only assume is soy sauce.

Food sounds wonderful right now.

I smack my lips and swallow the saliva forming in my mouth. "Of course," I say through gritted teeth and a forced smile and pick up the deceptively heavy container. I set it down with a thud and step back.

"Actually, put it under the table and set the pots and pans on the top."

Chewing on my cheek, I do as she says. *This is only temporary,* I tell myself. *Endure for one day.*

We go on that way until the sun starts to dip and my left leg is aching and chafing so badly that I want to cry. Both my arms shake from the exertion, yet through all her chide remarks and rude grunts, I never yell. I endure it all because I will not disappoint the gumihos, will not fail Inha.

A soft sound comes from outside. A crow lands on the porch, and I nearly collapse at the sight of Seonghwa.

Finally.

The ahjumma doesn't notice, instead looking out the window to the setting sun, the lowering rays of light illuminating her face. Sun spots dot her skin, wrinkles carving around her eyes and mouth. She has lived a hard life, but I truly hope that some of those lines are from laughter. My heart warms towards her for some reason. Maybe this ahjumma came out of the womb mean like the Song sisters, but maybe she had hopes and dreams and kindness, too, ones that were crushed and dashed by life. Maybe it is because I could be her one day, and if I was, I would want a kind girl to help me, too.

"Farewell," I say with as much kindness and respect as I would to Halmeoni Hyesun.

She does not turn to look at me, just glances out of the corner of her eye and grunts. I dip my head before turning towards Seonghwa. He hops backwards when I step out onto the porch. Peering over my shoulder one last time, I see the ahjumma rubbing her hands. They're swollen, much like the way Halmeoni Hyesun's do, especially when the weather is bad. I walk down the steps and back down the path I came, Seonghwa flying just above my head.

"Your trials are strange," I murmur, limping and massaging my cramping forearm.

"They are not mine, but yours," he replies, his wings casting a shadow in front of me as I trudge with the sunset to my back.

Brows furrowing, I ask, "What is that supposed to mean?"

"If you've ever asked the Heavens for patience, you'll know that the answer comes in the opportunity to develop some. Virtues are made like strong muscles, slowly and intentionally. Every trial you have faced, and will, are specifically designed for you."

"And what were the trials like for the others?" I recall the conversation I overheard when I first arrived and that only one had attempted the trials at all. But one out of how many? We are a decent distance away from the village now. I hope Seonghwa will open the portal soon; I'm exhausted.

He doesn't reply right away, and I have to peer up to confirm he hasn't left me. "That is something you need to ask the Gumiho King about," he finally answers.

Clicking my tongue, I grumble, "You're no help."

"Well, if I am no help, you can just walk all the way back to the palace," he screeches.

I reach towards him, calling out before he can fly away, "Wait!"

He circles around me, tilting his head and fixing a golden beady eye on my face.

"I'm sorry. Forgive my ungratefulness." I mean it, too. We often banter, but it seems I've crossed a line. More than I care to admit, the samjok-o and I are similar. Yearning for appreciation—to be valued—is something I understand well.

A caw echoes through the air, and a portal appears in front of me. I suppose that is his way of acknowledging and accepting my apology. Before I step through, I twist my head to look back once more. "Only five more left."

"They cannot finish soon enough," he squawks.

"I know you'll miss me. Isn't that why you're giving me more time between each trial?" A wry smile tugs on my face.

"Certainly not," he replies, and a great gust of wind slams into me, shoving me into the portal.

I come out on the other side, finding myself in my room. *Sweet little samjok-o,* I chuckle to myself.

14

AFTER I FINISH THE trial, I am too tired to check in on Inha, or maybe it is because we left our last encounter with a near-kiss and my head hurts too much to discern why and how our relationship is changing. But the next morning, I go to visit him, knowing I cannot avoid him forever. Having asked Changbin to fetch some tea, we now sit across the table from each other. The windows are open, the weather weirdly warm despite being winter. The ahjumma will not have to worry about snow just yet, and her laundry is certainly dried by now.

I sip the steaming herbal liquid, not sure what to say to Inha. Glancing at his clothed chest, I wonder how his wounds are, but when the memory of my fingers gliding across his skin enters my mind, I tear my gaze away. Once again, I am grateful that gumihos cannot read thoughts.

"Would you like to learn how to ride a girin?" Inha suddenly asks.

Tea spurts from my mouth, Inha deftly dodging the burst of liquid. "What?" I sputter.

He grabs a nearby cloth and hands it to me. "Gunoo told me you were trying to ride one when he met you."

Accepting the offered cloth, I dab the tea droplets dry. I'd forgotten about my poor planning for a potential escape, but it turns out Gunoo remembers our awkward acquaintance. I no longer have the desire to run away, but riding sounds interesting, if not intimidating.

I reply with a smile, "Very well. If you promise to catch me when I fall, I'm willing to try."

"Do not worry, Jiwon. I shall not allow you to fall in the first place," he says, lips smirking and ears perking.

Nerves that did not exist before sprout now. Grasping for any words that come to mind, I blurt, "Are you sure you can handle it? Are your wounds fully healed?" The concern is genuine, seeing as it has not been long since the bulgae attack. Does he heal faster than mortals even in his cursed state?

He stands in a swift, steady motion, holding his clawed hand out towards me. "Perfectly so. All thanks to my attentive caretaker."

Tucking my palm in his, he helps me to my feet. I hold my breath, wondering if he will drop my hand or hold it the whole way to girin pastures. When he turns towards the door, he lets go, my anticipation falling to the ground and disappointment settling in my heart.

As we make our way outside, our arms brush against each other in the hall, and each time we make contact, I inhale, heart beating with soaring excitement. Yet it crashes back to the earth each time the touch leads to nothing. Does he not feel the warmth and buzzing of each brush of our shoulders? Does desire not fill him when the back of our hands meet in a brief passing, whispering words that our mouths dare not speak? Perhaps the pain of his injuries caused him to imagine something that night, some delusion that led him to ask to kiss me. Otherwise, why does he not take my hand? Why did he drop it once he had it?

I scold myself for expecting anything in the first place.

Love has made a fool of me too many times, and I fear it is mocking me once more.

I've never lacked courage, yet in the face of these new feelings, I find myself a coward. If this is love, then I can understand how it destroyed my father when my mother died, but I can never comprehend his loathing of me. I was the offspring of their love, but the object of his disgust. Even if it is hard for me to believe in that tangible way that sits in our hearts and affects our thoughts and choices, I know, in some shallow form of belief, that there was something wrong with him and not me. Hopefully one day, that belief will reside as truth within me, replacing the guilt and feelings of unworthiness that continue to creep in like a thief sneaking in to steal all that is precious and worthy.

Without realizing it, my expression has turned sour, a scowl scrunching my face.

Inha, however, notices, his ears rotating towards me. "Are you alright?"

Smoothing my features, I shake my head and smile. "I'm fine."

He cocks a brow, eyes revealing that he does not believe me, but he doesn't press me further. Instead, while we continue our walk, he keeps close to me, our arms rubbing. His touch, soft as it is through the layers of clothing, chases away the previous bad thoughts. It is then that I realize he has slowed his pace from when I first met him. When I'd freshly arrived at the palace, his strides were long and quick, and I struggled to keep up. My lips curl into a pleasant crescent.

The girin huddle in the middle of the pasture together. Do they need heat like snakes and lizards? I ate a snake once... I shake my head, banishing the memory of that hungry spring long ago. Now that I am well fed, there is no need to recall such rough times. I don't know why my memories haunt me so harshly today. Inha guides me over the fence, his hand hovering over my head as I duck under one of the cross beams.

"Careful," he warns after a close call with the wood.

As I rise on the other side, I smile. "Thank you."

He moves much swifter than I, vaulting himself through the fence in a flash. He grins and gestures to the girin. "Shall we?"

A chuckle dances out of my mouth, and we head towards the mythical beasts that brought me in the carriage all those weeks ago. It seems like a lifetime has passed, yet the seasons have only recently changed. My life certainly has, too. If someone had told me I was to stand beside a handsome gumiho—the king of them to be exact—and ride a girin, I would have prayed for divine intervention to heal whatever mental illness ailed them. Yet here I am, next to Inha, and so very happy, even if it is for but a brief season of my life.

My gaze turns to him, only to find him watching me intently, his ears twisted forward, eager to listen. My heart skips a beat. Can he hear it, the way my breathing hitches and my blood rushes when he looks at me like that? The way his golden eyes twinkle incline me to believe he can. Embarrassment chases my gaze away, and I stride towards the nearest girin to hide my blushing cheeks.

A grass-green girin greets me first, his golden mane protruding like wheat and his ox-tail dancing in lackadaisical circles. I place my palm against its flank, stroking its smooth scales. A hand covers mine, warmth seeping from Inha's skin and tingling dancing up my arm and into my core. He is explaining something, but I don't hear the words, fixated only on his touch.

"Jiwon?" a voice asks, a hammer shattering my trance.

"What did you say?" I twist to look up at his face.

Amusement glows in his eyes, the corners of his mouth curl up, and his tail raises behind him. "I was just wondering if you had ridden a horse before. Although now I am more curious as to what was occupying your mind so much that you did not hear the question."

Clearing my throat, I shake my head slightly. "Nothing." I realize his hand is still on mine, making my mind cloudy. My fingers crawl out from underneath his with great reluctance, but if I want to focus, we can't be touching. "I've never ridden a horse before. It's something only the wealthy would be able to do."

Out of the corner of my eye, he smiles, and it only reddens my cheeks further. His tail brushes against the back of my legs, and I have to lean into the girin's flank to steady myself. Is he teasing me? I glance up at the sky, half-expecting Seonghwa to be soaring overhead to oversee this test.

"Well, if it helps, you can think of a girin as a large horse." He grabs the barley colored beard of the beast and caresses its muzzle. The creature does not fight him; they all seem rather at ease around him.

"I just said I haven't ridden one," I say, a little too sharply.

He ignores the thistle to my tone. "How about a large deer?"

We both break out into laughter. "Very funny," I say and bump my shoulder into his.

"I cannot say I have ever ridden a deer either. Only eaten one," he muses.

A new bout of laughter begins.

Once we regain our composure, he suggests, "Shall we ride together, then?" The side of his hand settles against mine on the flank of the girin.

My pride wants to say no. My heart wants to say yes. My weak left side demands the latter. "I'd feel more comfortable with that," I admit, brushing a loose strand of hair from my face.

He comes up behind me and whispers, "I was hoping you would accept." His breath tickles my neck, warm in contrast to the cold winter air. "Ready?" he asks.

I'm not sure what he plans to do next, but I trust him. "Ready," I reply with a confident nod.

He places his hands at my waist and lifts me into the air. "Swing your right leg over," he orders.

I do as he says, using the momentum of the lift to swing my leg over the beast's back, Inha twisting my body in impressively perfect timing, but if he has done this before, with another woman, I wish to remain ignorant. My fingers grab a thick lock of the girin's mane, and I try to keep my balance. A warm body quickly joins me atop its back, and Inha's arms wrap around me, one holding the mane while the other holds me to him.

"Do you feel steady?" he asks softly in my ear.

"Yes." The word comes out quickly and breathy, and I hope he doesn't notice.

The warmth of his body sweeps over mine, flowing deep down to my soul, enveloping that intangible residence of dreams and fears, of life and love. It whispers promises of safety, and I trust its soothing voice completely. This must be a myth, some fantasy, and I am content to believe in it even if it lasts but a mere moment.

He kicks his heels into the flank of the girin, and we jolt forward. I teeter towards the neck of the great beast, my heart beating like a wild river, the feeling of falling gripping my stomach, but it lasts for only the briefest breath before Inha pulls me into him, tightening his arm around me.

"Did I not tell you to be careful?" he chides in a playful tone.

"That was with the fence. You gave no such warning about riding a girin. Besides, didn't you promise to not let me fall? I'd hate for you to turn out to be a liar." I retort lightheartedly. These are different jests than before, although our previous verbal exchanges are better suited to be called threats. And yet, these current jests feel far more dangerous to me.

He scoots forward, his chest pressing into my back. "I will not let you even tip from now on."

Leaning into him, I smile and say, "I expect you to keep that promise."

We start slowly by padding around the pasture. The girin snorts, its deer-like hooves softly hitting the earth. A few shrikes and magpies watch from atop the walls, occasionally calling out in tweets and chirrups.

After a while, my confidence grows. Knowing Inha's arm is around my waist, I lean forward, reaching out to touch one of the girin's antlers. It is smooth like a bone with faint rivets and lines. Twisting my neck to look over my shoulder, I ask, "Can we go faster?"

Light sparkles in his eyes, and he grins. "So brave for a mortal."

He taps his heels into the girin again, and we set off into a smooth, swift gait. My backside bounces against the creature's back, but every time the thought of tumbling off enters my mind, Inha readjusts his grip on me, and all fears of falling float away. The world dances around us, air tickling my face. This is the closest to flying as I can get. Is a girin faster than a samjok-o? Beating Seonghwa in a race would bring me great joy, and I chuckle at my imaginations.

"Are you having fun?" Inha asks.

"More than I ever have before," I gasp, jubilation ripping the words from my mouth and into the winter air.

I hear the smile in his voice. "Anytime you wish to ride, let me know."

Nestling into his chest, I reply, "Alright. Thank you." Unfortunately, the bouncing begins to hurt too much. "I'm sorry," I say, wincing, "but can we stop?"

He pulls on girin's mane, and the creature slows to a halt, giving a small snort and shake of its large head. With an agility I cannot help but envy, Inha swings himself off the girin, landing on the ground as if the height were nothing. To a gumiho, perhaps it is the same as a small stair step. How powerful would Inha be with his fox pearl?

"I am so glad you enjoyed it." He reaches for me, and I lean into his outstretched arms.

He bears the full brunt of my weight, gently settling me on the ground, and I peer up at him, heart full despite my aching legs and back. "It was wonderful." I don't tell him how badly my backside hurts.

The girin we just rode trots off towards his friends who graze on some straw under a shelter on the far end of the pasture.

Inha's bright smile could rival the sun. Even after he helps me dismount, he doesn't let go of my hand this time.

Seonghwa appears to take me to my next test. We begin rather unceremoniously, our greeting and portaling a near habit at this point. This time, we appear on the other side of the portal to a familiar place—on the roof of the Song Estate. I do my best not to think about falling, calmly crouching and sitting on my backside before I get dizzy. I thought I had already addressed my fear in the second trial, and although heights are not anywhere near the level of dark and cramped spaces, it is not exactly pleasant either. Does he intend to test me on all of them?

"Why couldn't we portal to the ground?" I whine, clutching my knees.

"I assumed you would prefer not to get too close to those two," he replies dryly.

I follow the direction of his beak. A cold, not from the winter air, chills my bones, a stone dropping in my stomach. Taeri and Taehee sit together under a pavilion, the same Yoon boy with them.

"Why did you bring me here? To them?" My voice comes out feeble. I hate what just the sight of the Song sisters does to me. The spite that helped me survive them over the years has slowly melted from the safety and warmth of the palace in the Mythical Lands. Like a fawn before a tiger, there is a fear and a loathing—although I'd prefer a tiger to Taehee. She is far more malicious than an animal.

"Whatever you wish for them, so it will be," the crow coos almost sweetly.

"Whatever?" I ask, ashamed that my mind is already thinking of several ways I'd love to get back at them. Locking them in a rice chest is the most prominent of the options.

"Warts all over their face, their marriage proposals falling through, turning them into some carp…"

The last makes me laugh, but the humor quickly drains as I realize the severity of the situation. I eliminate turning them into carp—or any animal. Such mean women deserve to be alone, to suffer the way they made me. Or perhaps making them ugly, as they made me feel on so many occasions, so that at least their outsides would finally match their insides.

I realize what this is.

A trial on justice. My favorite one so far.

When I turn to look at Seonghwa, I open my mouth to give my answer, but the words freeze on my tongue.

He is gone.

In his place is the same black serpent of an imugi from one of my earlier trials. Gasping, I lurch backwards against the tiled roof. What is it doing here? Where is the samjok-o? Is he going to trap me in another dark cave? Yet the cave, no matter how unpleasant, no longer holds the same frightening power over me as it once would have.

The imugi smiles—or at least what I think is its way of a smile—but the expression is not one of joy, rather of malice and sick amusement. Its voice is so saccharine and seductive. "Do your worst. Take your vengeance. The euphoria is ensured, their ruins well deserved. Perhaps a curse?"

I grit my teeth, grinding them together. They *should* suffer. They should bow at my feet, begging for forgiveness. They should experience the pain they inflicted upon me. The image of them losing their status and fortune, of being forced to live in the shabby shack of a house that I used to live in fills me with a frightening pleasure. Them losing the ability to walk, that they might taste the cup of my own affliction, tempts me to tell the imugi to make it so.

A dark blanket of clouds covers the sky, thunder rumbling and promising a storming wrath. Is it a sign of their coming judgment? Is this the way of the Celestial Realm showing their approval of such punishments?

"The skies beat the drum of displeasure, such a delectable treasure," the imugi says, but his voice is not worried, just dark and sultry—sickly sweet like rotten fruit.

Displeasure? At the Song sisters? At the nobles who shirk justice for the sake of protecting their families? Or at me, for wanting to bring down the blade of vengeance upon their heads? But they deserve it, and nothing I could do would be too much, for me, for Yuna, and for everyone else they've wronged.

Somehow, I can hear the sisters' conversation now, some invisible power funneling their voices towards me. They do not seem to care about the coming storm.

Taehee slaps Taeri's hand that reaches for a pastry, the sound like the crackling thunder above us. "The pink ones are my favorite. You can have the green."

Taeri clutches her hand, sniffling. "You know I'm allergic to mugwort..."

Plucking the three pink cakes from the plate, Taehee plops one into her mouth. "That's not my concern."

The Yoon boy says and does nothing, just sits, slouching and silent.

The thunder cracks overhead. Even with their expensive fabrics draping their body, the jeweled pins in their long, smooth hair, and the table full of food that before coming to the Gumiho King's palace I would never have dreamed of eating, they are unsatisfied. A selfish and sad heart can spoil any amount of wealth. Halmeoni Hyesun was happier and more generous than the richest merchant or noble, and despite the loss of her daughter, her soul did not turn bitter.

"Well?" the imugi asks impatiently. "Give me your reply. Perhaps you would prefer them to die?"

The thunder pauses, as if waiting for my answer.

My hands curl into trembling tight fists. "I-I—" No words come out.

I can't do it.

My fingers slowly unfurl. I cannot curse these women even after all they've done to me. As I watch them bicker, I can see for the first time how miserable they are. They want for nothing material, and they have a family that loves them enough to find a replacement sacrifice for the Year of the Maiden, yet they possess not even a drop of joy. Of course, nothing excuses what they've done to me, to who knows how many others. For once, I consider that they're lonelier than I ever was, isolated on an internal island of misery. Perhaps that is the best fate for them. Their lack of remorse will only make them suffer more in the end, and when they do pass from this life, they will receive their punishment.

Afterall, vengeance is a vicious cycle, and each individual could just as easily justify their vigilante justice until no one is left in the world. The laws of the land failed me back when Halmeoni Hyesun reported that the Song sisters locked me in a rice chest. Although I could have died, the local official—most likely after a visit from the Song patriarch—determined it was a child's prank gone wrong. Not even an apology was given. But to indulge in such dark desires so easily dismissed as righteous retribution would be failing myself. Is that not what every murderer does, justifying their wrong with the wrong that was done to them? My own father deemed me the murderer of my mother—his beloved—and he spent my entire life avenging her death.

The path to a hardened heart is gradual, one step, one choice, at a time, and I will not follow my father.

A single sunbeam peeks through the roiling waves of thundering gray, a faint breath of freedom greeting me, an invitation to drink of its dregs until I am full, if only I dare to grasp it. I remember what Halmeoni Hyesun once said to me.

"Forgiveness is a key. First, you unlock your own chains, and then you offer it to the offender. It is up to them if they choose to free themselves. Some cannot even see their own shackles, and in the next life, they will be dragged down by them."

I don't wish to be bound by bitterness in this life or the next. If my father chained one leg then the Song sisters bound the other. No more though. I am free to walk away from them all, ready to embrace my future and the gumiho I hope is in it. The life I have lived has been full of sorrow and pain, and some remains for the future as well. But I have a warm home and clothes, friends like Seonghwa and Shinhye, and...something with Inha. If those on this earth will not hold them accountable, there is nothing to be done except to wait for what's in the next life.

"Vengeance is a divine blade, a weapon I am unworthy to wield. If they are remorseful, may mercy find them, and if not..." Letting out a breath, some of the tension in my body leaves with it. "I leave their fate—their punishment—up to the divine," I state sternly, thinking that the imugi will try to convince me otherwise.

But he attempts no further conversation. Instead, he opens his large jaw, revealing a dragon's mouth with rows of large and sharp fangs dripping in gray saliva. He launches towards me, but before I can move or shout, the storm clouds disappear, taking the imugi with them. Light fills my vision, casting its brilliance over the whole land, the sight of which begins to calm my pounding heart. A caw sounds above me, and I look up, shielding my eyes as I search for the samjok-o. I trace his figure as he glides down, settling on one of the shingles next to me.

"I thought you were finally going to fail one," Seonghwa says. His tone is not mocking though. He almost sounds...relieved?

"What would happen if I did fail?" I ask, a slight shake to my voice.

"I hope that you will not," he replies.

"That is not an answer."

"It is the only answer you will receive concerning the matter. For now."

"For now?" I narrow my eyes and point a finger at his face. "Are you implying that I will fail?"

"With that temper, you are bound to eventually," he retorts, mirth mixing in his words. But when he speaks again, his voice is more serious—sincere even. "I am proud of you, Jiwon. It is a simple matter to repay good with good. It is a more complicated one to repay evil with good. To have mercy on those who do not deserve it, to forgive those who have no remorse, it is not for the faint but the strong."

"Then should I have never stood up to them like I did previously?" I inquire, my tone sharp and defensive. "Are we all to allow those with power, whether physical or political, to harm us?"

Clicking his beak, he replies, "Of course not. There is a time for peace and a time for war."

"How can one know which time it is?"

If he could smile, he would be doing so now. "That is the question."

Staring through narrowed eyes, I say to myself, *Cryptic, cocky little crow.* But then a conspiratorial grin lights my face. "That was you on the day Taehee got pooped on."

Seonghwa shuffles on his three legs. "I cannot confirm nor deny that."

My finger moves to his back, gently stroking his feathers. I say nothing, turning to look at the Song sisters and Yoon boy. They're laughing now, completely unaware of the storm that loomed over them mere moments ago, ignorant to their almost doom.

"Will you regret not taking revenge?" Seonghwa asks, feathers ruffled at the sight of the Song sisters. He, too, seems angered at their flippant arrogance, and part of me still wishes for him to summon lightning from the sky to strike them.

"I cannot be certain, but I will not allow them to chain me and keep me from my future. I will not wait around for their apology. Sometimes, one must shake the dust and continue on their journey, leaving behind the bad people and bad memories." To live my life well would make Taehee absolutely livid. The thought tugs the corner of my lips upward.

"Often the difference between justice and vengeance is the heart with which punishment is given, and with the latter, one is often tempted to return double what was taken, in which case both lose." Once again, the samjok-o speaks in a convoluted manner, one that I do not care to decipher right now.

"Take me home, please," I say to Seonghwa.

This time, he portals me to a hallway in the palace. I spin around to see the door to Inha's room welcoming me.

That conniving little crow....

15

THE WEEK OF REST before the next trial is greatly needed. However, after nearly a whole day of napping, boredom sets in rather quickly. Since the cold causes my body to ache more, strolls outside have lost their enjoyment. In the past, I would still busy myself with cooking, cleaning our small shack, and listening to Halmeoni Hyesun regale stories of her life. Here, my meals are prepared and my rooms cleaned by servants. Shinhye has lived long, but she does not prattle the way Halmeoni Hyesun does. As for Minji, well, every anecdote must be pried from her lips.

Other women might sew or embroider, but with only one dexterous hand, those tasks are nearly impossible, certainly more tedious than entertaining. I look at the painting on the wall of my room. That is something I am capable of with one hand.

Shinhye follows my stare. "The Master made that. He enjoys painting."

My brows shoot up. "Really?"

"I am certain he would relish the opportunity to teach you."

"Shall we go ask him?" I stand a little too quickly to mistake my mood as anything other than eager.

Minji opens her mouth, but the opportunity to speak is stolen. "We actually have some matters to attend to, but you should go ask him now," Shinhye says and rushes out the door, dragging a puzzled Minji, before I can call her out for her obvious scheming.

There is a high probability that Shinhye and Seonghwa are working in tandem to bring Inha and I together. And if they are, I find myself without the will to fight them, content to let this river current carry me. Following Shinhye's suggestion, I head to Inha's room.

When I reach his quarters, I raise my fist to knock, but suddenly it opens. Inha stands in front of me, ears pointed forward. Did he hear me coming? My eyes are drawn to the fox pearl dangling from around his neck. With each trial the pearl glows brighter red, like a shining drop of crimson caught in the sunlight. My feelings falter, flickering like a feeble candle light against the wind. Have I been misreading his kindness? Has he simply been flattering me for the sake of his pearl and powers? But assuming the worst of him led to a near lethal mistake before, so I shove the doubts deep down. He saved my life, and it is only right that I return the favor. Whether or not he only sees me as a friend or something more, his kindness has soothed much of my past pain. Will he allow me to stay once the trials are complete?

His voice brings me back to the present and away from my realm of thoughts. "What brings you here?"

I cock a brow. "Disappointed?"

"Only that you did not come sooner." His tone sounds sincere, and there is no sultry smirk on his face. They are sweet words spoken softly. Not seductive, just the simple truth of how he feels.

A smile tugs my lips. "Shinhye told me you know how to paint, and I was wondering if you would teach me?"

Grinning, he dips his head. "It would be my pleasure to teach you."

He steps out into the hall unexpectedly, and we bump into each other when I'm too slow to scramble back. One of my knees buckles. An arm slips around my waist. My breath catches in my chest, our gazes clashing. Each interaction with him intensifies my feelings, every touch reigniting the embers within me, and as I swim in his honey pools, I wonder if the same blaze burns within him. All these emotions are a fire that threatens to consume me, and I wish for nothing more than to quench it before I turn to ash. No matter how many times I tell myself I will be fine if he does not reciprocate these feelings, the lie withers when we touch or when our eyes meet.

Afraid of being singed, I untangle myself from him. "Thanks," I mumble. *This all ends when the trials end,* I remind myself.

Even if it is a lie, I must make it the truth. I am not sure how many times one can break and put themselves back together. One day, my pieces may be too tiny to fix.

A shadow of disappointment darkens his expression for a moment before it disappears just as fast as it came. "This way," he gestures to a door further down the hall.

We walk in tandem, only one pair of footsteps sounding in the corridor. Even after all this time, the silence of their steps is strange. In the quiet, my mind wanders to exciting and frightening places, and I ponder if my relationship with the Gumiho King is one of mutual benefit, friendship, or the love that saps all the wisdom from one's head. Inha cried for me, so does that mean he cares for me? Or is my life so pitiful that even ancient creatures can cry when they hear of it? I peer at him from the corner of my eye. If only I could hear his thoughts.

He catches me looking, the corner of his lip curling up, and his tail swings forward, brushing my skirt. "What are you thinking about?"

"You said gumihos don't cry," I blurt.

A huff of air bursts from his nose in an almost laugh. "What an interesting thing to ponder."

We've reached the door. I turn on my heel to face him. "So why did you cry that night?"

His ears turn to the side. "It is not never, simply uncommon. When one lives long, a certain level of apathy is gained concerning the ephemeral and inconsequential. Mortals wage war as if the very earth depended upon it while mythicals watch on knowing another war will start a generation after the previous one ends."

"Mythicals are not so superior to mortals. We each have our faults," I retort, my words coming out harsher in my rush to defend my kind.

His ears turn down. "Mortals are too emotional."

"Maybe gumihos aren't enough." I cross my arms and lift my chin.

Inha's face softens, his ears tilt back up, and a smile that almost begs for an argument curls the corners of his mouth. "I shall concede because it is you."

"Not much of a fighter," I tease, letting my arms drop to my sides.

His voice changes into something soft and serious, dropping all jest. "Not of late."

"What changed?" My breath stills in my chest, anticipating his answer.

Inha stares silently at me, speaking without saying anything aloud, but I am scared to believe him, scared of what happens after this all ends, scared that this is a farce, his kindness the tool to spur me on in the trials. Turns out I am afraid of more than just being alone in the dark and water and heights. Maybe it is for the best that he doesn't answer.

Ignorance is a shield, and fear bids me to bear it.

A small voice whispers, *Coward,* but I pretend not to hear it.

I break the silence first and turn my face away. "So what lays behind this mysterious door?"

"Ah. Yes." He pivots on his heel and slides it open. "This is my painting room."

I enter after him, eyes widening and mouth dropping open. Every space on the wall is consumed by pictures, some long landscapes, others tall portraits, and a handful of petite squares of an array of animals and flowers, but the biggest painting hangs in the middle adjacent to the entryway.

Two gumihos, nine tails sprawling behind them like a peacock's plume, prance around a magnolia tree. Their white coats look like snow in the wind, flames of red flowing from the tips of their tails. With the way Inha stares at them, longing and sorrow inked in his dimmed eyes as if he wishes to leap into the picture and join them, these are not some random muses. He knew them. His parents, I assume. This feels much more personal than being invited into his rooms. For art is often a heart laid bare, and he has invited me to see it.

"Do you miss them?" I ask softly. My hand searches for his, but just before I grab his fingers, I freeze.

Coward, the same quiet voice says again.

And once again, I ignore it.

"Very much," he croaks. "They would have been ashamed of what I became." He tears his gaze from the painting, turning his back to the wall on which it hangs. His voice shakes, and his tail droops, dusting the floor. "They would be disappointed."

I follow him, taking his hand in mine, the desire to comfort him stronger than my desire to guard myself. "They would not have been ashamed. You were lost. Wandering. Even if you made mistakes, they'd want you to be happy, to not let their deaths or your past get in the way of your potential. I may not have had the best example of what a parent should be, but from what I've heard, they were good rulers. And they entrusted you with the throne. That means you were good, too."

"*Were,*" he scoffs.

He does not need to say the rest, yet I feel inclined to remind him that his past holds no power over his future. over *who* he can become. "Look at me," I order gently.

He stays still, the only movement that of his chest breathing.

"Look at me, Inha," I say more sternly.

Head turning slowly, he finally faces me. Such sad eyes. Shame drags his shoulders. I wish to banish both feelings for him.

"I will not pretend that you're perfect, and I don't know everything you've done the past several centuries before me. Since you've been cursed, you must have done something to incur the wrath of the Celestial Realm, and I doubt Seonghwa visits just for his own amusement. However, I know the gumiho who rode a girin with me. The gumiho who silently comforted me by my father's grave. The gumiho who saved me from the bulgae, nearly dying in the process." I pause, inhaling. "And…" Light flickers back to life in his eyes. "I believe that you are good now. Not perfect. But good."

"Do you remember the day we met?" Inha asks abruptly.

I nod, although I still don't understand how this pertains to our current conversation. "Of course. How could I forget? Even though I was wary of you, you were the most gorgeous creature to ever enter my life." I force a smile, hoping it will chase away his frown.

A faint blush brushes his cheeks. "Do you remember what happened in the throne hall?"

"If I recall correctly, you scolded me for trying to touch your throne," I tease.

He is not amused.

Realizing this is something serious, I straighten my posture.

"The reason why is, one who is unworthy cannot rule from it. One may sit, but it only sings to the ones who are worthy." His voice drops. "I had not heard it sing for centuries. So when a mortal was deemed better than I…" He glances up at me. "Well, I was upset to put it plainly."

"I am confident you will hear its song again," I say sincerely. When I complete these trials, all will be well; the throne will sing to Inha once more.

"Thank you," he whispers.

Giving his hand one last squeeze, I drop it, turning back to the paintings. "So all those paintings were done by you?" I ask, tone dripping in admiration.

"I have been stuck with these mortal hands for so long, I figured I should make good use of them. Eight centuries of practice," he explains, gesturing to the gallery.

While my eyes take in each picture, studying each brush stroke, I whisper, "They're breathtaking."

"I thought you were not fond of pretty things," he comments.

My chin raises. "I never said that. I don't like things that are only pretty, specifically temporary beauty. But paintings are a practical pretty, something that lasts."

His gaze follows me as I wander around the room. "Are you ready to learn?"

Gesturing to my left side, I reply, "I'm not sure how good I'd be at it."

"In order to paint, you only need one part of your body to move. Your mouth always moves quite well."

Heat blooms across my face, blossoming down to my core.

He must have noticed me blushing because he rushes to say, "I-I did not mean it like that. Just that you are quite good with your words."

"Oh. Thank you." Clearing my throat, I touch my cheek in order to chase away the heat.

Embarrassment quickening his steps, he heads to a shelf and pulls out parchment. He turns and sets them on a wide table where inks of different colors wait with brushes of different sizes laying nearby and waves me over. I sit next to him, and he hands me a medium brush with black bristles.

I point to two bowls of water. "What are those for?"

"The left is for washing the brushes while the right is for diluting colors. It helps achieve different shades."

The blank paper stares back at me, mocking my abilities—or lack thereof.

He smooths out a few creases in the paper. "Is there anything you would like to paint? Any landscape or animal you'd like to capture?"

"Nothing comes to mind," I mumble, shifting in my seat.

Clawed fingers clicking against the table, he suggests, "Hmm... why don't you try painting me then?"

Again, that heat dances across my skin. I cough. "Sure." My voice is anything but casual.

Inha gets up and sits on the other side of the table, propping one elbow upon it and resting his chin on his palm. His eyes remain fixated on me.

I scrunch my face, confused. "Aren't you going to teach me?"

He smirks, tail curling around his body and resting on his lap. "I need to see what skills you possess first."

None, but I suppose everyone has their own methods of instruction. If we had done this when I first arrived, I'd have thought Inha intended to mock me, but I know he would never do such a thing now. Well, at least not about my skills, my humanity, however, that is always going to be a source of enmity. Seeing how powerful and beautiful mythicals are, I cannot say I do not find my own mortality undesirable, especially with my left side being how it is.

Suddenly self-conscious of how uncomely I must be compared to Shinhye and Minji, I squirm, my gaze finding every place but his face to be. "Can't you look out the window or something?"

"Why?" he asks, his tone a teasing lilt. "Afraid of something?"

A spark sets off inside me, and I look straight into his eyes. "Of course not."

He does not move. He does not breathe. Or am I the one not breathing? At last, he points with his chin towards the blank parchment.

"Are you going to begin?" A faint smugness flashes in his face, apparently satisfied to see me so flustered.

As I return to attempting to paint, Inha asks, "Do you have any dreams?"

I think for a moment before replying, dipping the bristles into the black ink first, "Not really. I just wished for a little more food, a little better clothing, and a little bit of love in my home. Between my leg and my father, I didn't think the soil was suitable for lofty dreams."

"That is...sad," he comments carefully.

Putting the brush to the paper, I begin drawing his head, inking two triangles for his ears. "That's my life. Or was. I'm not sure what I will do after these trials, and it may sound callous, but now that my father is gone, I feel free in some ways. No one to provide for, no one to run off with my wages and squander them at a gambling house." Except, of course, I wish to take care of Halmeoni Hyesun. The desire to stay here, with him, after the trials is a dream I will not say aloud, at least, not while I remain unsure of his feelings for me.

"After the trials..." Inha murmurs, his voice fading into the air.

My heart thumps against my chest. Will he ask me to stay? I wait for his answer, but when he doesn't, disappointment washes over me. "What about you?" I ask, turning to look at him, hoping that maybe the words I want to hear will be written on his face.

He is already looking at me though, perhaps never having stopped, his voice soft as he says, "I recently obtained a dream."

I scrunch my nose. "Aren't you going to tell me? Or is being vague and cryptic part of being a gumiho?" To hide my desires, I drop my head, focusing on the painting and dragging the brush down in swift strokes for his hair.

"I will tell you later."

My hand doesn't do what my mind is imagining, his lips more sinister rather than a sweet smile. "That's not fair." I pout, both at his lack of an answer as well as how poorly this painting is turning out.

His voice is a mixture of sorrow and wistfulness. "If I speak it aloud now, it may break. Mine is a rather fragile one."

I do not ask again. Because what if his dream has nothing to do with me? In my ignorance, I can imagine his dream is me. Dipping the brush into the red ink, I do my best to paint and avoid his piercing gaze.

No matter how hard I try and no matter how many times Inha tries to explain it, my hand will not do what my mind orders it to. Heat begins to boil inside. When I accidently smear the paint with my less coordinated hand, my vision goes as red as the smudged paint. With a screech of frustration, I throw the brush to the floor, ink splattering like blood. It's been so long since I've had an outburst. I cannot meet Inha's eyes, afraid of what I will see in them. Will he be disgusted? Will he be afraid?

My bottom lip quivers. *I don't want to be like this either.*

"Jiwon," he says softly.

"What?" I snap. Why did my voice come out like that? I sound mad at him. Does he think I'm mad at him? I'm not. I'm mad at the world, mad that I was made with an abnormal body, but I cannot get myself to explain that to him.

"May I touch you?" he asks, voice still soft, still patient, which almost feels worse because I don't deserve it.

A nod is my reply, afraid that if I say something it will come out wrong again.

His fingers grab mine, and he sets our joined hands into his lap. If I wasn't so upset right now, I might enjoy his touch more, but my chest is tight from irritation, not infatuation.

"It is okay to get frustrated. I know this is hard for you. All that I ask is that instead of taking it out on my poor little brushes, that you would take a break before your frustration boils over," he says in a soothing voice.

A fair request.

"I'm sorry," I mumble.

"I forgive you. Now, will you let me help you?"

Looking up at him at last, I reply, "I suppose."

Picking up the discarded brush, he places it back in my palm, wrapping his hand around mine. He guides me to the ink, where we dip the bristles just to the tip. "A little can go a long way," he explains, tone even and calm. "Be patient with yourself. It takes time to learn, and it is okay to make mistakes." He pauses, and I can feel him staring at me when he says, "Someone taught me that."

"Thank you," I reply as he guides my hand over the paper, the lines wispy, each stroke a little wobbly but much improved from my own attempts.

❀ ❀ ❀ ❀ ❀ ❀ ❀ ❀ ❀

We paint until the sun goes down, the lanterns our only light as darkness creeps in the corners of the room. My strokes are still sloppy, and somehow I keep ending up using too much or too little water. I get up, stretch my arms and legs, and go to the window for some fresh air. I open the shutters, and white falls from the sky, fluffy snow fluttering to the ground. Inha appears beside me, our shoulders touching.

"Do foxes like snow?" I wonder aloud, holding out my hand. A white crystal lands on my palm with a cold kiss.

"Depends on the gumiho," Inha replies, ears flicking as snowflakes cascade onto his head. "Although I loathe the cold that winter brings, the snow is quite pretty."

"I would have thought that foxes don't mind the winter. So much fur to keep you warm."

"When I could shift as I pleased, I was indifferent." He gestures to himself. "But in this form, I feel the cold similar to other mortals. Perhaps slightly less than you."

Does fur cover parts of his body like Shinhye? I've seen his torso but— Heat begins to creep along my skin, and I shake my head to banish the thoughts. "I've never been fond of it. It's frigid, and walking in it is difficult. Work was harder and my home colder." I glance at him, the flakes the same color as his long hair. "But...now that I have warm clothes and a better place to stay," I pause, returning my gaze to the weeping skies. "I can see its charm."

"Would you like to run?" Inha asks suddenly.

I give him an incredulous look. "Are you drunk?" I know he is not, seeing as we've spent the last four or five hours together, only pausing to eat the meal Changbin brings us.

"I cannot get drunk. Cursed to be a human yet not able to partake in the blissfulness of inebriation." He wipes a nonexistent tear from his eye.

"If you're going to act like this, I am going back to my room," I grumble, my eyes rolling as I turn to leave. *I thought we were sharing another sweet moment, but maybe I am just imagining the kindness. It is nothing short of cruel to flaunt that which I am incapable of. Infuriating fox.*

He grabs my wrist, gently pulling and turning me back to face him. "I am being serious. Do you want to run?"

I don't understand his question, but there are many strange things in the land of mythicals. "Of course I would." I hike up my skirt, catching a glimpse of Inha blushing before I point to my brace. "In case you have forgotten, I walk briskly at best."

"There is not a single thing about you that I could possibly forget," he murmurs so low that I nearly miss it.

Had he said such a thing when I first arrived, I would have taken it for some kind of subtle insult about how annoying I am—how one cannot forget a thorn in their side—but now... He means it, and I hate what my heart is doing because of him. How many times has this nearly immortal gumiho felt love? Am I but a brief pleasure amidst his many others? What happens after I complete the trials? He is a gumiho, and I am a mortal. He will live a long life, likely another thousand years, while I grow old and die in five decades. He has loathed mortals for so long, so how could he love one?

In his current state, he is more human than fox and unable to shift. But what about when he can shift into his fox form? I doubt he would enjoy spending significant time as a human. The worries weigh heavy upon me, and wisdom whispers to reject him. It would be folly to continue diving deeper into our dalliance, for there is no option where whatever we have, or are, lasts.

Say no and go to your rooms, my common sense says.

I should not be doing these trials, for I am too impulsive.

"I want to run," I say.

His eyes light brighter than stars. "Front or back?"

"What?" My face scrunches in confusion—an expression I am sure is entirely unattractive.

He lifts his arms in front himself. "Shall I carry you in front?" He juts a finger behind him. "Or would you prefer to ride on my back?"

I ponder the proposition, considering which maintains my dignity the most, but sometimes, joy is more important than dignity. Besides, who would ever believe a story about the Gumiho King carrying a limping mortal woman around in order to make her smile?

"The back."

He bows deeply. "As you wish." Turning around, he bends one knee to the ground.

I climb onto his back, and starting with my stronger one, wrap my arms around his neck and straddle his torso. He hooks my legs, his steady arms keeping me lifted and in place. After standing, he twists his head towards my face.

Gazing at me with a smile on his face, he asks, "Are you ready?"

Who knew stars could fall to earth and make their home in a pair of eyes? Who knew moonbeams could make hair and red flowers could form lips? He is breathtaking, something of myth and not reality. Perhaps this whole time has been a dream, but if it is, I don't wish to wake up from it.

"Yes," I whisper.

Then we are off.

He launches himself through the open window with deftness far too great for mortals, the remnants of his fettered powers, and my heart leaps up to my mouth. Clamping my teeth together, I hold in a scream, but it lasts less than a breath before we are outside under the night sky, the world brightened from the snow.

Despite his mostly human appearance, he is faster and stronger than any man I have seen. I bounce against Inha's body, but his grip on me is sure and his stride steady. Wind nips playfully at my face, brushing stray hairs behind me while snow hits my skin with cold kisses. I've never ran so fast that my peripheral vision blurred. My legs and lungs burned from walking long distances, but now I am moving so quickly and without any pain.

Even with the snow, my body is warm, my lips spread wide in a grin. Then the next thing I know, I am shouting. Howling, full of joy, dances through the night. Inha's ears must be hurting, but I don't stop. For once, I am selfish, and my bellowing laughter continues. No matter what happens after the trials end, I will always have this night when snow fell and the Gumiho King carried me.

16

Frost coats the trees, making tiny crystal leaves, and the sunlight hits the snow, the whole world aglow. Has the world always been so beautiful, or do I peer at it through new eyes and a new heart? One that dares to hope, braves to see beauty while acknowledging the pain. Perhaps this is what courage is.

A new day and a new trial awaits.

I wait outside for the samjok-o, seeing as he always comes for me in the morning. Inha stands beside me, our cloaks tangling and our arms touching. His tail is hidden beneath his cloak, but I can see it moving like an animal trying to escape from a sack.

"How did you sleep?" he asks, the words coming out fast and his ears fidgeting.

"Well, thank you. After our..." What should I call what we did the previous evening? "Run last night, I took a warm bath. Then I had a serene slumber. Yourself?"

His gaze darts to me for a brief moment. "My sleep was tumultuous."

"Why?" I turn my face to him, searching his facial expression for clues as to what caused his distress.

He brushes a stray strand of hair from my face, careful with his long claw, and my heart skips a beat. "My dream kept my mind occupied."

"The one you refuse to tell me?" My brow arches, and my lip curls in a questioning smirk.

He opens his mouth to reply, but a caw interrupts. We turn to watch Seonghwa swoop down and land on the snow covered branch of the tree in front of us. Little specks of white sprinkle to the ground.

"Good morning, Seonghwa," I say with a smile.

His feathers ruffle. "Is something wrong with you? Did something happen?"

"If my new mood doesn't suit you, I can return to the old. How about I throw a ball of snow at you?" I slowly bend down towards the snow.

"I take my words back," he squawks.

Grinning, I tease, "Ah, so one of the messengers of heaven *can* be wrong."

His head tilts upward towards the sky. "I am not a divine *deity*, just a divine *messenger*. I am privy to many Celestial matters, but I am not perfect."

"With your attitude, sometimes I forget and think it is the former."

He clicks his beak. "There is the Jiwon I know."

I shrug. "You bring it out in me."

"Today's test will bring me great pleasure." If he could grin wickedly, he would be doing so now.

A low growl emits from Inha, but when I reach for his hand and give it a squeeze, the sound ceases.

Smiling, I say to the samjok-o, "Then I'll make sure to succeed just to spite you."

"No time like the present to gain some humility," the crow coos. And just when I move to grab a handful of snow to throw at him, the insipid crow launches off the branch and gives a great gust of air with his wings, causing the white powder that covered the tree to rain down upon me.

An exclamation leaves my lips as I shake my head and cloak to cast off the snow. Inha rushes to me, wiping the flakes from my head.

"Careful, Seonghwa. I do not mind adding another curse upon my existing one," he snaps at the samjok-o.

"A little snow will not hurt a human," Seonghwa fires back.

"I'm fine," I assure Inha, casting a cold glare at the most immature messenger of the Celestial Realm to ever exist.

"Be careful, Jiwon," Inha murmurs, brushing off the last of the snow from my head.

Giving his hand a squeeze, I smile and turn to step towards the portal Seonghwa has opened. When I glance over my shoulder, I see Inha still waiting and watching me.

"I will be here when you are finished," he says, his tail curled around his legs and peeking out from beneath his cloak as if it, too, is watching and wishing me well.

I nod, face forward, and step through the portal, eager to complete my task and return home to Inha. We have more painting practice to do.

Seonghwa and I come out onto a cliff by the ocean. Salt assaults my nostrils, the air sticky and the wind biting while waves crash against the rocks below with a roaring raucous. Blinking, I take a tentative step forward. I have never seen the ocean before. It stretches on and on in three directions, blending with the gray clouds of the horizon. Sea birds squawk overhead, a few brave ones daring to float further out on the water, unworried about the waves. They bob up and down, content to follow the flow. I glance over my shoulder, familiar forest standing behind me, although they lack any snow. I wish Inha could have been here for my first time seeing the sea. It would have been a pleasant memory to share.

Peering back towards the ocean, I ask, "What must I do?"

Seonghwa juts his beak towards the sea. "Jump."

Shock pries my mouth open and stretches my eyes wide. "Off the cliff?" I gawk in disbelief.

"Yes," he says casually as if he was ordering me to complete a much simpler task such as fetching him a cup of water and not instructing me to throw myself off a cliff into cold crashing waves in the middle of winter.

My voice raises, and I cross my arms. "Are you aware that I cannot swim?"

He has the audacity to say, "Have some faith, Jiwon."

"I have faith in reality, and the reality is that I cannot swim. Even if I could," I pause to peer over the edge of the cliff, my head growing dizzy from the sight of the long drop to the rocky waters below. "I would break my body on the rocks and die before the ocean could drown me."

"That which shall save you is not always seen," Seonghwa tells me.

"Take a leap of faith" isn't supposed to be this literal. I don't voice my thoughts aloud if only to avoid another long lecture full of Celestial wisdom.

At this point, I know that I cannot die in the trials, not with more still to come, but I do not look forward to being soaking wet in such cold weather. I'd complain more or try to argue if it was anyone but Seonghwa with me. No use dilly-dallying. I take a deep breath and summon all the strength into my good leg and jump.

The feeling of falling fills me with fear and excitement, my limbs tingling as my stomach flies to my throat. The ocean roars beneath me, my body plummeting towards the whipping waves that reach up like arms ready to catch me. Although I won't die, I can still get hurt. My teeth clench together, my eyes squeeze shut, and I brace for the harsh impact.

But it never comes.

Instead, something like wet grass cushions my body. I slowly open my eyes, my hand searching my surroundings. Something cold and smooth, almost like a fish, meets my fingers. I sit up, and then I am able to see what kept me from colliding with the rocky and rough waters.

A dragon.

It's a teal scaly pillar protruding from the sea, its enormous head turning around to observe me, golden eyes shimmering. Unlike the imugi I met in my earlier test with the cave and the Song sisters, this creature inspires no fear. Seonghwa flies down and perches on one of the dragon's cream colored antlers.

"I told you not to sit there," the dragon grumbles, air and water droplets bursting from his nostrils that are as big as my fist.

"You cannot expect me to hover while talking with you," the crow complains.

The dragon's long whiskers bounce as he retorts, "Is that not what your wings are for?"

I am still too shocked at the sight of the great scaled beast to speak. The dragon turns its attention to me, seemingly giving up on getting the samjok-o off his antlers.

"I heard you tried to kill the Gumiho King," he states plainly, intelligent eyes boring into me.

I gulp. "Sort of. One time. But I didn't really." It's the best explanation I can muster at this moment.

A deep rumbling vibrates through me. Is the dragon laughing?

He says in a gravelly voice, "If you tire of him, you are always welcome to come to my palace. I am also in need of a bride."

My jaw drops.

"Jisang, I think you have scared her," the crow cackles.

I stammer, "N-no. I am..." What word should I use? I do not wish to insult the only thing keeping me from falling into the ocean. "Flattered," I choose to say.

The dragon moves us towards the cliff edge, positioning his neck so I can get down. On hands and knees, I scramble ungracefully off of the great beast, the back of my cloak damp from the water soaked dragon-mane I landed on. I reach behind me and start flapping the fabric, feebly attempting to dry it.

"If you ever decide to accept the offer, come to the ocean and call my name," the dragon says in a serious tone that indicates his words were genuine and not in jest, which I am not sure how to feel about.

A squawking laugh erupts out of Seonghwa. "If Inha finds out you said such words—"

The dragon snorts. "I would like to see that furball try to do something to me. He will need to get over his fear of water first."

Well that is something Inha and I have in common.

"Not enough she-dragons to choose from?" Seonghwa asks as if it is an inside joke, one that I cannot comprehend completely.

The dragon curls his lip at the question.

Unlike Seonghwa, I think it best not to upset a dragon, so I dip my head, bringing his attention back to me and away from the snarky samjok-o. "Thank you for your help. It's Jisang, correct?"

Something flashes in the dragon's eyes, although I don't know what emotion it is. "Yes. I do hope we meet again, Jiwon."

And then the great creature turns back towards the sea, the water swallowing his scaled back, gone just as quick as he came. I wish I could tell Halmeoni Hyesun about this. She was always enamored by the myths of the great beasts of the water, and she'd be enthralled to hear of how I met a dragon—let alone received a marriage proposal from one.

The dragon knows my name, and he also knew I tried to almost kill the Gumiho King. Word must travel fast in the Mythical Lands. Do Seonghwa and his fellow samjok-os spread it? I eye the three-legged-crow, knowing that with his personality, he'd find great pleasure in gossiping. But for fear that he will refuse to portal me, I keep my speculations and quips to myself.

"Well, that concluded quickly," I comment with a light chuckle.

"Indeed. I did not expect you to jump with so little encouragement." I cannot tell if the crow is pleased or disappointed.

"I happen to have faith that you wouldn't let me die," I reply, beaming.

Seonghwa doesn't reply right away, but when he does, his voice is soft and tinged with a somberness. "I will take you back now."

"Is something the matt—"

Opening a portal, Seonghwa shoots through it before I can finish my question. *Strange creatures, samjok-os,* I muse to myself and step through.

When we return to the palace, Inha is waiting.

He rushes towards me, eyes searching for signs of injury. "How was it? Are you hurt? Hungry? Tired?"

I shake my head. "I am perfectly fine. It was surprisingly quick and easy. All I had to do was leap off a cliff and into the ocean. Except I didn't even fall far because a dragon caught—"

"You had her jump off a cliff?" Inha snarls, fangs flashing at the three-legged-bird.

"There was water at the bottom," Seonghwa retorts.

Inha swipes with his claws at the crow. "She cannot swim!"

Seonghwa dodges him, squawking, "She is fine. No harm done."

Inha jumps into the air, claws flailing as he tries to hit the crow, but Seonghwa flies out of his reach with ease. A giggle bubbles forth at the sight.

"Inha," I call out, trying to contain my laughter, "leave the bird alone before he makes me do more trials."

Ceasing his futile attack, Inha glares at Seonghwa before bringing his gaze to me. Scanning for any signs of scrapes or bruises, apparently unsatisfied with his first assessment, Inha mutters something about foxes being the natural predator to birds. When he finds no injuries, his expression relaxes into relief, his shoulders unknotting the taught tension.

A small smile forms on my face, a warmth blooming throughout my chest. His concern about my wellbeing means more than he will ever know. "I'm truly alright. But I am famished." I lay a hand on my stomach.

He grabs that very hand and hauls me into the palace. "I will take you to your room, and we can have Shinhye bring it there so you can sleep right after."

Chuckling, I say, "The dining hall will be just fine, Inha. Thank you for your consideration though." Now inside, I take off the still slightly moist cloak, grateful that the skirts beneath are dry.

Taking the cloak from me and draping it over his arm, he says, "As you wish. I had the cooks start preparing early just in case you came back. We will not have to wait long."

A gurgling sound comes from my stomach. "Wisdom befitting a king," I reply, laughing.

Inha chuckles. "Turns out I still possess some. It was just lost and forgotten on a shelf. Needed a little dusting off."

"Gumihos may not cry often but at least they can joke," I jest, still not believing that they're as stoic as they claim to be.

He glances at me, eyes sparking with an emotion I can't quite discern. "We can also—"

His words are cut off when we run into Shinhye in the corridor outside the dining hall.

"Master. Jiwon." She rushes over, guiding us into the dining hall and to our seats. "I came from the kitchen, and they were just finishing up. The food should be coming out shortly." She takes the cloak from Inha and scurries back out, leaving us alone.

Inha and I look at each other, the tables between us a sudden unwanted barrier. I wonder what he was going to say before we were interrupted, but I don't have the chance to ask because the first servants, the same trio as the last time, bring our food out. They place ox-bone soup and a mixture of barley and rice in a bowl on my table, dishes of braised lotus root and roasted chestnuts following after.

When the servants bring out Inha's meal, the meat sitting atop the platter is cooked. Noticing my stare, Inha explains sheepishly, "I thought maybe the smell and appearance of the raw meat was off putting to you."

"That's very kind of you, but if you prefer the uncooked—"

He shakes his head faster than flapping wings, ears wiggling endearingly, and I can't keep the smile from my face. I find myself smiling often these days.

He insists, "It is fine. I do prefer meat in its natural state—with a bit of blood–but roasted meat is alright, too."

Looking down at my dish, I try not to cry. That someone would care so much about not only my physical wellbeing but also my preferences is touching, and it makes me all the more determined to not fail these trials. I cannot offer him a palace, luxurious goods, or feasts of fine food, but I can at least break the curse for him.

I lift a spoonful of soup to my mouth. The food tastes more flavorful, each ingredient more poignant. It's the best thing I've ever eaten, but I am not sure if it is because I am hungry or if it is the cause of the company I keep. My insides warm, not solely from the stew.

Inha waits for me to eat most of my meal before he begins inquiring about today's trial. "So you met a dragon?"

So he did hear that part.

I plop the last lotus root in my mouth. "Yes. His name is Jisang, and he was huge. He even chided Seonghwa. A man—or dragon—after my own heart."

A scowl shadows Inha's face, and his ears flatten. For a moment, I don't understand why, then it dawns on me. Is he jealous? If he is in fact already jealous, then it would be a bad idea to share the part in which Jisang offered to marry me and called Inha a "furball".

Changing the subject, I explain, "It was my first time seeing the ocean, but I'd like to see it again, just for fun and not some divine test of virtue." Judging by his face, he does not seem to understand what I mean, so I add, "I'd like to go together."

His expression changes instantly, ears perking and eyes brightening. "I would be delighted," he says, smiling at last.

Silly fox. I toss a chestnut in my mouth to keep from laughing at his sudden—and adorable—change in countenance.

After I finish eating, we part ways, and I return to my rooms. When I enter, a rolled up tapestry sits on top of my bed, cradled by the plush blankets. I slowly unfurl it to see a painting of a tree on top of a mountain, its roots digging deep and its branches reaching high. I brush a finger against the painted leaves, imagining that they're real—smooth and fragile. Tracing the boughs down to the trunk, I picture the rough bark, the rivets and crests that rub against the skin. The scent of soil and musky foliage fills my nostrils as if I am there on the mountain.

It is then that I notice a small flower peeking through the roots, green stem and red petals nestled by the trunk. It may not have been his intention, but all I can think of is Inha and myself, the beauty and resilience and the dependence upon each other. I don't think I could ever see flowers the same after him. A sudden pain pangs my heart. I try to ignore the thoughts of "after".

I go to sleep that night clutching the rolled up painting to my chest.

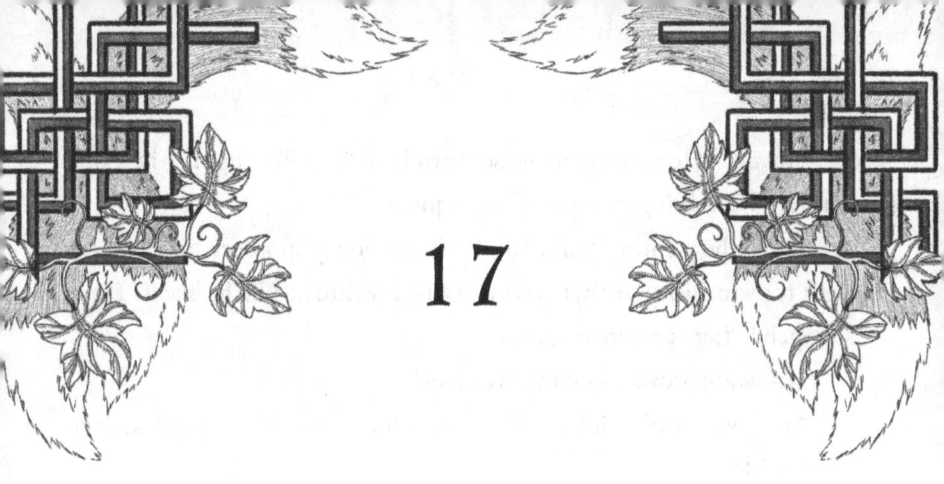

17

TRIAL SEVEN

AFTER RECEIVING THE GIFT from Inha, I work hard every day for a week on a painting for him. I have no money to buy him something—and even if I did, I have no market here to peruse—but I have a lot of time. With each stroke, I picture the Gumiho King. His eyes bright as the sun, hair like a spill of moonlight, and warmth that embraces me every time we are together. The claws that filled me with fright upon our first meeting now represent comfort—not tools of terror but of protection. So much for a malicious mythical who eats humans.

He has consumed my heart in a way I never expected.

I add the finishing touches, letting the paint dry before I take it to him. After I am confident the paint won't weep, I hold it up to the light filtering from outside. With a satisfactory smile and nod, I whisper, "Not too bad, Jiwon."

Carefully rolling it up, I stand and walk out the door to Inha's room. I dip my head and grin in greeting to a few passing fox-human servants. I make quick work of walking to the Eastern Wing, having memorized all the passages and halls between my room and his. When I reach his quarters, I don't even have to knock since he opens the door just as I turn the corner. Impressive hearing with those fox ears of his.

"Jiwon." He says my name so warmly; it feels like dipping in a hot spring. "What brings you here?" he inquires.

I hold the painting behind my back and slowly approach him. "I have a gift for you," I say softly, nerves clogging my throat. Will he like it? He is so much better at art than I am.

His white brows shoot up. "For me?"

"Shall we go in?" I jut my chin behind him where his room peeks over his shoulder.

He steps back, gesturing for me to enter. "Apologies. Please, come in."

I step inside, my shoulder brushing past his chest. He slides the door shut, and we are alone.

"Is there a special occasion I am unaware of?" he asks, one corner of his lip lifts upwards while his eyes glance down to where my hand hides behind my back.

"I appreciate the painting you gave me, so I simply wanted to give you one in return." My feet shift beneath my skirts.

"I wonder what it could be," he muses, tail twisting in a curious curl.

Inhaling through my nose, I bite my lip and present him with my painting, and his mouth parts ever so slightly. Surprise slows his movements, his arm raising at the pace of a tortoise. He takes the gift in his hand, holding it like it is something fragile—or precious. He unravels it with great care, but his features pinch together at the picture.

He glances between me and the painting. "What a beautiful..." He blinks and cants his head. "Phoenix?"

A scowl scrunches my face. "It's a gumiho."

A chuckle that he fails to muffle echoes in the room. "Then why is it all red and pink?"

"I accidentally used all the white to make the pink," I mumble, heat crawling from my cheeks down my neck.

"You could have asked for more," he comments, eyes still fixated on my failed art. "And what are those circular splotches on the head?"

"A crown of flowers…"

He does his best to stifle a laugh, but it is too late. Embarrassment and regret have already arrived, twin birds mocking me.

I reach for it, lip pouting. "Well if you hate it—"

He yanks the painting out of reach. "I never said that."

"You said it's bad." I attempt to jump, but end up falling into his chest instead. My breath freezes, our lips hovering a few inches apart, and our eyes fixate on each other's faces. Even if I become the best painter in all the lands, I will never be able to capture the beauty of the Gumiho King.

"I do not return what is given to me," he whispers, golden eyes burning into me like a pair of tiny suns.

But I've labored in the harsh summer sun, sweat soaking my skin while the scorching heat saps all my energy. This is the complete opposite. This is a pleasant and refreshing heat. I feel ablaze, like I could run for miles if not for my leg.

"May I kiss you, Jiwon?" he asks in a husky voice, gaze glowing with desire.

I swallow, gathering the courage to say yes, but instead I tease, "Do gumihos know how to kiss?"

His replies in a growl of yearning, "I am all too happy to show you how we foxes do things."

Unable to speak, I give a shallow nod, and the movement spurs him forward, our mouths colliding together after days and days of desire slowly simmering. His lips contain the sweetness of a ripe persimmon, his tongue flaming with the heat of warm tea sweeping down one's throat. Despite the sharpness of his canines, he is careful not to break the skin, nipping softly at my bottom lip. Without words, his mouth finally confirms  what I have been wondering this entire time. I hear the painting fall to the floor, and hands grip my waist, pulling me closer.

A caw shatters the moment, and we break apart, panting, as the samjok-o lands on an open window sill.

"Your timing is impeccable as always, Seonghwa," Inha hisses, but it is not anger that reddens his pale skin. He quickly bends to pick up the painting, rolling it up and tucking it at his side as if he doesn't want to share the image with the samjok-o.

I cover my smile with a hand, my finger brushing against my pleasantly swollen bottom lip.

Seonghwa clicks his beak. "It should not be a surprise that I am here. It *has* been a week, and I always come in the morning."

"To be fair," I retort, "You have shown up at night, too."

His feathers puff out ever so slightly. "That was to comfort you. After all, you fed me quite well when we were in the Mortal Lands."

"So you do like me," I exclaim, a mischievous smile on my face.

I feel Inha's tail resting against the back of my legs. Glancing at him, I find him already staring at me. Is he jealous of Seonghwa too?

Seonghwa draws my attention back to himself. "Let us depart."

A portal appears, but this time it is darker, like looking at a pond in the middle of the night, little lights like stars swirling in the darkness. Seonghwa flies through first.

Looking over my shoulder, I smile. "I'll see you after I am done."

He returns the smile and nods. "I will be waiting."

As I turn around and wade through the portal, I can't help but laugh, for I could have never imagined a king waiting for me. What a strange path life has led me down.

My feet sink into warm soil, a meadow sprawling around me, surrounded by a forest of godwood trees. A woman sits in the middle of it all, braiding flowers into a circle. Her form is plush, pink kisses her face, and her raven hair shimmers in the sunlight.

I step forward, but something is wrong.

There is no limp.

Scrambling to lift my skirt, my leg is bare, no brace, and the muscle of my calf is well defined, the line of my leg perfectly straight like my right side. I've never known what a normal body is like until now, but the shock and fascination quickly wanes as my attention shifts to the woman. Something deep inside me recognizes her. As I approach and sit down next to her, she turns to me. It's almost like looking into a mirror.

This is a woman whom I have never met yet always knew.

"Hello, daughter," my mother says, chestnut eyes sparkling.

My voice breaks. "H-hello, Eomma." Something wet falls down my cheek.

My mother reaches up and wipes the tears from my face. "I know, Jiwon-ah. I know."

That's all it takes for the sobs to pour out of me, and I collapse into her. She hums a comforting tune and strokes my back while the weeping overtakes me, mourning for all the memories I wished we shared and wondering how my life would have been different if she hadn't died. We sit there for a time before I finally get a hold of my emotions, and I untangle myself from her arms and lean back to look at her. I don't want to waste a single moment.

"Are you happy?" she asks, the back of her fingers brushing my cheek.

"Although life has been hard, I have known kindness. I had the village woman when I was little, and then Songhee and Halmeoni Hyesun. I was never alone, and I always managed to get by. And now I have new friends. I even live in a palace."

"It isn't easy to be grateful; complaining comes much more naturally," she says solemnly, a shadow of guilt clouding her eyes.

I nod. "I can't say I haven't cried or lashed out or screamed at my unfair lot, but I have tried to still find joy, Eomma. I have never given up no matter how dark it has gotten."

Smiling, she reaches for my hand and replies, "And that, my darling, is a joy that cannot be stolen. To be grateful in the hardships means you can weather any storm. I am proud of you."

I intertwine my fingers with hers, desperate to hold onto this brief breath of time. For once, I do not want the test to conclude quickly. Her words crack open a cave I'd thought I'd sealed, tears threatening to return, for she has said the words I've longed to hear my whole life. "But, Eomma, it is so hard. And father..."

Her lips pinch into a line, and she slowly nods. "I'm sorry that you were left alone with him. It broke my heart in double, seeing the man I loved lose heart and seeing my daughter suffer even more because of it. And all those nights you went hungry, all those moments in which you cried alone, each one was a knife to my chest."

"I thought there was no pain in the Celestial Realm," I mumble, wiping my nose.

"Indeed there is not. But here," she pauses and gestures to the meadow we are in. "This is where the past, present and future converge, where life and death mingle like the sun on the horizon. And it is here that all the pain has hit me. And how I wish I could prevent you from experiencing any more of it." Now her own eyes glisten, a teardrop trickling down her cheek.

So this is not the Celestial Realm, just a reflection of it, another glimpse. My left side is normal but so is my heart, and tears—which I thought I'd used all up—spring forth once more.

She continues, "No matter what obstacles you encounter in the future, please do not forget that it is all temporal and that there is a realm waiting without pain or tears."

She must know then, the dark thoughts that have entered my mind in the midst of my despair. She must know of that night on the river bank where I considered ending my life. She must know how much of my life

I spent lamenting it. Even though I could not see her, she saw me. It will never make up for her absence, but it does bring me some sense of comfort.

"I miss you," I rasp, a fresh wave of emotions welling.

"Me too. But we will meet again when you join me in the Celestial Realm. Until then," she pauses, placing her palm over my heart, "hold onto that joy."

"Yes, Eomma," I rasp, the vision of her beginning to blur. "I promise not to give in to despair."

"Good girl," she says, her figure nothing but a mirage now.

I reach for her one last time, but only empty air meets my hand.

It turns out the vision—or whatever it was—was only half the trial, because I awake in the depths of the dark night without seeing Seonghwa and no memory of portaling back to my room. I am back to a body that does not function normally and back to a life without a mother. If life is about learning to grieve, then I am its most well taught student. Tears spill from my eyes unbidden, and I bite my lip to silence the sobs, not sure if it was better or worse to meet her. The image of her in my head is no longer blurry, yet the pain in my heart is all the more poignant.

A soft rapping on the door.

I do not answer, but after a few more quiet cries, someone slides it open. I don't look, but I know who it is. Inha sits next to me without saying a word. Slowly, his hand crawls towards mine, pausing before making contact. I glance at his face, and his eyes ask for permission to touch me. In response, I grab his hand and tug him towards me. He seems to know what I mean, and he lowers himself, laying down beside me. I turn into him, burying my face into his chest. His heartbeat is a steady song, singing in tandem with my tears. He says nothing, just like I asked him to the first time.

After a while, my face is still wet, but I've cried out most of my emotions. "I met my mother," I rasp.

"What was she like?" he asks.

"Beautiful." My voice breaks while speaking. "She had such gentleness in the way she spoke and a light in her eyes."

I cannot picture her with my father, the two as different as fire and ice. Was he really that different before she died? Or was my mother the one who was different, her celestial person more perfect than who she was on earth? Either way, I feel robbed. My father was a broken man, and I had no one to depend on except for the kindness of strangers like the village ahjumma and her husband who made my first brace and Halmeoni Hyesun who braided my hair. A bitterness creeps into my heart. I thought I had removed all my hatred for him back at the graveside, but apparently a seed remains.

"I think my father hated that I was better than him. He lost a wife, but I lost a mother. I didn't have a normal body but I worked harder than he did. I think he looked at me with such disdain because he hated himself. I was a reminder of what he lost and what he wasn't, and in the end, I lost my father, too," I say quietly.

Inha nuzzles his face into my hair. "I know it will not replace what you lost, will not fulfill all that you desire, but I think you are beautiful and resilient. Your strength to endure and show kindness is a rarity. Like a plum blossom."

"Why a plum blossom?"

"Like you said before, trees are tough, but flowers are pretty. You are both."

A lump forms in my throat. I do not know what to say, so instead I twist my head up and press my lips to his cheek. His pale skin flushes pink.

"What was that for?" he stutters.

"A silent thank you."

There is joy to be had, if only one is willing to search for it. I burrow back into Inha's chest, holding tightly onto the happiness he brings me, doing my best to adhere to my mother's wish that I would not despair despite death and disability. It feels like a trial that will not be complete for as long as I live.

18

AFTER A NIGHT OF taunting dreams haunted by the mother I never got to know, I wake but stay in bed well into the day. Minji enters, bringing me a midday meal of steamed eggs, grilled fish, and pickled vegetables. I thank her and start eating while she busies herself with dusting around the room. She opens the window to allow some fresh air into the room, the warm floors keeping the cold away. Fresh snow has fallen.

"Do mythicals celebrate the Winter Solstice?" I ask. I have not kept good track of the elapsing days since arriving here, but I'm certain it must be near if not already passed.

"We did. But not since the curse," she replies with a sad sigh.

"What about birthing days? Speaking of which, when is Inha's?" I take my last bite of fish.

"Master's is today," Minji says as if it were any other normal day.

The empty dishes clatter as my knee hits the table. "Why didn't you tell me sooner?"

She hesitates, dusting cloth dangling from her hand. "Master does not celebrate it. He has not since the previous Master and Mistress passed."

I get to my feet and put on my thick cloak and a special pair of winter shoes. "Well, we don't need to celebrate if he doesn't wish for it, but I still want to do *something*."

"Mistress, where are you going?" she calls out as I'm nearly out the door.

"To obtain a present for him," I reply over my shoulder.

"Oh. Alright," she says. "I will be cleaning your room if you need me."

"Thank you, Minji." And then I'm limping briskly down the hall.

My mind grasps for an idea. Another painting? So soon after the first, it won't feel special enough. Although flowers are not my favorite, Inha is fond of them; they'll be the perfect gift for his eighth hundred and something birthing day. However, the fierce fiery bulgae remains fresh in my mind. I definitely need someone to accompany me. I'd ask Inha, but it would ruin the surprise. Shinhye or Gunoo might be a good option.

I go to the girin pasture where I've seen the he-fox most often and find him bringing out buckets of grain for the girin to eat. "Gunoo," I shout from afar.

His head jerks towards me, snout parting to reveal a full set of fox fangs—an endearing smile. He sets the buckets down and rushes towards me. I'm jealous at the swiftness of his strides through the snow, especially when my steps have become more laborious with the white blanketing the ground.

"What can I do for you, Mistress?" Gunoo asks, beaming.

"Jiwon is just fine," I remind him.

His face turns serious. "Forgive me, Mistress, but I cannot disrespect you like that."

Shinhye nor Minji have qualms about calling me by name, but I suppose it doesn't harm anything to allow him to continue to call me that. Now that Inha and I have confirmed our feelings, I feel more confident where I will be after the trials are completed.

Instead of correcting him, I say, "You have a kind heart, Gunoo."

He bows at his waist. "You flatter me, Mistress.

"Not flattery, but the truth." I touch his shoulder, signaling for him to rise. "I came to ask if you could accompany me outside the walls."

"I am not sure that would be appropriate..." His voice trails off, eyes darting between me, the palace, and the gate leading outside.

Leaning in, I whisper, "It's for your Master. I want to surprise him."

"Let us depart at once, Mistress," Gunoo hollers, already skipping towards the gate.

A quiet laugh sounds from me, and I follow after the most enthusiastic servant of the Gumiho King.

Birds sing a melody to keep us company, and the snow crunches softly under my footsteps. Although the cloak keeps me warm, cold nips at my nose and ears, and I adjust my hair to cover the tips.

"What has it been like under the curse?" I inquire, careful to keep to the main path towards the river where the sun has melted some of the snow.

"Master suffered before it, and he has suffered much under it," he answers, sadness tinging his tone, and I am sure he would be frowning if he could.

"I wasn't asking about Inha. How has it been for *you*, Gunoo?"

He is quiet for a moment, and he reaches up with his furry fingers to scratch behind one of his ears. After several steps, he replies wistfully, "I miss being able to shift as I please. I actually had a preference for my human form. At first, I found this form" —he points to human legs and fox head— "to be a mockery. And then when Master banned those in their full fox form..." He glances at me before turning his gaze away, voice soft, almost shameful, "I was angry. We were forced into isolation. I have always been excited to find a mate, but while I was unable to, Master had women sent to him. It seemed unfair, like salt in a wound."

My heart squeezes in my chest, yet I am also impressed with Gunoo. Despite his feelings—which are quite fair given the circumstances—he is still so loving and loyal towards his Master. I hope Inha appreciates him.

His tone lightens, and he lifts his face. "But then I started taking care of the girin. We needed a better form of transportation, especially when the mortal women came. Those girin kept me company through the centuries."

Shinhye had mentioned before the forbiddance of foxes from entering the palace grounds. Inha, although I have grown to love him, is not perfect, but I have also allowed my own misery to blind me from seeing other people's pain.

"Perhaps I can suggest that he revoke that command?" I ponder.

Gunoo stops walking, and I follow suit. He turns to me, eyes brighter than the sun reflecting off the snow. "Oh, Mistress! That would be wonderful," he exclaims, nearly bouncing on his feet.

Smiling, I say, "I am certain he will agree." Especially after I give him his birthing day gift. And the same Inha who decreed that edict is different from the one who carried me in the snow on his back and cares about whether the sight of raw, bloody meat unsettles me.

We resume our walking, Gunoo explaining in great detail how he has cared for girin. From combing their manes and beards to what kind of grain they prefer, he spares nothing. Those girin are fortunate to have a kind stablemaster, and the thought sprouts a small, sour weed. Gunoo treats his girin with more love than my father ever did me. A bitter tang hits my tongue. I should have reconciled all those feelings, but the recent trial with my mother has unearthed them again.

At last, the river comes into view, more quiet than the last time I was here, ice silencing the water. I am not sure if any flowers will be in bloom, but I assume that any that have survived the snow will be near water. Or should I be looking inland under trees? Flowers are not my area of expertise, since I only know plants as far as I can consume them or use them for medicinal purposes. What flowers bloom in winter is knowledge I do not possess, but even if I cannot find any, it is not a wasted trip. I was able to go out for a walk, even if my leg is sore, and Gunoo and I got to know each other better.

As we continue chatting, I search the area for any signs of flowers. There. A camellia shrub, petals crimson, peeks through the white snow.

"Shall I retrieve it for you, Mistress?" Gunoo offers, eyes darting between the flower and the nearby river where only the middle stream flows free of ice.

Hiking up my skirt to trudge into the deeper snow, I shake my head and reply, "No. I want to pick it myself."

"Very well, Mistress. Just please be careful."

The snow hides where the soil ends and the ice covered river begins, so I walk slowly, listening for sounds that would indicate I've stepped on frozen water. Nothing but snow gives beneath my feet though. Leaning down towards the camellia, I support myself against the nearest tree and brush the snow away, finding one more along with the initial one I saw. I pinch the stems until they give way.

Clutching the two flowers, I look up at Gunoo, who waits nervously on the shore with wringing hands, and start walking again. "I got them. See, I told you—"

A crack ripples through the air and under me. The ground I'm standing on disappears beneath my feet.

Gunoo lurches forward, reaching out to me, and shouts, "Mistress!"

I gasp as cold water hits my legs. All the air freezes in my chest. Although the river is not deep here, my knees buckle from the shock, water soaking my clothes and dragging me down. Frigid fingers crawl up to my chest, biting my skin and seeping deep into my muscles. Gunoo is quick to come to my rescue. His furry hands slip under my arms, and he hauls me up and over the snowy bank.

Body shivering and words shaking, I stammer, "Maybe next time you should pick the flower."

Gunoo does not find my quip amusing. "Mistress! You must take care of yourself. Master would rage like never before if something happened to you."

Despite the tremors racking my freezing body, a small warmth blossoms inside my chest. "I think you may need to carry me home."

"Of course." He stands and scoops me up in his arms, his fur smooth and comforting, yet it is not enough to combat the cold claws digging into me, my blood like ice refusing to thaw.

My teeth clatter together, and after a while, I cannot think clearly. The only thought that fills my mind is *cold, cold, cold*. Eventually, the palace comes back into view, Gunoo racing to get me inside. He carries me into my room, shouting for assistance. Minji hears him, sliding open the door as Gunoo barrels down the hall, and he brings me to the hot spring pool, setting me gently beside it.

"What happened?" Minji demands, rushing to my side.

"I-I fell in the r-river," I stutter, revealing the two drenched camellias in my hand. "P-present."

"I am so sorry, Mistress. I will go get Shinhye," Gunoo says, concern casting a shadow over his golden eyes. He looks far too guilty for something that was entirely my doing.

"It wasn't your fault," I tell him through rattling teeth. I know he will not believe my words and will feel like it is his fault, the poor sensitive soul.

He says nothing more, his ears flattened and a barely audible whimpering coming from his throat as he rushes out. Minji begins stripping my soaked clothes off of me. The steam from the hot spring teases me with its heat, and I don't want to wait for her to finish taking off my inner garments. As soon as I am naked, I crawl towards the pool, but Minji stops me.

"Apologies, Mistress, but you cannot go in. It will do more harm than good." She rushes around the screen, quickly reappearing with a fresh set of clothes. "We will get you into these and then wrap you in blankets."

Too weak to protest, I let her dress me, my gaze lingering on the tempting warm water. She works in urgency, slipping the pants that serve as undergarments on my trembling legs and forcing my arms through the sleeves of a wrap top. She ties off the strings and then runs back around the screen to bring a thick blanket.

"We will stay next to the water to help warm you up," she says, palm pressing to my forehead. Her face scrunches, her lips pinched into a firm line. "I will be right back. You need some tea." Then she leaves me alone.

But my solitude does not last long, Shinhye and Inha's voices echoing outside in the hall before they both appear, each with worry painted on their faces.

Even though I changed out of the cold, wet clothes, a chill clings to my bones, my body shivering no matter how many blankets I wrap around myself. "I'm fine. No need to panic," I say, doing my best to comfort them. The stuttering still plagues me, and it is obvious by their expressions that they do not believe me.

"Why would you do something so foolish?" Inha chides, hand pressing to my forehead. "You are burning up like a bulgae." He frowns, and his brows pinch together hard enough to hold a paint brush.

Another shiver shakes my body, either from the fever or from the mention of the fire dogs. Neither are particularly pleasant. "Can't you save your scolding until after I am feeling better?"

He removes his palm from my face and wraps another blanket around me. "We have an agreement. You cannot die before it is fulfilled," he growls but does not release his hold of the blankets. I try to squirm away like a worm, but he won't allow me to retreat. "I am serious, Jiwon. You should not have been so foolish to go near the river, especially knowing you cannot swim."

I look away and mumble, "I had a good reason..."

"There is no reason good enough for you to get injured or ill," he snaps.

Is this how a child feels when their parent scolds them? Not from anger but from fear?

He opens his mouth to continue his admonishment, but before another word can leave his lips, I tell him, "You."

He blinks. "What?"

"You," I repeat softly. "You are worth falling into the river for."

He cocks his head. "I was not drowning in the river, though."

I shake my head, my patience frayed by whatever illness infects me. "I don't mean it literally. I mean, I was doing it for you."

"I never asked—"

"I just wanted to get you something special for your birthday," I shout, head pounding and body trembling from the fever, and perhaps, anger. At times, his ignorance to how humans speak is endearing, but right now, it is making me regret ever reaching for that flower in the first place. But when I see his face soften, I know that I don't mean it. His hand sneaks under the blanket, searching for mine. Although I am the one who is sick, it is he who sniffles. With my other hand, I reach out from between my cocoon of fabric and cup his cheek. He leans into my touch, twisting his head to press a kiss into my palm, his lips warm against my skin.

I'd fall into a hundred rivers for him. Another wave of shivers rack my body, my muscles cramping under a new set of aches. Maybe just ten rivers.

His voice is so quiet, so broken. "For centuries, I have been told time and time again how unlovable I am, that I am not worth weathering any storms."

My heart feels like it is being crushed, for the sentiment is shared. "I cannot swim, but I would still do everything I could to save you from drowning."

"I never thought I could love a mortal, one coming from the kind which killed my parents and plagues the Mythical Lands through poachers and thieves." He lets out a long breath. "Actually, I was drawn to you from the beginning, which made me dislike you all the more, and it was that initial fondness that made the presence of the pin all the more painful. Despite trying to guard myself from your mortal wiles, I was completely enraptured by you, and here you are, holding not only my fate, but my heart, in your hands."

Am I delirious from the fever? Is he really saying what I think he is saying? We kissed, yes, but to hear him bear his soul so openly is another matter. To hear him use the word "love" does something to my heart. Or maybe that is from the cold.

Continuing, his hand cups my cheek, thumb whispering along my skin, "I will not lie to you, Jiwon. I have loved someone before, but I hope you will be the last." His eyes glow like little embers and like a moth to a lantern, I am drawn to them, even unto death.

The last.

How deeply I yearn for the same.

"We are both a bit broken, but perhaps that is why we fell for each other, seeing ourselves in each other's eyes. You were the cold, constructing icy walls for your own protection, while mine were barriers of fire, burning any who came close. By pushing people away and isolating ourselves, we thought that was peace, a wholeness that no one could chip away at, but isolation is not peace. Instead of someone else hurting us, we were hurting ourselves."

Is that water in his eyes? That would be twice that I've made a gumiho cry.

"Two broken souls make one perfect whole," he mutters quietly. "It is something my sire used to say. He was more romantic than my dam." Seeing my confusion at the former word, he quickly adds, "My mother."

Knowing more about his parents is more I know about him. Since he has let me in, let me see his paintings, it is only right that I reciprocate. "I don't know that I am ready to take down my walls, but there is a gate. And I grant you entrance," I whisper, worried that this little courage I have will crumble into dust.

He leans in, pressing his warm lips to my forehead, sending my heart fluttering. "I would say the same to you, but you snuck in weeks ago. And I possess no desire to kick you out."

Minji shuffles into the room, half bowing and eyes awkwardly averted. "Master, forgive me, but I think Mistress needs some rest."

Inha nods and reluctantly releases my hand to stand. His eyes linger on me as he walks out until he closes the door.

❈ ❈ ❈ ❈ ❈ ❈ ❈

Inha visits me every day, checking on my condition, but even after my fever breaks, he continues to come. Instead of the normal bowl of medicine, he brings with him a whole box, the attached strap slung over his shoulder.

"I used to be interested in the art of healing," Inha explains, pulling out a box full of ceramics and tiny vials. "This is ground oyster shell." He shows me a small ceramic that looks like a miniature vase and sprinkles the powder onto the skin of my lower leg. Then he takes out a long sock, one that goes all the way up my calf with strings to tie just above my knee. "This should help to prevent chafing in the future."

I can't believe I've never thought of that before. I've shoved pieces of cloth in between the wood brace and my leg, but it would always shift when I walked. If I wore my brace on the outside of my pant leg, my father would get angry and once Taehee even cut the straps of it while I was working. I purse my lips, holding in the tears. Wearing two pairs of pants was a luxury I never had, and the short undergarments I've been wearing here only go to my knee.

That he would consider me in such a way...

Receiving more love in the past month than I have my entire life from my father, it's bittersweet, but better love delayed than none at all.

Setting the sock on my lap, he pulls out another tincture of dark honey-colored liquid. "This is a concoction to help with the rest of your pain. You can place a few drops daily under your tongue."

Tracing the sock with my finger, I say quietly, afraid that talking too loudly will dislodge my dam of tears, "Thank you. I don't know how long you spent thinking of ways to help me, and the fact that you even noticed my pain at all..." I close my eyes. "From the depths of my heart, thank you."

"There is no better way of using my time than using it to think of you," he says, and my heart melts like snow under the sun.

I can picture his face even though my eyes are closed, the soft smile and simmering in his eyes with his ears tipped towards me.

Because I know that he is not just trying to flatter me, that he genuinely means it, I feel comfortable enough to share more of my past. "One time when my father was drunk and particularly enraged, he smashed my brace into pieces. Said, 'walking around with that contraption is a disgrace.' I cried and cried, pleading for him not to. It took me weeks of begging for coins to get enough to replace it."

"If he was not already deceased, I think I would have killed him." Inha glances at me and winces, clearly regretting his words. "Apologies. I should not have said that."

Once more, my emotions overwhelm me in a wave. My hand finds his, and we intertwine our fingers. I cannot believe he cares enough about me to be angered on my behalf, to be indignant at those who have wronged me. I love this gumiho, and he loves me—of that, I am certain.

Inha is not my only visitor. Gunoo and Shinhye visit me often while I recover, and Minji is practically a piece of fixed furniture in the room by now. Seonghwa even comes one day, telling me he's granting me another three days before the next trial. It's the first time all of us have gathered in a group, the atmosphere feeling festive. Minji and Shinhye sit on my left, constantly asking if I need anything: more medicine, another blanket, or some soup. Seonghwa perches on the table, eyeing the bits of rice left in my bowl, and Gunoo sits across from me, gaze fixated on his master with a furious loyalty while Inha sits beside me, hand often caressing my arm or brushing my hair out of my face.

"May I ask what you used to do back in the Mortal Lands?" Shinhye inquires, tucking my feet back under the blanket.

"My time was mostly spent working at a noble's estate; they kept some animals nearby on top of their tenant farmers outside the city as a precaution. The Yuan Empire has increased its attacks the past decade, so although we are far from the northern border, the Song clan prepares for all possible problems. And then I would forage leaves and roots that could be eaten, fermenting many of them during the fall to consume over winter."

"Hunting for plants—not so different from animals. You would make a good gumiho, Mistress," Gunoo says in all seriousness.

A giggle sounds from my lips. Minji and Shinhye do their best to muffle their laughs, but Seonghwa squawks in a raucous bout of amusement.

Meanwhile, Inha leans in and whispers in my ear, "I agree."

My laughing ceases. I turn to look at him. "Are you saying—"

Gunoo interrupts my question, pouting. "What is so humorous? I was complimenting our Mistress."

Looking back at Gunoo, I smile and say, "Forgive me. I wasn't mocking you. It was very sweet of you to say."

His sulking lessens ever so slightly.

"What about you all? What did you do before the curse? I know Gunoo said he only started working after it, taking care of the girin that were newly needed."

Shinhye speaks first, absentmindedly stroking her tail, "I was always working in the palace. My parents served under the previous Master and Mistress, and I wanted to follow in their footsteps. I suppose in a way, I was fortunate to be in this form when the curse came upon us so that I could continue serving Master."

I glance at Inha. I had forgotten about what Gunoo had said and the promise I'd made to ask Inha to allow the gumihos who are in their fox forms to return and reunite with their families. Now, in front of all the others, it is not a good time. I must remember to ask him when we are alone. Not that I think he'll refuse, but no one revels in their mistakes being pointed out in front of others.

Minji speaks next, "I was always more comfortable in my human form." She gestures to herself. "As you can see, I am one of the few completely in a human form. I used to go into the Mortal Lands to trade goods that were harder to acquire in the Mythical Lands." Pausing, she glances nervously at Inha, as if unsure if she should continue.

Out of the corner of my eye, I see Inha nod, granting her permission to speak freely.

"After the previous Master and Mistress passed, we were forbidden from going into the Mortal Lands. That was when I started working as a maid in the palace, and that is where I was when the curse happened."

"Would you like to return to trading? After the trials are complete," I ask.

Everyone in the room freezes. I look around at each of them. Only Seonghwa moves, pecking at the rice grains in my bowl.

Shinhye is the first to break the silence, her voice wistful. "I do not know that any of us have considered what happens *after*. This has been our reality for so long, our hopes dashed every century, that perhaps we resigned ourselves to our fate."

A hand squeezes my heart. I never would have thought of Shinhye as fatalistic. That seemed more like Inha—or me. Time after time, disappointment after disappointment, it has a way of chipping away at one's faith that things will get better until there's nothing left but hope's dust.

"I want to continue caring for the girin," Gunoo declares.

A smile visits every face in the room. Even Inha.

"I think the girin would miss you," Inha says.

"Does that mean we will not get rid of them?" Gunoo asks, eyes brightening.

Inha nods. "After so many centuries of service, they deserve to be well taken care of, and I trust you to do that."

"Then could I go back to trading with the mortals?" Minji inquires with some hesitancy, but excitement is clearly painted on her face and in the way she leans forward while clutching her skirts like hope itself.

Inha nods again. "Of course. You all have taken such good care of me even when I was unworthy of such loyalty. When all this is over, you are all free to do as you please."

Shinhye is the only one who looks troubled, a frown forming on her lips and her brows pursing. "Are you saying you do not want me to serve you anymore, Master?"

"Of course not, Shinhye," Inha replies gently. "It would be my honor to continue to have you here."

Her frown floats away, replaced with a pleased expression and loose shoulders as she dips her head.

"Do you have any more rice?" Seonghwa questions suddenly, and everyone bursts into laughter.

But part of me thinks it is because the samjok-o doesn't want to imagine life after the trials. I think the little crow has grown fond of us and is reluctant for his mission to end. Of course, he can always come to visit us. As for the others...

When they look at me, their eyes fill with the radiance of anticipation, and I don't want to disappoint them. When I meet Inha's eyes, I see even more, a swirling fire of emotions. The golden sunlight of hope, the honey of sweet affection, and the dark brown flecks of desire.

Yet a small thorn pricks my thoughts.

What if when the trials are over, so is their love for me?

I look once more at Inha's face, and all such worries wash away.

19

AT LAST, THE DAY of the next trial arrives. After this, only one remains, and my stomach will not settle. Should I ask Seonghwa if we can commence the final one right away? There is no need to wait a week between; once they're all completed, I can rest for as long as I desire. With Inha. A thousand birds flutter through my core at the very thought of it.

Speaking of birds, Seonghwa caws, alerting to his arrival. He is late. It's the first time he has come at night for a trial. I open the shutters to one of the windows in my room, and the crow swoops inside, bringing in a whisper of cold air. He finds a comfy perch atop the screen between my bedroom and the hot spring bath.

"Are you ready?" He shifts, talons clicking against wood.

I nod, looking around the room. "No portal?" I ask, brows raised.

"Your trial will take place here," he explains. Then he flies out the window, disappearing into the dark night.

That irritating bird didn't even give me the chance to ask a question. Gaze going around the room, I wonder what kind of test could take place here? How long it will take me to get bored? Am I not allowed to leave the room? Seonghwa should have explained more before leaving. Perhaps patience is the theme of this test? To see how long I will sit and wait in a room alone before I leave it out of boredom?

A soft thud sounds against the door, and I race over and slide it open. A small gasp leaves my lips. I am not sure if this is real or not, if the test has started or if this is something...else. A dream?

Inha's garments are untied, his chest peaking between the dark red fabric. His sculpted torso beckons my eyes. I force my gaze upwards, but what I find there is no better. Wisps of white doused in moonlight, there is a sudden urge to tangle my fingers in his hair. Inha's eyes are golden pools of honey, promising sweetness, and his persimmon lips entice my own. "Jiwon, I am sorry to bother you. I just—I just cannot get you out of my mind," Inha says, voice low and gravelly.

I gulp, doing my best to swallow the desire welling inside me. I've seen plenty of handsome men in the city, but none of them have ever talked to me, let alone *looked* at me like this. Yet yearning is painted clearly on Inha's face, and when he reaches for me, I do not move. I hold my breath as his clawed finger gently grazes my collarbone. This feels far different from our other encounter in which we kissed. If Wisdom is speaking to me, I cannot hear her, desire drowning out her voice.

Stepping inside my room, he leans forward, and my breath hitches when he presses his lips to my neck. He pauses after the first kiss, pulling back to search my eyes. Is he asking permission? I give my answer with a short, breath-holding nod. Then his lips return, this time with a greater fervor. He guides me backwards until my back hits the wall. A fire blazes through me, and suddenly, my hands are on his back, fingers digging into him. His hand sweeps across my outer thigh, sending pleasant chills through me despite the fabric between our skin, before settling on my waist. I bite my lip when his body leans into mine, my back arching against the wall. He works his way from my neck up my jaw and his mouth finally meets my own. Our lips clash in a desperate dance, and for a moment, there is nothing else in this world but me and him.

We take a second to breathe, and it is when our heads part and the moonlight shines on his face that I see myself in his eyes. It's a precious moment that brings me to my senses. I know that I am willing to go all the way with him, to lose myself to this pleasure when I have endured so much pain in my life. But I know what I need, recalling the promise I'd made to myself those years ago.

I put my hands on his chest and gently push him back, and I'm grateful that he does not resist, as the wall between my desire and my wisdom is weak right now. "I have given myself to another before and got burned," I rasp. "So the next time, it will only be with the one I will be bound to for life."

"Bound until death," he whispers, fingers drawing on my waist, a tortuous touch. "Forever," he vows.

Every part of my body is heated, and I want nothing more than to give my all to him. But I will not trust sweet words. "If you mean what I think you do, then you will prove it to me," I say with all the sternness I can muster in this moment.

"How? How can I prove my devotion?" His eyes search mine earnestly. No one could mistake the passion in his face, but passion burns bright and fierce, quickly dying out into embers and ash.

"You will wait for me, and after the trials are over, if you are still sincere, then..." I am not sure what to say. Marriage? Mates?

"I understand," he whispers, pressing a kiss to my forehead. "You are the first warm day of spring, and waiting for you is like anticipating the melting of the snow and the blossoming of flowers. Spring is more precious because winter forces one to wait for it. I will wait, and then you will become my mate."

My heart leaps at the word. But I need to leave now or the little discipline I cling to will slip from my arms, and I'll fall into his. "I need to go," I rush out and hurry out of the room, taking deep breaths of air to cool my heated blood. I don't stop until I am outside, the snow helping me regain my composure. This was the shortest and yet hardest trial of them all.

A familiar flapping of wings.

"I really thought you were going to fail that one," Seonghwa comments.

Hasn't he said that before? Does he think so little of me? I don't bother looking at him when I grumble, "Pervert."

He clicks his beak. "I would have stopped watching if things got that far."

"What was this trial supposed to be?" I ask, trying to banish the lingering feeling of Inha's body.

"When presented with pleasure, our vows and values are tested. Whether over indulging in sweets, controlling one's impulse to strike a man, or denying the urge to find comfort in the arms of another when he with whom you are bound to is being inattentive or argumentative, self-control is a virtue very quickly discarded. Yet it is essential for the health of a relationship, both as an individual and as a society. For a marriage to thrive, one cannot have an affair, and for society to survive, one cannot have unfettered anger and attack fellow people over slights. Many have betrayed promises and people in order to take a taste from pleasure's ephemeral cup. And in your case, you made a vow to yourself, and tonight it was tested."

"How did you know about it? I've never told you or anyone here," I snap, arms wrapped around myself.

"After that night—which I am certain you remember the details of quite clearly—you went to that halmeoni."

I close my eyes as if it could ward off the memory.

Seonghwa ignores my obvious discomfort. "You made an oath and shared it with her, vowing not to allow yourself to be swayed by sweet words ever again, that you would not lay with another in a bed that was not intended to be shared forever."

"I passed. Is there a need to continue to bring this up?" It's not that I have changed my mind on the promise I made myself—love and lust lure many into folly—but I don't want to recall the cause of that oath. I don't care what other women do, but I have been burned by a boy before. It won't happen again. The irritating samjok-o douses the last of my flaming desire, only the fire of my ire remaining. "I can't wait to be done with these trials and never see you again." I reach down, taking a handful of snow.

"Oh, you do not mean that," he coos. "I know you will miss me."

"You underestimate how much I dislike you." The snow slowly shapes into a sphere.

"Just know that I am equally eager to complete this mission."

The snowball barely misses the samjok-o. Seonghwa screeches, feathers ruffled. "So audacious for a mortal. Maybe you will get cursed next and need that fox to break it for you."

Speaking of Inha. "Was that really him? Did you force him to…" I can't get myself to say it. My chest tightens. Was he coerced to say those things? To do those things? Did Seonghwa entrance him or drug him into doing all that?

"Some trials need no divine orchestration. All creatures have will."

"Can't you just speak plainly for once?" I bark.

"I did nothing to Inha. As he mentioned before, he cannot get drunk. His desire came from neither drug nor drink," the crow explains.

The tension in my chest fades. Then he really does want me. And since he respected my decision to wait, it is not lust but love. Not empty words like the hollow promises of a noble man whispering to a courtesan he has no intention of actually marrying.

Letting out a breath, I say, "At least there is only one more test remaining."

For some reason, the samjok-o's voice sounds sad when he says, "Yes. I will be back in two weeks for your final trial."

"Two weeks?"

"I must go." And refusing to answer my question, the samjok-o flies off.

Shaking my head as I stare at the branch he had just been sitting on, I mumble, "I'm going to miss that peeving little crow." Although I will never miss the way in which he avoids answering me. I predict he enjoys possessing information I do not have.

❁ ❁ ❁ ❁ ❁ ❁ ❁ ❁

The next day, Inha arrives at my door again. This time he is fully clothed, ears flat and tail drooping. "I wanted to apologize for my conduct the other night," he tells me, head dropped down towards the floor.

A promise I have yet to fulfill enters my mind. "If you'd like to make it up to me, you should allow the gumihos in their fox forms to come to the palace."

"Yes. I should have done that long ago," he murmurs.

I didn't think he could appear any more pitiful, but he looks like a poor puppy scolded and drenched in the rain. "Thank you."

He glances up at me. "No. Thank you. For encouraging me to be better."

I grab his hand and give it a squeeze. "Both of us have our flaws, and it does neither of us any good to pretend they don't exist or to excuse them. Some things, you let go. Others, you confront them, like tearing down a decrepit building and constructing something new."

"I hope we will continue to build for each other then." He presses his lips to my forehead, a tendril of warmth seeping deep inside, embracing me like a pair of arms.

20

W ITH ONLY ONE TRIAL remaining, Inha throws a banquet, and it is the perfect time, too, the snow having melted and the worst of winter behind us. The plum blossoms will bloom in another month or so. In the Mortal Lands, commoners such as myself always welcome the end of winter. Once, Halmeoni Hyesun took me into the forest to pick azaleas and make little fried flower-rice-cakes. It was back when we were both younger, and she had enough energy to forage and even found some honey—obtained at the cost of a few bee stings. My heart aches at the thought of her. I hope she is well and that her bones do not ache too badly from the cold. Hopefully the garments, blankets, and food I had asked Inha to send kept her warm and full through the season.

Maybe I can even bring her here to live with me at the palace.

My mind drifts to what "after" looks like, my stomach twisting. Whether in dread or excitement, I cannot tell—perhaps a bit of both. Is he more excited about getting his tails back or being with me? I glance down at my left hand curled in its preferred fist and the leg that requires a brace. Every once in a while, the concern creeps in that he does not truly love me. How could someone love all *this*?

Going to the cabinet, I find the painting he gave me all those weeks ago. Staring at the tree with the little flower nestled in its roots, I remind myself of all the kindness he has shown. Words are easily whispered, but actions are harder to fake, especially for a prolonged period of time. He was patient as he taught me to paint, carried me on his back, and risked his life to save me. That is why I can weed out these worries. Taking one last look at the picture, I curl it back up and set it back in the cabinet.

Minji enters the room, Shinhye trailing in after.

"Master has ordered a special set of garments for the banquet," Minji explains.

A she-fox with a snout on an otherwise human face appears, carrying a basket full of fabrics and threads. When she gets closer and her skirt swishes upwards, I catch a glimpse of furry feet, as if they're somewhere between a fox's and human's—similar to Gunoo's hands. I wonder if she has difficulties walking like me. Her gait is awkward and lumbering, and she is the first gumiho I've met who makes a sound while walking.

She sets the basket on the ground and pulls out a white ribbon marked with black lines, spaced about a thumb-length apart. For the first time, I ponder if gumihos have magical clothes that appear when they shift into humans or if they're nude after changing forms. I cannot picture gumihos prancing around with a little bundle of clothing tied around their fox forms.

Shinhye seems to know me well, for she says, "If there is something you are curious about, you may ask."

A blush blooms across my skin, an embarrassed smile spreading on my lips. Should I voice both of my queries? Would the seamstress she-fox find it rude? I start with the question pertaining to gumihos in general. "Well, I see that you are wearing garments now, but I assume that you don't when you're in your fox form."

"That is correct," Shinhye replies, oblivious to where my thoughts are going.

"But does that mean your clothing is magical? Disappearing when you change into a fox and reappearing when you're a human. Do you have to hide clothing around in holes in the ground or carry them with you?"

The seamstress snorts, surprised by both her own laughter and my question. Minji gently hits her arm, shaking her head in a silent scold.

Shinhye also looks taken aback, blinking in rapid succession, but she quickly gains her composure and replies, "All gumihos possess the power to create clothing when we shift into humans, and those are the only two abilities gumihos have. Only our kings and queens, as you refer to them, have special powers such as the Master's teleportation. I am not certain, but I assume the same is for all mythicals with pearls."

I glance at the seamstress who is measuring my torso. "Then why would you need to learn how to sew?"

The seamstress pauses, her expression darkening, but the unpleasant thoughts that flash in her mind from my question quickly dissolve. She resumes her work with a placid expression, lifting my arm up to check the length of my arm.

"Under the curse, we do not have the ability to make our clothes with magic. One of our girls besides Minji was completely human when it came upon us, so we sent her into the Mortal Lands to learn," Shinhye answers, her voice filling with the somberness that always comes when she speaks of the curse.

"I'm surprised Minji did not go," I muse, recalling her love of exploring the Mortal Lands.

"My sewing skills are nonexistent," she explains. "I went first but could not quite comprehend it. We decided it would be best for someone else to try. Okbin has always been more adept with artistic endeavors, and that is how I ended up a maid." Minji dusts down the cabinet, her tone a tad sad.

How painful it must be, for all these gumihos to be trapped in bodies they do not desire. My heart hurts along with them, for I know the tortuous feeling all too well. Without realizing it, a tear escapes my eye, racing down my cheek before I can catch it.

The seamstress's black nostrils flare, her nose seeming to notice before her eyes do. "Why are you crying?" Her voice is hard and husky, as though each word is pried out with great effort.

Shinhye scrambles to her feet upon hearing I am crying. Her worried gaze bores into me. "Jiwon, are you alright? Are you sick? Did you need to sit down?"

I wipe my face and shake my head. "It is only a pain of the heart, not the body."

"Gumihos do not cry often, but we know the aching of a heart," Shinhye murmurs, grabbing my hand and giving it a squeeze.

"It's just..." I begin, working the words past the lump in my throat. "I know what it is like to want a different body, to *feel wrong*." More tears trickle, tickling my skin. "Ever since I can remember, I've desired a different set of limbs, to be normal, to not be in pain. I could not run and play with the other children, would be left behind while they swam and climbed trees." Sorrow drags my head down, my gaze glued to the floor while my chest tightens so intensely that it hurts to breathe. "And I am not a lazy person, but working is so much harder for me. It isn't fair. I can't carry as much, and I am almost always in pain. It's not just that. Why me? Why does everyone else get a normal body with a normal life and not me?" The words are becoming more difficult to say as sobs take over, salt kissing my lips.

I hear sniffling and look up. Minji, Shinhye, and the seamstress all are in different states of distress, Minji's face already nearly as wet as mine. "I thought gumihos didn't cry easily?" I attempt to joke, wiping my nose with my sleeve.

Shinhye says nothing, just bites her lip as a shimmering line forms on her pale skin.

"You are one of us," she rasps in that same voice that matches the rustling of leaves, eyes glistening from the lantern light hitting her moist eyes.

Minji says nothing, and instead wraps her arms around me unexpectedly as she sniffles.

Shinhye finally speaks, her voice a quiet murmur, almost hopeful sounding, "You are *the* one."

I assume she is speaking about the curse, that she is confident that I am the one who will break it. And I wish that it is so. I want to break it for them, to give them their powers back. I may be stuck with my body, but they needn't be. Without giving them the option, I use my arms to bring them into an embrace. They give grunts of surprise as our bodies smush together. They are warm. And kind. I cannot comprehend how the myths of mortal eaters ever began.

Maybe I do belong with the gumihos.

Five days ago, Inha had declared that all gumihos no matter their form were welcome to attend the banquet, giving enough time for the message to spread—with the help of Seonghwa. It will be the first time in centuries that Shinhye will get to see her mate and daughter. Shinhye's eyes are fixated on the entrance of the palace ground, rocking back and forth on her feet. Gunoo also waits next to us, chewing on a furry finger.

"Are you going to gnaw your finger to the bone, Gunoo?" I ask, smiling at his excitement.

The question breaks him from his focus, and he removes his fingers from his mouth and shuffles, flustered. "I have not seen my sires for so long. We are quite close for gumihos," he explains.

The seamstress—Injeong, as I'd learned—whispers with one of the cooking staff, both of their tails swishing.

Inha at last arrives, coming to a stop next to me, ears twitching.

I lean towards him and whisper, "For what it is worth, I am proud of you."

He looks down at me, face relaxing. "It means more than you know." Returning his gaze to the gate, he continues speaking, voice soft and full of sorrow. "I made the decree out of hurt and selfishness, and by the time I realized how foolish and cruel it was of me to keep my gumihos apart from each other, shame silenced me." His ears and tail droop.

Reaching for his hand, I intertwine my fingers with his. "You were wrong for what you did, but you cannot change the past, only the future. You've shown great courage and kindness today."

"I thought all mortals were liars, but you are, perhaps, a little too honest," he replies with a weak chuckle.

"If I were any other way, I don't think you would have liked me," I shoot back, smirking.

In front of everyone, he presses a kiss to my temple, heat rushing over my skin. The gumihos around us muffle giggles and cover smiles. Then quiet grips the air, everyone's breath held preciously in their chests. The first white form pads through the gate, bringing hope and life with it. The gumiho is bigger than the foxes found in the Mortal Lands, crimson painting the tip of its tail and ears, and the one who walks behind it is completely white save for a scarlet diamond on its forehead. Gunoo whimpers and takes off into a run, his presumed parents doing the same. The three of them collide into a furry embrace in the middle of the grounds.

The scene repeats itself again and again as the fox-human hybrids reunite with their fully fox loved ones. Shinhye's mate and daughter are last, and the sound she makes at the sight of them pinches my heart. She runs to them, her tail and hair whipping behind her.

I squeeze Inha's hand. He is the only one without anyone to meet, his parents murdered by poachers. I lean my body into his, and he presses his side into me in return.

He misses his parents, his anger rooted in shame and guilt. I miss my parents that never were—albeit for two different reasons—my anger fueled by the unfairness of life, the pain of my body not functioning and my father loathing me for it, but it is because of the reflection of ourselves that we see in each other that we match so well. Something about our fractured souls sings to each other, harmonizing into one whole masterpiece.

Inha swallows his sorrow and announces in a bellowing voice that echoes within the palace walls, "The banquet will begin shortly. You are all welcome to stay as long as you wish, to come and go as you please from now on."

Then he does something I never would have expected. He bows. The Gumiho King is kneeled on the floor, forehead pressed to the ground. "Forgive me for keeping you apart. It was a foolish decree."

"Oh, Master," Shinhye and Gunoo exclaim in tandem, rushing to his side and tugging at his elbows for him to stand.

He stays in his prostrate position for a few more moments before finally standing, and when he does, the other gumihos bend down in turn, those who are foxes resting their chins to their front paws in reverence, a beautiful reconciliation between ruler and subject. My heart warms towards Inha even more, for in his humility, he has found his greatness. This curse has changed both of us in so many ways.

"Please rise," he announces, gesturing behind him towards the palace entry, "and join me inside."

Excited voices buzz through the air as reunited family and friends trickle inside. I walk hand in hand with Inha to the dining hall, which has been decorated for the special day. The massive room that felt so empty when Inha and I would eat alone is now full and vibrant with low sitting tables covered in rice wine, dried fruit, nuts, and pastries sitting in front of teal cushions on the floor. Lanterns and ribbons dance and dangle from rafter to rafter, fabric weaving up each pillar in a curling splash of crimson. Lined along one of the walls, musicians of drums, zither, and lutes prepare to play their instruments.

Inha takes his seat in a portable cushioned chair that resembles his throne, a tree-like back cast in gold. He helps me settle in beside him. The others take their assigned seats, and after a few final words, the servants scurry off to attend to their duties. But now they will have the time to catch up, never to be separated again against their will.

However, the gumihos trapped in their fox-forms are not the only guests, a trio of haetae, a pair of phoenixes, and even a dragon all are attending in their human forms. Still, they retain elements of their animal appearances. Lone horns protrude from the middle of the haetaes' foreheads, a fiery feather plume cascades from the phoenixes' heads and down their backs instead of hair, and a pair of horns adorns the sides of the dragon's head, much like the antlers of the girin. The one commonality they all share is their golden irises.

The haetae approach us first, two women and a man. If I remember correctly, Seonghwa said their leader was a queen. If only Goryeo allowed such things, but a sole ruling queen has not happened since the Three Kingdoms Era, Shilla having three queens during her existence, if I recall what Halmeoni Hyesun told me correctly. A band of jewels adorns the head of the larger woman, tiny gems and threads of gold covering her large horn like a glittering net. The other two with her are also adorned, but not to her excessive extent. She must be the queen then.

"I was quite surprised to receive the sudden invitation, Lord of the Forests," she says in a husky tone, inclining her head.

Lord of the Forests? Is that one of Inha's official titles?

"You honor me with your attendance, Guardian of the Earth," Inha replies, dipping his head.

"And is this the mortal woman I have heard so much about? The one who tried to kill the Gumiho King?" Her expression is one of amusement, much like Jisang's was one of respect.

"I didn't try to kill him. I simply considered it, and brought a weapon in which to kill him with. Still, a subtle yet important difference," I say, smiling and hoping I read her levity correctly.

A big, bellowing laugh startles me, and the Haetae Queen's whole body shakes with her laughter. "Boyoung did say you were an audacious little thing."

My brows furrow, and I tilt my head to the side. "Boyoung?"

"A samjok-o," the other female haetae explains.

So there are many of those three-legged crows, all equally as talkative as Seonghwa it would seem.

"You will have your hands full with this one," the Haetae Queen says, finally reining in her laughter. With a final dip of their heads, the trio head off to their seats.

The pair of phoenixes are next. They both wear white robes trimmed in gold—a color that would indicate mourning in the Mortal Lands, but I suppose that mythical traditions would differ from our own. Their feathery tresses are far stiffer than normal hair, yet beautiful nonetheless, appearing like flickering flames under the lantern light and contrasting pleasantly with their dark, sun-kissed skin. One female and one male, they're both equally ethereal, a glow to their bronze skin as if they eat stars and drink sunlight.

These mythicals are also ruled by a queen, and it is the female who speaks, her voice like chimes yet her words entirely unpleasant. "I came to see if it was true, that one of the great mythicals has deigned to fall for a mortal."

It's as if someone shattered a plate right in front of me, the pieces beautiful but sharp and ready to cut. The Song Sisters emerge from my memories, and I shift closer to Inha.

"Keeper of the Skies, I would like to remind you that this banquet is in great part for my lovely Jiwon. I hope you will not sour a celebration with such sentiments." Inha's words are polite but his tone borders on threatening. I feel his tail twitching behind me, tapping my lower back.

"If you wish to demean yourself, then so be it. I came to warn you not to allow yourself to be beguiled by this mortal, to maintain the dignity as leader of one of the pearled mythicals."

The Phoenix Queen spins on her heel, her comrade in tow, and strides out the door. For birds of fire, they sure do suck all the warmth out of the air.

Inha turns his face to me, expression and tone full of worry. "Are you alright? Do not take her words to heart. Her daughter fell in love with a mortal and ran off with him, and she has been bitter ever since."

"I'm fine. Her words cannot shake me when I have yours to lean on." Had such an interaction occurred months ago, I would have argued with her—queen or not. But indignance does not burn so strong as it once did, for I am content to keep my own peace, made all the more easier with Inha at my side to encourage me.

"Sorry to interrupt," a voice that sounds familiar interjects.

I turn to see the lone dragon. Why does his voice scratch my mind as familiar? His golden eyes are shared by all mythicals, and his black hair only shimmers with green under certain beams of light.

I tilt my head. "Jisang?" I ask slowly.

His face alights with delight. "You remembered."

"You two have met?" Inha inquires, his arm snaking around my waist.

"In one of the trials," we both answer in tandem before breaking out into chuckles.

"Do not fret, Inha, for she rejected my offer of marriage," Jisang says nonchalantly.

Inha's claws dig into the table. "Your what?"

A grimace grips my face. Maybe I should have told Inha about it. "I didn't even consider it for a second," I say, tugging Inha's attention to me lest a gumiho-dragon war break out. "By that time, another mythical had already snuck into my heart. Even if I didn't want to admit it then."

It seems to calm Inha as his expression softens, his claws ceasing their assault on the furniture. "Well, I will forgive you this once, Jisang, for the sake of the relationship our sires had."

"I was not asking for your forgiveness," the dragon protests.

"I think it is time for the food to be brought out," I declare.

"Yes. Please take your seat, Watcher of the Waters," Inha adds, jutting his chin towards the table next to the haetae.

Jisang bows, whispering quickly, "My offer still stands."

"I don't think that is very appropriate," I say back, a little bite to my words to emphasize that I've no desire to hear of his offer again.

He raises from his half-bow, smiles, and turns to take his seat. Inha shoots arrows at his back, and having seen his skills with the bow, Jisang should be thankful Inha doesn't have his weapon with him. The female haetae accompanying her queen is quick to strike up a conversation with the handsome dragon, and Inha seems to relax now that Jisang's attention is elsewhere.

"Is he a king?" I ask Inha.

"No. Not yet at least. The dragons have a strange custom where one has to have a mate in order to receive the throne. Jisang only has a year to find one or anyone with royal blood can make a claim to his throne."

I nod. "Makes sense why he was willing to propose without knowing me."

Inha's stare feels like a gentle flame seeping into my skin, a tendril of warmth slithering through me. "Maybe he was enraptured by your beauty."

Heat blossoms in my core, and the desire to kiss him, to return to what we did not finish in my room those nights ago, bubbles up inside me. I reach for my cup of warm tea, shoving my cravings deep down. The servants enter with trays full of food, saving me from myself. After all the dishes are served, Shinhye instructs the musicians and dancers to perform, both of which are a mixture of mythicals: gumihos, haetae, and what I assume are two dokkaebi with small horns and markings inking their skin in swirls and lines.

The fans the dancers use are white as snow, their tips tassels of scarlet, as if they were dipped in blood. When they move, the figure of a gumiho emerges, the fans reminiscent of sprawling tails. I glance at Inha, his eyes heavy with longing while his gaze follows the fans. It hurts my heart knowing he is in pain, and I wish I could banish the sadness. One more trial, and I will. One more trial, and he can get his tails back. One more trial, and we can begin the next part of our lives—together.

21

AFTER THE BANQUET, ALL the other mythicals have returned to their homes, but the gumihos stay, spending time with their family and friends after so many years apart. Shinhye brings me to meet her mate and daughter.

"This is Doyeon." Shinhye places her hand on her daughter's head, scratching between her ears.

Grinning, I greet the gumiho, "Hello, Doyeon. It's a pleasure to meet you."

Shinhye crouches down next to her. "This is Jiwon. She is going to be our new mistress soon," she explains, rubbing her cheek against her daughter's snout.

Her daughter presses the front part of her body to the ground, her rear end sticking up in the air, much like a puppy playing.

"She is paying her respects," Shinhye stands and whispers in my ear. Pulling away, she says more loudly, "Well done. I see your father has taught you manners."

Taejoon replies in a demure tone, "I am sure it will be insufficient to your standards, my darling, but I have tried my best in your absence."

Shinhye repeats the gesture with him, pressing the side of her head to his muzzle. Although I am not a gumiho, the meaning of the action is clear. Should I do the same? Or is it something only those of blood or close relation do? What other customs do gumiho keep?

"Doyeon, how do gumihos greet each other?" I crouch to ask the she-fox.

Taejoon and Shinhye pause their conversation to watch us.

"In our fox forms, we greet each other by touching our noses together, and for those who we love, we rub our cheeks together. It is a show of trust, leaving our necks vulnerable, unable to see what the other is doing with their mouth. Every gumiho knows the neck and belly are lethal locations," she explains with such enthusiasm, her nine tails brushing the ground like a broom, that I cannot help but smile.

Thoughts of Inha fill my mind. Is he sad seeing all the gumihos with their families? Did he eat or is he hiding in his rooms refusing food?

"Well," I say, standing, "it has been an absolute pleasure meeting you both, but I want you to enjoy your time together after so long." It must have been so difficult for Shinhye to bear, being away from her child for centuries. She would have left her as a barely more than a babe and is now seeing her as an adult.

"It was an honor to meet you," Taejoon says, dipping his head.

Despite being nearly the same size as Taejoon, Doyeon bounces up and down with a youthful energy. "I hope to see you again soon, Mistress!"

A smile spreads on my face. "You know where to find me."

Shinhye dips her head as well. "Thank you for taking the time to talk with my family."

I reach out and stroke her back. "I hope you enjoy your time together. No need to worry about serving me. Minji said her sires have passed and doesn't have anyone to see, so she will take care of me."

Shinhye nods and turns back to her mate and daughter, Doyeon breaking out into the story of her first hunting experience—something about a wild boar who ended up chasing her into a hole. I head towards Inha's room, my feet quick with worry. I don't wish for him to be alone with his sorrow. He comforted me multiple times in my grief, and I want to do the same for him.

But when I reach his room, no voice answers my knock. I slide the door open, peeking my head through only to be greeted with his absence. Perhaps he's found solace in the solitude of his art gallery? I head down the hall to the next door.

There he is.

Inha sits on the floor, the painting of his parents no longer hanging from the wall but in his lap. His claw traces the images tenderly. A single ear twists towards me. "I found my sires bodies." His voice is so cold, more frigid than the deep of winter. "Their tails had been cut off and their heads severed."

Taking soft steps, I slowly approach him. "How did you know it was them?" I ask, hoping he does not deem my question insensitive.

"Their scent. Every gumiho knows each other's scent. And I followed theirs, all the way into the Mortal Lands. First it led me to the poachers' place, and I killed them, tearing their heads off like they did to my parents. Then it brought me to the ones who bought the products—my sires heads mounted on the wall and their tails sewn together into a luxurious coat. I tore them apart as I did to those vile poachers. Perhaps that is where the myths you mortals have of vicious gumihos come from."

"I-I don't know what to say. That's so horrible. I can't imagine—" A lump in my throat clogs my words, my heart hurting on his behalf. I wrap my arms around him from the back, tucking my chin in the nook of his neck.

We sit like that for a while, and I only move when my legs match the aching of my heart. Sitting beside him, I wait for him to speak further.

"Let us talk about something else," he mumbles, folding the painting over itself.

There is only one other topic that comes to mind, and as we near the final trial, it is a question that demands an answer. It is a curiosity that has plagued the back of my mind, even without Woosung's planting. "I know the timing isn't the best, but I have something that I've been pondering for a long time. And you promised to answer my questions after the sixth trial."

"Indeed I did. What do you wish to know?" He stares at me, letting me search his eyes for deception.

"What about all the other women?" I ask, my chest tightening and fingers digging into my skirts like little rabbits running from the frightening truth.

Is this what jealousy feels like? It is a foreign emotion to me, and I don't enjoy it, the way it makes me want to curl up into a ball and simultaneously fight someone. Yet the question burns within me, and it will not be quenched until I hear the answer. He mentioned he had loved someone before. Perhaps it is foolish of me to want to know.

He gets up and takes out a painting from his cabinet, sprawling it on the ground in front of us. In the center is a gumiho, nine tails proudly splayed. By seven of them there are flowers, each one unique and so beautifully painted that the gumiho seems insignificant and plain.

"I had a century for each tail, and if the ninth century passed and my tails and pearl were not restored, then I would be turned fully human and live out my days as a mortal," he explains solemnly, his expression somber and his shoulders sagging. He starts at the bottom left, his finger tracing the outline of the blush pink peony. "Kim Seonui."

Kim. It's a noble clan further west, I think. And if Inha is in his eighth century of life, then it means that there was the potential for another woman after me. It brings me some sort of comfort knowing that our love was not based on desperation from being his final chance. However, I will be the final mortal woman sent to the Gumiho King, of that I am certain.

He continues, "She was the first, and maybe it is because back then that I was still too arrogant to accept a mortal's help, but I was mean to her. Never cruel, but cold. I never even told her about the trials or my tails. She simply kept a garden of flowers in the courtyard and spent her days embroidering. She accepted mythicals quite well, actually. Shinhye was close with her, even cried when Seonui passed of old age."

My eyes go from his face back to his hand where his finger strokes a falling petal from the peony. If she accepted the mythicals, then perhaps she could have also been the one to break the curse if only Inha had been humble enough to try. Sometimes good people come at the wrong time.

Then he drags his fingertip to the next—a sky-blue hydrangea. "Yu Uihwa."

Yu. They've had queens come from that clan. Even *they* were not spared from sending a woman as a sacrifice to the Gumiho King.

"After Seonui, I realized the gravity of my situation and how my curse would affect not only me, but also my fellow gumihos. I decided I would try with her. Shinhye said Uihwa spat at her, and she refused to speak or eat. Shinhye had the cooks try every human meal they knew of, but she touched none of them. After a few days, Shinhye went into her room with a new dish and found her hanging."

I gasp. Perhaps for a woman from a clan who produced queens, she could not endure being bound to a mythical king. Maybe she even had someone she loved back in the Mortal Lands. Either way, I do not find contempt for her, only pity. Despair can claim the lives of the high and the low alike.

Inha moves to the sunset camelia, petals a deep pink and center a sunny yellow, the same flower he showed me in the meadows and the ones I picked for his birthing day. He smiles this time, even as sadness lingers in his eyes and voice. "Ahn Wonyoung actually arrived with her hands tied behind her back and a gag in her mouth. Shinhye had never received a mortal woman like that and did not know what to do, so she left her bound on the ride here. My Wonyoung was a fighter."

My.

Jealousy flares back to life, but I do my best to squash it. It's an ugly emotion, and it has no place here while Inha bears his heart to me. If Inha refers to her with such affection, then she was a wonderful woman—no need to be insecure about those who are no longer here.

"She kicked and threw punches, but I made a bargain with her. If she helped me, I would release her. She agreed, and we became allies, then friends. By the time the second trial ended, we were even becoming..." he pauses, glancing at me to gauge my feelings.

I reach out and place my hand over his, our palms pressing onto the painted flower. "It's alright."

He gives a soft smile, a thank you of sorts. "We were falling for each other, at least I thought so." His tone changes, transitioning from the warm nostalgia of summer to the cool melancholy of autumn. "But after the third trial, she changed. Something she saw or had to do, it was too much for her. She withdrew into herself, the light inside her dimming each day. I could not bear to see her like that, so I told her she was free to go." Dark and frigid winter now. "She left as soon as I said the words. Did not hesitate for even a breath." His face falls, his shoulders slumping.

Slowly, I lean my body towards him and rest my head on his arm. I do not know what to say, so I silently offer my comfort. Lament is a lover I am intimately acquainted with, and the more I learn about Inha, the more I recognize the same sorrowful kisses left by it, the kind that taste bitter and salty, sometimes even a bit bloody.

He moves to the white lily. "Shinhye encouraged me not to give up, and for the next one, I was going to try, albeit my heart ached for Wonyoung despite decades passing. But when the new mortal arrived..." He hesitates, and I remove my head from his arm to better see his face. From his expression, it appears his reluctance to speak is for a different reason.

He seems...worried?

"Are you afraid that I won't like what happens next?" I guess.

He nods.

"I will not run," I whisper, reaching for his hand once more, this time interlocking my fingers with his. "I've met many a monster before, and they don't look like you."

His expression, albeit still sad, is no longer shadowed with shame. With a tight smile and nod, he begins again. "When I went down to welcome her and help her out of the carriage, she leaped at me with a dagger. I did not even realize what I was doing—it all happened so quickly—but when I instinctively brought up my hands, I cut the life line in her throat with my claws."

"Is that how you got the scar on your chest?" I ask, recalling the mark I'd seen while tending to his wounds from the bulgae.

"Yes," he croaks, hiding his gaze from me.

I will not force him to look at me, for my words can only encourage him to come out of the cage of guilt he has built. He must choose to come out. Nevertheless, I hope he knows I am sincere when I say, "I do not judge you for defending yourself. I tried to do something similar to that woman, and yet you showed me mercy."

My words must be of some comfort because he leans his body into mine.

For the rose, azalea, and canola, he simply lists off their names. "Choi Inpyeong, Hwangbo Sinjeong, Jo Wisuk. I was tired of the curse, tired of it all. I told each of them about my curse and the trials, asked for their help, but none of them offered. When they refused, I told them they could stay and I would ensure they were well taken care of, or they could leave. They all chose to leave, presumably back to the Mortal Lands. I cannot say I blame them." He lets out a long breath.

There is no jealousy now, just sadness for all the women who came before. Whether they loved or loathed Inha, I mourn them and the lives they never got to live despite coming from noble clans. And for those who got to leave, I hope they found love and happiness. I look up at Inha, knowing I have found mine. I admire that he honored them in his own way, not forgetting their names. One would think that a mythical with such a long life would forget something as trivial as the name of a mortal with a short lifespan, yet it is the mortals who have forgotten the women sent here. I don't want to be on the receiving end of a mythical's grudge then.

Their love on the other hand...

Peering back down at the painting to where the eighth tail sits devoid of a flower, I say, "I want mine to be a plum blossom."

I feel his warm lips press against my temple. "As you wish."

Since he shared his previous love, it feels only right that I share mine. Even if it is a poor comparison. Mine was much more foolish.

"I loved a boy once. He promised to marry me, to provide for me. I'd want for nothing: food, jewels, honor. I'd become a noble lady. But it turned out to be a lie, a set up for his pleasure and the Song sisters' amusement. Thinking he was a blessing, someone who would save me, I went to his bed only to be discarded right after." My voice fades as the memory coalesces.

I still recall it as if it happened last year instead of four years ago. The boy whispered such sweet words, but they were hollow in the end, a vile ruse. I remember waking up naked next to him, and for a brief moment with the sun coming in and shining on our bare skin, I was certain my life was finally going to change, that Favor had at last embraced me.

And then the Song sisters burst into the room, waking him. "You didn't really think he was in love with you, right?" Taehee asked with a satisfied sneer, and the boy got up, untangling himself from my body and the blankets, dressing in the clothes he had so quickly taken off last night.

"You are good for warming a bed once, but you'll never stay in one," he had said, all the gilding from his words peeling off to reveal the rotten wood beneath, and my hopes crumbled.

I cannot get myself to tell Inha all the details though. Piece by piece, I will slowly show him all my shattered bits. "I vowed to myself that I would not so easily trust in a man's sweet words, and grew wary of love while guarding my heart."

Inha's tail curls around me. "So that was why you asked me to wait, so you would feel sure and safe."

I nod. Does he think me naive and foolish? To an ancient creature such as he, I might seem silly, but it is important to me nonetheless.

"Then wait I shall," he declares, grabbing my hand and pressing his lips to my fingers. "Even if it be for centuries."

"You don't have to wait to kiss me, though," I rush out before I can stop myself. My free hand covers my face, embarrassment warming my skin. *Why'd you say that, Jiwon?*

"If you had asked me to wait for even that, I would have honored your request, but I must admit," he pauses, his voice taking on a more flirtatious tone, "I greatly look forward to the next time our lips meet."

Despite part of me wanting such a meeting to take place now, I cannot quite wipe the bad memory I just spoke of away.

It must show on my face because Inha frowns.

"Do you happen to know the boy's name and the general area where he lives?" Inha asks, a fiery wrath flaming in his eyes. At least the shadow of sadness has disappeared.

That boy's name was discarded in my mind in the same way he discarded me. "He is in the past," I say, eyes tracing the lines of his face, all the way up his fox ears and back down to his golden eyes that light my world like a pair of lanterns in the night. "I am only interested in the future." I shift the way I sit, my tone turning more serious. "Speaking of that, what happens when I complete all the trials and you get your pearl and tails back?" Success looms, yet a heavy weight presses upon my heart.

"Well, I will be able to shift again and regain my full powers," he says casually, unable to recognize the thoughts that trouble me.

"And then?" I pry, hoping he will see where my concerns lay.

He looks at me with a puzzled expression. "What else is there? We would rule together, hold regular court again, live happily as I carry you on my back."

That he speaks of me at his side helps ease the pressure, but something else still plagues me. I just have to speak bluntly, for even a mythical gumiho king cannot read minds. "But you will continue to live a long life while I..." The sentence dies on my lips.

His brows bunch together, golden eyes darkening as he finally understands. "I had not thought of that, had not thought I would ever fall in love like this again or that a mortal would love me in return. Perhaps there is a way to extend your life. I will talk to Seonghwa about the matter."

Although I do not know if Seonghwa will be able to help, my chest warms because he wants to try, wants to be with me for a long, long time. Before, the thought of a long life was more tortuous than anything, but Inha makes me not only want to survive, but to live. I have no delusions that the path ahead will be easy, but with him, I know we can endure anything the world throws at us.

We seal the hope of the future with a kiss. Our first tasted sweet, like standing in a grove of fruit trees in summer. Safe and serene. Our second tasted of passion and desire, like an all consuming fire. A burning need. Our third tastes like forever, and I am ready to drown in its delicious depths.

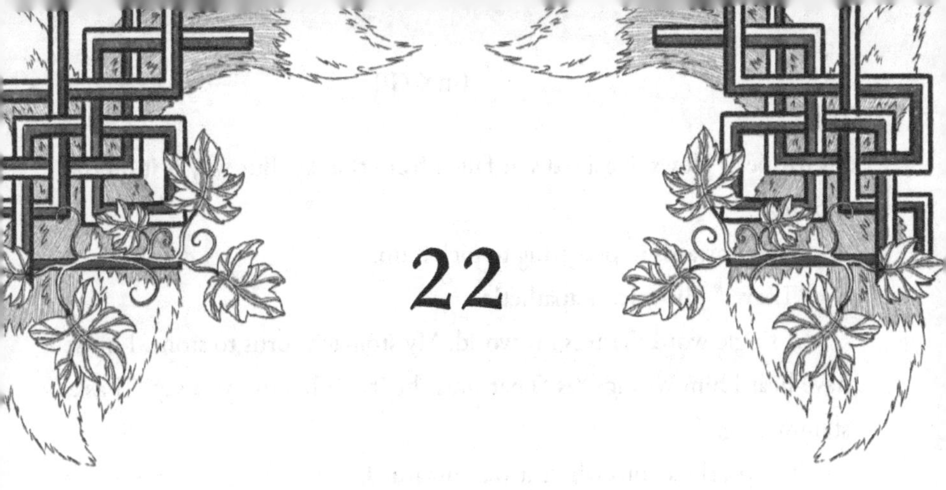

22

T HERE ARE ONLY A few days left before the final trial. I still wish Seonghwa hadn't delayed it for seemingly no reason. I wonder if Inha has discussed with him a way around my mortality. As I make my way to Inha's chamber to invite him to play baduk with me—a board game that Shinhye has been teaching me, although I have yet to beat her—I ponder all the plans for our future.

I can show him how to make flower cakes when the azaleas bloom, and we can go on picnics and paint together, maybe even bring Doyeon along with us. And of course, I will bring Halmeoni Hyesun here. Actually, I should request for her to be brought here today, for there is no need to wait until the final trial since Inha has made it clear that this is my home. So many things I want to do, and hopefully with the help of Seonghwa, Inha and I will have centuries to fulfill all of our wishes.

Elation lightens my steps, and I'd be skipping if not for my leg.

I reach his room and slide open the door, forgetting to announce my entrance, but since his hearing is so superb, I'm sure he already knew I was coming. Early morning light pours in from the open windows, the weather dancing on the verge of spring.

My steps falter when I see Inha.

Something feels wrong.

Inha stands, hunched over the window sill and looking out into the morning, his shoulders jutting up like two jagged mountain peaks, and his fox pearl glows like a red star fallen from the sky. But why is it on the ground?

I step towards it, preparing to pick it up.

"Leave." His voice is apathetic.

A single word shatters my world. My stomach turns to stone. I must have heard him wrong. Yes. That must be it. "What did you say?" I ask, stammering.

The pearl remains where it was discarded.

"Leave. *Go*," he commands, each word a sharp, stabbing blade.

It feels like someone has reached inside my chest and is crushing my heart. Even my good leg wobbles. "What?" I ask again, refusing to believe he said those words. This shouldn't be happening. I should be asking him to play baduk with me, and he should be smiling and accepting my invitation, our hands intertwined as we walk down the hall to my rooms, maybe even a few kisses shared between us.

He whips around, canines revealed as he growls, "Get out. Leave the Mythical Lands and never return." His gaze dances back and forth between cold and warm, the past apathetic Inha clashing with the affectionate one that I had come to know.

I don't know what's changed. Did I do something to upset him?

I take a step forward, reaching for him. "Did something happen? What's wr—"

His face freezes over into something hard and cold, like all the walls that had melted have been restored suddenly, and my body panics and pains in a similar manner as when I had fallen into the icy river. He avoids my touch and cuts off my words, "You should have never come here. You are not even of noble blood, just some filth swept in from the streets."

The hand squeezing my heart releases, and now a fire burns in my belly, my blood boiling. "Right. I'm not good enough for a *King*," I snap and spin around, striding out of the room.

He does not call out to me, does not try to stop me.

I rush to my quarters and throw a few sets of clothes and accessories Inha gifted me. My pride commands me to leave them but my practicality knows I will need something to sell for money to support myself in the Mortal Lands. A painful irony, how quickly I went from planning a bright future with Inha to planning on how to support myself after leaving him. My eyes pause, lingering on the painting he gave me, but a pang of pain hits my chest like an arrow, knowing that the gumiho who gave it to me is the same one banishing me now. Thinking I was a tree, it turns out I was the flower, withered and trampled by a pair of cruel feet. I rip my gaze from it and tie off the bundle with my teeth and strong hand, turning the cloth into a makeshift bag, and sling it over my shoulder.

When I turn to leave, Shinhye bursts into my room, chest heaving, Minji scurrying in after. They scramble towards me, kneeling in front of me.

Minji pleads, grabbing the fabric of my skirts, "Mistress, do not go. You are our only hope."

I gently tug myself free from her grip. "I am not your Mistress." I do my best not to say it with venom, for it is not her fault she serves a vile master.

Shinhye bows her head to the floor. "Please, wait a moment. We can talk about this. He has a reason for—"

When I pause, she looks up, hope flashing across her face, and my chest tightens, knowing I am going to crush it. "This time it *is* personal, Shinhye."

She starts to say, "There is something you should—"

"There is nothing you can say that can change my mind," I shout, regretting raising my voice at her immediately.

All the light sputters out in her eyes, as if I've thrown water on a fire. She stands slowly, voice full of sadness and shoulders slumping in resignation. "At least let me get the carriage and take you back. It is too far for you to walk." She does not argue, does not beg me further, and I am not sure if I am glad or not.

"No, thank you." I brush past them and stride out into the hall.

Inha thought lowly of mortals, that they cannot be trusted, but he is the greatest liar of them all. I want nothing more from him. Walking the extra hours will do me good, distract me from the pain piercing my heart.

Luckily, I come across no one else as I leave the palace. If I saw Gunoo or Injeong or even Shinhye's mate and daughter, my resolve would falter. They should not be serving such a selfish master. They're too good for him.

Inha deserves to be alone.

The trek to the river is spent raging, for I will not allow myself to cry over that gumiho. Each memory is spoiled now, as if I look through each one with a furious fire, smoke obscuring what was once bright and beautiful. My blood blazes with indignation, spurring my legs forward with a determined cause. A caw sounds above my head, and I look up to see Seonghwa. Is he going to try to convince me to stay too? He says nothing, only watching with those golden eyes, keeping me company all the way to the border of the Mortal and Mythical Lands.

The river that I crossed those months ago swells with an early spring melt, water roaring beneath the wide bridge. I stomp towards it, but when my foot steps onto the wooden structure, I pause to gaze across to the Mortal Lands. What is there for me? More maltreatment from the Song family? Certainly I cannot return to my home city, as they will not take kindly to their ruse being figured out. No father waits for me, not that I'd want to go back to him even if he were alive. However, it will take some time to be noticed, so I should be able to get to Halmeoni Hyesun and go to another city. The worst of winter will be behind us, and the things I packed should be enough for an ox or maybe even an old horse with enough left over to start a new life in a new place.

I twist around, peering at the path I came, pondering if there is anything for me in the Mythical Lands.

The answer is clear.

Inha left no room for misinterpretation; he does not want me.

Turning my back on the Mythical Lands, I walk across the bridge, leaving my heartbreak behind. *Forgive me, Shinhye. I'm sorry, Gunoo, Min-ji and Injeong, but I won't stay where I am not wanted. I am, after all, no gumiho. I feel, and I feel deeply.*

After I cross the bridge, the finality of it all hits me like a landslide. I have to pause, leaning against a tree trunk as my breathing becomes labored and my head dizzy. How could he do that? How could he say all those things, show me all those things, just to turn around and stab me in the heart. His final words were as good as killing me; it certainly killed the flowering love between us.

Except it was all an illusion.

Our love was like those flowers, beautiful but quick to die. Or perhaps it is more accurately a painting. Not real. Just a figment of dreams, a facade to shield from the harsh reality of the world and the people in it.

It takes me the whole day to reach my old city, and I'm grateful that it is so close to the border. I shouldn't have been so stubborn and refused the carriage ride that Shinhye offered. As much as I hate to admit it, Inha's sock is the only reason my skin is not raw beneath my brace. I stumble into the sector of shacks, everything the same as how it was when I left last fall, but I know when I head straight and turn left, my old house will most likely be occupied by another. Adjusting the makeshift bag on my shoulder, I take a deep breath and begin weaving through the shacks.

I hope that the Song family will not hear of my arrival until after I am already gone. Besides, it's not like they'll be visiting this part of the city. I just need a few days to figure out what to do now. Well accustomed to these alleys, my feet carry me as my mind wanders.

The mother I met in the trials, is she watching me now? Perhaps I should have taken Jisang up on his offer. Then again, maybe all mythicals are fond of deception. Jisang could just as likely desire to eat me. When he met me, I was no longer the scrawny girl of the slums, but a healthily plump woman, perhaps even pretty in the garments provided by the Gumiho King. A pretty, plump snack for a vicious dragon. A gormless girl who fell for a gumiho.

Despite my best efforts, love has turned me into a fool once more.

My misery pauses when I arrive at Halmeoni Hyesun's place. At least there is one ray of light in the darkness.

"Halmeoni," I call out.

Silence.

When I poke my head in, no hunched, wrinkled lady greets me. I shuffle inside. Maybe she was able to move somewhere with the things Inha sent? *If* he sent them, that is. My answer comes in the form of a note. I cannot read its contents, but I recognize the stamped sign: the red outline of nine tails. He really did send her supplies then. At least he is not completely evil.

My eyes scan around the room. There is something new, something that was not here before I was sent to the Mythical Lands. Charcoal characters dust the wall, some of the letters smeared in small sections, but it is the only word I ever learned how to read. Scrawled several times on the walls and even once on the dirt, my name stares back at me.

지원 지원 지원

She didn't forget me, or rather, she wrote my name so that even if her memory faltered, she would not forget my name, a name to match the aching feeling of a missing loved one. Tears tickle my eyes, and my chest hurts, but in this moment, it is a good kind of hurt. A grin on my face, I sniffle and look around further.

Dishes still sit on a leaning table, one leg shorter than the others, and well worn blankets lay in the corner. I go over to her bed, searching for confirmation that she hasn't moved to another abode.

Lifting up her straw stuffed pillow that Bora had gifted her last year, I find what I'm looking for. A chestnut colored wooden pin with white pebbles forming a flower on the end. It was a present from Songhee, and Halmeoni Hyesun, even in her incoherent states, never would have abandoned it.

I wait for her all evening, eventually falling asleep where my dreams are haunted by a lying fox and man with a godwood pin telling me I should have listened to him. The Song sisters appear as well, fingers pointed while their bellowing laughter thunders around me. I am naked in the bed again, the boy whose name I refuse to remember sneering, *"You are good for warming a bed once, but you'll never stay in one."*

When I awake the next morning, there is still no sign of Halmeoni Hyesun, and a cold stone hits my stomach.

Halmeoni Hyesun did not leave this shack; she has left this life.

I am truly and utterly alone.

23

TEARS FALL FREELY, MY face wetter than the southern province during monsoon season. Everything hurts, my limbs from the long walk of the previous day and my heart from all the loss. Will good ever drift my way? In one moment, I rage against Fortune and her lack of favor for me, and the next I beg, pleading for just a morsel of her blessing.

Eventually, the anger of yesterday is replaced by despair of today.

Dread digs into me; grief provides clarity. I have enough materials—jewels and garments—to start a new life in a new city. I could do it, if not for the fact that my heart remains in the Mythical Lands. Logic often appears in the ashes of emotions, and a realization hits me. What if that was my final trial? Did I fail it so easily? My quick temper is a curse of its own, but it was getting better, slowly, with Inha. But those words he said to me, they hit too deep—hurt too much to bear. But isn't that what the trials were about? I rub my palm against my forehead. What he said was wrong, but perhaps I gave up too quickly.

And Halmeoni Hyesun has gone to the Celestial Realm. There is no one and nothing for me here in the Mortal Lands. I think of the little myodusa. Will it miss me? And Shinhye, she became a friend, at least, I'd like to think our relationship existed outside of my ability to break the curse.

Inha...

Why did he have a sudden change of heart? Gumihos were supposed to be loyal to their lovers, mates for life. Although we were never bound,

I thought we would be. Why had he cast his fox pearl to the floor? Even if our love was a lie, the curse was certainly real. There was only one trial left, so why would he send me away when his restoration was within reach?

Now that my anger has had time to melt, I cannot help but wonder if there is another reason for his command for me to leave—something he is trying to protect me from. He rebuked the Phoenix Queen for me. It isn't far-fetched for him to be willing to hurt me if it meant saving me from something worse. That makes more sense to me than everything being a lie, and deep down, I know something is amiss.

Maybe I am a fool for wanting to return, but I will only know if I try.

Is it too late to go back? Would they even want me back after I gave up on them like all the other mortal women? I have to try. Even if my relationship with Inha is over, I will not be the reason the other gumihos suffer. Minji should get to come to the Mortal Lands, Gunoo should get to run alongside the girin that are so precious to him, Injeong should not have to suffer—walking on legs that are not made for a human form—and Shinhye should get to shift alongside her daughter and mate.

My whole life, all I wished for was for my father to fight for me, to love me.

Perhaps that is what Inha longs for, too.

That which I feared becoming, has been my state all along. Perhaps Yuna and I would have been better friends had I not been so judgmental, for although I was just surviving, I judged people who were also surviving. I never asked what they were going through, too focused on my own pain and assuming they were better off.

The walls that I thought made me so strong were in fact the very thing that made me a coward. I thought cowardice came in the form of people like my father—thought that courage only looked one way—but it turns out they both have many faces. Too busy condemning others, I was unable to recognize my own flaws. Afraid of being hurt, I kept people at a distance.

The spite that burned within me, flames snapping at others both deserving and undeserving, was no bravery.

I have been my father's daughter more than I cared to realize it.

But he died the way he lived, while I still have a chance to choose to change.

And I choose Inha.

Tucking Songhee's pin into my bundle of belongings, I head out into the alley, winding my way through the slum streets for the final time. No more running away, only running towards something. *To someone.* The trek towards the border feels longer this time. It's only been a day, but when separated from the ones you love, a day is like a year.

The rushing river tickles my ears, the familiar sound urging me on despite my tired muscles. Once I reach the bridge, it will only be a few more hours until I reach home.

Home.

I don't think I ever had one until him.

The bridge comes into view, and I nearly run, my leg creating a strange gait. My shoes smack against the wooden bridge, and a smile blooms on my lips. As I cross, I hear that familiar caw again. Peering up at the dusk sky dusted in pink, a three-legged bird with gold eyes soars above me. I knew that snarky samjok-o would miss me. Maybe he was watching me this whole time, even in the Mortal Lands, hoping I would return. The thought widens the smile on my face. For once, I am happy to prove that cocky crow right.

A flash of brown streaks through the air, hitting Seonghwa in the wing. My smile falters, falling from my face as his black body plummets to the earth, and all the breath leaves my chest. I drop my bag and sprint as fast as I am able towards the place I think he landed, hoping he isn't seriously injured. Before I can get far, something big comes crashing through the forest. A beast I prayed I'd never see again looms in front of me, fiery fur matching the setting sun. The bulgae snarls, and I slowly back away. I hit a tree. But the tree is soft. The tree is wearing clothes.

A hand shoves a cloth over my mouth, and then the world goes dark.

Fog still clinging to my mind, I slowly open my eyes. Where am I? It does not take long for my head to clear, and the final moments before I lost consciousness flood back to me. Now there really is a tree behind me, ropes binding me to it. I squirm, but they don't give, tied so tight I can't even slip out from under them. The sun has set, the moon taking up its post as guardian and guide of the night.

I gasp.

Night?

Too much time has passed.

No, no, no.

Inha is going to think I actually left. I mean I did, but I was just angry and hurt. I could never leave those I love. Not permanently. He is going to resign himself to his fate. He is going to give up and become human. I don't know who took me, or why, but it cannot be for anything good. Someone wants to keep me from him, but I will not let them succeed. I will escape and find my way back to him. He is a flower, beautiful and easily broken, and I must protect him so that no one tramples him. I may not be a sword, but I make an excellent shield.

I twist my wrist, reaching feebly at the ropes. The effort proves fruitless, and I hit my head against the trunk in frustration, bark biting my scalp. If only I was stronger, if only my left side wasn't so useless. Gritting my teeth, I banish those thoughts because they will not help me now. Self-deprecation can wait until later.

Lifting my eyes to the sky where stars dance across a court of ink, I whisper, "This is not the end."

Taking in a deep breath, I force myself to calm, to think. If I wriggle back and forth, will the ropes fray against the rough bark? That could take hours, but without a dagger, it seems like the best option. Moving left to right, I try to lean forward, putting the greatest tension on my bindings. Fatigue overcomes me quickly, and the idea is forfeited. My eyes catch on a rock. Perhaps it can cut through them?

My leg stretches as far as it can towards the one with the sharpest looking edge. I twist my ankle, hooking the rock with my foot, and bending my knee, I bring it within arms reach. It's cold in my hand. I adjust my grip and strain my arm towards the ropes and begin sawing. The moon is slowly crawling towards the apex of the sky, and I have barely begun cutting through. Fear prickles my skin. Is Inha alright? Is the person who tied me up after him? They certainly weren't after my things, seeing as my bundle is on the forest floor a few strides away.

Suddenly, the rope gives way. My heart leaps in excitement, only for it to crash when I realize that multiple bindings were used to restrain me instead of one single long rope. There are at least two more. A grunt of frustration bursts through my clenched teeth, and water begins to form in my eyes, blurring my vision.

A twig snaps, my head darting towards the sound.

Is the bulgae back? Panic prickles my skin.

A small tan furry face with black markings emerges from the shadows, its serpent tail slithering behind it. The myodusa.

With a smile spreading on my face, I sniffle back the tears. "Hello, friend. Would you be willing to help me?"

The myodusa tilts its head, golden eyes glowing extra bright in the darkness surrounding us, but just when I think it did not understand me, it crawls forward and begins chewing on the top rope, cute cat paws leaning against the tree trunk.

"Thank you," I say, letting out a big breath of relief, and begin cutting at the middle rope.

The myodusa finishes before I do, coming to complete the half-sawed middle rope for me. As soon as the last binding falls, I scramble to my feet, using the tree trunk to brace myself. My legs buzz from the position I was forced in for the past who knows how many hours. The rest of my body aches from so much walking the previous two days, but my worry for Inha spurs me on despite it all.

Reaching down to pat the myodusa's head, I say, "Thank you for your help. I need one more favor from you. There is a three-legged crow somewhere nearby. Please find him and make sure he is alright." I have to trust that the little mythical understood as it slithers off into the dark woods to search for Seonghwa.

I hope the samjok-o will forgive me for not finding him myself, but something inside me tells me that Inha is in even greater danger. Then I am running as fast as I can manage, stumbling through the forest and bracing against tree trunks and large rocks when my limbs weaken and wobble. A spring breeze rustles the bare branches of the forest, whispering encouragement, *Go, go, go*.

What I lack in physical prowess, I make up for in stubborn strength. The sole recipient of all my determination—of my love—is a cursed fox king who fell in love with a mortal woman. No matter how broken my body is, I will find him. No matter how far the distance, I will not give up. No matter what awaits me, I will not shy from it, for I am no coward. Not anymore.

24

THE GUMIHO KING'S PALACE peaks above the trees, the top of the tiled roof waving from a distance. Its greeting gives me one final burst of energy. When I see Inha, my heart leaps, and I smile in relief. He is alright. *He is alive*.

It feels like coming home, like a warm embrace after a long day. Even the foxtail whipping back and forth and flattened ears have become so familiar. He is pacing just outside his palace walls, the two lanterns dangling from the arch of the gate like two golden mythical eyes keeping watch. What is he doing out here though?

Suddenly, he freezes. His ears perk. He turns towards me, and when he sees me, he breaks out into a sprint, barreling in my direction. Even now his steps are silent, yet the speed at which he races to me shouts loudly. The eagerness with which he greets me confirms my suspicion that something else is involved in this matter. The reason behind his final harsh words to me, although no excuse, must be more than just a cruel heart.

He skids to a halt in front of me, his hands cupping my face. His eyes drink the sight of me in, as desperate as a man dying of thirst. A small part of me—the angry part—wants to shove him away, but my aching heart bids me to stay, to lean into his touch. I doubt my temper will ever be fully tamed, but his mere presence calms the normal blaze into a manageable flame.

His features contain a mixture of emotions, conveying so many messages. His voice cracks when he croaks, "I longed for you to return, yet I loathed that you would. For I could not bear to send you away a second time. Although I could not go to you in the Mortal Lands, a selfish part of me hoped you would return. So I waited and watched." The look in his eyes lets me know he would have continued to wait and watch until the end of his days—until he became a mortal and died like one.

"There should never have been a first," I say with a stony voice.

A string draws my attention. He is wearing his pearl again. Does that mean he wants me to finish the last trial? Does he want me?

"You are right," he rasps and swallows a lump of shame.

My hands find their way to his, palms pressed to the back of his hands as he continues to hold my face like he is afraid to let go. "Then why did you send me away? Why did you say the words that would wound so deeply?" I ask in a whisper, staring into his eyes and searching for truth.

He opens his mouth to speak, and my breath stills in anticipation of his answer. The words he says will either confirm that I made the right choice in returning or cause me to regret giving him another chance. I pray desperately that it will be the former, but a voice I have not heard or thought about in a long time interrupts.

"You always amaze me, Jiwon. Full of surprises."

Our hands drop to our sides, and we rip part to turn and face the man emerging from the woods.

"Woosung, what are you doing here?" I ask, perplexed, my brows furrowing. There is no reason for him to be here, especially in the middle of the night. I peer around, looking for his masked guard, but he is nowhere to be found. It is dangerous to be a lone mortal in the Mythical Lands, especially at night.

Did Woosung always have markings on his skin? Perhaps I just never saw them, his body well covered by clothing. My eyes widen as he steps into the moonlight. I know for certain he didn't always have those two horns protruding from his head like a young goat, and just as new are the two sets of fangs jutting from his top and bottom teeth. Although unlike Inha in his human form, all of Woosung's teeth are sharpened to a point. I would have noticed *those* before.

I recall what Shinhye said when I first arrived in the Mythical Lands. *"Illusion. Dokkaebi have the power to create short but powerful illusions. Usually they use them to play pranks, but some of the more sinister sort use it for more nefarious purposes."*

Panic flutters like a frightened bird inside my chest. My gut tells me that Woosung is the latter kind of dokkaebi—if that is in fact what he is. There is so much I am ignorant of about mythicals, and he could be something even worse. My gaze turns to Inha as my mind works to puzzle together what is happening.

Hurt flashes across Inha's face. "Did you bring him here?" In his eyes, shock and suspicion wrestle with his desire to trust me. He takes a few steps back.

If I hadn't brought that godwood pin with me into the palace, his mistrust would not have such a solid foundation on which to now build. Shaking my head, I urge, "No. *No.* I promise, I didn't know. I—"

Woosung clicks his tongue. "Come now, Jiwon, did you not tell him about us?"

"He's lying. I knew him, but I am not *with* him. I would not hurt you." I limp towards Inha, but he takes another step back, hands curled into fists barely peeking out from his wide sleeves.

"If she is fit enough for the Gumiho King, then she is fit to be the wife of the Dokkaebi King," Woosung declares.

I twist to look over my shoulder, giving him a cold glare. He's never voiced a desire for me before, and I'm certain he is saying it to turn Inha against me.

Eyes full of greed and devious delight, Woosung stares back at me. "You surprised me in many ways, Jiwon. You are strong for a mortal, and you would fit in quite well with the other dokkaebi with that temper of yours."

How much has he seen? How does he know me so well? He has to be lying. But that doesn't matter, only what Inha thinks does. I shake my head, my eyes searching Inha's, begging him to listen—to believe me. "I promise, Inha, you are the only one I love. I did not bring him here. I came back for you. For us."

Inha's nostrils flare, his eyes narrowing and white brows bunching. He stands on a cliff of trust, unsteady and unsure, and Woosung is trying to push him over. I can't allow it.

"Inha, listen to me, please." I infuse all the love, hope, and desire I possess into my voice. "I love you. I have been honest with you ever since I've started the trials. Don't trust a stranger over me."

Snarling, Inha explains, "He is not a stranger. He is a dokkaebi, one I know of quite well. He has a band of fellow dokkaebi who hide in the Mortal Lands because even the rest of their kind don't trust them. They cause trouble, covet that which is not theirs, and what he desires most of all are pearls."

"What," I gasp, looking back at Woosung who is occupied by the sight of the fox pearl around Inha's neck.

"Woosung, is it?" Inha asks with a sneer. "Care to tell her your real purpose, Kwangil?"

That seems to shake Woosung—no, Kwangil—from his fixation on the fox pearl. He smirks. "You pearl bearing mythicals are so arrogant, think you deserve to be keepers, lords and guardians." He turns his attention to me, holding out a hand. "Join me, Jiwon. You know what it is like to be deemed inferior. Would you not relish the chance to *take* instead of *serve*? You could have power. I could turn you into a mythical."

Shaking my head, I step back, for it is an easy choice to refuse him. "Never. I will not harm others for my own benefit."

Kwangil's hand drops to his side, disgust clear on his face, his lip curling back. "That is not the girl who accepted the godwood pin."

Lifting my chin, I reply, "You deceived me, said I was going to be helping other women. I no longer believe your lies, and I have changed a lot since then." When I take a step towards Inha, he does not retreat from me this time, much to the chagrin of Kwangil.

The dokkaebi runs his tongue across his teeth. "Well, then, shall we get down to business?" He lifts his hand, his fingernails sharpened to a point, although shorter than Inha's claws.

"Get back, Jiwon," Inha warns and pushes me behind him.

Kwangil scoffs, "You are going to protect her even after she has betrayed you?"

Inha bends his knees, ready to spring forward. "I can die by her hands, but never from yours."

"We shall see about that."

In a burst, Kwangil barrels towards us, but Inha's reflexes are fast, charging forward to meet the dokkaebi. They clash, throwing brutal punches and swiping with sharp claws. Red lines mar Kwangil's cheek after a hit from Inha, but he is quick to repay it, Inha shouting as Kwangil's tapered nails cut his neck, although the wounds are, thankfully, shallow.

I don't know what to do, how to help. Looking over my shoulder, I wonder if I should run to the palace and call for help. Another howl of pain draws my attention back to the brawl. Inha is clutching his arm, having taken a few steps back from Kwangil. If he had his pearl, I am certain Inha would be more powerful and this fight would have ended already, but without it, even a pearless dokkaebi is able to outmatch him. Bouncing on my feet, I know I must choose quickly whether to run to the palace or use my pitiful amount of power to help Inha fight Kwangil.

Shinhye. I need her. And there must be other gumihos in their fox forms here. Before I start making the long sprint to the palace, I look back once more, worried about what has transpired in the precious seconds of my indecision.

When I glance back at Kwangil, he now has a bow and arrow in his hand. Where did it come from? Another illusion? Wait. Seonghwa was shot down by an arrow. Not an illusion, then. Fear like I've never known before grips me, dread heavy in my stomach. Everything slows, my mind already arriving at what is going to happen next.

I am powerless to stop Kwangil, and so is Inha. Because I never finished all the trials, he cannot shift, can't fight back well enough. I don't know if Inha believes my words, but even if he hates me, I won't let him die. Although I didn't bring Kwangil here, I did conspire with him initially. And I left, leaving Inha vulnerable, so when Kwangil points the arrow made of godwood directly at Inha's heart, I don't hesitate. Throwing myself in front of Inha, I hear the whizz of the arrow before I feel it. My legs give out, and I collapse into Inha. All suspicion and hurt melts from his face, his expression now one of horror, eyes and mouth round as the moon above.

Together, we slump to the ground.

Kwangil tsks. "You should have given up back when I sent my bulgae after you, but you are too stubborn for your own good, Jiwon." His tone rises, more dramatical now. "And if you had just stayed away, if you had not tried to return, you would have been just fine. I sent my guard to detain you. Is it really that hard to stay away from that fox?" His voice changes once more, lower and full of disappointment. "I always thought of the love of you humans to be fickle, yet here you are dying for a *gumiho* of all things. Such a pity. I would have given you wealth. You could have lived by my side, yet instead you die by his."

Inha thought all mortals a liar, and Kwangil thinks us all greedy for wealth. While it is true for some, I for one, have no desire but for love. I had it, too, for a while at least. I got to feast upon the beauty, love in all its forms from platonic to romantic. I can take the memories of Seonghwa and Shinhye with me and cling to the kisses of the Gumiho King. If my death means the gumiho are free, then it is a happy death indeed. With sticky, hot blood seeping from my wound, I smile up at Inha. He is just as handsome as the day I met him, even now when his eyes are watery and his lips are parted in shock and sadness.

Inha's face hardens with rage, his jaw clenched and his arms shaking. Suddenly, a red glow coats his entire body, his golden eyes lighting up like the sun, outdoing the moonlight that showers us. One by one, nine white tails tipped in crimson sprout behind him, his nostrils flaring as the power fills him.

I smile despite the burning blazing through my body.

No painting could capture the brilliance; no storyteller could relay the magnificence.

In the middle of a chilled night, the Gumiho King has returned to his full might.

Inha wastes no time shifting, human features giving way to fox ones. In the blink of an eye, a nine-tailed fox the size of a cow stands in front of me. He is so much bigger than the others I've seen; it must be the power of a king. Kwangil is just a dokkaebi and no match for Inha. With a snarl of thunder, Inha launches himself at him.

Grunting and grimacing, I manage to twist, a yelp escaping my lips as the feathered end of the arrow bumps against the ground and digs deeper into me. Suddenly, there are three of Kwangil. What is happening? Inha swipes at each of them, but two of them are naught but air. The two forms dissolve while the third tries to dodge, but Inha is quicker. His paw hooks Kwangil's legs, and Inha pounces upon his prone form.

A shout echoes through the night, followed by a snarl. Kwangil begs for mercy, but Inha's palpable wrath leaves room for none. Slamming my eyes shut, I know what will come next. A crunching wet noise. Then there is silence. I don't open my eyes until I feel soft fur brush against my face. Inha leans over me, back in his half-human-half-fox form, although all nine tails now sprawl behind his back, and he brings me onto his lap, his breathing labored and his body trembling. His claws are covered in crimson, but I do not know if it is Kwangil's blood or my own.

"Hold on, Jiwon," he urges, and a familiar feeling overtakes me, the world blurring for a breath before we coalesce in a new location. The tiled roof of the palace peeks over Inha's shoulder. He must have teleported us.

"Shinhye! Bring me my medicine box," he screams. It is not the confident command of a king but one of a desperate and panicked person. He brushes hair from face, leaving sticky streaks of blood behind. "It is going to be alright. You are going to be fine."

The words fail to convince either of us no matter how many times and ways he utters them. My breathing is becoming more difficult, my thoughts are becoming harder to form, and my vision is dimming.

Seonghwa's silhouette appears, the moonlight carving him from the night sky. He swoops down, his wings flapping erratically. One of them is warped. He is wounded. *My poor friend.*

My body doesn't hurt now. Everything is numb. *So tired.*

"I understand why you missed your tails so much. Your fox form is truly magnificent, so I'm glad I got to see it once," I rasp, coughing. There is a strange tang on my tongue. I think blood came up from my coughing. Or was the blood already in my mouth?

"You have not seen all that I can do yet," he whimpers. Then Inha looks to Seonghwa, face full of desperation and voice so pitiful, not commanding—just anguished and pleading. "Take my tails back. Take them all. Make me human. Just save her."

I feel myself fading, but even then, I do not regret how I lived, *who* I lived for, and now, who I die for. I fulfilled my end of the bargain. Inha has his pearl and powers back, and the other gumihos are free again.

"There is no greater love than one laying down their life for another," Seonghwa whispers, golden eyes peering at us with a heavy sadness.

"Don't be bitter. Find joy. Be kind," I fight to say, using the last of my strength to wipe the tears dripping down his cheeks. Instead, I accidentally leave streaks of crimson, red rivers marking his face. "Promise me."

"I-I promise," he croaks, hand caressing my head.

"Good. I won't be here to break another curse for you." Smiling feebly, I whisper, "I love you."

He is crying.

That is three times now that I've made this gumiho cry.

Pressing his hand to my face, as if he held hard enough it might keep my soul in my body, his reply sends me off into the afterlife. "I love you, Jiwon."

25

A BLACK ABYSS DOES not greet me, and instead I am met with a brilliant light. Then soil kisses my feet. The aroma of flowers waft through the air, and the silence is not the eerie sort, but rather of serenity. I am in the same meadow that I met my mother in in the previous trial, but this time, another person greets me. Even though she appears forty years younger, I'd recognize those kind eyes and soft smile anywhere.

"Halmeoni!" I shout and run towards Halmeoni Hyesun.

"Jiwon-ah!" she says, arms open wide. I fold into her embrace, warmth seeping deep into my bones. She smells of life, of summer trees and buzzing bees, blooming flowers and the earth after rain showers. It is an aroma that I cannot quite compare to one single thing.

Her breath tickles my ear when she says, "Songhee is here." Her voice is strong, not that of an old woman like I last heard. She is the same soul in a new body.

Tears prickle in my eyes because this place is not the Celestial Realm, just a glimpse of eternity, thus I can still feel the aching of my heart. "I'm glad you found each other again." And I am glad she does not have to suffer from swollen joints that are sore nor empty stomachs anymore.

We pull apart, and she explains, "I am here not just to greet you but also to give you a choice. You may go with me to the Celestial Realm and keep this body" —she gestures to my brace free leg and relaxed left hand— "or return to your Gumiho King and your old body."

Everything happened so quickly that I hadn't even noticed the change at first, but now I *feel* it. When I ran towards her, it was not in the lurching gait that had been present all my life. My arms feel equally strong. My whole body is different, just like when I met my mother. However this time I am offered with the option of keeping this new and strong body. I could run. I could swim. I could at last live like everyone else got to. There is no pain in the Celestial Realm.

The choice is an easy one.

"I want to go back," I say, grateful that I get the chance to return to Inha.

"I'd ask if you are sure, but I know from that stubborn light in your eyes that you're determined to return to him." Her laughter echoes beautifully like the sound of a song.

I nod, a grin making my cheeks ache.

"Very well," she says, letting out a long breath, the first and only sign that she wishes my answer was different. "I will see you later." When she notices my confused expression she adds, "Time is different here. What is a day here, is years down there. Later for me is a lifetime for you, until you join us, that is."

I wipe a tear that manages to escape my eye. "Thank you, Halmeoni, for taking care of me all those years. If I possess any virtues, they were cultivated by you. I'll miss you, but I am glad you're with Songhee. Tell her I said 'hello'. My mother, too." I trust that the two will have acquainted themselves with each other already.

Halmeoni Hyesun nods, her aura effervescent and her skin smooth as one in youth. Her mind is sound once more, too. A bright light embraces her, and then she is gone.

But I am not alone in the mystical meadow.

"Seonghwa, I see even *your* wounded wing won't prevent you from doing your duty," I tease.

He unfurls his mangled wing, feathers jutting in opposing directions. "Tis but a flesh wound."

"We share the same stubbornness. Perhaps that is why we get along so well—and argue even better." I'd poke him if he wasn't injured.

Clicking his beak, "I do not argue. I—"

The amused look I give him stops him mid-sentence. He clears his throat and begins again, "I am here to complete the final part of my mission."

"Does that mean I passed the final trial?"

"Indeed. Love is sacrifice. Not always something as large as a life, but even small sacrifices such as saying sorry when you do not feel like you have done anything wrong but have hurt someone or giving your food to another. Love takes many forms, but it is always about putting another above yourself." As if he can predict the question poised on my tongue and wishes to get ahead of it, he adds, "That does not mean you should neglect taking care of yourself or allow someone to abuse you. One form love takes is allowing someone to experience the consequences of their actions so that their character can develop."

"Like a curse?" I propose.

Seonghwa chortles. "Exactly."

I cock a brow, my curiosity piqued. "So what is the final part of your mission that you mentioned?"

"Do not move," he orders, and with a thrust of his wings, he launches off the ground and into the air. He flies towards me, hovering at my chest. "This is going to sting."

My brows pinch together. "What are you—"

He stabs his beak at my heart, penetrating past the fabric of my clothes and into my skin.

"Ow!" I lurch backwards, swatting at him with one hand and rubbing the spot with my other.

Seonghwa darts away just as quickly as he came, and I pull my garment down just enough to see the area he pecked. A small bead of blood forms. Wiping it with my finger, I open my mouth to ask what the point of him pricking me was, but the words die on my lips. I wipe once more to make sure I am not imagining it. It appears my eyes are not the problem, for beneath the blood is a red dot the size of a fox pearl, as if a small flower petal fell and sunk into my skin.

I look up at Seonghwa, a dumbfounded expression on my face. "Does this— Is it—"

"I hope you and the fox boy enjoy a long and lovely life together," he answers in a feigned apathy.

"Thank you," I whisper, water forming once more in my eyes.

He looks away from my tears, and I wonder if birds can cry. "I am glad you came back to him. Free will made a fool of him."

"What does that mean?" My face scrunches in confusion.

A chuckle comes from the crow, and he looks at me at last. "You must go now, Jiwon. Thank you for all the rice."

Without a chance to reply, everything dissolves, the darkness only lasting for a breath before moonlight filters through my eyelids. I gasp, gulping in air as my eyes fling open.

A gumiho greets me, and not a half human one this time. White fur, ears and tails dipped in red, and golden irises fill my vision. Even though all the mythicals share the same color, I could never not recognize him. My Inha. His body is wrapped around me, nine tails blanketing my body. Even in death, he did not abandon me.

He senses my movement, whipping his head up. A sound emits from him, one of relief and grief. "I must be dreaming. This is worse than any curse, tormenting me with hope of you," he rasps, nose nuzzling my hair. He closes his eyes, unable to believe that I am alive.

I reach my hand up, stroking the smooth fur of his face. "Inha," I whisper softly. "This is real."

His eyes slowly open, ears turning towards me, perhaps listening for a heartbeat to confirm his hopes. "Jiwon-ah. My Jiwon. *Jiwon*," he says my name as if to convince himself of reality.

He rubs his cheek against mine, much like I saw Shinhye and her family do. A smile curls my lips into a crescent, and I press the side of my face against his in equal affection.

Inha's voice is broken and desperate, each word spilling out in a rush. "I am so sorry for what I said to you. Seonghwa told me that the last trial would require a sacrifice, and I could not bear to lose you. Forgive me. I thought I had to sacrifice us in order to save you."

He was going to give up everything for me? He was going to allow himself to become a human? Tears well in my eyes. "You fool," I hiss, lightly hitting his shoulder with my fist. "Coward. You're a coward." My fist falls back down. "But so was I." My voice is full of remorse, sorry and shattered. "I ran. Twice I ran from you, from us, because I was scared. I should have stayed, should have tried harder."

"I am so sorry," he whispers into my hair. "Never again."

My punches resume. "How could you take that choice away from me? And-and all the others. They would have become mortals, too." It wasn't fair for Shinhye and her family, Injeong and her legs, or Gunoo and Minji with their dreams. "How could you do that to them?"

"I asked them."

I pause my pitiful punching. "What?"

"I gathered all the gumihos of the palace together and explained. We chose to save you."

Water trickles from my eyes, and a hoarseness clings to my voice. "You all...wanted to protect me?"

He nods. "Besides, you are a human, so we thought we would all be just fine becoming one, too."

I wipe the tears from my face. "Foolish. I am not worth it."

"You are to us—to me. I told you all those weeks ago with the bulgae that I would fight them all over again—that I would die for you, and I am no liar."

"You lied when you were trying to get me to leave," I point out.

He sighs before a half-chuckle comes from his throat. "You are right, but aside from that *one* time, I have always been honest."

"So you really did want to shoot me with that bow?"

His voice is full of a gentle warning. "Jiwon..."

"Sorry," I mumble. Part of me is still hurt by what he said the other night, even if it was a misguided attempt to save me, but if he can forgive my temper, I can forgive his poor bid at protecting me. "I've been quick to judge and slow to trust my whole life. Partially out of survival, partially out of a deep sense of unfairness in life, and mostly to keep my heart from harm. You taught me how to see the good again." My voice keeps cracking, but for once, I do not fight my emotions. "But I want to try, even if I get my heart broken."

"I will not allow it to break. I cannot fix your left side for you, but I will not be the cause of more pain for you." His cold, moist nose nuzzles my ear.

"I wish I could go back to the night we met, wish I would never have tried to kill you, had been more open to who you were and not just believe the stories." My fingers burrow into his tail that is draped across me.

"I do not regret a thing because it led us to where we are now, to each other. It just took me eight centuries to find you."

Looking up into those eyes that seem as magical as the sky, ones that have haunted my dreams in the best kind of way, I say, "It seems fate would have us together, then."

"Or a curse," he muses, his lips twitching upward in a fox's way of smiling.

I lift my hand, placing my palm against his head just under his eye. Soft fur swallows my fingers. "Whatever it was, I am grateful for it. I would have wandered until I found you. You are a haven, a sanctuary of rest and respite from the hardships of life." I say everything I've ever felt about him, knowing how precious our time is and how fickle life can be. I will never miss a chance to profess how I feel about him, even if that entails telling him I love him every single day.

"You are not a burden, Jiwon. You could never get out of bed again, and I would never resent you for it. You have labored your whole life for love, for independence, for fear of being a burden, but you are safe now. You may rest."

If he is trying to make up for those words that wounded me, he is succeeding.

A wetness tickles my face, my nose stinging as my lip quivers. I don't know what to say, so I simply reach out and grab his paw, bringing it to my chest and holding it tight. Had he not said those words, I don't think I'd ever admit it. I worked because I knew we needed to eat, but I also thought I could earn my father's love, that by working hard enough, he'd see my value despite my weaknesses. I never thought of myself as a beggar, yet that's what I did my entire life, begging for my father's affection, begging for the world to see the value in me. Closing my eyes until my vision is a black void, I shut out the rest of the world except for Inha's touch that anchors me.

"Let's go inside. I've missed home," I say at last, opening my eyes.

"Home," Inha repeats, smiling. He shifts into his human form, save for a set of ears and a tail. Picking me up, he carries me back inside, winding down the familiar halls.

"Where are all the others?" I wonder aloud, realizing no one else was there when I awoke.

Inha grimaces. "When I thought you were...gone, I may have told them to leave me alone."

"I'm gone for a few minutes and you already returned to old habits?" I ask in a lighthearted exasperation.

He presses his lips to my forehead. "I guess you cannot leave me, then." The way he stares at me as if enchanted, I am amazed at how much can be conveyed in one's eyes.

"Never again," I promise, grinning. Content to be carried in his arms, I tuck my head into his chest, his heart a steady rhythm of comfort. But curiosity is another, at times peeving, trait of mine, and my mind starts thinking of that dokkaebi and his motives. "I feel like a fool for ever listening to Woosung—er, Kwangil. What was his purpose anyways? It's not like he could take over as the king of the gumihos," I ponder aloud.

"He did not want to just kill me; he wanted to take my fox pearl. I think he believed that by stealing mine, he'd gain the ability to shift—into what I do not know," Inha muses, his tone hardening at the mention of Kwangil.

"How do you know?"

"He used godwood arrows, like the pin."

"He said it was the only way to kill you." The sentence burns in my mouth, for I loathe the very thought of it.

"I think the bulgaes proved him a liar. We can die through the same means of mortals, albeit we do not get ill so easily. Rather, godwood can be used to remove pearls. Although I do not think he was aware that mine was outside my body until he saw it hanging from my necklace before we fought."

A shiver snakes down my spine. "Well, I'm glad it is over." Kwangil is dead, and there is no need to continue to guess at his heinous plans.

When we get to my rooms, the sound of sobbing sneaks through the door. I look up at Inha and cock a brow, wondering who is weeping. He shrugs and adjusts his grip on me so he can slide open the door, and we enter to find Minji, Shinhye, and Injeong crying together.

"I think my power is making those who don't normally shed tears cry," I mutter to myself. But my heart blossoms with heat, touched that they care so much for me. "Ahem." I clear my throat, drawing the attention of the three she-foxes.

They turn their head in tandem, shock flashing in their eyes. Minji and Shinhye scramble to their feet and rush towards me, Inha's arms tightening their grip.

"You can set me down now," I say amusedly.

He hesitates but acquiesces. "I still need to check your wound. I took the arrow out while you were unconscious, but it still needs to be treated."

Now that he mentions it, there is no pain where the arrow hit. "I'm fine. I think?" But I know the expression he gives me means he nor his worries will rest until he checks it for himself. A blush blooms on my cheeks at the thought of him checking the spot on my chest. I shake my mind clear and focus on the three female gumihos in front of me.

"How?" Shinhye questions, wide eyes roving from my head to toe.

Inha and I glance at each other. "I am not quite sure myself. The how or the why. But I was given a choice." I grab Inha's hand. "I think my answer is obvious."

If they had been mortals, perhaps they would have asked more questions, unable to accept uncertainties, but mythicals are used to magic. They accept the mysterious as a part of life instead of treating them as enemies, not striving to defeat them in the manner of mortals.

A memory suddenly surfaces at the front of my mind. So much has happened in such a short amount of time, and even though I am now a mythical, the mortal trait of inquisitiveness still plagues me. "Shinhye, you were trying to tell me something before I...ran away."

Her eyes flicker between Inha and I. Inha answers on her behalf, wincing as he explains, "When I said everyone agreed, it was not without counterarguments."

My mouth drops open. Shinhye didn't want to save me? My chest tightens, and I frown. However, I know that my hurt is illogical. She has a daughter who she wants to run alongside of, to greet in the custom of gumihos in her own fox form. I cannot hold it against her, so I force the frown from my face. "I understand, Shinhye."

Her guilty expression eases. "Thank you for understanding. It is not that I did not want to save you, but I thought that you should be included in the decision and that we could all come up with a solution together. I must admit, I wished to save the both of us."

I reach forward and give her hand a squeeze. "I understand. Truly. It was a difficult situation, and it was not only myself at stake."

Injeong stands, and I notice human feet peeking out from beneath her skirt. A smile pulls at my lips. Catching my stare, she says, "Thank you for freeing us. I am glad you are back and safe, Mistress." Her voice is clearer, no longer strained now that she can shift completely.

"Oh, yes," Minji agrees, nodding her head enthusiastically. "I will prepare a new set of clothes." She gestures to the torn back of the top I am wearing.

Shinhye adds, "I will fetch the Master's medicine. Just in case." She gathers the other two gumiho and shoves them out the door. "We will be back soon." Her eyes reveal her intent to give Inha and I a moment alone.

Smiling, I shake my head. It feels like how things used to be.

"Oh, Mistress," Shinhye says, pausing in the doorway. "You should go to the girin pasture when you get the chance. Gunoo is beside himself."

Although it is inappropriate, a laugh loosens my lips, and I do my best to gain control over it. "I will do that. Thank you, Shinhye."

She gives me a strange look due to my outburst but closes the door behind her without another word.

"Why was that amusing?" Inha asks, forehead creased and head canted in confusion.

"I don't know. Just the thought of Gunoo sobbing in a field and hugging a girin was a bit humorous."

"Perhaps that is a peculiarity of mortals that a mythical cannot understand," he muses.

"About that..." I turn to face him. "I have something to show you." I pull the collar of my top to the side, revealing the scarlet spot on my skin just over my heart, assuming he will know what it means.

His mouth drops open. It turns out I still enjoy making mythicals speechless.

"You—" His eyes dart between my eyes and the mark. "You are—" He touches it with a finger. "You are a gumiho?"

I nod. "Do you have one, too?" I haven't seen Inha's bare chest since he received his pearl and powers back.

Still in shock, he says nothing, untying the knot of his top. I swallow as the fabric flutters to the sides of his body, framing his bare chest. Forcing myself to focus, I look for a red dot. There, in the same spot as mine.

At last, he regains his composure. "What about your left side? Do you still need a brace?"

I nod. "Unfortunately, that was not a part of the offer."

He is already striding out towards the door. "I shall talk to Seonghwa. If something like this is possible, then—"

"Inha," I interrupt, reaching out to grab his sleeve. "It's alright. I've accepted how things are. And more importantly, I am grateful that I get not only a second chance at life, but a long one." I grab his hand. "With you."

"Jiwon," he whispers, gaze full of awe, anticipation, and an abundance of joy.

He slips his hands around to the back of my head and pulls me into a kiss. His bare skin is warm to the touch, heating my own insides. I drink of his love for me, and it is sweeter than honey. I could spend centuries kissing the Gumiho King and never grow weary of it.

After a few moments, he pulls away. "What should we do now?"

I take the opportunity to ask, "How do you shift?"

"You simply want it and it becomes so. Although it normally takes some practice to be able to do partial shifts." He gestures to his ears and tail.

"Controlling singular parts is a skill. But lucky for us, you have centuries to perfect it."

Just want it? I close my eyes and picture Inha's fox-form, imagining nine tails sprouting behind me, four paws and two furry ears, and lastly a snout full of fangs. My whole body buzzes, tingling in every limb, but it doesn't hurt at all when my body changes shape. I open my eyes to see Inha's smiling face.

"Absolutely stunning," he rasps, his eyes alight with dancing flames.

Although his voice is soft, I hear it so clearly. And the smells. I can smell the food being cooked all the way in another section of the palace. I wonder what it would taste like in this form. I twist around. Nine white tails with streaks of bright red running from the tip and tapering towards the base peek behind me. Testing out my four legs, I take a step forward. My left foreleg feels weak but not so much that it can't support me. However, my back left leg buckles easily.

"Do you think there is a gumiho who will be able to make a brace for me?"

Inha replies, finger tapping against his sharp chin, "I must admit, I have never tried it, but you might be able to create it yourself. We have the power to make clothes for when we shift to humans, so I do not see why it would be any different in your fox-form."

His reasoning makes sense. I focus again, imagining the stiff and smooth wood stretching along the length of my back leg. After a few moments, something hard surrounds my hindleg, and I duck my head under my belly, elated to see that it worked. Whipping my head back up, a grin spreads along my snout, but suddenly my tongue falls out. Inha chuckles. It will take some time adjusting to this fox body. For now, I think I will stick to my mortal form.

When I turn back into a human, Inha gawks. Did I do something wrong? Is there a snout on my face? Am I unclothed? I glance down, panicked. But everything looks normal, and a new skirt and top, black and trimmed in red much like Inha's, covers my body. I should inform Minji that new clothes will no longer be necessary.

Inha approaches and reaches towards my head, bringing a chunk of hair into view. Now it is my turn to gawk, for it's white as the moon. My hands frantically pull the rest of my hair so I can see it, but it is the normal raven black I've always had.

"Just another reason you are special," Inha says with a soft chuckle. He pulls me into an embrace, and I tuck my head under his chin. Even his tail curls around my legs. "Remind me to paint that plum blossom," he murmurs into my hair.

"We should plant some, too."

"As you wish, Mistress."

26

NOW A MYTHICAL WITH new abilities and a new life ahead of me, there is one more thing I wish to do, one final string I want to sever from my past. The last visit to the Song estate was for the trial, but this time it will be for me. Although I forgave them then, I find myself needing to renew it.

Just as Seonghwa said, there is a time for everything.

Previously it was peace, for the pain was too raw for me to confront them without losing control over my temper, but one thing I have learned is that kindness can come alongside confrontation—one that does include the choice of turning them into a pair of fish. Now that so much has changed, including myself, I feel ready to talk to them.

At least on this occasion, my love will be accompanying me instead of a snarky samjok-o or sinister serpent. That is, if he agrees to take me.

"Inha?" I ask while watching him paint a plum blossom on the foxtails picture.

"Mhm." He doesn't look up, focused on a thin, watery stroke of his brush.

Inhaling, I ask, "Would you take me to the Mortal Lands?"

He pauses his painting and lays the brush down in a smooth, elegant motion, tucking his long sleeve back with his other hand. "Impeccable timing. Actually, I also wish to see them."

My brows furrow, and I tilt my head. "Who?"

His voice is calm despite the words he says, "The girls who tormented you, who made you fearful of the dark."

My thought wanders to the myth that gumihos eat human hearts or livers. Will it become truth today? My eyes narrow. "What do you plan to do?" Is he planning on avenging me? We do not need another curse.

"Nothing you do not want me to." He presents me with a calm look and soft smile.

Muscles relaxing, I exhale, scolding myself for worrying in the first place. That was Inha before the curse. "Well, I also wanted to see them one more time."

"Allow me to carry you," Inha says, arms held up.

Eyes narrowed in a faux suspicion, my lips refuse to participate and curl in a smile. "Wouldn't teleporting be faster?"

"Indeed, but I would not get to hold you for as long," he replies, smirking and sweeping me into his embrace before I can protest—not that I'd want to.

"Are you going to carry me the whole way?" I ask, amused by his affection.

"Only until we are outside. Then we can teleport," he explains.

I tuck my head into his chest. "Take your time."

He presses his lips onto the top of my head. "How about a century?"

Chuckling, I reply, "Why not? What is a century to a gumiho?"

"Well, without you, torturous."

"You know, I am not sure how you became known for eating hearts and livers in the Mortal Lands. You are more flirtatious than threatening." I trace his collarbone from atop his clothes, dropping down to where I know a little drop of red marks his chest.

His hold on me tightens. "Only for you."

When we exit into the newly spring air, Inha portals us to the same rooftop Seonghwa did all that time ago. He keeps an arm around my waist, his eyes fixated on me as I stare at the Song estate where the Song patriarch is welcoming wealthy looking men into his home while servants scurry around, hurrying to go about their chores. They're still wealthy, completely unaware of all that's happened, of my challenges and new fortune. I doubt they spare a single thought on the poor girl from the slums bought with a small pouch of coins and sent to die.

Inha's fingers draw lazily on my waist. "I am curious as to why you came to me in the first place and why you did not just run away."

"Well, I thought if I returned here, the Songs would be angered and kill me or take their wrath out on Halmeoni Hyesun if they knew we were connected—they explicitly threatened to kill my father. And I didn't have the means to start up a life elsewhere. Of course, after my almost assassination attempt, it's not like I had a choice."

"I would have let you leave. I was not going to kill you," he murmurs, lip pouting.

"How was I supposed to know that?" Ire sparks inside, flames of indignation spreading.

Lifting his hands in surrender, he says with sparkling eyes, "You are right. I reacted poorly in that situation." He leans and presses a kiss to my temple, and just like that, the fire is doused.

Satisfied, I give a curt nod of my head. "Anyways, in the face of forever, the pain of the trials was but a glimpse of my life, one well worth it." Because at the time, I may not have cared for him in the way I do now, but I cared for the gumihos as a whole. Their state was so similar to my own. In that compassion, I found the desire to try to help them.

He glances at them once more. "Well, they" —he gestures to the Song family— "did one good thing in their miserable mortal lives."

"And what's that?" I peer up at him.

His gaze returns to me, the corner of his lips curled up. "They sent you to me, and it is the greatest gift I have ever received."

"The feeling is mutual, although I still could have gone without being locked in a chest." I rub my arms.

He hisses, ears flicking and tail fidgeting furiously. "Do you want me to punish them?"

"No. You may lose your pearl again, and I have no desire for another trial."

"Do you want to talk to them?"

"Yes. Even if they have no remorse, I want to do this for myself." I look up at him and point at his ears. "You might need to lose the fox-ears and tail." They disappear instantly. I smile and add, "Now can you portal us to the front entrance?"

"Your wish is my command, Mistress," he replies with a wry smirk.

We reappear near the bustling front gate of the Song estate where maids and male workers scurry in and out, a single armed guard positioned just outside. I take a deep breath, calming my heart. I've walked through it as a servant, but now I am returning as the wealthier woman, wife of the Gumiho King—well, almost. And with me is a man—gumiho—who loves me dearly. His handsome looks and wealth are just a satisfying addition. When my stomach begins to gurgle with nerves, I hook my arm through Inha's, tethering my erratic heart.

"Ready?" he asks softly, peering down at me, searching for signs of discomfort.

I nod, setting my jaw in determination. "Let's go."

Walking arm in arm, we approach the gate, Inha's pace slow to match my limp. I recognize some of the people, fellow laborers I chatted with in brief segments while working. Some were wary of me and my brace, others were sympathetic and smiled often at me, but none of them acknowledge me as Baek Jiwon, servant and daughter of a drunk, instead only casting curious glances at Inha and I. Then I understand. They do not recognize me—although that could be due in part to my new gold eyes. They see a noble appearing woman in expensive garments next to an equally lavishly dressed man.

The guard intercepts us at the entrance. "What is your business?" he asks firmly yet with respect as one would when addressing nobility.

"I am an old acquaintance of Taehee," I reply, dropping the honorifics I used all my life in this place. My station is above hers now; I am royalty. Even if it is only in the Mythical Lands.

He bows, gesturing for us to enter. "Taehee-nim is in the pavilion, I believe."

"Thank you." I dip my head, and we stride through the gate.

Taehee is where the guard said she would be, Taeri sitting across from her sister as they both practice their calligraphy under the pillared pavilion where two servants stand nearby, waiting to carry out the wills of their mistresses. That reminds me.

I lean and whisper, "Inha, will you please teach me how to read and write?"

His brows shoot up. "Of course." His smile is warm and comforting, stoking my confidence.

There are only a few steps remaining between us and the Song sisters, but their backs are turned to us, their bickering loud.

"I told you not to copy me," Taehee snaps at her younger sister.

"I had already started this poem. *You're* the one doing the copying," Taeri argues.

A sigh. They haven't changed at all. Truly pitiful.

"Excuse me," I call out.

The sisters whip around, annoyance written on their face before their eyes sweep down to the fine fabrics we are adorned in, and when their gazes land upon Inha, smiles light their features. Now I am annoyed. Part of me wishes we were by the pig pen so I could splash their faces with mud.

Taehee rushes to her feet, her sister following suit, and smooths her top and skirt. "Forgive me, but I do not recognize you. Are you perhaps friends of our father?"

Taeri won't stop gawking at Inha's face.

I speak, drawing her attention away from him and to myself. "I am shocked that after all the years of knowing each other, you do not remember me."

A puzzled look scrunches her face, but my words must have sparked recognition because her lip curls back ever so slightly. "Jiwon." She says my name as if it is sour in her mouth. Eyeing me up and down, this time with disgust instead of appreciation of my clothes, she sneers, "How many men did you *attend to* to afford all of that?" Glancing again at Inha, she says in a way in which to wound me, "You'll never keep a bed, just warm it a few times before being discarded."

My fingers dig into the fabric of my top, my legs beginning to shake with a desire to kick her. How dare she mention that.

Inha stills beside me, his voice low and threatening. "You should be wary of the way in which you speak of my wife."

I stand straighter when he says it, for although it is not official yet, in our hearts, we are bound to each other. We have both proven our devotion, willing to die for each other. After facing fiery bulgae and dokkaebi with godwood arrows, the Song sisters are so insignificant in comparison. And yet, despite being human, they are monsters nonetheless. Arrogant. Cruel. Selfish.

"Wife!" both sisters exclaim in tandem.

"You thought you were sacrificing me, sending me to my death, but you actually gave me the best gift." I twist my head to look up at Inha.

"Don't tell me that he is…" Taehee's eyes dart between the two of us.

Inha flashes them his sharp fangs. Taehee's eyes bulge, and Taeri's mouth drops open. There is satisfaction to be had in their shock, but it is not the purpose of my visit.

"I came to show you the fruit of your scorn. You loathed me and the Gumiho King, but in fact, the only ones losing are the two of you. I had hoped that perhaps guilt for sending me to what many assumed was my doom would inspire some sense of remorse, but alas, the same pride then lives in you now. Nevertheless, I have forgiven you. I hope you will both learn and live better in the future for it."

Taeri pouts, but Taehee's eyes darken, a coldness consuming the air around us despite the warm beginnings of spring. "I don't need forgiveness from a *pig*," she sneers.

A growl grumbles from deep inside Inha's throat, a sound more mythical than mortal.

I pull gently on his arm, signaling for him to hold his anger. "Well, if you refuse it, I will still give it. For my sake," I reply, grateful that I mean it and that my body does not tremble in fear nor rage any more. The final string snaps. My past as a mortal will be buried here.

"Not even worthy of my pity," Taehee grumbles.

But Taeri looks near to tears. She was always the kinder one. If only by a hair.

"Let's go home," I say, and Inha wastes no time.

The Song sisters' shouts of surprise send us off as we portal back to the palace.

Inha teleports us into my room. "I know you do not like to cry, especially in front of others, but I thought after all *that* that you might need to," he explains, stroking my head.

"Actually, I am not sad. Or mad. Just...done. They are no longer a part of my life, only my past, but they sent me on the path to you. For that, I am grateful."

He presses his lips to the crown of my head. "What do you want now?"

"To live well." I pause, twisting to stare up into his golden eyes. "With you."

Wrapping his arms around me, he says, "I promise to make you so happy that the pain they have caused you will fade."

"I think only time can dull such things," I mutter solemnly, but when I see his frown and drooping ears, I add, "But your love will speed it along." It seems to cheer him up, his ears perking.

"I did tell you I was interested in the art of healing," he says, a smirk coated in mirth curling his lip.

Darting forward, I press my mouth to his. When I pull away, his lips are parted and his brows arched high, and a satisfactory smile forms on my face. There is endless amusement in making mythicals speechless.

"Maybe the healer is you," he muses, ears twitching and tail brushing against my leg.

"Why do you say that?"

"Because you saved me." His voice is so soft, so sincere.

After all he has done for me, I am glad to know I have done the same for him. "Well, you made me feel safe." Not just because he offered me a place to live, clothes to wear and food to eat.

He brushes a stray strand of hair from my face. "Looks like we were both in need of some rescuing."

The way I feel for him is beyond words. No artist could paint it, and no storyteller could express it, but it would be worth a try, if only to grab glimpses of the grand love we share. "We were both in need of love, of learning how to receive it and give it."

"Love is a light in the dark," he states, a phrase that is reminiscent of something Seonghwa or Halmeoni Hyesun would say.

I nod slowly. "Perhaps love is more like the flowers you adore, something fragile yet resilient. Even when killed by a scorching summer sun or a cruel cold frost, it will return, growing anew."

"I do not know about that. I am quite fond of your idea, of a love like trees, steadfast and thriving for hundreds of years." His finger tangles with my tresses, white and black hair curled around his finger.

Maybe this will morph into a myth of its own: the story of a mortal and mythical, a love that broke the chains binding both of them. I'm not much of a storyteller, but I trust the great writers of the world to embellish it into quite the romance.

27

To my surprise, Seonghwa comes to visit. He claims that it's a final meeting for his mission, but I think he just misses me. We sit outside under a winged pavilion, enjoying the first blossoms of spring, in which pink clouds cling to the trees, and flowers dot the bushes like a sprinkle of pretty paint. The floral scents dance to my nose while the birds sing, their song echoing through the air.

"How's the wing?" I take the lid off of the rice bowl, setting the steaming grains in front of Seonghwa.

He hops forward, gold eyes glittering excitedly at the sight of his favorite food. Unfurling his wing, he says, "All healed. How is your chest?"

I smile as he pecks at the rice and barley mixture. "It healed when I came back from the meadow."

"Glad to hear it." His voice is muffled by the beak full of food.

"Now that your wing is healed, I assume you can fly fine, so I need a favor." I place a jeweled hair pin that is finer than anything I've seen in the Mortal Lands and a note that only has a single word written in wriggling lines: *Jiwon.* "Could you take this to a young woman in the Mortal Lands? Her name is Kang Yuna. She was a...friend. Well, she would have been if I hadn't kept her at such a distance."

"Glad you can see that now. If I had been allowed to talk to you back then, I would have screeched some sense into you," Seonghwa chides.

Rolling my eyes, I fetter my retort. But my self-control does not last long, the desire to return to our comfortable bickering defeating it. "I completed all the trials, so does that make me eligible to become a divine messenger?" I muse, giving him a look that I know will irritate him.

Seonghwa does that same strange squawking laughter. "Hardly! You are not perfect, not even close. You would need a hundred more trials to tame that temper of yours."

I cross my arms, my eyes narrowing. "Well, you could have corrected me in a nicer manner."

His laughing dies down, tone turning more serious. "No living being is perfect, neither mythical nor mortal. It was not about finding a sinless being, but someone who despite their past sins, does not give up on trying to be good. You may have a temper, Jiwon, but you try to be kind and honorable no matter how hard life tries to drag you down."

A lump of emotions forms in my throat. "I never thought I'd hear you compliment me." His words make me wonder if Inha would have still received his powers even if I'd failed some of the trials—the trying more important than the success. Or more accurately, the success lies in the trying.

"Do not get used to it." He pecks at the rice.

"I'd be worried about you if you did it too often." My finger finds a stray grain of barley, and I press it into my fingertip and twist my wrist to give it the samjok-o. I can't believe how much time has passed since I fed him from my hand all those months ago.

"You are a mission I shall never forget," he replies after gulping down the barley.

"A mission? Not a friend?" I cock a brow.

Swallowing another beak full of grain, he says, "It is good to be self-aware."

I take a swing at him, but he dodges and flies high into the sky, the letter to Yuna and the pin secured in his talons. "Live well, Jiwon. And keep Inha humble so we do not have to repeat this whole process," he caws, his words echoing into the sky.

I wonder if his other mission is finished as well? Seonghwa won't do well being bored.

"What is this about keeping me humble?" Inha asks, appearing silently next to me.

Despite being a gumiho myself now, I am not as quiet when I move as the others, thanks to my bad leg. "Nothing. Seonghwa was just saying we are made for each other," I reply.

An arm slides around my waist. "It is one of the few times I agree with him, then."

I twist my head, looking up into the golden eyes of my love. Life is full of broken people, and you know you've found the right one when your jagged edges fit together.

But something catches my attention.

Arching a brow, I ask, "Are the tails really necessary?" All nine of his foxtails are out on display, obnoxious as a peacock's plume.

In a red mist, they all dissolve except for one. His face crumples along with his shoulders. "Do you find them hideous?"

I grab his hand. "Of course not. I am never ashamed of your tails, and they even have a certain charm to them. But all *nine*? They're a little cumbersome and keep us too far apart if we stand side by side."

His face brightens. "How about six?"

"How about three?"

Two more tails sprout back. "Deal."

A smile lights both of our faces, and we seal our bargain with a brief kiss.

Ever since I was given a second chance at life, he has not shifted into his fox form very often. Granted, neither have I, as it is still rather awkward to walk around in. "I thought you hated your human form."

He shrugs, a mischievous twinkle in his eyes. "It has grown on me."

"I wonder why," I tease.

He stops, grabs my hips and spins me on the cushion to face him, his warm body pressing against mine and his returned three tails shielding us from the view of potential onlookers. "I shall show you."

He leans forward, lips parted ever so slightly. As much as I'd love to enjoy it, I push him back with my hand. "Wait a few more days for the ceremony, and then you can show me all that a gumiho can do."

A fire of desire sparks in his eyes, golden flames glowing in anticipation, and I wonder if my own reflect the same.

"So disciplined in all but your temper," he chides playfully, presenting a pretend pout.

"I must make up for what you lack," I retort with a chuckle.

Suddenly he asks, "Do you remember that dream I refused to speak aloud?"

I nod and lean forward.

His finger traces my cheek. "My dream is this. My dream is you."

"I did not dare to dream before, for it felt like it was pointless, but I am ready to dream now."

He smiles, grabs my hands, lifts it slowly to his mouth, and presses a kiss to my fingers. His golden eyes glitter with excitement—and a promise. I hope the next few days pass soon because it is getting harder to tame the flaming desire inside of me.

All the gumihos are gathered to celebrate the broken curse and a coronation—an event very similar to what I imagine the human ones are. Another banquet will take place, but first, we assemble in the throne room. I haven't been here since I was first shown around the palace, but the high ceiling, jade floor, and tree-like throne still inspire a sense of awe. Unlike the flame colored fall leaves of last time, pink blossoms cling to the branches like a cloud of blush sky. Lanterns with shapes of nine tailed foxes cut out dangle from their stands, gumiho shadows cast around the hall, and a crimson carpet leads from the entrance to the dais. Without realizing it, I've grown rather fond of the color red, my own garments a dark scarlet with white flowers embroidered along the hems and collar. I'm still not quite in control of subtle shifting, so I choose my human form for today.

Inha stands next to me, his own garments the opposite of mine, white and trimmed in a plum red with large wings of fabric dangling from his arms. Gold leaves crawl along the collar, and three tails peek from beneath his voluptuous robes. The Gumiho King is quite stunning.

He leans in to whisper, "I hear it again."

"What?" I ask and wave at Doyeon who prances into the hall, Taejoon and Shinhye following all in their fox forms. Shinhye looks so beautiful, her coat of fur more red than white.

"The throne. I can hear its song," he says, so many emotions clogging his voice.

I whip my head to look at him. "When?"

"I had heard whispers, faint melodies, after the bulgae, but I thought them only wishful imaginations. After I sent you away, I heard it slightly stronger, but today, its melody is unmistakable."

"You are worthy," I whisper, grinning as the magical music plays in my own mind.

"As are you," he replies, returning the smile with his own. "Are you ready?"

I nod.

The hall is nearly bursting with gumihos in fox, human, and hybrid forms. Their soft murmuring rumbles like low thunder in the room. Up in the shadowed rafters, I swear I can see the silhouette form of a samjok-o. Perhaps I am mistaken—a trick of the lantern light.

Inha's voice grabs my attention. "My dear fellow gumihos, it has been centuries since all of us have gathered like this, centuries since joy has been present in the palace. And the reason," he pauses, gesturing to me, "is this breathtaking creature beside me. A mortal more honest and brave than most mythicals, and now a gumiho like us. Today is both a celebration of a broken curse as well as a declaration of a new start."

I ignore his backhanded compliment to my previous humanity—some habits take longer to break.

Yipping and shouts of jubilee echo in the hall, and Inha begins to walk down the steps.

"What are you doing?" I ask with a hissing whisper, my brows puckering.

Smiling, he whispers back, "Just trust me."

When he reaches the bottom of the steps, he lifts his hand towards me. "Your new Mistress—Queen of the Gumihos," Inha declares, standing tall with eyes sparkling with pride and joy.

Rows upon rows of gumihos bow to me, snouts pressed to the ground and tails fanning in the air. Shinhye peers up at me with such happiness it warms my heart, her daughter's tails twitching as her paws shift impatiently. Injeong is also on all fours. Minji and Gunoo are both in their human forms, grinning and glancing at each other, blush coloring both their faces. Then there are the multitude of ones I have not met yet but look forward to.

My focus shifts to Inha. My mate. Our eyes meet, and our lips stretch into even wider grins. But then Inha does something that makes me want to weep.

The Gumiho King shifts into his fox form and lays on the floor, belly up, in the way gumihos show reverence to their ruler. The others follow suit, bellies pointed to the sky in the ultimate act of vulnerability.

If I was a mortal, I might think it a strange sight.

But I am not.

I am a mythical, bride to the Gumiho King.

This is the legend of the Gumiho King's Bride.

When fall is on the cusp of winter, the people tell of a pair of foxes, eyes gold as honey and fur white as snow. Prancing through the forest, one, a piece of wood on its left hind leg, all indeed know.

Their yipping is heard in the twilight, the two always found in the same sight. Their love and loyalty is the lore of the land, an inspiration to all of man.

Acknowledgements

I can't believe we are on book number seven. First of all, I am so grateful to my family for supporting me, always believing in me and telling people about my books. I am thankful for my husband for being so stinking amazing that he inspires my romances. I am thankful for my author friends who recommend my books and support me as well as all the readers who take the chance on my books.

Shout out to my Cave Dwellers; you are my sisters forever. Thank you for putting up with my need for words of affirmation and my constant barrage of art (some of which shall never see the light of day).

A special thank you to my beta readers—without you, this book would be a hot mess... Well more of one. XD (Are emojis unprofessional in books? Oh well.) Thank you Evelyn, Claire Kohler, Brittany Adie, Reverie Moon, and H.K. Brooks for your feedback. They are all fellow authors by the way, so feel free to check their books, too, or, if they are still working on their debuts, follow them on social media to stay up to date on their story progress. Hehe.

And last but not least, thank you Jesus.

Thank you for reading!

If you enjoyed *The Gumiho King's Bride*, please leave a review as it really helps authors. <3

Other Books by Bex

THRONE OF ANGUISH DUOLOGY
-Throne of Anguish
-Crown of Sorrows

DAUGHTERS OF THE SUN

BOUND TO THE TYRANT KING

DEEP-FAKE IN LOVE

Glossary

Abeonim: father (formal)

Ahjumma: title for middle aged/married women

Appa: dad (informal)

Bulgae: fire hounds said to chase the sun and moon

Daltokki: moon rabbit

Dokkaebi: goblin

Eomma: mom (informal)

Girin: Korean mythical creature that mostly resembles a dragon mixed with a deer

Gyeryong: dragon with a chicken head

Goryeo: Korean dynasty succeeding the Later Three Kingdoms and preceding the Joseon dynasty (918-1392)

Gumiho: nine tailed fox

Haetae: Korean mythical creature often referred to as a "unicorn lion"

Halmeoni: grandmother

Imugi: baby dragon or a serpent that failed to become a dragon

Kaesong: Goryeo capital

Maeum: heart

Myodusa: half-cat half-snake

Samjok-o: three legged crow

Shilla: One of the three kingdoms of Korea, later unified Shilla

-ah: informal attachment to a person's name

-nim: formal title added onto a name